TOO CLEVER BY HALF

A DAVIES & WEST MYSTERY

Will North

This is a work of fiction. Names, characters, places, and incidents either are the product of the author's imagination or are used fictitiously. Any resemblance to actual persons, living or dead, events, or to businesses, locales or institutions is entirely coincidental.

Published in the United States by Northstar Editions.
Too Clever By Half: A Davies & West Mystery / Will North — 2nd ed.
Library of Congress Control Number: 2015908375
Cover Design by Laura Hidalgo

ISBN-10: 0-9989649-4-8
ISBN-13: 978-0-9989649-4-2

For my son Eric and grandson Baker,
of whom I am so proud

The Major Crime Investigating Team

Detective Chief Inspector Arthur Penwarren
Detective Inspector Morgan Davies
Detective Sergeant and Crime Scene Manager Calum West
Detective Constable Terry Bates
Police Constable Adam Novak

Prologue

IF THE SURFACE of the English Channel off Cornwall's Lizard Peninsula had not been as smooth and glossy as wet enamel that soft Thursday, seventeenth May, the snub-nosed beam trawler, *Catherine P,* would never have spotted it.

They'd pulled nets late into the night, and now the skipper, Mike Perran, was running his vessel southwest, roughly five miles east of the peninsula's cliffs, bound for the port at Newlyn with a hold full to bursting with cuttlefish, monkfish, and gurnard from the inshore fishery off Lyme Bay. Tide was slack and his boat made good progress. Perran was young for a ship's owner. With a sun-bleached head of curls and a face already weathered beyond his years, he'd been working the fishing grounds off Dorset, Devon, and Cornwall since he was fourteen as a hand on his father's boat. And when, six years later, Jack Perran suddenly died of a pulmonary embolism after minor knee surgery, Mike stepped into the wheelhouse. He had just turned twenty, but his father's crew, twice his age and more, stayed with him. It was a matter of respect for the old man. And it was a job.

The sky over the Channel was a bell of milky blue. The sun-sequined swells were so gentle it was as if the bejeweled sea were in deep sleep. Far off, toward France, a scud of clouds white as batts of sheep's wool hung low on the horizon.

It was Perran's newest crewman, stocky and eager Ronnie James, just turned nineteen, who spied it first, alabaster white against the royal blue water, drifting on the swells. It could have been a thick slab of white Styrofoam from some yachtsman's floating dock.

Except for the head.

James signaled to the wheelhouse, and the skipper, catching sight of the floater, turned the boat to starboard. As it drew abreast of the corpse, the rest of the crew clustered along the rail. Young James, without waiting for orders, dropped overboard with a line. When he'd wrapped it around the body, the other crew members hoisted it aboard. Perran watched all this and decided Ronnie James was a keeper. He set the gyro compass and climbed down to the deck.

Perran knew that it was common for someone who pitched overboard to have their clothes pulled off by the drag and wash of the chop, but the sea had been glassy, as if oiled, for two days. He scanned the horizon for a drifting boat but saw none.

"All right, you lot," he said, turning back toward the bridge, "I'll get on to the Coastguard in Falmouth. Cover him, but don't touch the body." The older crew members hesitated; Ronnie James fetched a canvas tarp.

On the wheelhouse radio the Coastguard operator squawked, "Change course and return to Falmouth."

"Not a chance, mate," Perran replied, his voice even. "Not unless you're ready to buy my entire catch; I'm inbound for tomorrow's auction at Newlyn, last of the week. I've got one dead body on deck, but I have hundreds more dying by the minute in my hold. By Monday I'll have a total loss."

A pause: "Understood then, captain. We'll send a high-speed RNLI rescue boat out to collect the body and take it ahead of you to Newlyn. Penzance police will collect it there. The vessel does 25 knots; we should be with you shortly."

"Roger that. We'll keep you posted on our location."

One

ONE MINUTE ARCHIE Hansen was jouncing across the stony field in his aging, rust-red Massey Ferguson tractor, the next minute he was airborne. Like a stumbling horse, the lurching tractor had pitched him right out of its cab.

"Son of a bitch!"

It was Thursday, twelfth March, and Hansen was doing a shallow weeding of his field of Maris Peer potatoes. Now, right shoulder wrenched, his side bruised by the jagged granite shards that studded his ancient field on Cornwall's Lizard Peninsula like a crop of their own, he struggled to his feet while the tractor, still in gear, labored helplessly to move forward, its big rear power wheel turning uselessly because the right front wheel was deep in a hole.

Hansen, on the wrong side of fifty and beginning to show it, was rawboned as a goat but for a developing paunch that spoke of too many nights spent downing pints of Doom Bar at his local, the New Inn at Manaccan. He fetched his cap from the ground and slapped it on a skull that was as bald to its crest as a half-peeled orange. He offset this tonsorial desert with a greying beard which, fastidiously trimmed to a sharp point at the chin, gave him a vaguely Mephistophelian air. The leader of a local group of Druids, he'd lately been straying from the faith and experimenting with spell-casting and darker magic. The devilish beard was, he thought, only appropriate.

He climbed up to the cab, shut off the motor, and cursed himself for not owning a four-wheeler that could have pulled itself out of this dilemma—not that he'd ever spring for something that pricey. Depending on the year and the field he was rotating during Cornwall's mild winter months, Hansen cultivated daffodils, cauliflower, early potatoes, and followed with grains—barley or wheat—in the spring. He was as successful as any farmer in Cornwall could say he was these days, but he was tight as a Shylock, and therefore better off than his neighbors.

Now he knelt beside the sunken wheel. The ground he'd farmed for years here on the Lizard, and that generations of Norwegian immigrant Hansens had farmed before him, inexplicably had given way beneath the tractor. Looking down on either side of the knobby, black front tyre, he saw only darkness. He climbed back into the cab, started the engine, and gunned it, only to have the front wheel dive even deeper.

"Son of a bitch."

Hansen's verbal expressions of both disgust and surprise were limited. He yanked his mobile from the pocket of his dirt-encrusted navy blue coveralls and rang up his young neighbor, Bobby Tregareth. The two of them farmed adjacent fields just inland from Nare Head, on the soft, undulating hills above the pastoral reaches of the Helford River on Cornwall's English Channel coast.

A half hour later, Hansen had a chain hooked between the front axle of the tractor and Bobby's beat-up, tan Land Rover Defender. Burning up the four-wheel-drive Defender's clutch in low gear, Bobby managed to pop the tractor's wheel from its trap and pull it away. Archie grabbed a torch from the cab, and like a terrier after a fox gone to earth, tore away turf and stone and managed to get his head and the light into the hole. What he saw, to his astonishment, was a rectangular stone-walled chamber. At the eastern end, two roughly five-foot granite pillars suggested an entrance tunnel, long since collapsed and filled with rubble. Directly opposite, to the west, a six-inch-thick slab of granite the size of a small, misshapen door lay flat on the earthen floor, its surface studded with white quartz crystals that glittered like diamond chips as the beam of his torch swept it.

"One of them ancient chambers, Bobby. Fetch a ladder; I'm going down an'll need a way back up."

"But Mr. Hansen, surely this is a matter for the archaeologists at the county council…"

"Don't be wet, Bobby; nothing comes to ditherers."

Bobby did it. He'd little choice: he leased much of his farmland from Hansen and depended upon his good will.

After Bobby left, Hansen shoved the torch into a pocket, swung his legs into the ragged mouth of the hole, held himself suspended above the gap on wobbly arms for a moment, then dropped in, his arms extended above his head.

He fell farther and hit harder than he expected; the roof of the chamber was a good six feet high. Groaning, he rolled to his knees, stood, and looked around. The four walls of the chamber were curved inward ever so slightly until they met three granite roofing slabs, roughly four feet wide, a foot thick, and five long. The tractor wheel had dropped through a weak spot at the edge of one of these slabs.

The day was clear, and a shaft of light pierced the musty chamber from the hole above like sun slicing through cloud. Hansen sat on the edge of the thin slab on the floor for some time, scanning the perfect walls, looking for anything of interest—not that he had a clue what "interest" might look like. It was like being inside the belly of a beast.

A restless, impatient man, as he studied the walls and waited for the ladder, he thumped the rubberized butt of his torch absently on his stone seat as if keeping time with his pulse. It took a few moments before he noticed a tonal difference toward the center of the stone that didn't exist around its periphery. He stood up and tapped again. No question: hollow.

"You down there, Mr. Hansen?"

"You see me anywhere else, Bobby?"

"Right, right; I've got the ladder. You need help down there?"

"I'm done here. Just send the ladder down."

"What'd you see, Archie?" Bobby's enthusiasm was almost childlike as Hansen squeezed to the surface.

"Not a damned thing. Just another of them Iron Age fogous. Bloody nuisance, they are, just like them big standing stones we got to plow around. Not to mention that Roman mosaic floor poor Johnny Sayer found in his field over Porthallow way. English Heritage were all over that and they'll be all over this, too, wanting to protect it for God only knows what reason, which means I lose one of my best fields."

"That's just not right, Mr. Hansen."

"Too true, Bobby, because it'll mean I'll need one of the fields you're leasing from me back again."

"Straight up? But I can't get by..."

"Hush now, lad; I know. I've a simple solution. We don't report this; we just carry on as per usual and no one's the wiser, yeah?" Hansen said, tapping a knowing forefinger to the right side of his nose.

"You won't report it?"

"Dime a dozen these underground chambers are hereabouts. What they don't know about they won't miss, am I right?"

"Sure. I guess. What about the hole?"

"Bit of corrugated roofing to cover it and then dirt so's it looks like everything else, only I don't plow near it again. Take me a couple of days and then—hey, presto!—it's just our little secret. Few weeks, it's grassed over. Invisible. Right, Bobby?" Archie looked at the young man, hard.

"Right, right. Invisible."

LATER THAT AFTERNOON, though, Hansen was back in the chamber, alone. He'd slipped webbed strapping around one corner of the stone slab and was cranking a come-along winch anchored with spikes he'd driven into the hard pan of the chamber floor. It was brutal, hot work, even for late March. The sweat from his forehead left small black craters in the dim dust. Several times he'd had to re-anchor the come-along as the slab inched away from its resting place in a slow, rasping arc. His back and arms burned. He could have got Bobby to help, but he didn't want the company.

Having moved the slab some sixty degrees off center, Hansen shone the torch into the hole he knew would be there. It was roughly two feet square and the same deep. Nestled in its center was a lidded clay vessel. Belly down on the slab, he reached in, and lifting the lid, shone the light on its contents.

"Son of a bitch," he whispered.

JUST BEFORE MIDNIGHT, Archie flicked on his most powerful torch, and descended into the chamber. Prone again on the displaced slab, he made to lift the earthenware vessel nestled in the underground compartment and then gave up. He had no idea gold could be so heavy.

The clay container was the color of weathered slate, grey and ribbed as if made from coils. It was roughly eighteen inches high, a foot wide at its shoulder, and narrow at the bottom, like an upside-down pear. The lid was an upended bowl and covered an opening at the top he guessed was about eight inches in diameter. He'd thought to bring a burlap seed sack from his machinery shed and had planned to lift the container into it, but there was an ominous crack along one side of the vessel and he decided to remove the contents instead. Hands trembling with excitement, he lifted two large, intricately-braided, nearly circular gold objects he reckoned were neck ornaments, six gold and bronze pins, *brooches* his partner Charlotte probably would call them, two gold rings with embossed signets, and what looked like an ornamental gold belt buckle. He was stunned to find that the bottom half of the vessel was filled with small grey coins. Hundreds of them.

Working in darkness, he loaded his trove into the back of his own Land Rover, strapped the ladder to the rack on the roof, eased the vehicle into gear, and moved off across the field as quietly as possible, lights off and navigating by habit and the penumbral gloom of a quarter moon.

Two

WHEN THE CALL about the floater came in from the Coastguard just before noon, seventeenth May, the Comms division of the Devon and Cornwall Police immediately contacted the Major Crimes Investigation Unit headquartered at Bodmin. Detective Chief Inspector Arthur Penwarren was at a briefing at Devon and Cornwall Police headquarters in Exeter, so the call fell to newly-promoted Detective Inspector Morgan Davies.

Davies was already speeding south on the A30 in her unmarked, white Ford Escort estate wagon when she finally called Detective Sergeant Ralph Poldennis, the senior CID officer at the Penzance Basic Command Unit. Newlyn, where the Coastguard would off-load the body, sat cheek by jowl with Penzance on the scythe-like curve of Mount's Bay and was Poldennis's jurisdiction.

"Ralph, it's Morgan," she barked into her mobile. "I'm just clearing the Hayle roundabout."

"Imagine my excitement. Did I call you?"

"Comms did."

"Splendid."

"Control your enthusiasm, Ralphie."

"Should I be enthusiastic? Look, the RNLI boat isn't due here for at least half an hour. We have nothing so far but an apparent floater…"

"A floater is enough to get my juices flowing."

"Takes all kinds…"

"Don't be coarse. When your ship comes in, as they say, we'll transport the body to the mortuary at Treliske."

"Splendid."

"You said that before."

"As you say, my enthusiasm is unbridled."

"Look, Ralph, I'm not trying to pirate your patch."

"Could have fooled me."

"Come off it; the body was found off the Lizard Peninsula. That's Falmouth's patch anyway. You're receiving it because Newlyn's where the RNLI boat's landing; that's all. Where will it be unloaded, by the way? Which quay?"

"I suggested the old north quay. Little used these days; skippers prefer the newer Mary Williams Quay. Better services."

"Good thinking; fewer sightseers that way, too. Funeral director's wagon on its way?"

"No, Morgan, I hadn't even thought of it..."

"Jesus, Ralph, I'm just trying to do my job."

Poldennis sighed. Davies had been his boss at Penzance before her promotion. "I know you are, Morgan. Wouldn't have thought it possible, but we sort of miss you down here…like we miss being rubbed with sandpaper."

Davies laughed: "Be there in fifteen."

"We'll put out the welcome mat."

"Electrified, no doubt."

And now Poldennis was laughing, too.

DAVIES WALKED TO the end of the nineteenth century stone quay and looked out over Mounts Bay. It was a fine mid-May afternoon. In the far distance beyond the harbor, water and sky merged as if without boundary, the one indistinguishable from the other. This far tip of Cornwall was accustomed to freshly-laundered air delivered daily from the Atlantic, but today was a rare one, with the wind from the Continent. The atmosphere was hazy and the water calm, as if catching a breath before the next onslaught from the west. Away to the east, the castle atop the rocky offshore pinnacle of St. Michael's Mount shimmered in soft focus, as if it sat behind a lacy curtain suspended in the still, sunny air. Above Davies, grey and white Fulmars screeched and wheeled and the stench of fish guts and diesel fuel filled her nostrils. The stench smelled like home.

Across the broad protected anchorage, at the larger and longer Mary Williams Quay, trawlers and long liners, their hulls painted every color of the rainbow, were unloading for the next day's pre-dawn auction. Forklifts stacked with red plastic bins filled with iced fish skittered about like wharf rats. Morgan knew these fishermen; they'd been her friends and neighbors from the days when she lived here in a renovated stone sail loft above the quays, before her promotion moved her north to Bodmin. Catching sight of her when she arrived at the car park, several of the slicker-clad men called out or waved. She waved back and grinned; she'd arrested more than one of them, and yet missed their rough and tumble company.

But now she was thinking about Calum. Calum West was the senior crime scene manager for the Scene of Crimes unit at the Bodmin Operational Hub, where she too was now based. West was the sort of chap who gave the impression of being perpetually and benignly amused, as if the everyday absurdity of life were a source of quiet joy. No matter the extremity of the crime scene, and his cases were always extreme, there was a brightness, almost a playfulness about him, as if he'd managed to preserve a childlike sense of wonder at all things, including murder. In the early days, Davies had taken this for a lack of *gravitas*. But after working together closely on the Chynoweth girl's murder in Penzance the year before, she'd changed her mind: each new body was, for him, a new adventure, a new knotty problem to solve, and he went at it with enthusiasm and brilliance. She admired him immensely. But now she worried he would be annoyed with this new case: no scene to examine, no site to search, no clothing to test for distinctive fibers, no fingerprints. The body itself would be his only "scene." Then she smiled. Knowing West, that would just make the problem all the more intriguing.

Finally, in the gauzy distance, she spied the Severn Class RNLI vessel with its navy blue hull and bright orange superstructure. It hurtled across the water, dragging its churning white wake behind like a long bridal train. Beside her, Detective Sergeant Poldennis stood with his hands thrust in his trouser pockets. A young, uniformed police constable waited just behind them. He'd been introduced as PC Claire Reynolds, and she had given him a sympathetic pat on the shoulder. Thanks to their given names, he'd forever be assumed to be a woman, just as Morgan would forever be assumed to be a man. For more than twenty years she'd had to deal with policemen who were instantly dismissive when they discovered she wasn't male. Try as they might, though, they never reached her and they soon learned that she gave as good as she got…and then some. Silently, she wished the young constable best of luck in the force.

While they watched the approaching vessel, Poldennis regarded the woman beside him. Davies was tall and big-boned, just three inches shy of six feet, he guessed. Handsome rather than pretty. And though she wore inch-high pumps with her plainclothes pantsuit, Davies didn't strut as she walked like most women did in heels; instead, she strode, heavy-footed and leading with her chin as if perpetually recovering from a near-stumble. What made her arresting, besides her plush figure, was a sharply sculpted head—high cheekbones, knife-cut jawline, fair skin largely unwrinkled for a woman of forty-five, spiked hair streaked blond, and eyes blue as the interior of an iceberg and not much warmer. He'd heard she was Welsh by birth, but she looked more like a Scandinavian warrior goddess. She was blunt and acerbic, but also passionate about policing, and he often thought that if anything ever happened to someone he loved, he'd want Morgan Davies on the case.

As the RNLI vessel approached, Davies marveled at the breakneck speed the skipper maintained even as the boat approached the quay, then watched in amazement as it came to an abrupt halt thanks to suddenly activated bow thrusters. The boat wallowed for a moment in its own chop and then a uniformed crew member made it fast to the quay. She admired the boat jockey behind the wheel, imagining some rakish lad. But when the skipper who emerged turned out to be portly and old enough to be her father, she smiled at that short-lived fantasy.

Davies climbed down the rusting iron rungs set into the granite face of the quay, reached the vessel's bobbing deck, turned, and punched her hand out to shake the skipper's.

"Detective Inspector Morgan Davies, Captain: Major Crime Investigation Team, Bodmin."

The dapper captain bowed slightly: "Rory MacDonald, and may I say it would certainly be more of a pleasure to meet you, Inspector, under more salubrious conditions."

Morgan nodded and smiled: *We all have our private fantasies…*

Beckoning PC Reynolds, who held her bag, she pulled out a white Tyvek jumpsuit, shrugged the protective garment on over her clothes, and shoved her fingers into latex gloves. The body lay under a shroud on the deck.

"How'd you handle the body?"

"Can't say about the fishing crew, but we used gloves," the captain said.

"Well done."

She lifted the cloth and took record photos with a small digital camera. She said nothing as she moved around, but noted the dead man's peculiar wounds. She touched nothing. From time to time she knelt to look closely. Finally, she stood and nodded to the constable, and the two of them, the PC also now in Tyvek, wrapped the body in white sterile sheeting and then zipped it into a thick, black plastic body bag. She locked and tagged the zipper, and then Poldennis signaled for the body to be winched quayside where the undertaker's van waited, engine idling. She stepped out of the Tyvek coveralls, thanked the captain, turned to the iron ladder, and then paused.

"Up you go, Ralphie," she said, waving Poldennis ahead of her. "Don't want you staring at my arse as I climb, you old rogue." She knew Poldennis would blush, and he did.

Three

CHARLOTTE JOHNS HAD been Archie Hansen's partner for coming up on five years. They'd met through Druidry, not long after his former wife divorced him and took their two children north to Cumbria where she had family. His wife, Margie, had charged that Archie was addicted to violent, pornographic videos and that she and her children were in danger. Though no direct evidence was presented to substantiate these charges, the court nonetheless awarded her custody. Hansen never saw the kids again, and had no idea how or where they were now. To Charlotte, it seemed Archie had a wound that scabbed over but kept oozing. And he told her the porn tapes had merely been a business sideline. He'd sold them by mail order and had made a tidy sum. Thankfully, from his point of view, neither Margie nor the court knew just how tidy a sum it was. Nor did Charlotte.

Charlotte believed Archie's passionate embrace of Druidry was driven by a hunger to fill the hole left by his divorce and the loss of his children. As for being dangerous, that was nonsense. He liked his ale like any Cornishman, but was no drunk. He was strong minded, yes, and even autocratic sometimes, but also somehow compelling. Archie was a man you noticed, not because he was handsome, for he wasn't, particularly; it was just the aura radiating from him.

They'd met at a pagan moot in Falmouth, and the sexual energy passing between them that evening reminded her of the arcing discharge between the globes of a capacitor in an old movie from the early days of electricity: flashing, crackling, blinding white, like lightning. They'd spent that night together, in frenzied abandon, and had been partners ever since. Physically, he was sinuous as a feral animal, but also balding, his wispy, red hair swirling around the back of his head as if in a windstorm. Not that forty-nine-year-old Charlotte, also divorced, thought herself a beauty deserving of something better. She was shorter than Archie and slightly built, almost elfin. Her close-cropped, curly hair was a light brown already threaded with silver—the color, she often thought when looking in her mirror, of an ailing field mouse. Her eyes were grey tinged with green at the edges, the same deep green as the Serpentine rock at Lizard Point from which local artists made shiny jewelry.

Charlotte overcame what she saw as her physical shortcomings with an erotic energy that was unquenchable. She'd captured and held Archie by worshipping him with her body and soul as if he were a god. She called him Thor, because he brought her thunder, at least in bed, but in her heart she saw him as Erik the Red, the mariner, the searcher and, in the end, the fugitive searching for emotional safety. His own carnality was a gnawing hunger she threw herself into satiating. In this, at least, they were well-matched.

In the years since, however, certainty about their relationship always seemed just out of reach. He had never wanted to marry or even be hand-fasted within their Druid circle. Nor did he want them to live under one roof. He lived at his family's ancient farmstead; she lived alone a few miles away in a bungalow on the southern flanks of Goonhilly Downs.

A committed vegetarian, Charlotte had a small garden on the sloping hillside beside her bungalow that she worked daily. The Lizard's mild climate meant that even in winter she was able to raise and store crops—carrots, beetroot, parsnips and other root vegetables, cabbage and cauliflower, kale, even lettuce and spinach, provided she covered the tender leaves with a sheet on the rare occasions when frost was predicted. The garden, and a modest settlement from her own divorce, made it possible for her to scrape by. For extra cash, she worked part time as an orderly at the Helston Community Hospital, close by the Culdrose Royal Navy Air Station. When she needed money, Archie sometimes helped her, but she always had to beg...and there was always a price.

Over the years, she'd persuaded herself that real intimacy with Archie—not physical, but emotional and domestic—was beyond him. Working at the hospital in Helston, where death was a frequent visitor, Charlotte had developed the turtle-tough outer shell required of anyone who regularly has contact with patients in advanced stages of age or disease. They were there one day and gone another, leaving behind only a freshly remade bed. Enduring emotional stress was second nature to her, so she stored her pain about Archie in a sort of cave in her heart, a bloodless chamber. But sometimes, in bed, the two of them cresting, she still dreamed they would be about more than just the banishing of each other's emptiness. And year after year, she ignored the distance between them for one simple, unalterable reason: she needed him. That urgent need had never diminished and, in the heat the two of them created, her doubts always evaporated, like a fog upon the sea at daybreak.

Late Friday afternoon, thirtieth March, she arrived for the weekend as usual at Archie's farm, Higher Pennare. Though they sometimes spent the odd weeknight together, weekends were their scheduled "together time." That was also when most of the ceremonies of their Druid group were held, and that always added a certain magical edge to their nights.

She parked her aging silver VW Polo around the back in the yard of the old whitewashed, slate-roof farmhouse, and entered through the low kitchen door, her arms laden with the last of the winter crops from her garden—fat leeks, frilly kale, snowy parsnips, as well as groceries she'd picked up from the Sainsbury's supermarket in Helston. The bag included a coil of fat and savory Cumberland pork sausage for Archie. She'd never been able to convert him to vegetarianism.

The house was empty, but that wasn't unusual. Like most farms in the area, Archie's fields weren't contiguous; they'd been acquired over centuries, a small parcel here, another parcel a ways away, as land became available. She reckoned he was off in one of the distant fields. The farm at Higher Pennare was so old she could hardly credit it: it had been recorded in the Domesday Book, the survey initiated by William the Conqueror and completed in 1086. The present building, replacing who knew how many predecessors, was a thick-walled mix of stone, wood, and cob. It was built in the late seventeenth century and had gradually been expanded. Archie's Scandinavian ancestors were themselves relative newcomers to the farm: they'd only owned the property for just over two centuries, and had made their living from it ever since. Archie, the eldest of three children, two of them girls, had inherited the land at his father's death. The house was backed by a low hill above the Helford River that protected it from the winter winds from the Atlantic, and it had a panoramic view eastward to the English Channel. Archie had a crop of thousands of daffodils planted in the field beyond the front door, and Charlotte watched the sunny blossoms dance in the light evening breeze. He grew them to sell the bulbs. Later, she'd try to remember to bring in a bouquet of the useless blossoms.

It was a big house, and meant to be what it long had been: home to a sprawling family. Charlotte felt the generations all around her. Archie had lost his own family, and she'd been too old to begin one with him when they met, much as she might have liked to at some abstract level. Sometimes it was as if the house knew all that. She wanted to warm the house with her presence, as if with blazing hearths in every room, but she wondered sometimes if she even warmed Archie, other than at night.

Initially, at least, Archie's sexual repertoire had been limited. She put that down to all those videos he'd once sold. But she had studied the spiritual magic of extended arousal and had managed to knit those practices together with Archie's Druidry, gradually bringing him around. Oh yes, she had brought him around.

Upstairs, she stripped off her daytime clothes, opened a wardrobe, and selected Archie's favorite: her Viking Wench outfit. Naked, she stepped into a short, tan suede skirt with a handkerchief hem, the points of which she'd trimmed with bits of rabbit fur. Then she slipped on a thin, white linen blouse with a drawstring peasant neckline, the strings left loose for maximum décolleté. Over it she cinched a burgundy velvet lace-up "balconette" corset, which lifted her breasts as if on a platter for Archie's personal delectation. Then she pulled on a pair of black, lace-top stockings and finally stepped into a pair of calf-length, brown suede boots with heels that made her ever so slightly taller than him. As she clipped a black velvet choker with a silver Viking rune around her neck, she turned in the full length mirror they kept by their bed and smiled. Archie'd never twigged that she controlled him by her very eagerness to please.

That was the beauty of their intricate erotic dance: she acted the role of the submissive because it turned Archie on, and when Archie was turned on she got what she needed, which was long hours of lovemaking. Carefully, gradually, she'd initiated him into the finer points of domination and surrender, and he didn't even know she was leading him, poor sod. If she dressed in a revealing outfit in the evening, he thought it was because she was hungry for him, because she wanted to submit to her "Thor." But the truth was she loved luring him, having him perform for her, loved having her puppet think he was pulling the strings.

He was so into his fantasy of being descended from the Norse gods that he had taken lately to carrying an antique broadsword to the meetings of their Druid grove—in fact, he had a collection of swords mounted on the wall of his ground floor office. And he had become obsessed with the legends and occult practices he believed these gods practiced. The swords made Charlotte laugh; the symbolism was so obvious.

But she tolerated his eccentricities because what she needed, what she craved more than anything, was financial safety. Charlotte had been the eldest of five in a motherless family headed by her father, Brian, a laborer at the Delabole slate mine in the north of Cornwall. Her mum had died giving birth to her last child, another daughter. Her dad was proud to work the mine: "roofed most of London from this mine over the years," he'd crow. But even when her dad was working, they struggled to make ends meet, and when cheaper roofing materials began appearing and the mine began to cut back, they struggled even to be fed. She loved her dad, cared for her brothers and sisters, and had given up much in the doing of it. She was the vigilant one who got the bills paid, the one who got the younger kids to school, the one who shored up her failing dad, the one who made him believe he was still in charge, right up until he was gone. Lung cancer.

This was the only way she knew to be in a relationship with a man. Her blueprint, her template, the role she'd always played, was watchfulness and control. It worked just fine with her first husband, until he found someone younger. And it was a role she played still. For she was a miner, too, working on a promising lode called Archie.

Archie rumbled into the farmyard that Friday evening and parked the tractor beneath the shelter of the old slate-roofed stone outbuilding that served as his barn. Though he must have known she was there from her car, he rummaged around in the back of the machinery shed, out of sight, longer than usual.

There was a damp chill to the late March evening and Charlotte had set a fire in the kitchen fireplace, a hearth so wide she could step inside it and yet not touch its sides with her arms outspread. It had a massive and blackened oak beam as a lintel and there was still a forged iron arm hammered between the stones from which cooking pots would have been suspended long ago. Archie'd had a small coal grate set into the maw of the hearth: more efficient than burning wood, but far less romantic. It saved money on heating elsewhere in the house and made the big kitchen their warm lair. Later, supper done, she'd turn out the electric lights and there would be only candles and the light from the glowing coals. And the sturdy oak kitchen table to play upon.

But now, while she prepared their meal, Charlotte watched through the kitchen window and wondered what was taking Archie so long.

Finally he emerged, crossed the forecourt, and came through the back door, whistling. When he entered the kitchen and saw her outfit, he grinned and slipped a hand high up her leg.

She shivered, but slapped his hand away. "Go on, ya' randy bastard, and wash the farm off your body. Plenty of time for that later!"

That got him. Archie sloped off into the house to bathe and change. She had a pint glass of Sharps Special ale waiting on the little cricket table beside the fire when Archie came back downstairs. He settled into his favorite chair and downed the pint like a man who'd been lost in a desert.

"What's for tea, then?" he growled.

"We call it supper now, in this century, Arch."

He made a face.

"One of your favorites," she continued, bringing him a refill. "Cumberland sausage smothered in caramelized leeks with potato and parsnip mash. Will that satisfy my Thor?" She bent at the waist to display breasts barely contained in her loose linen blouse.

"Only one thing satisfies Thor. An' Thor knows you like your sausage, he does. No wonder we call 'em 'bangers, eh?"

She giggled. "But first, my lord, you must be fed, to renew your strength..."

The play had begun. They knew their lines. And Charlotte knew that when he'd eaten and had his third or fourth pint he would either bend her over the table or haul her upstairs and make demands of her she was only too eager to fulfill…because she'd set the rules.

She served and poured. This was going very well. One day, soon, he would be hers completely. Patience. Submission. Control. These were her weapons.

Four

ON MONDAY MORNING, second April, Archie Hansen gulped his coffee, tore off a bite from a buttered hunk of brown granary bread slathered with orange marmalade, and looked out through his kitchen window and across the yard to the building opposite. Not for the first time, he wished he'd had a proper enclosed barn. The stone outbuilding across the concrete yard was more a large slant-roofed shed, stone walls closing it on three sides but open to the sheltered courtyard. He didn't have animals to protect or bags of perishable feed to store so the massive slate-roofed structure, its lichen-encrusted granite walls dating from the eighteenth century, was sufficient to keep his tractor and its accessories sheltered from the elements and protect the other supplies necessary for the crops he cultivated.

But it was a poor place for hiding treasure.

Still in his slippers, the leather of which was crackled like an alligator's hide, he shuffled into his "office," barely a pantry off the kitchen, which housed his aging desktop computer and, mounted on one wall, his collection of antique swords. He turned the computer on and, when the aging monitor finally awoke, pecked away at the keyboard, once ivory but now grimy from his farmers fingers. Normally he used the machine to check the weather forecasts, follow commodity prices, and order seed, bulbs, or equipment. But not this morning. This morning he was using it to search for dealers in antiquities. That was the word: *antiquities*; it had taken him a while to find the right search term. He peered at the screen, then pulled out his mobile and punched in a number.

"Good morning, Bonhams London," a young woman's posh voice answered. "May I connect you with one of our departments?"

"I, ah…I'm not sure which one."

"Was there something in our catalogue or auction schedule you wished to discuss?"

"No, it's to do with Roman jewelry, I reckon."

"Buyer or seller?" the chipper voice asked.

"Seller, actually." Archie was trying to sound posh, too, but feared his thick Cornish accent belied his efforts.

"I'll just connect you, then, shall I?"

Archie wondered if it was really a question.

He went through roughly the same drill with the next receptionist before being connected, finally, to a curator.

"This is Hugh Edwards," a plummy voice purred. "How may I be of assistance, Mr.…?"

Archie blurted the first false name he could think of: "Tregareth."

"Yes, Mr. Tregareth?"

"I have what I reckon may be some Roman stuff, in gold, and some other things, coins mostly. Found them plowing one of my fields. In the Southwest."

There was the slightest intake of breath. "I see. Yes, that would most certainly be of interest, Mr. Tregareth. You have reported these objects, of course, under the Treasure Act of 1996?"

"The what?"

A pause: "I'll take that as a 'no' then, shall I?"

Archie wanted to reach through the phone and throttle the poncey bastard.

"You see, Mr. Tregareth," Edwards continued, "one has a legal obligation to report finds of ancient artifacts to the county coroner's office where one resides and to do so within fourteen days of one's discovery. The coroner will hold an inquest sometime in the next six months. If the coroner's inquest declares the artifacts treasure under the meaning of the act, then they, in turn, will contact the Department of Portable Antiquities and Treasure at the British Museum, which will arrange a valuation."

"Yeah, but what about selling them straightaway?"

"We could not possibly offer at auction the pieces you have found, sir—assuming they are genuine. That is illegal. On the other hand, under the terms of the Act, you could be due a reward equal to the full market value of the find, in which case no sale would be involved. The treasure reverts to the Crown and is held by the British Museum, you see."

Archie didn't see and didn't much care: "How long's that evaluation take, then?"

"Oh, it's a meticulous process, as you might imagine with items of great antiquity and value. The museum will choose one or more experts…like myself"—Archie did not miss the tone of superiority—"to appraise the pieces, determine their authenticity, and ascertain their value. It involves much research and easily could take another year or two, depending on the rarity of the items. Our responsibility is to the Crown, you see, Mr. Tregareth."

"Mr. Tregareth? Hello?"

But Archie had rung off.

Hugh Edwards sat for a while in his richly-furnished, wood-paneled office and finally called a private number at the British Museum.

"Roger? Hugh here. Just thought you should know I had some rustic give me a bell just now wanting us to sell what he claims are pieces of Roman jewelry and coins he's found on his farm somewhere in the Southwest. No, he hasn't reported it. Yes, I informed him, of course I did. Said his name was Tregareth; that's all I got. I also got the impression he didn't want to report and was looking to sell quickly. Of *course* I bloody well turned him down, Roger; what do you make me? No, I didn't get more of his particulars; he rang off while I was in mid-sentence, if you can believe it. No, I *didn't* bore him to death! Jesus, you stuffy old queen, why did I bother? Consider yourself forewarned."

Roger Montague, director of the British Museum's Department of Prehistoric and Romano-British Antiquities, stood at his rain-streaked office window overlooking Great Russell Street and very nearly sniffed, like a hound, trying to catch the scent of gold from the far-off Southwest. The game was on, there was treasure to be located and returned to the Crown. The problem with

Hugh and Bonhams was all they cared about was what they could sell at auction. Crown treasure was nothing to them, but everything to him. His job was to do with heritage and history. It was a noble assignment.

Tregareth. Strange name, he thought.

ARCHIE HAD BEEN pacing his kitchen ever since his call to Bonhams, worried he'd given too much away. He'd chosen Bonhams simply because, alphabetically, it was the first dealer listed on Wikipedia. But the Treasure Act? Who'd ever heard of such a thing? Bloody government meddling in his private affairs, on his own land, is what that was. He voted Conservative to rid the country of this sort of officious meddling and look where it had got him!

Then, he thought of eBay. But when he tried to list his finds, he hit an electronic stone wall, an eBay "Restricted" warning: *Sellers listing items of potential Treasure found in England and Wales on or after 24 September 1997 should be able to provide proof that the items were reported under the Treasure Act.*

"Son of a bitch!" He kicked a leg of his desk, walked out into the kitchen, and stared across the courtyard to the shed. Then he picked up his mobile again.

"Reg," he said when the call connected.

"Archie, you old Cornish knave, what rock you been hidin' under? Wantin' back into the dirty videos game, are you? One of our top distributors, you were, but that game's over, my friend, done in by the bloody Internet, not that we haven't adapted a'course…"

"Like I don't know? No, this is different. Bigger."

"Oh?"

"I need somebody who deals in antiquities, Reg."

"*Antiquities*, is it? What's that mean in English?"

"Ancient jewelry and artifacts. Roman, I reckon."

He heard a whistled breath.

"A bit out of my league that is, you know, Arch."

"But you might know someone?"

A pause.

"I might do."

Five

"WEIGHT?" DR. JENNIFER Duncan demanded. On her home turf, the Royal Cornwall Hospital mortuary in Truro, the forensic pathologist did not mince words.

It was early Thursday evening, seventeenth May, several hours after DI Davies had received the floater from the Coastguard at Newlyn. Scotty Thomas, the bearded and bearish mortuary manager, read the weight of the body, white and shiny as a huge slab of filleted Atlantic halibut, from the digital read-out at the head of the stainless steel trolley.

"Eighty-three kilos, Doc."

"Height?"

"One point seven three meters. Little chap."

Duncan laughed. "Only compared to you, you beast."

Thomas grinned. "Why thank you, ma'am. Didn't think you'd taken notice of my splendid physique."

"I haven't, you randy ape. Don't get any ideas."

Duncan, one of two contract forensic pathologists serving the Devon and Cornwall Police, had worked with Scotty for several years now. They'd had a rocky start, principally because Duncan, though in her mid-thirties, was impossibly young-looking and, to make matters worse, a silken blond of very fine construction.

Her forensic skills notwithstanding, it had taken her quite some time to be taken seriously by the old boys. But no one misjudged her any longer: she was all business. And the only thing sharper than her scalpel was her tongue.

From a perch on a stool near the door, DI Davies smiled: *Sisters under the skin, Jenn and I are…"*

"We await your convenience, Calum," Duncan called now, her impatience echoing in the white tiled autopsy room.

"Listen here, young lady," crime scene manager Calum West said from atop the tall folding ladder from which he was taking digital record photos of the body, "my job is as vital as yours, just not as bloody, thank God."

"Don't get all high and mighty."

"It's the ladder."

"Then get down here."

"Patience is a virtue."

"Virtue is overrated and bodies deteriorate."

"You're still single, am I right?" West said, finishing and climbing to the tiled floor.

"What's that to do with anything?"

"Just suggesting you might be a bit more tolerant of the men in your life."

"Most of the men in my life are dead, Calum."

"Mine, too, Jenn," said Davies from her perch, "but the difference is they're still breathing."

Duncan gave Davies a thumbs up and chuckled.

"Jaded, you ladies are, more's the pity. Plenty of fine gents about." This from Roger Morris, West's best exhibits manager. He sat on another high stool beside a stainless table, ready to receive and preserve tissue and organ samples from Duncan. A trim, gentle fellow just turned forty, few women had been able to see past his face, which, thanks to rampant adolescent acne, looked like a bomb-cratered acre of the Somme from World War One.

"Send me a list when you have a moment, Roger," Duncan snapped.

Theirs was a gruesome job, and their banter made it less so. They were, in fact, close friends and a well-matched team.

West and Thomas, both dressed in green scrubs and blue paper booties like Duncan, Morris, and Davies, pushed the trolley across the room and lifted the blanched body to the autopsy table where Duncan waited. There were three such tables, just over waist-high, in the long room. Each high-rimmed ceramic platform was shoulder-broad at one end and ankle-narrow at the other, not unlike a lidless porcelain coffin with short sides. Each was supported by two white stanchions thick as tree trunks. West often wondered what sort of local calamity would require all three tables to be in use at once; his cases had only ever required one.

Duncan had a small digital tape recorder tucked into the breast pocket of her scrubs. This was a new bit of technology; she'd previously taken written notes, shuttling back and forth from the autopsy table to a stainless steel counter where her paperwork lay. But that method was too inefficient for her now, a time-waster; she'd transcribe her oral observations later.

"I begin with an assessment of what appear to be ante-mortem injuries," she said into the recorder, "specifically, shallow linear slashes on the torso. There are no wounds about the face, as if that had been spared intentionally. Wounds are inconsistent with marine predator attacks. I suspect a straight or only slightly curved weapon. A machete, perhaps, but others are possible."

"Let's say the chap fell overboard. Could those be propeller marks?" Calum asked from the opposite side of the table.

"Thought of that when I first saw him, and called a pathologist at Cambridge who's an expert on propeller marks. He was one of my teachers. He says not a chance."

"You were at Cambridge?"

"Don't look so surprised, Calum…"

She returned to the tape recorder: "The buttocks and back are grazed as if the victim has been dragged across rough ground, concrete, or shingle. As for time spent in water, there is no sign of maceration of the hands or feet, no detachment of the skin, no bloating. No gull pecking on the back, either." Leaning hard, Duncan compressed the chest and only the slightest drizzle of soapy foam escaped from the victim's mouth. She crossed her arms and said nothing for a moment.

"This is, without question, a dry drowning," she said finally, "which is to say the victim, though alive, was unconscious and face-down when entering the water. The initial intake of seawater was small and his larynx spasmed. He suffocated. He did not ingest seawater. I believe the victim was in the water a very short period of time before being found. Not less than one hour, not more than four. Bloodstream diatom tests are unwarranted."

Taking up a scalpel next, Duncan cut a deep, clean incision down from each ear, around and beneath the jaw, stopping just above the sternum. From there, she drew the blade down the center of the chest, veering slightly to the left at the navel, then continuing all the way to the pubic bone.

Calum had always marveled at the absence of blood in post mortems. Dead bodies don't bleed.

Using scalpel and shears, she cut through the connective tissue along each side of the chest, retracted the skin, and examined the ribcage.

Next, she lifted the ribcage free, revealing the lungs and heart beneath. She set the chest cage aside to be returned to the body at the conclusion of the autopsy.

Working quickly but methodically, she began removing organs, starting with the heart and lungs. The lungs evidenced no excess fluid, reinforcing her conclusion that suffocation, not drowning, was the cause of death. From the heart, she took blood samples which she shifted to Morris. These and several tissue samples would be sent upstairs to the hospital's tox lab. With any luck they'd have results by the next day.

Moving on, Duncan removed, examined, and weighed other organs. Finally, she made an ear-to-ear incision across the top of the victim's head, pulled the scalp both front and back as if peeling a fruit, and then used her Stryker saw to remove the top of the skull.

As she always did at this stage, Morgan rose from her seat along the wall and left the autopsy room. She wasn't squeamish, but there was something about opening the skull which seemed to her a profound violation. She didn't hold much truck with notions of "the spirit," even after the last case with that witch, Tamsin Bran, with its apparent visitations from the spiritual "Annown," the after-world. She still hadn't fully got her mind around that experience. But the brain was a sacred organ to her, the place where reason resided. And reason—clear, icy, almost mathematical—was the mechanism by which Morgan coped with the world she encountered as a policewoman. It was also how she'd coped with the traumas of her childhood, and it had sped her advancement in the force.

Duncan cut free the victim's brain and, after taking tissue samples, placed it in a container of formalin.

As he assisted, much of this work seemed superfluous to Calum West. From his point of view as scene of crimes manager, the victim had died in the water. That was obvious, even if the man had not, technically, drowned. And the victim was assaulted, his body lacerated. That, too, was obvious. There didn't seem to be much more to learn. His impatience, he knew, was due principally to the fact that he had no crime scene to investigate: no bloody room, no patch of turf in a park, no damp alley: just a naked anonymous body afloat on an empty sea. The body, in fact, was his only "scene." Still, he respected Duncan's commitment to procedure and held his tongue. As he watched her work, she reminded him oddly of a seasoned barkeep at a pub: she moved fluidly and continuously, without a single wasted motion: slicing, sampling, turning, and slicing again, as if choreographed. The only thing missing were the punters at the other side of the bar, their pint jars raised to signal for a refill.

"Cause of death is suffocation, the wounds incidental," she finally said into her recorder, stepping away from the table after midnight and making room for Thomas to return the organs and rib cage and sew the body back together.

"But clearly not accidental," Davies said. She'd returned from the staff room.

"Not with those wounds, no."

"He didn't bleed to death?"

"No; the cuts are shallow, deliberate, and irrelevant to cause of death. A swipe in the right place—neck, leg, any major artery—would have killed him quickly. These wounds were intentional and designed to maim, not kill."

"It could have been torture, then?"

"Maybe. Or punishment. Same thing, really."

West cocked his balding head and smiled. "You moving up to detective, Jennifer?"

"You call that moving up?"

Like an actor in a silent film, West winced, hands up as if for protection. Davies and Thomas both laughed.

"Remind me, Jennifer, why we have you under contract?" West countered.

"Because I'm the best you've got." Then, tired as she was, she threw a runway model's pose: "And so decorative."

"I won't contest that."

She shot him a look: "Which?"

"That shall be my secret."

Davies had run out of patience. She wanted to go home, have a vodka tonic or three, and slump into her bed. "There's a Major Crime Investigation Team meeting with DCI Penwarren at the Falmouth nick tomorrow morning at nine. You'll attend, Jennifer?"

"Live bodies or dead?"

"Live. Mostly."

"I'll be there."

Six

"SO I MAY know of a chappie, down Bristol way..." Reg Connor said.

It was Wednesday morning, fourth April, and Archie was on his tractor bumping up a stone walled, single lane track to another of his fields. He pulled into a layby, switched off the throbbing engine, and pressed the mobile to his ear. His hearing wasn't what it used to be.

"I'm listening."

"Goes to these rare coin shows around the country, he does. Buys stuff found by detectorists..."

"Who?"

"*Detectorists.* Guys who go 'round the countryside with metal detectors looking for buried coins and such. Popular hobby, I hear. Anyway, this chap buys the stuff from finders and then sells it on to dealers and collectors who don't ask too many questions about provenance."

"*Provenance?* Who's that when he's at home?"

"Place it came from, is what that means, Arch...where it was found. Detectorists are not supposed to dig up this stuff on someone's land without permission. Some of them do anyway. *Night hawks,* they're called. They dig at night. You need to get up to speed on this, Arch."

"Found this stuff on my own land, I did."

"You weren't roamin' around somewhere with a metal detector?"

"Sod you, Reg; hit it with my tractor, didn't I?"

"Works for me, friend."

"So who's this chap and where do I find him?"

"Name's Richard Townsend. Goes by 'Dicky,' if you can credit it. There's a coin show at the Grand Hotel in Bristol this Saturday, the seventh. He'll be there."

"Bristol's hours away."

"Inconvenient, innit? Look Archie, you got something to sell? You go where they're buyin', see what I mean? And Arch, my lad, this ain't peddlin' naughty videos, you know."

"Yeah, I get that."

"I don't think you do, Arch. You're into heavy territory. Keep your head down, okay, pal?"

THAT SATURDAY, ARCHIE Hansen stepped into the lobby of the Grand Hotel on Broad Street in Bristol just before eleven, after an hours-long drive north lugging along in the slow lanes of the A30 and M5 in his aging Land Rover Defender. It was a farm vehicle, not a motorway rocket. He was wearing his best and only suit—an out-of-fashion navy blue worsted, shiny in the seat and worn at the elbows from too many boozy weddings and wakes. Within moments of stepping through the hotel's revolving doors, he was approached by a mincing young man in a tight-fitting black suit with the hotel's name and crest embroidered in gold on the jacket's chest pocket. A slender badge above the pocket said, *Concierge,* which meant nothing to Archie and sounded suspiciously French.

"May I help you, sir?" the young man oozed, his right hand smoothing back slicked blond hair too white to be natural, while at the same time noting Archie's suit and shoes with subtle disapproval.

"Coin show," Archie mumbled.

The concierge was visibly relieved, this alien visitor now slotted into an acceptable pigeonhole: "Ah yes: that would be the Cavendish Room, second level, left out of the lift," he said, taking Archie's elbow and whisking him out of the sparkling lobby toward the elevators at the back.

The Cavendish Room was like nothing Archie had ever seen before, except perhaps in shows on the telly about stately homes. He stood at the door and marveled at its high, coffered ceiling supported by six towering ivory and gold striped Greek columns with fanciful leaf patterns at the top. Three huge, pear-shaped chandeliers with hundreds of crystals hung along the center of the room, sending shards of light in every direction. Soaring multi-paned windows trimmed in the Georgian style flanked two exterior corner walls and were framed and capped with triangular pediments and draped in slate-blue fabric. The ruby red walls opposite the windows were hung with large, age-darkened landscape paintings. The carpet, in a vaguely oriental pattern, was of a matching red and slate blue. Arrayed along the walls of the long and crowded room were at least two dozen linen-draped tables belonging to dealers in coins and other antiquities. At each, modest printed signs of folded white poster board announced their names. The dealers, mostly men, lounged in chairs behind their tables and eyed each visitor, as if estimating the size of their wallets, rising and bowing to anyone who looked promising.

They ignored Archie.

It took him several minutes of elbowing among the well-dressed collectors and visiting dealers before he came upon Townsend Antiquities. The chap behind the table was short, a bit more fit than Archie, and balding at the temples, his hair grey there but ash blond elsewhere. He wore a sagging corduroy jacket the color of mud and an open-necked white dress shirt in need of pressing. A black jeweler's loupe dangled from a braided leather lanyard around his neck. He had no customers. He gestured to the artifacts displayed on his table:

"Something here of interest, my good man?"

"Yourself, I reckon," Archie said, his hands clasped behind his back in the manner of a browser.

"Oh, yes?"

"You Townsend, then?" Archie asked without lifting his eyes from the items displayed on the table. They looked very old and ill-used.

"Was last time I checked. And you'd be…?"

Archie ignored the question. "Pal of mine, Reg Connor, put me on to you, he did."

The dealer stood and extended his hand: "Dicky Townsend." The man's head was large and nearly bulbous, out of scale with the rest of him. Archie reckoned him late forties.

"Did he, now? Good old Reg!"

"He did. Old business partner, Reg is, you see. We go way back, right? Said I could trust you."

"And you most certainly can," Townsend said. He had the rumbly voice of someone bigger and he pitched it just below the hum of the crowd at the other tables. "But with what, is what I'm wondering, Mr....?"

Archie hesitated for a moment. No use lying; Reg would have put the chap wise by now anyway. "Hansen," he answered finally. "Archie Hansen. From down Cornwall way."

"Ah," Townsend said, as if that explained much. "And how may I help you, Mr. Hansen?"

"Found some items on my farm. Reckon they're old." Archie looked around at the other people milling about the display tables. "You get a break for lunch or something?"

"Did you have something to show me, Mr. Hansen? Something of interest?"

Archie stuffed a hand in his suit pocket, pulled out a dirty handkerchief, unfolded it, and revealed a tarnished bronze brooch cupped in his palm. Just as quickly, he returned it.

Dicky Townsend nodded, flipped his dealer's card face downward on the table, scooped the few items he had on display into a shiny black briefcase, spun its combination lock, and said, "The Commercial Rooms pub is just around the corner on Corn Street. Good food, good beer. Better than this bloody hotel. You wouldn't sleep in a restaurant, I always say, why would you eat in a hotel, eh?"

A few minutes later, Archie stood outside The Commercial Rooms gazing at the building's façade as if rooted to the pavement.

Dicky smiled. "Bloody gorgeous, innit?"

To Archie the pub looked more like a museum, or maybe a fancy old bank building. In the midday sun its limestone façade and pillars glowed as if coated in honey.

"One of the first neoclassical buildings in Bristol. Built 1810," Townsend explained. "See that triangular pediment over the entry with the four columns supporting it? That's high Georgian, that is. Most of central Bath, just up the road, looks like this, but Bristol was a working port. It took another thirty years for culture to arrive."

"And this is their idea of a pub?"

Dicky laughed and guided Archie up the worn stone steps to the door. "That's only lately, my friend. It was built first as a sort of private club for the wealthy shipping merchants of the day. Even had a special weathervane on the roof so they'd know when the wind was right to bring their ships up through the Avon River gorge to the docks."

Archie stepped through the door and gazed at the soaring interior, even more richly carved and decorated than the building's façade. The walls were easily eighteen feet high and divided by ornate Grecian pilasters into panels painted a pale yellow, outlined in deep burgundy red. Above the center of the room, a yellow- and orange-painted dome soared even higher, its sides ringed with glass segments and its summit supported by twelve columns in the shape of Greek goddesses. Like a tour guide, Townsend pointed it all out.

"How d'you know all this?" Archie asked.

"Read history at Oxford until I chucked it, didn't I? Decided I'd starve as a scholar and moved on. Been dealing in antiquities, more or less, ever since."

They secured a small round table and Townsend swept up three plastic cards that were wedged into a slot in a metal tray holding catsup, mustard, and HP Sauce. He palmed the one from which he'd learned the building's history and passed Archie a menu with pictures of the offerings. He'd been here before. The pub, despite its historic location, was now part of a chain: the beer good, the food execrable.

"My shout, Archie. What'll it be?"

Archie looked at the pricey menu and jammed it back into its holder. "Pint of Doom Bar and a bag of ready-salted crisps will do me."

"No Doom Bar in this house. But if you like Doom, I'd go with Old Speckled Hen. Similar, it is, creamy and amber."

Archie nodded and Dicky set off for the bar like a waiter expecting a big tip for his haste. When he returned, he had Archie's pint in one hand and a double whisky on ice in the other. The bag of crisps he held in his teeth, which were uneven. He sat, took a sip from his glass, and smiled so unctuously that he reminded Archie of an over-eager tractor salesman.

"So, about that item in your pocket. Might I have a closer look? No one in here will know or care, believe me."

Archie pulled out the brooch and passed it to Townsend, who immediately popped the jeweler's loupe in his left eye and squinted. After a moment, he looked up. "You an MD?"

"Doctor?"

"Metal detectorist."

"Don't be daft; I'm a farmer. Came upon this and more while working a field."

"More, eh? Your own land or leased?"

"What's that matter?"

"Somebody else's land; somebody else's property."

"Mine, then."

Townsend smiled. "And there are others like this?"

"Yeah, a few pins, big gold necklaces, bracelets, a buckle or some such, that sorta thing."

"So, why are you talking to me about this?"

"'Cause Reg said you could be trusted."

"Yeah, but why haven't you reported this to the Crown under the Treasure Act? You could be handsomely rewarded." Dicky had read up on the law.

"And be dead of old age before they get around to a valuation? Oh aye, I looked into it, I did. Takes forever, that does. Bird in the hand's worth two in the bush is what I'm thinkin'."

"I hear you, Archie. But here's the problem as I see it. Take that bronze brooch for example. Lovely piece, that is, especially with that abstract horse decoration on the face."

Hansen nodded.

"This piece here, I'm thinking, is pre-Roman. Romans always stamped the image of their emperor on stuff like that, like coins. Not abstract horse images like this one."

"So what?"

"The 'so what' is that, to the British Museum, that single piece, if it is indeed pre-Roman, might be worth anywhere between five hundred and five thousand pounds. Hard to say." Hard to say because, while Dicky had boned up on history, he had no idea about value. Yet.

He watched Archie's eyebrows jump.

"No way of knowing the total value of your find till the museum and their lads evaluate it and, like you say, that could take years. Depends on rarity, in part. There have been other finds around the country over the years. They're called *hoards,* because valuables like this might have been buried, or hoarded, in troubled times, like in underground safe deposit boxes.

"Now, say you try to sell them to an auction house. Because these pieces are ancient and unique and unreported to the Crown, auction houses won't take them on. Too risky, that. Violation of the Act. You following me?"

"Already know that."

"Then, let's say you sell them to me, yeah? When I sell them on, I have no legal responsibility to guarantee the provenance or the actual date when this stuff was discovered, see?"

Hansen nodded.

"But let's say that you tell me your beloved granddad found these items way back in, say, the nineteen fifties, and your family's just been holding on to them as, I don't know, keepsakes, maybe? And now you need the money they might fetch to keep your farm afloat, yeah?"

"Farm's doing fine."

"I'm just sayin', okay, Archie? This is what we might call a *scenario*, yeah? Hypothetical, it is. And let's say that what your granddad passed down in his story was that this stuff he found while plowing was part of a burial chamber, items meant to accompany an old chieftain or whomever into the afterlife. It wasn't just squirreled away for safe-keeping during, say, a conflict among tribes. Which is to say it wasn't a hoard, it's burial goods."

"Yeah. I get it. So what's that mean to me?"

"So under that scenario, you see, you and me, we can deal. And I can look for buyers for you. Now, let's be clear: no way you'll get near what the Crown might offer, and here's why: I have to find private collectors—very private—who want to acquire antiquities before the Crown gets hold of them, see what I mean? On the quiet. There are collectors who'd want to buy, don't you fret about that, Archie. And I know them. They're mostly in America, Switzerland, and Germany. Some in China, too. They're greedy, rich, and they don't ask questions.

"So, if you have me sell these items for you, you'll get maybe fifty percent of what you'd get from the Crown, maybe only twenty-five percent, depending on the item and the interest of the collector." Townsend tilted his orb of a head and winked: "Except you'd get all the dosh now."

Townsend let this register and then leaned across the table.

"So here's my advice," he said, just above a whisper, "if you're a patient man, report the find to your county coroner's office. That's what the Treasure Act says is your first step. Then they'll get on to the Crown. No question you'll have to wait, maybe a couple of years, but you might get full value in the end. Maybe. If all goes well. Who knows, eh? Plus there's the other problem…"

"What's that?"

"Your farm gets listed as 'archaeologically significant' and the government decides what you can do with it..."

Archie stared across the vaulted room. He thought about what he wanted and where he thought his life was going. Change was coming, that was already in the cards. A new life. That was his secret and it excited him. *Made good money on the black market before,* he thought, *real cash in hand. Why not give it another go? To hell with the bloody Treasure Act. To hell with the government!*

He turned back to Townsend: "I've got other stuff, too."

"Pardon?"

"Dull stuff, grey. Coins, I reckon, roughly round and stamped with images. Some of them kind of fused together, like."

Dicky Townsend's heart leaped but he maintained his bland frog-eyed gaze.

"I can't say as I'd hold out much hope for the dull stuff, as you call it," Dicky lied, "but I'd be happy to have a look-see. Perhaps we should set up an appointment for a private viewing?"

Archie was wary: "Have to think about that, I will."

"You think our pal Reg would have put you on to me if I wasn't your man?"

"That's as may be; you're the first dealer I tried."

"And the best." He leaned forward again, looked left and right, and added: "Thing is, another dealer might report you. I won't."

While Archie thought about that, Townsend looked off across the room. "Cornwall, eh? Used to holiday there as a lad. Down Newquay way. Great beaches there."

"That's the north of Cornwall, that is. Full of them surfers now. I'm in the southwest, Channel side."

"Where's that?"

But Archie figured he'd already said too much.

Townsend reached into the pocket of his old jacket and pulled out a business card, crisp as new money.

"When you're ready, friend—and I understand your caution, believe me—give me a bell. I'll take good care of you, yeah?"

"Right. Yeah. Thanks."

"Can't buy you lunch? Terrific steak and ale pie here."

"Got to get back to the farm, I do." He touched his cap, which he hadn't removed. "Ta."

Townsend knocked back the rest of his whisky, and followed. "Parked at the Grand, are you? I'll walk with you. Got to get back to my table there anyway..."

In the hotel's car park, Townsend waved Archie home, but not before taking note of his registration plate. He never returned to the hotel.

Seven

MORGAN DAVIES HAD never liked the Dracaena Road police station in Falmouth. She'd been there several times when she was head of CID in Penzance. The two-story nick was virtually windowless from the ground to halfway up the second story—a blank, unwelcoming face to the public painted a cadaverous white. High up, just beneath its wide overhanging roof, a band painted black as a scowl ringed the upper floor and the dark, tiny windows punctuating that level looked like machine gun ports in a wartime blockhouse.

The ground floor was devoted principally to reception, cell blocks, and storage rooms. Local policing and response and the district's tiny criminal investigation division were lodged on the floor above. It was the cramped CID office which served as the meeting room for the hastily-assembled Major Crime Investigation Team on Friday morning, eighteenth May.

Davies entered the crowded room, and Detective Chief Inspector Arthur Penwarren—"Mister," as the popular DCI was known privately among his subordinates—looked up. She was late. West was there, as was Dr. Duncan, along with the head of the uniformed policing service in Falmouth, a representative of the Tactical Aid Group for Cornwall and, to her delight, her former colleague from Penzance, Terry Bates, just back from training and newly minted as a detective constable. No longer required to wear the regulation hat of a police constable, she'd let her ginger hair grow to a wavy luxuriance that reached almost to her shoulders.

"Ah, Morgan; good of you to finally join us…" Penwarren said, lifting a long-suffering eyebrow.

"Sorry, sir. Traffic."

"Would that be the same traffic I encountered coming down from Bodmin? Curious, don't you think, that I managed to arrive on time?"

"You were no doubt wise to leave earlier than I, sir."

The plain fact was that Davies had left her newly-rented eighteenth century granite cottage in the high moors above Bodmin just before dawn. She had done so for the express purpose of being able to make a leisurely tour of the Channel coast enroute to Falmouth to the south, an area of her new jurisdiction she did not know well. This was the softer side of the Cornish Peninsula, sheltered from the screaming Atlantic gales by the high granite moors to the west: a world of lush, shallow inlets, valleys, and bays. The forested slopes on the Channel side of Cornwall were as prettily pastoral as the storm-wracked cliffs on the Atlantic side of the county were dark, cruel, and dangerous. And partly because of this stark contrast, this side of the county held a faintly mystical power over all who lived there.

Like a foundering ocean liner, the bow of which was the tip of Land's End, the whole of the Cornwall

Peninsula rose high along the cliffs on the Atlantic side and listed sharply down to the Channel side. The tidal creeks and rivers along the Channel that once had been havens for pirates and smugglers in the eighteenth and nineteenth centuries now were safe harbors filled with yacht moorings.

The waterways, though, were neither rivers nor creeks, really. That much she'd learned. They were *rias,* tidal fingers of the Channel itself that flushed nearly dry at low tide and rose full again at the high, as if receiving twice daily saline transfusions.

South of Truro, she'd slipped down minor roads, and paused first at Trelissick to watch the nineteenth-century King Harry ferry winch itself, like a waterborne inchworm, across the River Fal along the links of its submerged chain. Fulmars wheeled and screamed as the ferry crossed, and in the shallows of the mudflats and sandbars grey herons and snowy white egrets waited motionless on spindly legs to spear tiny fish. Farther out in the river, ducks flipped themselves beneath the surface as the ferry approached, reappearing many yards away, eelgrass hanging from their beaks.

Heading south on narrow, hedge-lined lanes, she crossed Restronguet Creek and Mylor Creek, finally detouring through Penryn before reaching Falmouth, the principal port on the Carrick Roads.

"What I was saying, detective inspector," Penwarren said, "is that the central challenge in this case…"

"…is that the body was nowhere near a vessel of any kind, other than the one that found him," Morgan finished.

Penwarren shook his head in amusement. Ever since their last case together, the Chynoweth murders, Morgan's quick mind and even quicker mouth often left him feeling like a figurehead. And that was fine; he liked his detectives to be aggressive, and though his own approach to cases was very nearly gentlemanly, Morgan's bulldog technique produced confessions and convictions even more effectively.

"Do we know who he is yet?" Davies asked the room in general.

"Kaminski, our forensic odontologist, will have a dental report soon," Calum West said. "We interrupted his surfing holiday at Widemouth Bay."

"Old Oleg surfs?"

"Some of us try to stay in shape, Morgan," Penwarren said.

When Penwarren arranged for Davies to be promoted from detective sergeant in Penzance to detective inspector in the major crime unit based at Bodmin, it had taken her two regimes at the gym to shape up.

"I could deck you in a heartbeat, Guv."

Penwarren burst out laughing and the tension evaporated. He took charge.

"Right, then, people: we have a middle-aged male victim found floating five miles off the Lizard. That's a long way offshore, but Dr. Duncan here says the body wasn't in the water long. A couple of hours at best. Maybe less. That rules out being swept to sea from the coast."

"The Channel was pond calm and the tide slack and low," Terry Bates said. "I checked."

Penwarren nodded to the new DC. Morgan had been right about her: this one was sharp.

"So, assuming chummy wasn't dropped from a helicopter, how does he get there? And if he fell from his own boat, where is it? If he fell overboard, couldn't swim, and both body and vessel were adrift, current and tide would have kept them in rough proximity."

Duncan spoke: "It was a dry drowning, sir. No water in the lungs. He'd have to have been unconscious already when he entered the water."

"So maybe he fell in his boat, was knocked unconscious, and then pitched into the water?" Penwarren asked.

"No corresponding head injury, sir, though there are several lacerations on the body."

"What's your assessment of those wounds?" Penwarren asked. "Your report says they are ante-mortem."

"They're superficial but consciously so. Inflicted to maim. Possibly over several days. I've seen something like this in sado-masochistic relationships gone lethal. It's torture. Then there's the lab report: the victim was heavily drugged: Lorazepam."

"Which means he didn't fall overboard," Davies said. "He was drugged, maimed, and then dumped."

"I half expected you to add, *'elementary,'* Morgan," Penwarren said, smiling. Gentle laughter around the table. "Do we have a miss-per yet?"

It was young Bates who answered: "There are hundreds of reports in the Missing Persons Index, as usual, but none answering to this chap's description and none yet reported during the time period involved here. Also, no reports from the Coastguard of trawler crewmen missing."

"Thank you, Terry," the DCI said, and he watched as Morgan smiled at her protégé.

"So let's say he was thrown overboard," Penwarren continued. "If someone was going to leave him to drown, why go to the trouble of cutting him?"

"Vengeance? Satanism?" Davies said.

"Do we have Satanists down here?"

Davies laughed: "Guv, here in Cornwall we've got satanists, druids, wiccans, witches, warlocks, shamans; paganism's going strong down here. Maybe this maiming was part of some ritual, who knows? Ever been to the witchcraft museum up Boscastle way?"

Penwarren gave a bemused shake of his head: "Can't say as I have, Morgan."

"You should…Sir. Proper museum it is with a terrific library. Went there with Tamsin Bran after the Chynoweth case in Penzance last year."

"Ah yes, the witch, Ms. Bran. Planning on bringing her in on this case too, are you?"

"Early days, boss. And I didn't bring her in; she was already a person of interest in that case, as you'll recall. And she helped break it."

Smiles around the table. Calling on a witch to help solve a murder was so typical of Davies. She never let protocol get in the way of an investigation.

Still, they all loved to watch Davies and Penwarren spar…and loved the fact that the DCI seemed to relish it. Different as moon and sun, they were, but both shone. There was affection and respect there, and they all saw it.

"Barely managed to keep your warrant card after that last escapade," Penwarren added.

"Results, sir. It's all about results: we got our murderer."

"For kidnapping, not for murder, as you may recall."

Davies shrugged. "Of course I bloody well recall. But we put him away for a good long while. And I don't fancy being him in prison when the other inmates learn about his crimes against children…"

"Well, let's hope this new victim's had dental work from the National Health," Penwarren said. "Right now we've got only Oleg for identification, until someone reports the floater missing. I don't mind saying, those cut marks are disturbing."

Morgan smiled. There were times the DCI seemed almost prissy. It was his upper-class upbringing, she knew; he was a Harrow School boy, a Londoner, his speech and manners impeccable. It was one more reason working with him was such a pleasure. He treated everyone with courtesy. It was ingrained in his moral code. And for that simple decency, there were higher-ups in the force who distrusted him. He didn't care.

"Morgan and Calum," Penwarren said, "as soon as we ID this poor fellow, you're in charge. Terry, you're with Davies, as before. You seem to be able to tolerate her…"

"What?"

He swung his patrician head toward Morgan.

"But no witches this time, detective inspector. Are we clear?"

West chuckled. Bates looked at the floor. Morgan said nothing.

Eight

BOBBY TREGARETH, BROAD shouldered and thick necked as a Devon Red bull, had been raised in the soft tidal valleys and high stony fields of the Channel coast of Cornwall and had never wanted to be anything other than a good Cornish farmer with a good Cornish wife. Now he had both, and his Joellyn, plump and ripe as a melon, her golden brown eyes glowing, was due to give birth to a son any day. He could hardly credit that she had agreed to be with him, a young farmer barely making his field lease and equipment payments.

It was Archie Hansen who'd brought them together. Joey was a member of the group—"grove" they called themselves—of Druids that Archie led. Bobby'd not known much about Druidry, but Joey explained that Druids had been ancient Celtic pagans, dating back long before the Roman occupation, as far back as the Iron Age. They were said to be seers, sorcerers, and philosophers. They revered the natural world and the cycle of the seasons. And they believed that each soul after death, like everything else in nature, came back in another form, regenerated.

As a farmer, accustomed to shaping his life around seeding, nourishing, growing, harvesting, resting, and seeding again, it made sense to him, in a way, even though he did not participate in the grove's rites.

Joey wasn't a natural beauty, but Bobby didn't mind. He suspected that she tarted herself up to compensate for that, and maybe perhaps because she hadn't gone beyond secondary school and felt she had to put herself out a bit to be noticed. Bobby had gone on to agricultural college and had excelled, but he'd never thought Joey his inferior. She was spirited and, fact was, the bright lipstick and long eyelashes made her look bloody sexy.

From the moment they "tied the knot" in a Druid hand-fasting ceremony above the Halliggye fogou on the Trelowarren estate near Helston more than a year ago, the ceremony presided over by Archie and his partner Charlotte, Joellyn had wanted a baby. Her wanting was fierce. Exhausted from the farm work, he'd come home for supper and, as soon as they'd finished, she'd drag him up to bed and pounce upon him. It made him happy beyond measure but for a long time it came to naught. Then she told him she was pregnant.

And now the baby was due.

Joellyn lay in their bed, her belly high as a smooth, sun-warmed hillside. It was Sunday, eighth April, a fine evening, the freshly plowed soil in the field opposite redolent and earthy.

"I want to call the boy Archie," she said, her voice strong. It was not a suggestion.

Bobby, who'd been undressing, stood in his skivvies, his trousers in one hand, his mouth opening and closing soundlessly, like a landed cod.

"We depend upon Mr. Hansen for so much, Bobby—for our land, for our living. It could help give us a permanency, don't you think? Security? A connection grounded here in the earth, in the glades along the river, in the cliffs along the shore, in the fields you work every day? Archie is our benefactor and my group's spiritual leader; he would be like a guardian to our son."

Bobby couldn't credit it. A son—*his* son—should take his name from their family, just as a daughter should. That was how it was done, down through the generations. Continuity. Tradition. What would Joey's parents think, in their snug and smug little thatch-roofed, whitewashed retirement cottage perched above the river at Helford? What would they think; they who'd never thought much of him from the start, but let their willful daughter join him to simplify their lives? What would *they* think if their grandson was named Archie?

"This is all that Druid nonsense talking. It's not about us, Joey," he said, finding his voice.

"But that is part of who and what I am, Bobby. And it is not a nonsense. It is a way of being, a way of believing, a way of understanding where we fit in the natural scheme of things, in our place in the universe."

AS HE EMERGED from the birthing pool at Helston Community Hospital, Archibald Robert Tregareth announced his arrival late Wednesday afternoon, eleventh April, with a scream roughly the pitch of a

Hawk fighter jet on approach to the nearby Royal Naval Air Squadron at Culdrose. The whole idea of being born in the water worried Bobby, but Joey'd said it was best for the baby and, as usual, he let her have her way. Later, in the maternity ward, his wife, rosy cheeked and still a bit feverish from the effort, clutched the infant to her breast. Bobby struggled to connect with them and failed: they were a fully complete unit, Joey and the babe. And him? A visitor. Feeling as useless as wheels on a bird, he told his wife he had to get back to the farm and would visit the next morning, hoping she and the child could come home then.

Leaden clouds had settled over the Lizard like a skillet lid as Bobby crossed the car park and hauled his bulk into his old Land Rover Defender. He stared out the windscreen for a few moments. Perhaps it would rain; they needed that. Then he pulled out onto the A3083 and headed south toward home, to where he knew he belonged.

WORD HAD SPREAD fast and Manaccan's New Inn was packed Wednesday evening. The polished wood tables and chairs in the low slung, stone-walled lounge, were fully occupied, but most folks were crowded up against the inn's short, beamed bar.

"Lift a glass, neighbors, for our Bobby," Archie Hansen called out. "Newly a father, a great honor and a great burden. Poor devil, he's a young and free lad no more! More comfort to him! May he settle into the new job easy."

A gift for you

Enclosed is your Zip Book. When finished, please return the item and note to the desk of any Sacramento Public Library. From Sacramento Public Library Zip Book

amazon Gift Receipt

Send a Thank You Note

You can learn more about your gift or start a return here too.

Scan using the Amazon app or visit **https://a.co/d/1yLBr0B**

Too Clever By Half (A Davies & West Mystery)

Order ID: 111-5214124-6089853 Ordered on September 25, 2023

amazon.com

SGk4rxccmd

Purchase Order #: Zip Books FY23-24
Order of September 25, 2023

Qty.	Item
1	**Too Clever By Half (A Davies & West Mystery)** North, Will — Paperback **0998964948** 0998964948 9780998964942

Return or replace your item
Visit Amazon.com/returns

0/Gk4rxccmd/-1 of 1-//TCY9-CART-A/next-1dc/0/0926-05:00/0925-21:00

SmartPac

The gathered crowd didn't quite credit Archie's speech, but they did his beer, so they applauded as he ordered a new round. He was on an antic roll, the unofficial master of ceremonies, and he kept the beer and snacks coming. There were cheers and jibes for Bobby in roughly equal measure, a mix of affectionate congratulations and ribald warnings. Bobby had known most of these people since he was a boy. The sweetest moment was when Charlotte gave him a full body hug and smiled up to him: "I am so happy for you both, Bobby. Truly." But by then his head was spinning.

"WHAT WERE YOU going on about back there?" Charlotte asked Archie as they walked up the darkening lane from the New Inn that evening. They hadn't stayed until closing; few farmers, early risers all, had.

"What d'you mean?"

"You didn't seem yourself, is all."

"Don't talk nonsense, Char; I'm fit as a fiddle."

"And spending money like a drunken lord: you bought pints for half the village."

They went over a stile in a stone wall and followed a footpath uphill toward Archie's property.

"Expansive mood is all."

"Expensive, you mean."

"Look, what I do with my money is none of your business. I've got it, and more to come, and I'll do what I want with it!" He didn't even stop to address her directly.

"More to come? From where?" she asked, trying to keep up.

"Like I said, none of your business."

"But Arch, we're partners. We share!"

"We're lovers and you'll do what I say," he barked.

Stunned, as if slapped, she let him stride ahead through the gathering darkness.

Nine

MEASURING HIS STEPS with exaggerated care that night, Bobby climbed the steep stairs to the attic bedroom of the home he'd renovated for his wife. The house sat above Gillan Harbor, less than a mile from some of the fields he farmed. The bedroom he'd created under the eaves of the eighteenth century stone cottage was draped and furnished, thanks to Joey, in cheery chintz, like a picture in that *Country Living* magazine she pored over every month. It had taken him awhile and more than one blinding crash into the low oak beams supporting the roof before he managed to negotiate the room without clocking himself. Petite Joey had no such problem.

But perhaps as soon as tomorrow there would be a third occupant, and the sweet sense of sanctuary he'd so loved about this room, the cossetted two-ness of them in it, the morning views across the tiny harbor when the only sound was birdsong and the susurrate whisper of tidal changes, would be shattered with midnight cries, colicky screams, and feeding demands. He wondered idly whether he should spend the next few months on the settee downstairs, but couldn't bring himself to abandon his responsibilities.

He was a better man than that, and sure he could be a better father.

Wobbly, but feeling he must do something to welcome Joey home and make her comfortable for her return tomorrow, Bobby decided to lay out one of his wife's nightdresses and her slippers. She'd never been away from him overnight before. In her absence, it was as if his chest, normally so full of her, was suddenly like that empty chamber beneath Archie's field.

He'd never before ventured to Joey's side of their bedroom chest of drawers, as if there were some unspoken yet inviolable wall of prudence between her four drawers and his. The simple but handsome Victorian-era piece had come down through his family: sturdy stripped pine that glowed from decades of being rubbed with Briwax, its fist-sized round drawer handles made of contrasting dark walnut. The joints were dovetailed like intertwined fingers, the work of a long-forgotten but meticulous craftsman. The drawers still slid on their runners as if greased.

Joey's top drawer, he discovered, held carefully folded knickers and brassieres, each cup neatly folded into its mate's. Though he'd removed them hungrily from her body on many nights, accompanied by her bubbly giggles, he shut the drawer quickly. He felt like a trespasser. The deeper drawer below held nightdresses: well-worn nubby flannel ones for winter, which he'd never liked, and white cotton gowns with eyelet lace for summer. He loved the way these became translucent as she walked through the morning sun flooding in from the dormer windows of their bedroom. On those mornings he believed he was the luckiest man in Cornwall. There were two other short gowns in lace, one pink, one black. Those were for play. He decided they were not appropriate for a new mother, but he fingered them nonetheless, remembering. It had been a while.

As he refolded these and returned them to the drawer, he felt something hard beneath and found a black, leather-clad book. Gold letters impressed in the cover spelled, "Grimoire." He had no idea what the word meant and instinctively shoved the volume back beneath the nighties. If it was a sort of diary, he felt it something he should not open.

Grimoire. The word sounded French to him. He pulled the book out again and lifted its cover. He realized immediately that it was not a diary but something to do with Druidry—a kind of record of rites and spells Joey had participated in or learned, beginning long before he had ever met her and running up to the very present. The pages were dated and the rites seemed to have distinct purposes. Some were related to seasonal pagan festival dates: the spring equinox, Beltane, the summer solstice, the autumn equinox, the winter solstice, and so forth all around the wheel of the year. But the more recent entries were more specific and personal: rites for appearing attractive to others, for getting pregnant, for giving birth, for healing oneself or another. A few of the notations seemed written in a kind of code of letters and numbers: A216, A287, A319, A2910, A212, among others. It was a mystery.

Having no particular religious beliefs of his own, Bobby had accepted his wife's embrace of Druidry, though at a remove. Now that remove had suddenly compressed. Had she been taking instruction from her group—her *grove*? Had she needed some special rite for getting pregnant? For giving birth? Was that necessary? Did it even make sense? Other couples did nothing of the sort; they simply rejoiced at the process of conception and the birth of a child. Suddenly his wife—the mother of his newborn son—was a stranger to him, a keeper of secrets.

He lay upon their bed, fully clothed, staring at the beamed ceiling until the ale took over and he slept.

Ten

ROGER MONTAGUE, WHO was well past what should have been retirement age, had chewed on Hugh Edwards's tip about the southwest farmer's alleged treasure discovery for several days. He was not the museum's most decisive curator. But finally his acquisitive heart won. On Thursday morning, twelfth April, he pushed a number into his new office mobile, holding it as if dealing with something which might suddenly explode. He missed the old rotary phone.

"Egerton."

"That you, Bonnie? Roger Montague here."

"You were expecting someone else?"

"No, no, it's just that it's been a long time since we chatted. Didn't know whether this exchange was still valid."

"We call them phone numbers now, Roger," Bonnie said. Detective Inspector Bonnie Egerton was the head of the Metropolitan Police's Art and Antiquities Unit at New Scotland Yard, just off Victoria Street on the Broadway. It was her job to investigate illegal trade in ancient objects and art.

Bonnie waited. She could hear Montague's breathing, as if the old man were trying to get up enough steam to speak again.

"Is this a social call, or had you something to discuss?"

"As it happens, Bonnie…ah, Miss Egerton…there may be a treasure find that's being shopped."

"I'm listening…"

Another pause. Then, finally: "Got the tip from Edwards at Bonham's."

"This would be Hugh Edwards, at New Bond Street?" Egerton, who held a first in British history from Oxford, had been with the Met for more than two decades. But she'd headed the Arts and Antiquities unit for only a few years. The Edwards-Montague rivalry was legendary, however, and had long been a subject of mild amusement in her department.

"The very same but, as usual, his intelligence was inadequate."

Egerton wondered if Montague referred to Edwards's tip or his I.Q. "Did you call to complain or to give me something I might find useful?" She stood at her window on the fifth floor of the Yard's Victoria Block and gazed out toward the upper stories of the Art Deco headquarters of the London Underground, built above the St. James's Park Tube station.

"Oh, the latter. Definitely the latter."

Another pause.

She pulled the receiver away from her ear, and looked at it as if it were something that needed a slap to keep functioning.

"And...?" She struggled to stifle her exasperation.

"He says some farmer called Tregareth gave him a bell, but all Edwards learned was he was from the Southwest. No address. The rustic rang off as soon as he heard about the Treasure Act. Wanted nothing to do with it, apparently..."

"By Tre, Pol, and Pen, shall you know all Cornishmen..."

"Pardon?"

"Old rhyme, that is, Roger." Egerton, the child of a naval officer, had been raised in Plymouth, on Cornwall's Channel coast. *"Tre-gareth* would be Cornish. Doesn't mean he resides there, of course. What's Edwards say the chap's found?"

"Roman gold jewelry and coins, he claims, though, honestly, how would a farmer know, eh? I mean, really..."

"Have you heard of the Internet?"

"Yes, yes, I know; but a farmer?"

Egerton sighed. "Are you asking the Met to intervene? A bit out of our patch, the Southwest is..."

"Well, shouldn't someone?"

Egerton, like everyone else in the Met, was buried in cases. While the Prime Minister, like all prime ministers, had promised a commitment to law enforcement, most of the government's policing resources were focused now on terrorism...and rightly so, she reckoned. But it left her department, and most others, gasping for staff and funds. And anyway the Met—Scotland Yard—served London, not the provinces.

"Tell you what I'll do, Roger: I'll get on to the finds liaison officer down that way—probably connected to the Royal Cornwall Museum—and see if they can locate this Tregareth, all right?"

"They'd report to the British Museum," Montague mused wispily. "I suppose I could have done that myself..."

"Except you didn't. No problem, a nudge from Scotland Yard might help get the ball rolling, yeah?"

"My thoughts exactly, Bonnie. Grateful for your help..."

Egerton rang off, thinking: *Who really needs the nudge here?*

DICKY TOWNSEND WAS not a member of any professional antiquities association. Indeed, he was a member of no recognized association whatsoever, except perhaps, that of con artists. What Dicky excelled at, and what his boss, Reg Connor, valued him for, was that he was a chameleon. He could take on the role of almost anyone Reg needed him to become, and he could do it with such aplomb no one questioned his credentials. Dicky had not read history at Oxford, as he'd claimed to Archie Hansen. The child of performers who'd toured music halls after World War Two, he'd become a young trouper in regional theatrical performances all over Britain, where his talent for becoming who he was not was rewarded, though meagerly. Discovered, finally, by Connor, he'd moved on to more lucrative roles: impersonating antiques dealers, estate agents, artists' representatives, or whomever else Reg needed him to be to snag a deal.

Each task involved a lot of study, but Connor paid him well and Dicky had a steel trap memory. He loved the research and he loved performing the roles. They'd been partners for years.

That Thursday night, Connor and Townsend sat in a corner of The Old Royal Ship Inn at Luckington, in Wiltshire. The pub was just on the edge of the fifteen hundred acre Badminton estate. Connor had an interest in the firm that handled the betting for the annual Badminton Horse Trials, one of the most important equestrian events in Britain. A recently minted member of the horsey circle, Connor kept his perfectly groomed silver head down, socially and professionally, but, thanks to the earnings of his various enterprises, he'd turned a crumbling, cruck-roofed, seventeenth century limestone tithe barn into one of the most-admired residences in the area. He was not yet fully accepted by the local gentry, but he was a patient man…and a man used to winning.

He and Townsend were huddled at a small table beside the pub's hearth. It was a raw and misty April night, a cold wind having dropped down from Scotland. A welcoming coal fire glowed in the grate. The pub, a classic with low beams and lots of atmosphere, was mostly empty but for a knot of boisterous young men at the bar. Connor was in full country gent kit: pressed brown twill trousers, green rubber Wellies, white Tattersall checked shirt, olive green waxed Barbour countryman's coat, and flat tweed cap. The clothes were right, but Connor didn't quite pull off the look. His features were too coarse: a broad ruddy face with pores large as pox marks and a nose that had seen too many fights. Reg Connor in country kit was like a thug at a costume party.

Dicky, in his customary worn corduroy jacket, had just returned from the bar with a foam topped pint of Wadworth's 6X bitter for the boss and a double whisky for himself. It frosted him that Reg never bought a round when they met, like it was beneath him or something.

Connor passed a slip of paper across the oak table to Townsend beneath his hand, a hand, Dicky noticed, upon which the skin was loose, puckered, and age-spotted. Reg was getting on in years.

"Name's Archie Hansen, just like he said. Sharp of you to get his auto plate. Mate of mine in the local force hereabouts tracked it for me. Handy he is, for speed tickets." Connor's sleek, charcoal grey BMW M5 sport sedan sat outside in the car park like a crouched animal waiting to spring.

"Lives on the Lizard in Cornwall, this Hansen does. Had to look that up, I did. Never heard of it. Bit of land that pokes into the Channel south of Falmouth. Has a farm there called Higher Pennare. Pretty remote, which could be a good thing. Got his phone as well; just his land line, not his mobile. You'll have to work with that."

"Photos next, Reg?"

"Use that little digital Sony I gave you for the antique furniture job we did in Wales a while back. The Swansea job? When you get the images, my people can assess the value—fair market for the Crown and private market for collectors. Got that?"

Dicky nodded. The boss liked to talk down to him. Dicky, who was nobody's fool, let it pass. All in a day's work, he reckoned. Him, he stayed focused on the goal, which was to break free of Connor completely one day, and Hansen was looking like his chance.

"So I pay a visit?"

"You tell him you need photos. Without them, you can't interest the private collectors who'll reward him big-time for his find. They will want photographic evidence."

"When?"

"Yesterday."

"I'm on it," Townsend said, draining his whisky. He rose, nodded to Connor, and slipped out the low door of the pub. Connor stared at the door for a moment. Suddenly, he felt less the director and more the advisor. He didn't like it. He went to the bar and ordered another pint and a supper of chicken curry. Waiting for the pint, he turned to the closed door again and thought, *What's the lad up to?*

THE FAST TRAIN from Bristol to London's Paddington Station took less than two hours, and by eleven the next morning, Dicky Townsend was climbing the broad marble stairs from the British Museum's light-filled Great Hall to the floor above in search of Room 50: *Britain and Europe 800BC to AD 43*. He found that the long, narrow space was filled with tall glass cases. As he moved from one display to the next in the hushed room, his rubber-soled shoes squeaked on the polished wood floor. Just before the opening to the next room, *Roman Britain,* he saw something familiar in a case filled with objects from the late Iron Age: a bronze brooch not unlike the one Hansen had shown him in Bristol. The case held other brooches, as well as bronze garment pins and bracelets, many incised with patterns or decorated with what looked like bits of coral. These were mostly from the period 300-100 BC. He was amazed at the artistry of the vines and flowers etched upon the back of one particular polished bronze hand mirror. There were also spear blades, ax heads, and knives, their wooden hafts long since returned to the earth. There were even iron scissors. He wondered if they'd been for sheep shearing.

Then he turned and saw a case that made him gasp. In it were displayed several glittering, nearly-circular gold ornaments from the same period—*torcs,* the display sign called them. They were heavy, rigid necklaces made of thick strands of pure gold plaited like braids, the ends of which, probably designed to rest just below the collar bone, were finished with sculpted finials, some shaped like animal heads, others more geometric. Dating to around 50 BC, the sign above them said they were worn like badges of office by Celtic clan chieftains and their wives. Given the narrowness of their diameter and their rigidity, Townsend wondered if they'd been modeled on the wearer directly and would then be worn until death.

A case opposite presented a display of small, somewhat irregularly shaped gold coins stamped with Celtic symbols. And in an adjacent case was an exhibit of similar coins, but this time made of almost charcoal grey silver or silver alloy, many of them fused together by time and tarnish. Some of these coins, Celtic *quarter staters* they were called, also had stylized horse images stamped upon them, as well as wheat sheaves and other images he couldn't figure out. Definitely no Roman emperors. The coins were dated to before 50 BC.

Townsend had a quick look in the Roman room next door, but instinct told him that if Archie's brooch was Iron Age, the rest of the hoard would be, too. He checked the time on his mobile phone: best head back to his computer in Bristol and research what relics like these were worth. He walked out through the museum's main doors and smiled as he thought about the grey coins: *Dull stuff, indeed.*

Eleven

IT WAS SATURDAY morning, nineteenth May, two days after the floater had been pulled from the Channel, when Comms finally received a missing persons report that seemed to fit:

Woman, Charlotte Johns, reports her partner, Archie Hansen, went fishing with a friend called Charlie, seventeenth May. Has not returned. Boat missing from usual mooring.

Davies immediately rang Johns and arranged an interview. When the detective swung her car into the farmyard at the rear of Higher Pennare, her partner, DC Terry Bates, squinted through the windscreen and whistled.

"That's one ancient cob house…"

"*Cob*?"

"Way of building houses back in the eighteenth century and earlier, cob is: clay, sand, straw and water mixed and rammed into forms for the walls. Chaps who did the ramming, they were called *cobbers*."

"Where I come from, in Wales, we build houses from stone. Slate. Solid."

Bates laughed. "This is beginning to sound like *The Tale of the Three Pigs,* but 'huff and puff' all you may, a cob house will hold. Plus, those walls will be two feet thick or more, I reckon; they keep out the chill of winter and keep in the cool in summer. Fine old house is this one. Rare."

"I feel like I'm in the middle of an article in *Country Living* magazine. Only thing you're missing is the Wellies and the golden retriever!" But as she parked the car, Davies marveled yet again at this novice detective. She'd worked with her on that case last year down in Penzance, the one with the pedophile murderer and the witch, but Bates kept surprising her with how much she knew…and how much of what she knew she kept under her hat.

As they pulled into the rear farmyard, a petite figure emerged from the back door of the farmhouse. Charlotte Johns wore sandals and loose, slightly oversized clothes: a colorful skirt, blouse, and loose waistcoat, the varying patterns of which seemed engaged in some kind of pitched aesthetic battle.

Looks like a waif escaped from a Gypsy encampment, Davies thought. Davies herself was in her usual blue pantsuit and starched white blouse, her streaked blond hair set in short, sharp vertical points, like a wire brush. Bates, in crisp raw linen trousers, low saddle-brown heels, and a white cotton jumper, looked like she was on holiday. Davies would have to have a word with the lass.

"I've made tea," the woman at the door said as the two detectives showed her their warrant cards. "Will you have some?"

"That would be grand," Bates said before Davies could decline. Morgan looked at her and smiled. *No keeping this one back…*

As Johns poured, they sat at a scrubbed oak table in a vast kitchen facing an inglenook fireplace as wide as a cave entrance, complete with inset bread oven. Once, long ago, different fires in the wide hearth would have been arranged for cooking several things at once, but now it held only a squat cast iron coal stove, the exhaust pipe of which disappeared up into the maw of the old stone chimney. The stove looked like a small fish in the mouth of a whale.

"So," Davies began, "…is it not Mrs. Hansen?"

The woman smiled. "It's Charlotte Johns. I have kept my name. I believe that is acceptable these days."

Seated away at a slight angle, Bates took notes in a pocket-sized black notebook.

"Of course it is, Ms. Johns." Davies watched her for a moment and wondered about the formality of the woman's speech.

"You reported Mr. Hansen missing, last night I gather," Davies continued. "He'd gone off fishing, you told police. With a friend called Charlie. In the Channel. That was when?"

"Thursday sometime. He sent me a text message. I'm new to this texting business; he made me get a mobile. Anyway, I said this in my report."

Davies smiled. "I know you did, Ms. Johns, I'm just making sure we've got it right. What made you think something had gone amiss?"

"When Friday noon he'd not returned, I figured maybe he'd spent the night with his friend, but later I drove down to the little cove at Flushing where he anchors his boat, *Saga,* and it wasn't there."

'But his boat would have been gone, wouldn't it? If he'd gone out fishing?"

"No."

"Pardon?"

"It's a fourteen-foot, open fiberglass fishing skiff with an outboard petrol engine, detective; it's not meant for overnight trips. When I'd still not heard from him by late Friday afternoon, I rang the police in Falmouth. He's a farmer, not a fisherman. It just wasn't like him to be away. Have there been radio reports? Have you sent helicopters out to search yet?"

"Was Mr. Hansen in the habit of popping off on these fishing trips, Ms. Johns?"

"Not often. Fishing is a sort of hobby, a break from the farming routine. It relaxes him." She smiled for a moment: "And sometimes it's supper, too, if he catches something. But mostly I think he just loves being out on the water for a change."

"So you did not find this outing unusual…?"

The woman adjusted her position in her rush-seated chair. "Infrequent, yes. Unusual, no. What with the late spring this year, it is a quiet time in the fields." She looked away for a moment and added: "Beyond that, I must confess that he does not often confide his plans to me. Often he does not even leave me a note."

DC Bates rose from her seat. "I'm sorry, Ms. Johns, but could you point me to the nearest loo?"

"The house is ancient and we're a bit short on toilets, constable. You'll find one in the upstairs hall, not very posh, to the right of the landing."

"Bates?"

"Sorry, ma'am, call of nature."

Davies watched her partner disappear down the hall and wanted to throttle her. She returned her attention to the woman before her and leaned across the table: "Please pardon me for asking, Ms. Johns," she said, her voice gentle, as if inviting a confidence, "but what exactly is the nature of your relationship with Mr. Hansen, if he does not confide in you?"

Davies watched her decide how to respond. The answer, when it came, was oblique.

"We are Druids, Archie and I. There are many in Cornwall, as elsewhere of course. It's an ancient Celtic pagan practice which lives still. We worship the cycle of the seasons in the natural world, of which we are but a part. We met through Druidry, Archie and I did. We became lovers. That was five years ago, nearly. Archie now leads a small grove of Druids based here in Manaccan. He is their priest. I am the priestess. We have several regular members. In the last year, however, Archie has become something of a student of the occult. He's read many books and has delved into what some might call the dark arts. He is very secretive about it. I think it all harmless and frankly rather silly, but there are some in our grove who are frightened by it, by his attempts to cast spells. There are people who want him driven out."

"What kind of spells, Ms. Johns?" Davies noted that Johns had not answered her question.

"I'm sure I don't know."

"Excuse me?"

"He scatters powders during our rites. Sometimes he focuses intently on one or another of our members. Beyond that, I know nothing."

"And these members are intimidated?"

"I believe some are."

"And you believe so, because?"

"They tell me it makes them uncomfortable. It's not what Druidry is supposed to be about."

"Are you suggesting, Ms. Johns, that these same people might have wanted to do Mr. Hansen harm?"

"I don't know what I'm suggesting, detective. Like you, I am trying to make sense of his disappearance."

"But unlike me, Ms. Johns, you know him and his followers."

"Members, not followers."

"I appreciate your sharing this with me, but you've not answered my question: If you are married, why does he not confide to you?"

Johns stared at the surface of the table for a moment. "It is just not his nature," she said.

Davies was losing patience. "Ms. Johns, I should like you to make a detailed written statement of what you know about Mr. Hansen's disappearance: when you saw him last and where, time of his text message, and your own movements during this two day period. And please include the names of the others in your—what was it...*grove?*—if you suspect them."

Charlotte nodded. She fetched a pad of lined paper from Archie's office, took her seat again, and began writing.

Upstairs not long after, the toilet flushed and Bates eventually rejoined them. Davies leaned against the back of her chair, crossed her arms beneath the shelf of her breasts, and glared at Bates when she re-entered the kitchen.

"Tell us about Charlie, Ms. Johns," Bates said, interrupting the woman's writing.

"I can't," she said. She did not look up.

"Pardon?"

"He's never mentioned him. Could be another farmer, a school chum, a business associate. No idea."

Davies uncurled for a moment: "You have been together for some years and you don't know his friends, Ms. Johns?"

"As I have said, Archie keeps himself to himself. But I do know that none of the men at his local is called Charlie."

"And his local is?" Davies pressed.

"The New Inn at Manaccan. Just down the hill."

As they waited, Johns finished writing her statement and then rose and turned to Davies.

"Are we done here now, detective?"

"I'm afraid we're not, Ms. Johns. Please sit down again. I have something to tell you."

AT THE MORTUARY behind the Royal Cornwall Hospital at Treliske, just up the hill from Truro, Davies nodded to an attendant, and a curtain opened upon a body wrapped in gold-braided blue velvet. Only the man's face was visible. The woman beside her stared for a moment, then turned away.

"Is that him, Ms. Johns? Is that Archie Hansen?"

The woman took a deep breath and straightened her spine.

"It is." Her voice was barely audible.

Davies nodded and the attendant closed the curtain. It struck her that Charlotte Johns had gone about as pale as any human being could who still had a pulse.

"I am very sorry for your loss."

"What happened to him?"

"That hasn't yet been determined."

"IN FUTURE, *DETECTIVE* constable, when we are interviewing a person of interest in a murder investigation, you will not leave for a "call of nature" or anything else. Your job is to take notes, be a second set of ears, and ask questions. Are we clear?!"

Davies and Bates stood in the car park behind the mortuary, having sent Johns home in a patrol car with a female Family Liaison Officer charged with making sure the bereaved woman would be all right.

Bates smiled. It was not the reaction Davies expected.

"Did you look around that kitchen?" Bates asked. Her voice had a hint of mischief in it.

"Yeah, a mess it was. So what?!"

"A man mess, Morgan, is what I thought. So I decided to snoop around."

"Without a warrant?"

"Needed the loo, didn't I?"

Davies cocked her head to one side and waited.

"No woman lives there," Bates said, finally. "Not a feminine touch anywhere. Except in the main bedroom, where there's an interesting collection of costumes in one wardrobe."

"Costumes?"

"Sex costumes, I'm guessing. Lots of sexed up stuff."

"This is so out of order, Bates."

"I've had a good teacher...but the point is that no woman lives there full time. They're not married; I'd bet my warrant card on it. She's nothing but Hansen's playmate. Funny she didn't say so."

"We are not amused," Davies snapped as she climbed into her car.

Twelve

ALMOST EXACTLY A month earlier, thirteenth April, Charlotte arrived at Archie's house as she did most Fridays. She was unloading groceries from her car when she heard the kitchen phone trill. She ran to answer.

"Higher Pennare," she panted into the wall-mounted receiver.

"Oh, hello! I was hoping to reach Archie Hansen," the voice said.

This was odd. Archie seldom received calls on the land line at the house; everyone he knew used his mobile. If you wanted to reach him, he'd most likely be out on his tractor.

"May I help?"

"This Mrs. Hansen, then?"

Charlotte was immediately suspicious. "Is this a commercial call?"

The man at the other end of the line hesitated and then said, "I suppose it is, in a sense. See, I met your husband a couple of weeks ago at an antiquities and coin show in Bristol. We discussed the artifacts he's found on your farm."

Charlotte blinked: *artifacts*?

She fought for a response and found one: "Oh, yes, of course. He mentioned you, Mr....

"Townsend. Richard Townsend."

"Yes, yes, of course: Mr. Townsend. It all comes back to me now. I am so sorry to have seemed abrupt. I was outside when the phone rang."

"Not at all, ma'am; is Mr. Hansen available?"

"I'm afraid he's not. Out in the fields, he is, but he told me about your meeting and said to expect your call." She was making it up as she went, as fast as she could.

"Well, good. Excellent. What I was hoping was to arrange a meeting with you folk to do an evaluation of these items he's found."

"Yes of course; let me just get his calendar, shall I?"

Charlotte made banging and shifting noises while she gathered her wits: *Archie's found something. On the farm. Artifacts of some kind. The kind a dealer would be interested in. Was he involved in some new illegal scam?*

She picked up the receiver again.

"Hello, Mr. Townsend?"

"I'm here."

"You're coming from where?"

"Bristol."

"Ah well, that's not so bad. End of the world we are down here on the Lizard. But not so long from Bristol: you just bang right down the M5 and the A30 and, in a couple of hours, here you are! When did you have in mind, Mr. Townsend?"

"I was hoping the next few days."

"Right. Now, let me see... Ah! How about this coming Monday, the sixteenth, at one? That will give you plenty of time to drive down, do your evaluation, and return home to Bristol at a reasonable hour."

"Excellent. And thank you, Mrs. Hansen. Archie will be there?"

"He'll just be finishing his lunch," she lied. "Did you need directions?"

"Got an Ordnance Survey map of the Lizard. Higher Pennare is marked very clearly."

"That should do you. See you Monday, then?"

"You will."

"Good. South of Manaccan, we are, just above the valley."

She sat at the kitchen table and stared out the window after the call. It took a while, but finally the penny dropped…

CHARLOTTE PROWLED AROUND Archie's thick-walled tractor shed looking for something that didn't belong there and was infuriated because, since she'd never been permitted in there before, she had no way of telling what was out of place. Archie lately had been spending an inordinate amount of time in the shed after returning from the fields. *Maintenance,* he'd explained. Charlotte was not inherently suspicious, but she was ever watchful. She'd learned to be so as a girl, looking after her father and her siblings. Vigilance was a trait established deep in the most primitive "fight or flight" part of her brain. And it had served her well over the years. It had warned her something was amiss before her husband had left her, and it spoke to her now. It was almost an electric vibration within her.

As she picked her way across the concrete floor of the old stone shed, she found, as she might have predicted, that Archie's farming gear, while aging, was clean and laid out in an orderly manner. The floor contained nothing but machinery, some of which looked unused for years: a hay turner, a rusting front end loader, an antique tractor with one wheel missing, a shiny new fertilizer spreader lined up next to two older ones, and another tractor older than the one he was currently using but still looking functional.

On one wall, a pair of metal shelf units held labeled boxes of chains, nuts and bolts of various sizes, grease guns, hydraulic hoses, wrenches, and other bits and bobs which looked to have been salvaged from one or another of the relic machinery on the floor. Maybe that was why the disused equipment was still there: for parts.

In the back of the building a steep and worn wooden stair, barely more than a ladder, led to a loft space, and there she found bags of fertilizer and soil additives, each stacked in neat piles. She stood for a moment on the landing, and then realized that from this level, Archie could simply dump the bags into the hopper of a spreader below instead of hauling them down the stairs and lifting them into the hopper from the ground. Smart, that was.

She stepped around the stacks and, in a far corner, noticed a group of loosely-woven burlap bags labeled to contain daffodil bulbs. The blossom season was over. The remnant foliage in the fields was left to soak in the sun to strengthen the bulbs beneath, which were the real cash crop. Cornish daff bulbs were in high demand. The bags, therefore, were empty, sagging limply against the loft floor. Except for one, tucked beneath the others.

She poked the bag with her toe and was surprised to hear a dull metallic clunk. She was about to pull it out, but caught herself just in time: there was a length of thin, clear monofilament fishing line, virtually invisible, laid along the folds of the burlap bags.

She smiled. *Oh, you clever clogs; you've left a tell-tale, haven't you…*

Careful not to disturb the lay of the line, she knelt and eased a hand beneath the pile, searching for the bottom bag's mouth without shifting its position. Presently, she found its lip, slipped her hand inside, felt something cool and hard, and withdrew an object so bright that, even in the dim light of the loft, it seemed to flame: a curved solid gold artifact shaped like a necklace. She recognized it immediately as a *torc*. Charlotte was a volunteer with CASPN, the Cornish Ancient Sites Protection Network, whose members, many of them fellow pagans, patrolled the prehistoric monuments that were thick upon the ground throughout southwest Cornwall: stone circles, standing stones, sacred wells, Iron Age forts and villages, Stone Age burial quoits, and underground fogous. They checked for vandalism and cleared trash left by tourists. She'd attended CASPN sponsored talks, led by curators at the Royal Cornwall Museum and the Cornwall

County Council's chief archaeologist, about objects that had been looted from some of these sites centuries before. It was thought there was nothing left to discover. Archie seemed to have proved them wrong.

She returned the torc to the bag, ascertained there was more within, and left the pile and the filament undisturbed. Then, using her palms, she shifted the dirt and dust on the loft floor to eliminate any footprints that would signal she'd been there. As she walked across the concrete yard from the shed to the house, she heard again Archie's dismissive voice after the party at the New Inn celebrating Bobby and Joey's new son: *What I do with my money is none of your business. I've got it, and more to come.*

And now the "more" made sense. But where did he find these things? And what did it mean that he had told her nothing about them?

THAT NIGHT, WHEN Archie'd finally come home, been fed, and had several pints, she led him upstairs for one of his favorite games: the one where she did a slow strip for him until he broke into a sweat. Then she climbed up onto the old oak bed and knelt above him, watching his eyes.

"Was there something my Thor required?" she purred. As always, she controlled and then satisfied his needs.

REG CONNOR WALKED through the manicured parkland of the Badminton estate near his house, following the public footpath. He stopped frequently to lean on his walking stick. He was often short of breath these days: congestive heart failure, the NHS doctor had explained. The doctor prescribed a change in diet, blood thinners, and regular walks. Connor ignored the dietary and medical advice, but did walk. Sometimes the walks felt like torture, but he kept at it. It was not like Reg Connor to yield to anything or anyone. He was as driven as a border collie herding sheep.

He had been brooding about Dicky Townsend since their meeting at The Old Ship. He punched a number into his mobile.

"Let's put a watch on Townsend, eh?" he said when the call connected. "Lad's up to something. I can smell it. Some farmer down Cornwall way's found some ancient relics he doesn't want the Crown to see. Looking for a quick bob, he is, apparently.

"No, not Townsend, Max, the bloody *farmer!* Then again who knows, eh? Maybe our Dicky's looking for a quick killing, too. Came up here for a chin wag, he did, then buggered off quick. Maybe he's thinking of branching out on his own. We want to disabuse him of that notion, understand? Yeah, I knew you would. Loyal soldier you are, my friend. There are rewards for loyalty…"

IT WAS LATE that same Friday afternoon, as she was just brewing a cuppa, when the phone chirped in Patricia

Boden's cramped cubicle in the bowels of the Royal Cornwall Museum in Truro, Cornwall's county seat.

"Miss Boden, is it?" a voice said when she answered.

"Ms."

"My mistake. Bonnie Egerton, here: Metropolitan Police Art and Antiquities Unit."

"Oh yes?"

"You are the British Museum's Finds Liaison Officer for Cornwall, am I correct?"

"I am, though there's not much call for it down here."

"Well, I might have a job for you now."

"Oh yes?" Patricia said again.

A few moments after she'd rung off with Scotland Yard, Boden called the Cornwall Coroner's office in Barrack Lane across town. She'd considered first ringing her museum director, Hilary Gracefield, but decided to take this inquiry upon herself. Patricia Boden was a slender woman, a little taller than average, and she had her shoulder length hair streaked in brown and blond to disguise the emerging grey. Though divorced and edging into middle age, her crystal blue eyes flashed with intelligence and enthusiasm. Her professional skills were underutilized at the museum, but the job was what was available for a single woman in Truro with an archaeology degree, and she was grateful for the post. She also curated their Bronze and Iron Age collection. A treasure finds case was a rare excitement, the first, in fact, during her entire tenure.

"This is Patricia Boden, the Finds Liaison Officer for the British Museum at the RCM," she said to the Coroner's receptionist. "I need to speak to the coroner's officer who investigates claims under the Treasure Act."

The woman at the other end of the line laughed. "We haven't had a coroner's officer for at least two years, luv. Budget cuts."

"Then, whom?"

"Have to talk to the police, you will, I reckon, dearie."

"Where?"

"Haven't a clue; not much call for such things, you see. Not so long as I've been here and that's been donkey's ears."

Boden looked at the phone in her hand. She hadn't heard Cockney rhyming slang in, well, donkey's ears...

When they learned that the finder lived on the Lizard, Truro police bounced her to Falmouth. A young receptionist put her on hold and, after a wait long enough for Boden to rewrite her will, finally returned.

"I'm told we can assign a constable to assist you, Ms...."

"Boden."

"Yes, of course. Ms. Boden. He's new. Name's Adam Novak." She lowered her voice. "And a handsome devil he is, I might add, Miss."

"That's Ms."

"Whatever, girl."

"When?"

"This Sunday, the fifteenth. No rest for the wicked, eh? He'll meet you here at the Falmouth nick.

Technically, the station's not open at the weekend. But just press the intercom button at the front door. Eleven?"

"Yes, I can make that. We'll be going to the Lizard."

"Ah, lovely it is down there. Nice outing. Lucky you, twice!"

Boden made a face and ended the call. The station was closed on Sunday; did crime take the weekend off?

Thirteen

"HE HAD FORM, our floater did," Terry Bates said to Morgan Davies. It was Monday morning, twenty-first May, and they were at the Bodmin Operational Hub, a south-facing steel and glass, three-story building so light-filled it made Davies wish she carried sunglasses. Compared to her cramped old nick in Penzance, Bodmin was like working in a tanning salon.

"Did he, now?" They were in the CID offices on the second level, Davies hunched before a computer screen. Normally, with a murder, the office would be abuzz. But they still had little to go on in the Hansen case, and it was driving the chronically impatient Davies quietly mad. DCI Penwarren wasn't pleased, either.

"How is it that I end up in front of a computer screen and you get to do all the investigating?" Davies sniped. "What's right about that?! But do go on, constable…"

"*Detective* constable, ma'am."

Davies rolled her eyes.

Bates grinned. "There's not much, to be honest: *Suspicion of trafficking in pornographic videos,* is what we have, mostly."

"Not kiddie porn, again!" Davies snapped. It was an echo of her last big case before she left Penzance, a case in which Bates had nearly been killed.

"Nah, just the usual garbage, near as I can tell, and a few years back, as well."

"Enlighten me: what exactly is the 'usual garbage'?"

"Oh, naughty videos, some professional, some amateur. Amateur sells best, is what I hear. Go figure. But, you know, the mail order porn video business collapsed because of the Internet."

"And I would know all this *because…*?"

Bates ignored the question. "Reading between the lines, I reckon he was ratted out during a nasty divorce. Lost his two kids, he did. Wife used his porn business to get sole custody."

Davies looked at the computer printout Bates had handed her. "*Possible minor drug dealing,* too, this says. What's that supposed to mean: *possible*? Was there or wasn't there? And what's minor? Who filed this bloody report?"

"DC name of Barton. Falmouth nick. Retired."

"Never heard of him. No wonder he didn't rise in the force."

"*She,* actually: a Shirley Barton."

Davies was even more disgusted. She was about to begin ranting about female detectives needing to be sharper than their much more numerous male counterparts, but Bates interrupted her thoughts.

"Ma'am?"

"Will you please stop that 'ma'am' crap?"

"Morgan, then."

"What's your take on Charlotte Johns, Terry?"

Bates considered a moment. "Stiff. Almost brittle. What was her reaction at the mortuary? You were alone with her at the unveiling."

"Same. Of course when the police haul you up to a mortuary you certainly have a hunch what's coming next. Maybe she just prepared herself."

"Maybe. But there's the other thing I was about to mention..."

Davies lifted an eyebrow.

"She's still not said a word about not actually living at the farm. She has her own place. Little bungalow a couple of miles away. I checked the county tax records."

Davies nodded, once again impressed. Then, thinking aloud, she said, "Look, maybe he was everything to her. Maybe pretending to have been his life partner is all she has left, you know? Maybe she's clinging to that."

"Yeah, I could understand that," Bates said.

Davies wondered why. Instead, she said, "All right: first thing is track down this Shirley, our retired DC. What kind of antique name is that, anyway? *Shirley?* Sounds pre-War, for God's sake. Find out what she knew. Next, see if there's a HOLMES II file on Hansen, though given this form is old I doubt it.

HOLMES was the acronym for the national Home Office Large Major Evidence System—a name idiotically cobbled together, as far as Morgan was concerned, to match the name of the fictional detective, like this was something on the telly. It was the system by which all cases were now tracked and all evidence cross-referenced. HOLMES II was its latest iteration. Much as the name annoyed her, the system was invaluable.

Twenty minutes later, Bates was back. Davies looked up from the computer screen and stretched her back.

"So?"

"So, Shirley Barton didn't just retire, she died. Breast cancer. Died six months after she left the force. She was only forty-two."

"Bloody hell."

Bates wasn't entirely sure whether Davies's reaction was about the dead woman or the dead end.

"Also," Bates continued, "there's no HOLMES II file on Hansen."

Davies sighed. "Right then, start interviewing the people Johns listed as members of her Druid…what did she call it?"

"Grove."

"*Grove*." She ran a hand through her spiky hair. "Jesus wept," she mumbled, shaking her head.

"Actually, Morgan, one meaning of the word *Druid*, is 'oak knower.'"

"Of course it is! How silly I didn't know!" Davies said, raising her hands in disbelief.

Bates turned to go.

"One other thing," Davies barked: "Get some professional-looking suits." Bates was wearing an ankle-length linen skirt, sandals, and a floral blouse. "You're a plainclothes detective now, yes, but this ain't a holiday at the beach."

Bates looked down at her outfit and then squared her shoulders. "On it, ma'am…uh, Morgan. And thank you."

Fourteen

PATRICIA BODEN GRIPPED the sides of her seat as PC Adam Novak wrestled his police car, a white Ford Escort plastered with the iridescent yellow and blue checkerboard side panels emblematic of the force, through the twisting single lane roads on the Lizard Peninsula. He was, she realized, the kind of confident driver who seldom needed to use his brakes. He anticipated every twist and turn and downshifted and upshifted constantly, letting the transmission do the work as they shot along the stone wall-lined lanes and edged around utterly blind, ninety-degree turns at field corners.

Patricia wished she were younger. The receptionist had been right: Novak was dishy: eyes dark as molasses; curly, nearly black hair cut close to his sculptured skull; skin already beginning to tan in the gradually intensifying spring sun. Late twenties, maybe; eastern European heritage, probably, with that name and those cheek bones. Trim in his constable's uniform, too. But he was all business—almost as if he could not permit himself to chat with his passenger. Or was he just shy? She watched and wondered.

They had rocketed down the A394, past fields mostly given over to grazing sheep, turned south just before Helston, and now were weaving their way through the Helford River valley toward Manaccan and the farm she'd identified as belonging to Robert Tregareth.

Tregareth. That was all she'd got from Scotland Yard, that and the probability he lived in the Southwest. But to her great surprise, her data search revealed there was only one active farmer with that name in the region and he was on the Lizard.

They came upon a tractor pulling a furrow cutter in the lane and swung wide at a passing place to overtake it. A few hundred yards later, the tractor followed them right into a concrete yard between a lovely old cottage and a barn.

The tractor driver pulled in behind them, leaped from his seat, and stalked toward them as they stepped out of the Ford.

"What the hell are you doing on my farm and where in bloody hell did you learn how to drive?" Bobby Tregareth demanded.

Novak dipped his head and touched the brim of his chequer-brimmed peaked PC's cap.

"You have my apologies, sir; I am not accustomed to your country lanes. You are in the right; I was in the wrong." He looked up and grinned. "Perhaps we should issue me a citation for reckless driving. You could sign it."

Bobby stared for a moment and then laughed. He nodded to Patricia. "Pardon my outburst, ma'am. Just startled, I was, that's all. Tractor's so loud I can't hear anyone overtaking."

Patricia said, "You are Robert Tregareth?"

Bobby looked around as if someone else were being addressed.

"I am, yes. What's this about?" he said turning to the uniformed constable.

"I have information," Boden said, redirecting Bobby's attention, "that you recently reported to an auction house that you'd unearthed some ancient relics while working on your farm, items which likely would be covered by the Treasure Act of 1996. This information comes to me from the British Museum. Such a find must be reported to the county coroner's office and cannot be sold privately. I am the county's Finds Liaison Officer."

Bobby stood splay-legged, pulled off his cap, and scratched his head.

"Haven't a clue what you're on about," he said.

"Are you saying you did not unearth a trove of Roman era relics last month and contact the London auction house, Bonham's, in an effort to sell them?"

Bobby tilted his head to one side as if by this action his comprehension might increase.

"Who's Bonham's? Look, would you like tea? I'm parched."

Without waiting for a response, Bobby plodded to the back door of his cottage and the two followed.

"Jo? Joey?"

There was no response, and when he peered out the kitchen window Tregareth saw that their car was gone.

Off to the Sainsbury's in Helston, babe in tow, to shop for supper he reckoned. He filled the electric teapot on the kitchen counter, snapped it on, and gestured to the chairs around the kitchen table: "Wife's away, it seems. Make yourselves comfortable."

It was after he'd poured the hot water into a teapot that it came to him.

"Hang on, hang on," he said holding up the sugar spoon upright like a tiny scepter. "My neighbor, Archie: Archie Hansen. He found a fogou beneath yon field beside mine. Weeks back, that was. I was to say nothing, he said."

Bates was taking notes. "Fogou, sir?"

"Underground chamber from before the Romans. They're scattered across this part of Cornwall, they are. There's another one right here on the Lizard. D'you reckon he found something in there, didn't say, and used my name, 'stead of his? Bloody hell: my landlord, he is! I lease most of my fields from him. Hard man he can be sometimes, sure, but he's been like an uncle since my wife birthed our son, and fact is we depend upon his good will to keep farming. I wouldn't want to rile him. Why'd he ever use my name? That's beyond me, that is."

Patricia Boden decided she wasn't buying it. "Beyond me, too, Mr. Tregareth. Makes no sense at all. Your neighbor pretending to be you?"

Like a light had suddenly come on, Tregareth looked at each of them in turn and said, "Wait, am I in trouble or something?"

"Only if you're lying, Mr. Tregareth," Boden said.

Novak looked up and closed his notebook. "Mr. Tregareth, do you suppose you could take us to that field?"

"'Course I can," Bobby said, rising immediately.

Patricia colored. It was something she should have thought of. They left the tea untouched.

BOBBY TREGARETH'S LAND Rover Defender thudded along the rutted edge of a field he'd recently planted in barley. The ground was well-tilled and tiny green shoots were just emerging. Patricia Boden was in the passenger seat, PC Novak in the jump seat behind trying to keep his head from hitting the roll bar. Bobby halted beside a beautifully crafted stone hedge, yanked on the handbrake, and pointed to the field opposite.

"That'd be Archie's field, where he found that fogou. But I never told you, see? Can't afford to lose my land now I've got a family to support. You understand?"

Patricia looked at the farmer beside her and saw his fear. She nodded. "I understand, Mr. Tregareth. I'll respect that."

Bobby's face relaxed, and when it did, Patricia thought it looked like a boy's: open, honest, naïve.

"You see that bright new grass over yonder," Bobby said, pointing. "That's fresh seeded earth, that is, with a bit of corrugated metal roofing beneath, protecting the hole. Or at least that's what Archie said he'd do. Reckon he did. But if he found what you're lookin' for, that I can't say."

"Can't or won't, Mr. Tregareth?" Patricia pressed.

Bobby turned to look at her. "Listen, lady: I've told you the God's honest truth here. If you're lookin' for someone whose got summat' to hide, I suggest you climb over that stone hedge and have a look for yourself, because I'm done with this. You want a ride back, I'll wait. You want to walk, that's fine with me, too. You got that clear?"

PC Novak said nothing. Patricia stared out through the windscreen for a moment, and then turned to the driver.

"Forgive me, Mr. Tregareth. I am new to this sort of investigation and no doubt clumsy. I—we—would be honored if you would wait. And I appreciate your honesty. It's an increasingly rare commodity and you appear to have it aplenty. Thank you, sir. We'll be right back."

Fifteen

AS IF HIS shoes had springs, Calum West bounced into Morgan's office at Bodmin on Monday morning, twenty-first May, and stood, grinning, in front of her desk.

"Oh, what is it now?" she said, barely looking up.

"I think you meant, 'Hello, handsome!'"

She made a face. Consummate professional that West was, there was also something helplessly boyish about him. She wasn't sure whether it charmed or annoyed her. But given the family tragedy he'd recently endured, she humored him:

"Hello, handsome…Now, what the hell is it?"

"Got a crime scene, we do. The *Saga*'s been found. Hansen's boat. Any interest in a bit of walking in the English countryside, admiring the wildflowers, down Helford River way?"

"This your idea of a date?"

"Is it yours?"

"Definitely not." But Davies had already grabbed her jacket. "Your car or mine?"

"Oh, I think we'll take the Rocket."

"That Volvo estate of yours? Let me check my life insurance first."

"And bring your Wellies."

"In my car. Meet you out back."

Ever since their last case, Davies and West had sparred like this—bumping shoulders and trading barbs like adolescents who hadn't a clue what to do about their mutual, if somewhat mystifying, attraction. Davies had been married but was long since divorced. She was still friends with her ex, another detective, but she'd been single for years, and had come to believe that it was her natural condition. West's wife had succumbed to cancer more than a year before their last case. He had two young daughters, Meagan and Kaitlin, who were devoted to him. Davies had met the girls, and their grandmother, Ruth, at a Christmas party at the Bodmin headquarters. Morgan had no family. She adored his. And yet their wholeness terrified her.

THOUGH THE ROUTE through St. Austell and Truro would have been more direct, Calum West took the western A30 instead, much of which was a dual carriageway. He seldom left the fast lane, the Volvo growling and clocking well over ninety most of the way. Then, at Camborne, he turned south onto a minor road, switched on the flashers hidden in the grille beneath the bonnet, and sped through several sleepy hamlets, reaching Helston in just under an hour. It took another nearly fifteen minutes of careening down single lane roads on the Lizard for them to reach the clustered whitewashed riverside village of Helford. One of West's Scene of Crimes vans was already in the car park just above the village. Davies stepped out of the car and nearly kissed the ground in thanks for being delivered safely. But the truth was West drove as if he and the turbo-drive Volvo were one entity. She'd never felt in danger...except that they'd get a speeding ticket. The man was a brilliant driver.

"Bugger: the lads got here first," West groused. Morgan knew that it wasn't that he needed to be in charge of his team. Indeed, he was admired by his staff for the freedom he gave them in investigations. It was simply that he liked to be the first on a scene so he could do absolutely nothing but quietly take it all in. She'd learned that about him in the Chynoweth case the year before. Reconnoitering was, for him, almost a form of meditation. It cleared his head and it was as if his vision became suddenly more acute. Crime scenes would speak volumes to Calum in these moments, even as they mystified others. It was one of a growing list of things about him that she'd lately begun appreciating.

West shouldered a small rucksack which, unlike those carried by other coast path walkers, included not water and energy bars but a Tyvek jumpsuit and rubber gloves, among the other tools of his somewhat macabre trade. He pulled an Ordnance Survey Explorer map from the pack's side pocket, and struck off down a lane that twisted among the thatch-roofed cottages huddling like mushrooms near the water in the tiny riverside hamlet. Davies followed him in her black rubber Wellies, clomping along like an animal noisily stalking prey. Soon they were following a well-marked footpath through the woods above the river.

Because spring was late, the ground beneath the twisted branches of the sessile oaks was carpeted with early wildflowers.

"That's lesser celandine," West said pointing to tiny yellow flowers alongside the footpath as he led on. "And that's stitchwort," he added, waving a hand at a patch of plants with delicate five-petal white blossoms.

The path turned away from the main course of the tidal river and followed a tributary arm upland and westward. The SOCO chief continued his commentary, pointing to a cluster of glossy green leaves with dimples in the center.

"That's navelwort, that is, for obvious reasons."

A few hundred yards farther, Morgan's nostrils were attacked by the smell of crushed onions in a section of woodland blanketed in starburst white blossoms.

"What the hell is that smell?" she barked. She was struggling to keep up.

West laughed. "Ramsons! Wild leeks! A culinary delicacy, I'll have you know."

Davies stopped to catch her breath. "How do you know all this stuff?"

West turned, the boyish enthusiasm gone from his face.

"Catherine. She taught me."

Davies looked at her feet.

West reached out and gave her shoulder a squeeze. When she looked up he was smiling again.

"Long ago and far away, Morgan," he said. "Almost."

And off he strode again.

How do you recover when your spouse dies young and leaves you children to raise alone? Where do you find the strength? How do you even keep going? Divorce was one thing, common enough as she knew only too well. But sudden, unfair, early death? Davies marveled at West's quiet strength. He must have dark moments. He must hurt. He was known as a passionately dedicated investigator. She wondered if that was the salve that soothed his pain. She wondered how he got through the night.

"Where the hell are we, Calum?" she called after him.

He stopped and waited for her again. "Frenchman's Creek is where we are. Tidal arm of the Helford. Daphne du Maurier country, this is. Wrote a book of the same name back in the 1940s, she did: tale of a pirate and a lovelorn aristocratic lady. Very romantic, I'm told."

"Are you the pirate? I sure as hell feel press-ganged into this operation."

Calum remembered a saying: women don't sweat, they *glow*. Morgan glowed like the lighthouse off Lizard Point. He let her rest a moment.

"Are you my lovelorn aristocratic lady?"

"In your dreams, you idiot," she panted.

"Yeah. I've had those dreams."

Morgan was momentarily speechless, then recovered. "Where's this bloody crime scene, dammit?"

West crouched in a drift of bluebells so they could see beneath the hanging branches of the Sessile oaks and pointed. It was low tide and the creek was empty. She saw boot prints leading across the flats and then spied West's SOCO team swarming around an open skiff tucked under overhanging shrubbery. Except for the boots, his people were dressed in their usual white Tyvek coveralls so as not to contaminate the site.

West and Davies climbed down to the shore and set off toward the four men investigating the boat. The mud pulled at Morgan's Wellies like quicksand.

"Romantic creek?" she called to West. "It's a bloody quagmire! That du Maurier lady ever even come down here?"

Morgan Davies was not a nature lover, she was an avid indoors-woman. Her idea of a perfect weekend was old movies on the video and several vodka tonics, not a walkabout.

If anything, the mud was worse where the SOCO boys had churned it into a greyish pudding as they moved around the boat. As Davies waited, West circled the open skiff, the mud making sucking sounds each time he lifted his boots. The vessel's hull was made of white fiberglass with a molded lap strake finish. It had a high, pointed bow, a stand-up wheelhouse amidships, and a big Honda outboard. Solid, powerful, and seaworthy. West reckoned it at about fourteen feet.

"What do we have, gentlemen?" West asked his team.

Rafe Barnes, his senior investigator, answered.

"Let's start with the obvious, Guv. The skiff's not been here long. Also, it's been thoroughly washed and rinsed. There is also the slightest tang of bleach. We've taken samples, of course. In fact, we're nearly done here. Nothing else to see, I'm afraid."

West ignored him and picked his way around the open boat, squinting here, sniffing there like a hound, but touching nothing as he hadn't donned his Tyveks.

Finally, he turned to his senior investigator, eyes twinkling. "Don't have a boat, do you Rafe?"

"Right the first time, boss, landlubber is what I am. I like my *terra firma*. The more firma the less terror."

Davies and the rest of the team laughed.

But West pointed to the line that ran from *Saga*'s bow to where it was tied to an overhanging branch.

"See that painter?"

"Painter?

"The line from the bow. It's called a *painter*. You see that knot on the branch?"

"Yeah. So?"

"Know what it is?"

Rafe smiled. "No, boss, I don't, but I reckon you're about to enlighten me…"

Davies watched all this and marveled at the easy way Calum had with his men. He wasn't correcting Rafe, he was guiding. And she didn't know the answer either.

"That's a granny knot, that is," Calum said, pointing to the branch. "No boat owner would ever use it. Too easy to slip. A reef knot would have been right. A couple of half-hitches would be better for a mooring like this. Or a clove hitch. Those knots, they get tighter the more they're stressed. But not a granny. Jiggle or tug on it the right way, like in a rising and falling tide, and it can unravel. Boat lost."

Davies was impatient: "What's the point here, professor?"

"The point is that no boat person tied this skiff here. The whole scene is amateurish."

"Maybe someone found it and tied it here for safe-keeping?"

"And didn't report it?"

"Who did report it?" Davies asked.

"Girl from Treveador Farm just uphill, Joyce Wilcox," Rafe answered. "Twelve, she is. Out walking her dog. Knows the creek well. Found the boat tied here as it is."

"Not a likely suspect, then," Davies said.

"The girl or the dog?" West asked.

The group laughed, and the tension evaporated like morning sea fret.

West stared across the flats. The tide was beginning to slip back up the channel. "So, what happened to *Saga's* owner? Well, okay, we know what happened to him. But how? Where?" And how'd his boat get here? Who tucked it under these branches? Who tied that incompetent knot?"

"You turning detective, Calum?" Davies asked.

He raised his hands in mock surrender. "Sorry. Your patch, Morgan. Just thinking, I was."

"You do scene, I'll do investigation. You okay with that?"

"Yes, dear."

More laughter from his men.

"So what were you thinking?" Davies asked anyway.

"Pardon?"

Morgan smiled. "Out with it: I'm listening."

"Right, but how about we do this at the Shipwright's Arms back at Helford? Tide's coming in fast and I could use a pint. Lads?"

"Guv?" Rafe answered.

"Won't be long before the tide lifts the skiff. One of you fine gents get back to Helford and have someone with a boat tow it out and then let's have it impounded and carried overland to Falmouth nick. But no further contamination, yeah? Gloves all around, including whomever tows it.

"And Rafe, when you get it to impound, treat the entire interior with Luminol. Also the surface of the gunwales around the edge of the hull. And let's do Superglue fuming for prints along the underside of the gunwale. Whoever it was pulled this skiff in close to shore may have forgotten they'd leave prints there underneath. Superglue fuming's the only thing that will work on a nonporous surface like this fiberglass hull. Off you go, then, lads and let me know what the lab results are as soon as you can. Or sooner."

"On it, Guv," Rafe said.

As they plodded back across the mucky flats of Frenchman's Creek, Davies asked, "You a boating person, Calum?"

"Too smart for that, I am, I assure you. Hole in the water, boats are, into which you pour money."

She stopped in mid-channel as the tide slipped in gently, almost invisibly, around her boots: "So all that knot nonsense...?"

Ahead of her, she heard him laugh. "Scouts!"

A Boy Scout. I should have guessed, she thought: *Mr. 'Be Prepared.'*

At the Shipwright's, they left their muddy boots at the door.

"A couple of pints of Doom Bar," West called to the hefty dimple-cheeked young woman behind the bar in the low-roofed pub.

"And a bag of ready-salted crisps," Davies added.

"You don't want to eat?"

"I'll stick with the crisps."

West shook his head. Morgan's routine to make herself seem plain and common was transparent to him. "Hold the crisps," he said to the girl behind the bar. "We'll both have your famous crab salad."

"Who the hell are you to—" Davies began to protest.

"Hold your water, Morgan. Crab's brain food. And we need to feed that splendid brain of yours."

"Vodka tonic's what feeds it," she snapped.

He spun around to the bar again: "That'll be just the one pint of Doom, after all, and a double vodka tonic for the lady."

"You two finished now?" the girl asked, hands on heavy hips. She didn't know what these two were on about, but they certainly were entertaining.

"We'll just step outside on the terrace, shall we?" West said, taking their drinks.

"I'll start a tab," the girl called after them.

MORGAN TOOK A long slug from her double vodka tonic. The mud flats in the narrow tidal creek below the pub were filling with the incoming tide. On the opposite shore, whitewashed cottages, some with thatched roofs, rose above the rocks. She was beginning to enjoy this rustic outing.

"Your man Rafe said he detected bleach in that boat," she said, her eyes closed as she basked in the sun. "But Luminol lights up bleach just like it does blood. How will you tell the difference?"

She opened her eyes and slid them in his direction like the pivoting cannon on a tank. "Luminol would be pointless."

West laughed. "Who does 'scene'?"

Davies stared daggers.

"Plus. You're forgetting about human nature," Calum continued. "Whoever tried to clean that skiff would have been in a hurry; they'll likely have missed a few spots. We'll look for the areas that don't completely light up and then look for the spots within those blank areas that do. That'll be the blood."

Davies looked out at the rapidly filling creek and shook her head. West was way ahead of her, again. She was trying not to hate him for it.

Sixteen

JUST BEFORE TEN on Monday morning, sixteenth April, Charlotte walked into the lobby of the Helston Library.

"Morning, Glynnis," she said to the reedy old librarian at the front desk.

"Charlotte Johns! Long time; how have you been keeping, then, dear?"

"Someone told me that anyone who says, 'I can't complain' has no imagination, but I'm fine, Glynnis. Your mother is well?"

"If you can say someone who has no idea who she is, where she is, or who I am is well, then yes. They look after her fine at the care home."

Charlotte patted Glynnis Martin's arm. "I understand."

"I know you do; I hear about your work at the hospital. Patients love you."

Charlotte smiled. "Just my job."

"But you're so much more than an orderly there. You take time to visit with the sickest patients. And after you've visited them, they're peaceful, is what I hear."

"I just comfort them, Glynnis. They're often left alone."

The librarian nodded. "Here for a computer, are you? Still don't have one of your own? I thought almost everyone did these days."

"Too pricey for my budget, plus I seldom need one. But I do need to look something up, if I may."

"Of course, my dear." She pointed to the bank of computers on a long table in the middle of the reference section. "Take any available seat; usual password."

Charlotte signed in and began researching ancient treasure in Britain. It turned out that there had been just a few discoveries in recent years, some by metal detectorists, some by farmers like her Archie. Many discoveries were Roman, but the rarest and most valuable were pre-Roman: Iron Age or earlier. She researched torcs in particular and sat, gobsmacked, looking at the screen before her: torcs like the one in Archie's burlap bag fetched hundreds of thousands of pounds Sterling, even millions! There was a reference to the Treasure Act of 1996, and when she searched for that and read the Wikipedia entry, she smiled. *That's why the dosh is in a bag: Archie would never put up with this sort of red tape. Never.*

IT WAS JUST after one that same afternoon when Charlotte heard the crunch of wheels in the gravel forecourt of Archie's house. As if she were the lady of the manor, she opened the house's massive old oak front door and waited on the steps to greet her visitor. She had no idea when it was that anyone had used this door last; she and Archie always came through the farmyard to the kitchen door. To greet her visitor, she'd chosen a vintage wrap dress by Diane von Furstenberg in a black and white diagonal stripe pattern she'd found at the Oxfam charity shop in Helston, smoky grey holdup stockings, and black inch-high kitten heels.

Dicky Townsend stepped out of a silver Mercedes S-Class sedan he'd hired from Avis in Bristol. Cost the earth, but a good impression was everything, he figured. He threw a black suit jacket, also hired, over his open-necked white shirt, grabbed his black leather briefcase from the passenger seat, and approached the house.

"Mrs. Hansen! Lovely to meet you at last!"

"Mr. Townsend. Welcome."

Townsend, who was roughly Charlotte's age and nearly as short, admired her trim figure and bowed slightly as they shook hands.

"A pleasure, Mrs. Hansen."

Charlotte regarded Townsend for a moment before ushering him into the house. The man looked fit beneath that lovely suit. An oddly attractive man, despite a head a bit too large and round for the rest of him. Losing his hair, too, like Archie, but doing so more elegantly, the hair receding at the temples and touched with silver there. A gentleman, she reckoned.

She settled them on the divan in the front lounge she and Archie never used but which she'd cleaned for the occasion. Beyond the deep-set windows, there were early flowers in the borders around the forecourt's edges: deep purple wallflower, white and lavender crocuses that should have been long gone by this time of year, and lemon yellow primroses. A stone hedge edged the forecourt, and beyond it was a field with the wilting blossoms of the last of the season's commercial daffodils. Bracketing the ends of the hedge, old rhododendrons as big as garden sheds were massed, their buds about to burst into magenta flower.

Earlier, to take the chill off the room, she'd set a coal fire burning in the grate of the lounge's ancient granite hearth. The room was now nearly tropical.

"It's been a long wait for the spring this year Mrs. Hansen, lovely to have a fire in this room."

"Why don't you take off your jacket, Mr. Townsend? Tea?" She gestured to a tray already prepared on the low table before them. There was a small plate of McVities biscuits coated with dark chocolate on the tea tray as well.

"Thank you, ma'am," Townsend said, shucking his coat. "Don't normally get such royal treatment. I am charmed. May I call you Charlotte?"

Like some Victorian coquette, she ducked her head and tipped it sideways: "Of course you may, Mr. Townsend."

He waved a hand: "Please, it's Richard. Or simply Dicky."

"Dicky is it!" Charlotte put a hand across her mouth and faked a blush. "That must be a burden…"

"Not really, ma'am. It suits." Townsend smiled, but kept his eyes locked on hers.

"Does it indeed? Well!" Charlotte said without looking away. "Milk and sugar…Dicky?"

"Please."

She bent to pour the tea into two white porcelain cups, so delicate they were nearly transparent, and let the V-neck of her wrap dress gap.

Townsend admired the view, which was unfettered by a brassiere. "And will Archie join us soon?" he managed to ask.

"I'm afraid Archie cannot; he had a meeting in Truro with the county agriculture people about going organic," she said as she sat again, her stockings whispering against each other as she crossed her legs.

"Only told me about it this morning, I'm afraid. No choice, he said, and I did not know how to reach you."

"Organic?" Townsend said trying to hide his annoyance. "Very admirable, that is, I reckon."

"You'd think so, but he doesn't have much faith in it. I've tried to tell him that he'd earn more in the end by converting, but it's the transition that troubles him: the years before his fields and practices are finally certified. Our neighbors are doing it, and it's working for them, but he's still holding out." She shook her head in disgust: "Stubborn old goat."

Townsend knew less than nothing about farming and simply sipped his tea. The woman seated beside him was not a classic beauty. But there was something she radiated, something earthy, which overwhelmed any other impression and aroused him. He tried to stay on topic.

"Can you tell me about what your husband has found?"

Charlotte averted her eyes and answered, as if to the room at large, "Mr. Hansen is not the confiding type, Mr. Townsend."

"A private chap?" Townsend volunteered, his sympathy like honey dripping from a comb.

She leaned forward. "And cold, Dicky," she lied. "Cold and private."

Townsend cleared his throat. "While coming to know you better is a special delight, Mrs. Hansen—um, Charlotte—I had intended to do a photo appraisal of Archie's discoveries so as to ascertain their value."

Charlotte ducked her head again. Townsend found this habit charming, and suggestive of submission.

"While Archie has hinted to me about his discovery, Dicky," she said, "he has not revealed its location yet. I suspect he has hidden what he's found in several places about the farm. That would be like him. Secretive, he is. But I have found one of his hiding places, and one of his discoveries."

From behind her chair, she pulled an orange plastic carrier bag printed with the Sainsbury's supermarket logo, and placed it upon the low table before them.

"Please," she said, gesturing to the bag.

Townsend reached into the bag and withdrew the intricately braided gold torc. His bulging eyes bulged wider. He pulled a jeweler's loupe from his jacket pocket and peered at the item closely. But though it had not yet been cleaned, its authenticity, based on his research at the British Museum, was unquestionable. He returned the loupe to his pocket.

"You are a very lucky woman, Mrs. Hansen," he said finally. "Your husband has found something of great value."

"Tell me about it, Dicky. I don't know if he will."

Townsend reached for the teapot to pour himself another cup but she slapped his hand away playfully. "That's my job, sir!" she said, her voice tinkling like bells.

Townsend sat back. Charlotte presented his refilled cup and saucer.

"This, Charlotte," he said pointing to the relic, "is a gold torc from the Iron Age, probably sometime around 50 BC."

"Before Christ?!"

"Yes, and before the Romans. Cornwall at that time was settled by a tribe called the *Cornovii*. That's where the name, *Cornwall*, comes from. Their clan chieftains, and their wives as well," he said, nodding to her as if she were one of them, "wore these neck ornaments as emblems of their status. Gold was not easily won from the ore hereabouts, so they are very rare. And very valuable."

Charlotte clasped her arms across her breasts in excitement, then lurched forward and kissed her guest full upon the lips. "But this is wonderful! Oh, thank you, Dicky!" she exclaimed, bouncing on her cushion like a child.

"Yes. Well. Um…congratulations." He was trying to recover from the kiss. It had been awhile for him. "The question, Charlotte," he continued, "is where the rest is, and of what is it comprised. Archie told me there was more."

"I have no idea, Dicky," she lied. "But I aim to find out. Imagine Archie hiding this from me! What does that say about fidelity?"

"If I may be so bold…Charlotte…"

She leaned toward him: "Be bold, Dicky."

He swallowed. "I suggest that, after I take photos of this piece, you put it back wherever you found it. That Archie would keep this secret from you does not, if you will permit me, bode well. And I should like to look after your interests…if you will permit me." Townsend had no idea what he was saying, the words came from him unbidden. He was promising things to this woman he'd just met that he was not even sure he could deliver. It was not clear to him which of them had the upper hand. He could feel himself being drawn into her orbit. Still, he kept on:

"So, here is my proposal," he said.

"You're proposing, Dicky?"

Townsend blinked. "You're already married, Mrs. Hansen…"

"Actually, I'm not," she said, arching an eyebrow and then winking. "Not legally, anyway. That 'Mrs. Hansen,' is just a convenience. It simplifies things."

"Ah," Townsend said. He didn't know what else to say.

After an awkward silence, Townsend retrieved the digital camera from his briefcase, placed the torc on the pine table, and took shots from several angles.

"I propose that you spend the next few weeks trying to discover, discreetly, where the rest of Archie's hoard is hidden. As for today, tell him I am sorry to have missed him and I look forward to hearing from him soon. When he does, and he and I meet, I'll take more photos of the artifacts he's found, establish their value, and then you and he will have to decide how you want to handle this discovery going forward. There are legal matters, like whether to report this to the Crown as official treasure. I talked to Archie about that in Bristol. He wasn't game. I could, however, arrange to sell these items privately. To wealthy collectors I know."

Charlotte placed her hand on his and gave it a gentle squeeze. "I understand. But what if he never tells me what he's found?"

Townsend thought for a moment and then smiled. "Tell him that an antiquities dealer called Townsend phoned to follow up on our meeting in Bristol, but nothing else and, of course, nothing about our meeting today. Ask him, in a general sort of way, what it's all about—no, wait: don't. Just relay the message that I called. That should light a bit of a fire under him."

"He will not be pleased."

"All you are doing is telling him about a phone call. Let him consider that and make the next move."

Charlotte squeezed his hand again. "You are trying to protect me. Thank you, Dicky. I am not used to having someone look after me."

Townsend rose. "So there you have it, Charlotte: in time you will have some decisions to make. You understand?"

At the open front door, he gave her his business card. Charlotte took his hand in both of hers. "I do understand. Come back soon, Dicky," she whispered.

A few moments after Dicky's Mercedes disappeared around a curve in the narrow lane, a cattle gate in a high stone wall fifty yards or so from the house opened and a low-slung dark blue Audi TT coupe emerged from a field. The driver stopped in the road, got out, and closed the gate again. He got back into his car, pulled into the next layby in the one-lane road, and flipped open his mobile.

"He's been and gone, boss," Max said when the call connected. "Very chummy he and the lady were at the door."

"The *lady*? I thought he was meant to meet Hansen!"

"Only saw the missus. No sign of the farmer. No tractor in the farmyard, and from my viewpoint, no other figures in the windows. Got right close, I did, thanks to a thick stand of old rhododendrons off to one side."

"Photos?"

"Just as he came out. No other angles."

"What else?"

"Just that I don't think he come away with anything. Just carried a thin black briefcase."

There was long pause, and then: "Okay, well done as usual, Max. Send me your hours when you return. We'll wait and see now."

"That is fine…"

But Reg Connor had already rung off.

Dicky backed the Benz into a blind farm lane at the top of the steep hill above Gillan Creek, got out, hunched close to the break in the high stone wall and waited. He'd sussed his tail hours earlier on the A30 as he drove to his meeting at Higher Pennare. The tail was a pro, slipping far behind in the stream of southbound traffic, then creeping within visual range again, mile after mile, the whole length of the spine of Cornwall. When Dicky left the A30 and took the A39 south toward Truro, Falmouth, and the Lizard, he'd caught the sporty coupe, barely visible, drafting close behind a long Sharps Brewery delivery lorry. He'd thought of shaking him, but decided he'd rather know more about the car. Someone on Reg's payroll, he was sure.

Now, at the point where the single lane road from Higher Pennare pitched over the lip of the hill down into Carne and then Manaccan in the Gillan Creek valley, the road was overhung by trees and a driver would have to adjust to the suddenly leafy shadows while, at the same time, negotiating the twisting tarmac. He would be focused on the curves, not the farm gates in the stone boundary walls.

As Townsend watched, the tail flew right by.

Seventeen

THE MAJOR CRIMES investigation team had grown beyond the confines of the Falmouth nick; they'd moved to the nearby St. Michaels Hotel and Spa, overlooking the beach at Falmouth. By Tuesday, twenty-second May, the day after *Saga* had been found, they'd set up in the hotel's "Starboard" conference room. Davies entered the hotel's maritime-themed lobby and was impressed by its clean lines. Unlike the fusty "Grand Dame" hotels which lined the slopes above Falmouth's long beachfront, the St. Michaels was unabashedly contemporary, its interior largely white with accents of sunny yellow and sea foam blue. It boasted a well-respected restaurant and a full spa, complete with indoor pool. Davies doubted they'd be availing themselves of these amenities.

In the Starboard room, four young Falmouth PCs were running phone and computer lines and moving in tables and chairs, white boards for notes, cork boards for posting images, the lot.

On one of the cork boards, Terry Bates was just placing a pushpin in an Ordnance Survey Explorer map for the Lizard Peninsula at a spot marked "Higher Pennare" when one of the young Falmouth uniformed constables stopped as he passed by with a coil of cable. She sensed him behind her and turned.

"Yes?"

"Been there," the PC said, pointing. She reckoned him about her own age. His brown eyes were lustrous as polished stone.

"The Lizard? Yeah, most of us have."

"No. Higher Pennare. Case I was assigned to last month. With the finds liaison lady from the Royal Cornwall Museum in Truro. It was a Treasure Act investigation. Not that it went anywhere."

"Treasure Act?"

"Farmer there apparently found some Roman artifacts and tried to flog them on the open market. But under the Treasure Act, they're supposed to be reported to the county coroner and then to the Crown. Only it turned out the chap whose name the museum lady had wasn't the one who'd allegedly found this stuff. Said his neighbor might have, though, nearby at Higher Pennare."

"Did you get on to the neighbor?"

"This liaison person, Boden her name was, she was supposed to follow up."

Bates looked around the conference room and saw Morgan Davies in conversation with DCI Penwarren, who'd come down from Bodmin to oversee the set-up.

"Can you wait here a moment, Constable...?"

"Novak. Adam Novak."

She put a hand up: "I'll be right back."

WHILE WORKERS BUSIED themselves around her, Davies sat at a folding table with Novak. Bates was at her side, taking notes.

"So this farmer, Tregareth, took you to a field where he claimed his landlord, Mr. Hansen, had found an underground chamber?"

"That's it. Said Hansen dropped into the chamber alone and told him nothing when he emerged, except to swear Tregareth to secrecy. Tregareth was right frosted Hansen later had used his name."

"Why the secrecy?"

"So the county archaeology people wouldn't shut down this field, is what Hansen told Tregareth. Could they do that?"

Davies ignored the question. "And what, exactly did you and Ms. Boden find in that field, constable?"

"Not much. Like Tregareth said, beneath a patch of new grass was a section of corrugated metal shed roofing. I dug through to it with my fingers."

"And?"

"Well, detective, there was no way I was going to uncover it and move it without authority. It wasn't a police matter. Ms. Boden said she'd make arrangements. And then we were done there."

"What's she done since?"

"No idea. I wanted to pursue the case, but I haven't the remit. I'm just a PC."

Davies did see. She also saw a policeman with brains and promise. She made a mental note and dismissed him.

Bates made a mental note, too: *Handsome devil...*

Davies was on the phone to the Royal Cornwall Museum immediately. Patricia Boden confirmed Novak's report, explained what Scotland Yard had told her, and sketched out the requirements of the Treasure Act.

"I've called the Hansen farm several times about this matter since our visit," Boden explained, "but I only ever get his voicemail and I don't have his mobile number. And the thing is, I am so overloaded with museum-related work I haven't had the time to follow up in person. Budget cuts, you see. I don't understand why he hasn't replied."

Davies made a face. Hansen clearly hadn't replied for any number of reasons, mostly having to do with not wanting to report his find, whatever it was; not wanting to admit he'd tried to flog his discovery to a major London auction house; not wanting to admit he'd used his neighbor's name as an alias; and not wanting to let anyone know he was looking for unofficial channels for selling whatever he'd found.

"Look, why don't I drive down there right after work," Boden volunteered. "Maybe he'll be home at suppertime."

"Unlikely, Ms. Boden. He's dead. Murdered."

Leaving the woman gasping, Davies rang off and turned to Bates.

"Since he contacted Bonhams in London, I think we can assume that whatever Hansen found, it's important and valuable."

"Motive."

Davies cocked her spikey blond head to one side and grinned. "You think?"

"But for whom?"

"You're catching on."

Her next call was to Calum West at Bodmin. "Got a job for you," she said when he answered.

"Sorry, who's calling please?"

"You know damn well!"

"Ah yes, I'd know the dulcet tones of that voice anywhere. And I'm fine, thank you, Morgan…not that you asked."

"Christ, Calum."

"Never been mistaken for Him before, but thank you for the compliment. And how are you this fine day, DI Davies?"

Outside, it was pouring with rain.

"You're giving me a headache…"

"Probably the weather. Did you say there was something about which you'd like to chat? My place, or yours?"

He heard her take a deep breath, calming herself.

"It seems our floater discovered treasure on his farm some weeks ago and was trying to flog it."

"Treasure? Doubloons? Pirates? That's *so* Cornish…"

"Roman treasure, you idiot. And reportable under the Treasure Act."

"Treasure Act? What's that when it's at home? Sorry, luv, I'm all about bodies, not plunder. But do carry on. I swoon at the mere sound of your voice."

"About time you sobered up."

"You intoxicate me, you siren. Can't help it."

"Do please shut up and pay attention: the Treasure Act's about how most everything gold and silver that's found from ages ago belongs to the Crown…"

"Doesn't everything in Cornwall belong to the Crown anyway, or at least to our dear Duke of Cornwall, Prince Charles?"

"…and anyone who finds stuff like that—they're usually metal detector hobbyists, but sometimes farmers like our floater—is required to report their find and pass it on to the British Museum for valuation."

"Except our boy didn't?"

"You aren't as dim as you seem, apparently."

"Don't overestimate, my dear."

"No, he did not. And now he's dead."

"Well, yes. Certainly seemed that way in the mortuary."

"Are you ever serious, Calum?"

Calum paused. "I try not to be, Morgan, because so much of what I see every day is so bloody serious..."

"You know what?" Morgan said finally, her voice softening. "I think I always knew that about you. It's how you get by in this job. Me, I just get angry and drink alone at home."

"I hear you. I'm sorry. So what's this job we've got?"

"It's time your lads went through Hansen's farm."

"Morgan, look: we do scene of crime, in case you've forgotten. It's your people who investigate."

"I'll wager it's a scene. It was you reminded me that some of the cuts on the floater were old and some fresh. Where'd those older cuts happen? I'm thinking maybe his own farm."

"Gone fishing, have you?"

"That some kind of a joke?"

"Don't play dumb, Morgan, it doesn't suit you. Using us like that is fishing which, even you, the force's resident rule-breaker, must know SOCOs can't do. We can only enter a house if it belongs to a suspect. Hansen's not a suspect, he's the victim."

"Oh, bugger."

"On the other hand, you've got the oldest laws of the land on your side: you can have your own people conduct a preliminary intelligence search under Common Law if you're permitted access."

"Which means getting the nod from Charlotte Johns..."

"Right the first time, but she has no reason to deny it; she's the one who reported Hansen missing in the first place."

"I knew all this, you know."

"But you're always in a hurry. You want a suspect who can be convicted, yeah? Then procedure's your protection, Morgan. Follow it, and it can't be questioned by the defense. Ignore it, and you'll never convict. Remember the Chynoweth case?"

"You love to lecture, don't you?"

"No, I love to protect you from yourself."

Eighteen

ON TUESDAY, FIRST of May—Beltane on the pagan calendar—the members of the Lizard Druid Grove met at noon, just as the late spring sun hit the mouth of the sacred well close by the Bronze Age burial mound at Roscruge, less than a mile from Hansen's farm. The well had been discovered in the late eighteenth century by the antiquarian W. C. Borlase. Acting on local lore, Borlase had followed a tributary of Gillan Creek upstream and found its source beneath a thicket of bramble and gorse: a spring in a low, manmade stone grotto barely large enough to accommodate a crouched figure collecting fresh water.

On this particular day, the moist joints of the prehistoric walls of the well were studded with pale yellow primroses and emerald maidenhair ferns. The ground above was carpeted with the bell-flowered indigo spires of native wood hyacinths. A gnarled blackthorn—a "May tree"—twisted skyward from the stony ground at a distance of three yards exactly to the south of the well. In full, frothy blossom, it was white as a bridal bouquet.

At Charlotte's insistence, Archie Hansen had been elevated to High Priest of their grove three years earlier, pushing aside the aging Philip St. Martin, whom everyone called "Gandalf," not just for his long mane of silver hair and beard, but for his wisdom as well. Charlotte had been St. Martin's lover before she met the much younger Hansen, and she used St. Martin's frequent heart-related absences to persuade him to step aside. St. Martin had begged off today's ceremony, too.

There were eight of them gathered at the well, and Archie was pleased with the symmetry. Besides himself and Charlotte, the celebrants included Don and Phyllis Braxton, a dithery couple of naturalists who oversaw the Lizard National Nature Reserve a few miles away. The erotically-charged spring Beltane celebration was an event which always made them blush, but that did not keep them from participating with the enthusiasm of hormone-charged teens. Brad and Cheryl Winters, husband and wife in their forties, who owned a florist shop in Helston, also attended. And Ryan Durgan, the young cook at the Ship Inn at Cadgwith Cove, was there with his twenty-something partner Katy Anthony, who ran the bar. Both of them were marking time, waiting for the aging publican at the Ship to pop off so they could take over the pub.

Though the day was warm, Charlotte had lit two small fires of dried brush and branches to the left and the right of a straight line between the well and the blackthorn tree. Hansen, cloaked in an ankle-length white cotton robe like the other members, used the tip of a double-edged steel broadsword to describe a wide circle in the ground encompassing both the well and the tree. He walked counterclockwise as he did so, and when done he divided the circle into the quarter ways: north, south, east, and west. Then, deliberately mixing the couples, he placed a man and woman in each quarter, finally taking his place with Charlotte in the southern quadrant. In addition to the sword, Hansen wore a horned leather Viking helmet on his balding head. The other grove members had never quite taken to Archie's curious merger of Druidic practice with Viking lore, but they did not voice their misgivings. It was Archie's grove now; he was their acknowledged leader. What's more, the newest members had only the vaguest idea of the history and practices of the Druids, about whom there was no written record. St. Martin had been the grove's teacher and he'd drawn from what little the Romans had written about the sect, but he was seldom involved anymore. Archie had other objectives for the members of this grove. He had been studying the blacker arts of witchcraft and experimenting with spells and potions. Indeed, had used a potion earlier this day.

Having placed the members in the circle, Archie raised the sword with both hands, swung it through the smoke of the two small fires, and touched its blade to his forehead in a sort of salute. Then he called out their traditional Celtic welcome:

"Sláinte agus failte!"

The group returned the greeting.

Next, he passed around a large silver chalice filled with honey mead generously spiked with vodka, and each member of the grove drank deeply as he blessed them.

Finally, he began the rite:

"Now the earth grows green, now the shoot has become bud and bud is flowering with the kindling of love's fire. Today we celebrate the heat of the lusty month of May, and the greater heat of summer yet to come.

"Long ago on this day, the elders extinguished their winter fires and kindled the two which burn here with us now, left and right, between the sacred well and the ancient blackthorn. They would dance between the two fires for luck and then they would re-light their home fires from these fresh embers to signal the renewal of life, the rebirth of the season of plenty. We are come to this sacred place to honor these ancestors, to bid goodbye to the God and Goddess of Winter, and to celebrate Aine, the Queen of the May and of fertility, and her consort, Aengus the Harper, the God of Renewal. In this season of new seed flourishing, of bounty beginning, we dance between the flames of these paired fires which represent the duality of all things, the male and the female, the light and the dark, the sun and the moon.

"And then, as did the elders"—Archie paused for effect—"we retire to woods and fields to bring those dualities together in ecstatic union! This is our festival of life renewed, of abundance ahead, of the fecund spirit of the coming summer and, as with every living thing, the sensual potential in us all."

Charlotte, dressed as the aging Goddess of Winter, her face made up to accentuate its lines and creases, watched her partner closely. She had never seen him so enthralled in a rite, so poetic in the words he chose, so overtly suggestive of what was, indeed a festival of the sensual. It thrilled her and she felt her desire rising.

At this point Archie splashed rose-scented oil from a small flask onto the embers and, as the flames flared, the paired couples skipped between the two fires. Then his voice rose again, and he pointed his sword to the ancient hawthorn:

"Now in the hinge of time
Wise ones are calling
Show us your wonder
O Maiden of May!"

A figure cloaked in a hooded white robe, face in shadow, emerged from behind the tree's thick trunk and approached the well. As it approached, Archie pointed his sword and cried:

"Hail, the Queen of the May!"

Everyone turned to the advancing figure. At the edge of the circle, the cloak dropped to the ground to reveal Joey Tregareth, naked but for a glossy girdle of rhododendron leaves at her hips, her new mother's breasts pendulous, her only other ornament a fistful of wildflowers.

Charlotte gasped, but the other members cheered, having got well into the spirit of the fest.

Joey circled the well with slow, clockwise steps, scattering her flowers: bluebells, primrose, white anemone, lemon yellow celandine, and tiny wild violets.

"In this season of renewal," she said, her voice just above a whisper, "we do honor to the goddess of the wells, for the sacred well is the eye of the earth, the giver and receiver, womb of creation."

When she arrived at the center of the circle between the two small fires, Hansen added more scented oil to each and, once again, they flared.

"Surely it is true," he called as he entered the circle's center to face Joey, placing his hands on her bare shoulders, "that when the Maid of May appears in any place or any heart, the delight of love cannot be far behind. So it is that Aengus the Harper, whose music awakens longing and fulfillment in mortal hearts, calling to all to come away from earthly care and join in the joy of May. Listen now to the elders calling the young lord!" he continued, facing Joey:

"The young son
Aengus the Harper
Son of the Dagda
Whose staff is the strongest

Born of enchantment
Son of the Mother
Sing, O enticer
Delighter of Maidens

Sap in the branches
All making merry
Bee to the blossom
Hei to the Maying

Raise now the May-rod
Aengus we name you
Wonder child rising
Come to our calling!"

At this, Joey Tregareth stepped forward, grasped the hilt of Archie's sword, lifted it upright, kissed the blade, and walked the circle bidding each woman to do the same. When she completed the circle, she thrust the blade into the earth, saying:

"Awake, Aengus, O King-to-Be! Enter now the maiden Earth and bring joy and blessing to us all!"

There was moment's silence, during which the only sound was birdsong from the surrounding heath, and then the members of the Lizard Druid Grove cheered, paired off, and slipped away. Hansen collected Joey's cloak and held it for her as she wrapped it around her body. Then she retreated in the direction from which she'd come. Archie, flushed with his performance, turned to Charlotte.

"Shall we join the others in play?" he said.

Charlotte's eyes narrowed. "I don't know what game you're playing, Archie Hansen, but I suggest you remember who takes care of your deepest, darkest needs." Then she turned and walked back toward the farm. Archie scattered the dying embers of the little fires, crushing them with his boot, pulled his sword from the ground, and smiled.

It worked...

Nineteen

AT NINE SHARP on Wednesday morning, twenty-third May, Morgan strode into the new incident room at the St. Michaels Hotel.

"Bates!" she barked at the young woman bent over a computer keyboard. "Whatever you're doing, stop."

Terry Bates smiled. She was getting used to working with "Miss Congeniality." She spun her chair and stood.

"At your pleasure, ma'am."

Morgan frowned. "Oh stop. It's Morgan. Got that?"

"Yes ma'am...*Morgan*."

"I want you to pay Hansen's partner, Ms. Johns, another visit. She's an interested party, and another interview is warranted. But what I really want is a bit more quiet reconnaissance of that house. Tell her we're trying to know Hansen better, to get the big picture of his life. She acts a bit of a cold fish, I know, but that also could be shock. She loved him, that's clear. She should be happy to help."

Bates nodded.

"Take a PC with you from the crime team here. Then have her walk you around the farm to learn how he worked. Meanwhile, make an excuse and have the PC investigate the house."

Bates smiled. "Have someone in mind, do you Morgan?"

"Novak. Plenty distracting. Plenty smart."

BATES AND NOVAK stood with Charlotte Johns at the edge of the field closest to Hansen's house. The desiccated yellow blossoms of the daffodils planted there nodded in a light breeze like sleepy pensioners at a rest home.

"He rotates; I mean *rotated,*" she corrected, placing her hands on the stone boundary wall and gazing across the field. "I don't seem to be able to get the verb tenses right. Can't get my mind around the notion that he's gone…"

Bates touched the woman's shoulder.

Johns nodded. "Yes, he rotated his crops in his various fields, so as not to wear the soil out, he said. So it might be daffs like these, followed by grain, followed by clover, and then maybe potatoes or cauliflower. Gave the fields time to rest, not planting the same thing, he said…"

"My Dad farmed," PC Novak said. "That's what he did, too. Good husbandry is what that is."

Charlotte Johns looked at him. "Husband," she whispered. And then her knees seemed to give out.

Bates knelt beside the tiny woman. "Ms. Johns, have you eaten anything yet today?"

The older woman shook her head.

"Constable," Bates ordered. "Get back to the Hansen house and put a kettle on and see what else you can rustle up. Sugary biscuits of some kind. I'll stay here with Ms. Johns. We ladies will talk."

"I could get the tea…" Johns said.

"Yes, but no. I suspect your blood sugar's perilously low. Let's us rest here a moment and we can talk more about Archie. Novak's just a PC, not a detective. Getting tea's the sort of thing he's supposed to do."

Johns watched Novak walk across the farmyard. "I work at the hospital at Helston," she said finally. "I'm only an orderly, but I've heard of that blood sugar thing. Takes the strength right out of you, it does."

"You'll be better in a moment or two if you rest. So tell me, are all of Archie's fields right here, around the house?"

"No, scattered, they are, but nearby. His family bought them up over the decades as they came available, but only the best ones. Clever devils, the Hansens are...were."

"Did Archie work alone? Did he have any hired help?"

"Archie? Hire help? Not a chance. Too tight-fisted for that, though I know the work was getting harder for him now he's—*was*—getting on in years. It's a hard, physical life."

The two of them sat on the grass, their backs supported by the dry stone wall behind them.

"I'm sorry to ask, Ms. Johns, but what happens to the farm in the event of Mr. Hansen's death?"

Johns shook her head and said nothing for a moment.

"I've no idea. He's—he was—so very private. I don't even know if he had a will. He had a family, years ago, a wife and two children. She divorced him and he never saw his children again. Up north somewhere, they are. Cumbria, he said. I suppose they're his next of kin. Margie, his wife was called, Margie Hansen. No idea whether she kept his name. Maybe she's remarried. The eldest, he was called Erik, after Erik the Red, I suppose. Archie was into that Norse legendry. The daughter's called Brynne. No idea how old they are or whether they'd inherit. Never said a word about them, they'd hurt him so. He'd locked the door behind them."

"But you two have been together for several years; wouldn't he have provided for you?"

Charlotte Johns rose, steadied herself, and looked back toward Hansen's house.

"I don't know. I just don't."

"Are you all right to walk back?"

"Yes, thank you. I'm sorry I collapsed."

"Don't apologize for being human, Ms. Johns. Can you show me around his barn?"

"'Shed' is what he calls—called—his main outbuilding, though it is so big. Where he kept farm machinery and such..."

NOVAK FOUND THE electric kettle on the counter beside the kitchen sink, filled it, switched it on, and raced upstairs. He and DC Bates had worked out a plan that whoever got free would have a look-about. Like a prowling cat, Novak padded around the main bedroom, but found only the man's personal belongings and nothing else apparently out of place. The other two bedrooms seemed little used. The bathroom was spotless.

From the window, he saw Bates guide Johns into the biggest outbuilding, and he slipped back down the stairs. The table in the formal dining room was coated in dust, and the adjacent lounge, while clean, smelled of disuse. It was as he was rummaging around the kitchen for something to go with the tea that he found the tiny room, not much bigger than a closet, that apparently was Hansen's office. It had a desk and computer with a grubby keyboard and a single overhead light bulb. On one wall there was a shelf of jumbled farm journals and file boxes. On the opposite wall was what looked to Novak to be a collection of antique swords, dominated by a polished broadsword straight out of a movie.

THE KETTLE HAD boiled and he'd just laid out mugs and plates as the two women crossed the farmyard. He had a cupboard open and was searching for biscuits when they entered.

"I'm at a loss, Ms. Johns," Novak said over his shoulder. "Can't find a box of biscuits anywhere!"

Johns smiled. "He hid them. On a shelf too high for me to reach. He knew I had a weakness…" She pointed to a round tin atop one of the cupboards ringing the big kitchen. That's it, up there. Dark chocolate whole meal biscuits, unless I miss my guess. His favorite. Mine, too."

At this, she seemed to wilt again, and Bates guided her to a chair beside the scrubbed oak kitchen table.

Novak poured the tea, added plenty of sugar and milk, and offered Johns the opened tin of biscuits. She took three.

"Who taught you how to pour tea, constable?" she chided, her eyes bright. "It's milk first, tea second."

Novak bowed and smiled. "My family is from Eastern Europe. I suppose we do it differently there. Shall I begin again?"

"Don't be silly."

Bates watched this little vignette with mounting disgust. The chocolate coating on the biscuit in Charlotte's hand was melting beneath her fingertips. She slipped two fingers and a thumb between her lips and slowly withdrew them.

Good Lord, she's flirting with him!

Now she took a bite and sipped her tea, winking thanks to Novak.

"I reckon now the blossoms have faded, Archie would next harvest the bulbs, yes?" Bates asked. "What would he plant next?"

"Grains, I should think, wheat or barley," she answered returning her attention finally to the detective. "Like I said earlier, he'd rotate, depending upon what that particular field needed or could provide."

"I see," Bates said, sipping her tea. Except she didn't. There'd been no seed bags for either wheat or barley in the loft above Archie's farm equipment, or anything else. The bulbs languishing in Hansen's fields would have been harvested by now had he lived, but she'd seen no evidence of preparations for either harvest or a following crop. It was as if he'd simply abandoned farming one day, like someone fleeing with his family from an impending invasion and leaving the table still set for supper.

THEIR CAR HAD just cleared the village of Manaccan and was headed for the A394 back to Falmouth when Bates finally said, "So?"

"So, an interesting house," Novak answered. "Sort of lived in, sort of not."

"Pardon?"

"Too clean, you know? At least the rooms that were used regularly—the upstairs loo, the main bedroom. Like a charwoman had been in to clean the place. The other rooms? Stuffy, unused."

"What did you think of the costumes in the bedroom wardrobe?" She didn't look at him; she was waiting to see how bold Novak was.

"Costumes?"

"The sex costumes. Don't play the innocent, it doesn't suit you."

Novak slid a look at her, and returned his eyes to the road ahead of him; he was driving just over the posted limit, eager to get home.

"That's some imagination you have, there, detective..."

"You didn't search that wardrobe?!"

"Of course I did: a few work shirts, denim and cotton flannel, a shiny old blue wool suit, and one dress shirt that once had been white. Pile of clean coveralls folded at the bottom."

"No Viking maid outfit?! No black leather dominatrix getup? Nothing like that?"

"Excuse me?"

"Oh, shit..."

Novak slowed the car a bit. "You all right, Terry?"

"No, I'm bloody well not! Someone's sanitized the scene. The sex costumes were there last time we visited, Davies and I. Only Johns didn't know I'd found them."

"And you found them...how?"

"Did a little walkabout on my way to the upstairs loo—which was filthy at the time, by the way."

"Which is to say," Novak said without taking his eyes off the road, "your search is inadmissible as evidence, just like mine?"

"Yes, and please shut up."

Bates watched the fields blur by and tried to think like her boss: Hansen disappears and is discovered dead. Johns, while apparently shattered, is smart enough to know that eventually the house will be searched. She doesn't want their private games exposed. Too embarrassing. So she clears the costumes out. Does she bin them? Somehow, Bates didn't think so. So she hides them. Not on the farm; too easily found. Where? Her own house, then? But what if her own house was searched? Bates pulled out her mobile and called Davies.

"Good work, both of you," Morgan said when she heard Bates's report. "But the costumes are irrelevant. What people do in the privacy of their bedrooms is not a police concern, however kinky…unless it is connected to a crime and we have no such connection as yet. Plus, there's another problem."

"Ma'am?"

"Stop that."

"Sorry. Habit. The other problem, Morgan?"

"If Johns is only a sometimes playmate, what's our boy do for fun the rest of the time, you know? Randy farmer like that? Does someone else use those costumes? Is it just our Ms. Johns?"

Bates made a face at the phone and rang off. One day, she'd be ahead of Davies. One day…

A FEW MINUTES later Davies called another number.

"Morgan! What a delightful surprise!" West answered. "Let me take my blood pressure medicine, just to be safe."

"Oh, shut up. Got a new twist in this Hansen case."

"Given how little we've got to go on, any twist is welcome."

Davies filled West in on the two previous "informal" examinations of Hansen's house, and explained Bates's latest report: "The house has been thoroughly cleaned. Do we think that's just to hide their role-playing? I doubt it. If Hansen was maimed before he was thrown into the Channel, where might that have happened, if not his own home? I think that's why the house has been sanitized.

"The maiming could have happened anywhere. His barn? A field?"

"Occam's Razor, Calum. Occam's Razor."

"Pardon?"

"Don't play stupid: Middle Ages English friar and philosopher, William of Ockham. He said, basically, the less complicated the solution, the more likely it will be correct."

Calum smiled to himself. He knew exactly who Ockham was, and what Morgan was saying. He just liked to wind her up.

"So I suggest Hansen's place is the scene of a crime which, as I recall, is your department, yes?" Davies said.

"Well, if you put it that way..."

"Which I do."

"…then I'll need to get Mister's okay. But honestly, Morgan, he might need to go upstairs for this one. It's a bit irregular."

"Then put him on a lift, Calum. I feel as if we're losing evidence every day…"

Twenty

AS DAYLIGHT FADED on Thursday night, third May, Bobby Tregareth walked with his colicky son along the stone wall bordering the field closest to his house. The baby was only just over three weeks old, but had already begun screaming, arching, and twisting his tiny spine almost every evening, not long after Joey had breast-fed him. Normal, she said it was, but she said she was fed up with it: she was off to her parents' cottage in Helford for a break. And so Bobby walked, the child in agony, and himself struggling to cope with the boy's piercing cry. There were moments like this when, helpless to calm the child, it was everything he could do to keep from dashing his brains out on one of the stone walls. His fury at his powerlessness frightened him, as if the emotion were a wild thing living just beneath the surface of his skin, a barely contained raging beast wanting nothing but peace. Did all fathers feel this way, or was he crazy? He wanted the noise to stop. He wanted the child to rest. He wanted an end to it. But though his brain was afire, he kept walking, patting the wailing baby's back and talking to him as they wandered in the grass beside the field. He talked incessantly to create an alternate noise, something that might calm the struggling babe, and calm himself as well, as if his own sonorous voice could be a balm. He talked about everything and nothing.

"Now, now, Rob, my boy," for he could not bring himself to call his son Archie, "this here's my fallow field, which I just plowed calcareous sand into. That's calcium and lime from shells, that is, and it'll correct the pH in the soil, make it sweet. And after that I'm seeding with clover to build up the nitrogen. That's the proper way to manage land and it keeps down the need for bought-in fertilizer, you see. And when I turn that clover under, all that goodness will go into the earth and the tilth'll be rich and crumbly for the bulb planting this fall.

"Our neighbor there, Hansen," he turned so the cranky infant could face the opposite field, "he does none of that. Just lays down more chemicals and his soil's going barren. Set in his ways, he is, and won't hear of other ideas. Us, well, it won't be long now before we're certified organic. Yields'll be lower at the start, but the cost of our inputs will be lower, too. No expensive chemicals, see? And the price we get will be higher. And the soil will get richer. Better for everyone, I reckon that is."

The infant was quiet now, finally, but Bobby stayed outside. He thought about the field where Archie'd found that chamber and wondered what mischief the man was up to. Treasure Act? Artifacts? Using his name? Bobby knew it wasn't right. He should confront the man, but he didn't dare. Archie could ruin him.

The early May night was fragrant with awakening earth smells. He walked back to the walled kitchen garden he'd built for Joey just out the back door of their cottage. Young lettuce, spinach, peas, and turnip and beet greens had already broken the surface. When the soil got warmer, which it would soon, he'd plant scarlet runner beans beneath the tripod trellis he'd built, and tomatoes he'd started in their little glass garden shed. He sat on the bench he'd set at the head of the garden, rocked the quiet child gently at his shoulder, and puzzled over another problem.

Fact was Joey had drawn away from him ever since the boy's birth, and he missed her, as if a limb had been severed. Maybe distance was normal after an event as painful as childbirth. He couldn't imagine what it might have been like for her. Maybe she blamed him for the pain. He wasn't sure. Then there was post-partum depression; the doc had warned him about that. But as for the babe, now it seemed to him she only did what she had to and left the rest to him, as if he didn't have a farm to tend.

What he did know was that it was as if there were an invisible wall between them in their bedroom now, the same room, the same bed that had been such a haven for them both. And the only thing that seemed to interest her these days were her Druid grove meetings, to which she had returned.

He didn't understand that, either.

JUST AFTER EIGHT that same evening, two days after the Beltane celebration in which she had played such a central role, Archie opened the kitchen door at the back of Higher Pennare farmhouse to admit Joey Tregareth. She wore a hooded white cloak, the very one she'd worn for Beltane.

"I am here for you, my lord Thor," she said, her voice strong, confident in herself.

"Good. You have done well. Tonight, we will celebrate Beltane in our own fashion, having been kept from doing so on May Day by…circumstance. But tonight we also celebrate a new beginning for the two of us, a life that will continue into the years ahead. A life together, far from here."

"Can it finally be?"

"It is being arranged. I will soon share everything and you will see. Shall we ascend?"

The woman nodded and turned to the stairs. She knew the way.

Up in the attic of the ancient house, a dim space packed with the clutter and dust of generations, Archie unlocked a low door, so old its frame and panels groaned when moved.

"Our place. Our sanctuary," she whispered as she entered. "Prepare it, my lord," she ordered. "Prepare our sacred place."

It was little more than an alcove tucked beneath the eaves, but a rosy light from two wall-mounted sconces with red shades suffused the room with a warm blush. A half dozen books on witchcraft were stacked along a low shelf on one wall, and on the shelf above were several dozen labeled plastic bags filled with herbs and other substances. There was a small table covered in black velvet upon which sat a granite mortar and pestle, a bottle of red wine, two glasses, and an antique silver candlestick, tarnished almost black. While Joey reclined on a low settee along the opposite wall, Archie lit the candle and began the process of grinding several ingredients.

"Did you do as I instructed?" he asked as he worked.

"I did, my lord. I sent the man I handfasted out to walk the child and drank the scented wine you hid in the box hedge beside the door."

"Well done," Archie said as he passed a glass of red wine infused with the herbs he'd just blended. While Joey drank it, he disrobed and wrapped himself in a white cloak matching hers.

Moments later, her eyes ablaze, Joey said, "Your magic is so powerful..."

He pulled her to her feet. She rose on tiptoes, kissed him, and then she repeated the words he'd spoken at Beltane, which perhaps only the two of them had truly comprehended:

"The young son
Aengus the Harper
Son of the Dagda
Whose staff is the strongest

Born of enchantment
Son of the Mother

might be eager to see those photos. Foreigners, they are. Love that old stuff, they do. Pay well, too."

"Right, the Jamaica at eleven, then."

Hansen rang off and stood in his kitchen, looking across to the old stone shed where the treasure rested. Rest. Yes. That was his aim. Farming no more. He and his new woman would be shot of this damp peninsula for good. Coast of Spain somewhere. Malaga or thereabouts. Practically a British colony these days, it was. English spoken. Sun. Good pubs. No worries. And free of Charlotte's addictive control, so hard to escape, like a prison of need. Free of that, like breathing again. And this time, with this woman, he would be in control. He'd had a good teacher, after all, and now he had a willing and submissive student.

Twenty-One

ON THURSDAY MORNING, twenty-fourth May, seven days exactly after the floater had been found, Morgan Davies stood in front of an upright cork board in the Falmouth hotel temporary incident room and stared at an Admiralty Office nautical chart of the English Channel pinned there. In her head, it was like she was in a helicopter hovering high above the Lizard coastline, everything in view. Somewhere out there, far beyond the Manacle Reefs, which had brought so many ships to grief, out where it was deep and where water stretched to every horizon, a body had been dumped the previous Thursday morning.

Then a light came on.

"Somebody get me the number for Culdrose!" she barked.

A PC in the incident room clattered at his computer keyboard, then called the number out. Morgan snapped open her mobile.

"Again!" she ordered. He repeated, and she punched in the number.

Culdrose, the Royal Naval Air Station situated at the northern edge of the Lizard, was the largest search, rescue, and attack helicopter base in Europe, and also home of the Royal Navy's 736 fighter jet squadron. It took several tries before Davies found someone at Culdrose who could tell her that if she wanted imagery of the Channel she needed to speak not to them, but to the Royal Air Force satellite imagery center in Lincolnshire, in eastern England. But that turned out to be a dead end, too. The RAF's satellites had no images for Cornwall on that or any other day; they were focused on strategic hot spots of concern to the UK elsewhere in the world. Cornwall wasn't one of them.

Davies slammed a fist on her desk. Everyone in the incident room turned, but said nothing. Powerlessness was a condition that drove Morgan to fury. She knew its genesis and had long struggled with its effect. Her brother, father, and mother all had been destroyed, in various ways, by the notorious 1966 Aberfan coal tip disaster in her native South Wales, when a mountain of saturated coal mine waste broke loose, buried part of her village, and killed more than a hundred souls, most of them children in a primary school. But no one associated with the National Coal Board had ever been fired, demoted, or fined. Because there were no regulations governing coal mine waste, none had been violated, the judge decided. In one way or another, Morgan Davies had been fighting authority and seeking justice ever since. It was why she was such a good cop; also, why she was a difficult one. She was driven, relentless, a rule-breaker. It helped that DCI Penwarren was her advocate, almost her protector, in the force.

Next, she tried the Internet. In minutes, she found a private company in Surrey that collected satellite images of coastal conditions in the UK on a daily basis. When the firm understood there was a murder investigation underway, they immediately saw a new source of potential revenue in police investigations and readily responded. But when the imagery Davies ordered appeared on her computer screen, it turned out there were more than a dozen boats in the several square mile area of the Channel that day. What's more, there was no way to zoom in to identify them. It would take weeks to track down these boats by investigating their sat-nav records, if they even had any. She didn't have weeks, but she passed the assignment on nonetheless. Someone else's responsibility. Meantime, she'd have to explain to DCI Penwarren how she'd bought the imagery without authorization. She smiled: *It's always easier to get forgiveness than permission.* It was practically her mantra.

She returned to the Admiralty chart and studied it yet again. Something about it nagged her still. Suddenly, her eyes widened and she slapped the standing cork board so hard it nearly toppled.

"Bloody Pythagoras!" she shouted. Everyone in the incident room froze.

Morgan had gone directly from secondary school into the police force as a lowly police constable, pounding the pavement. But the instructors at St. Dyffd's School in Merthyr Tydfil, the town where she'd been raised by her grandmother, had been rigorous.

It was Terry Bates who spoke up: "Pythagoras?"

Morgan shot her a look. "Hansen couldn't have been dumped from the *Saga*. Where was his body found?"

"Just off the Lizard."

"Five miles isn't 'just off,' detective."

Bates looked around the room. No one else moved. "It was a clear day," Bates said. "Very calm. Terrific visibility."

"That's where Pythagoras comes in."

"Sorry?"

"Where's your schooling? It's all about the curvature of the earth. Pythagoras sorted this out around 500 BC. Let's say I'm standing in the bow of the *Saga*. I've just chucked Hansen's body overboard, yeah? Now it's time to head home. But which way's home?"

"The coast, of course."

"But guess what? I can't see the coast. All I can see is water everywhere. The farthest I can see from the bow of the *Saga* is three miles. Pythagoras proved that. The curvature of the earth is such that three miles is as far as I can see on a clear day. So, if I'm in a boat meant for fishing just along the coastal cliffs, I have no idea which way Cornwall is. I'm lost."

"What about the cliffs? Couldn't you see the cliffs?"

"Too low. Lizard's basically a plateau; a hundred meters or so high at best."

Bates considered. "Okay, what if someone dumped Hansen in view of the Lizard and let the body drift out? The post mortem said that the body could have been in the water for as much as four hours. That's a lot of time for the tide to move it.'"

"Duncan also said *not less than* one hour, so it could be any time within that three hour period. And the fact is, you answered that question already, Terry, at the last MCIT meeting. The tide was low and slack, you reported. If the body went anywhere next it would have drifted *toward* shore on the returning tide, not away. And anyway, it was found before the tidal shift."

Bates was silent for a few moments, her eyes cast aside as if regarding something from a distance, a finger pressed against her left temple.

"A second boat," she said.

Morgan smiled. "Well done, detective constable. Exactly. Without navigation equipment, *Saga* could never have been that far offshore. Some other boat was. What else?"

"A second individual."

Davies smiled. "Ms. Johns says she got a text message from Hansen saying he was out fishing with someone called 'Charlie,' though Johns says she does not recognize the name. Maybe Hansen uses his skiff to meet up with Charlie's better-equipped boat somewhere, anchors or moors his, and climbs aboard the other."

Bates was silent again. "Yeah, Charlie…"

"Yes?"

"Look, *Charlie* is street slang hereabouts for heroin."

"Tell me something I don't already know."

"So maybe Hansen had moved on from porn videos to drug dealing. I'm wondering whether maybe he was making a heroin pickup and the deal somehow went all pear-shaped. Or maybe he owed them money he couldn't pay."

Davies looked at Bates and smiled. "You haven't got any dimmer in the year you've been in training, have you, Terry?"

Bates grinned. "Reckon you'll have to be the judge, Guv."

"Okay, let's push this forward: so Hansen motors out in the *Saga* and heads where? South along the Lizard coast it's too rugged for a rendezvous, so he heads north, toward Falmouth and the Carrick Roads. Lots of safe moorings there. Or maybe just to the mouth of the Helford River."

"Or he meets this Charlie, or whomever, and they just raft up anywhere to meet," Bates said. "Calm sea. No need for a mooring."

Davies stared at her for a moment, then punched her shoulder.

"That's it! You just figured it!"

"Sorry?"

"No need for a mooring! What if *Saga* was tied astern of the bigger boat and towed out far into the Channel and Hansen simply was pitched overboard from his own boat! No contamination to the other vessel. You are brilliant, Terry!"

"But who's Charlie, Morgan? Why did he want Hansen dead?"

LATER THAT DAY, Brad and Cheryl Winters sat, like two parakeets on a perch, upon matching stools at the high work table in Blooms, their florist shop on Meneage Street, the narrow, sloping commercial road in central Helston. Bates and Novak sat on the other side. At the news Bates gave them, the pair blinked as if their eyes were driven by the same mechanism. The police had not yet released the victim's name.

"Archie?" Cheryl whispered, as if others were listening. "He's dead?"

"Yes. Murdered, apparently."

"Good lord...."

"He were fine when we saw him last," her husband said in a tone so bereft of emotion he might have been commenting on the weather.

"And that would have been when?" Novak asked, his notebook open.

"Sorry?"

"When you saw him last. When was that?"

Davies had assigned Novak to Bates for the interviews of Hansen's Druid grove members because she was constantly on the prowl for candidates for the next generation of detectives. Novak was in her sights. This interview was their last. Their first three had been notably unproductive, the grove members being suspicious and guarded, as if the interviews were somehow a judgment about the legitimacy of their beliefs and not a murder investigation. They all had alibies for where they were the day Hansen was found, and none had a boat. Only Brad and Cheryl Winters seemed to be willing to cooperate. Or at least Mrs. Winters was.

"Beltane, that was," Cheryl answered, looking off as if to a movie in her head.

"Sorry?"

"First May," Brad answered. "May Day to most folks, but it's *Beltane* to pagans, including Druids like us: a celebration of the fertility of spring."

"Dancing around the Maypole and all that?" Bates joked.

Brad Winters frowned. "This is a sacred moment on our calendar, detective. No Maypole dancing. That's a much more recent invention, more symbolic than real. Nothing to do with Druidry."

"So, how do you celebrate it, if I may ask? I'm sorry, I don't know much about Druids,"

She watched Cheryl's face color.

"There is a solemn ceremony during which we bid farewell to the God and Goddess of Winter and welcome the Queen of the May and her consort, the fertility God," Brad answered, as if quoting from a script.

"And, as your leader, Mr. Hansen presided?"

"Yes," Brad said.

"But he were acting strange," Cheryl added quickly.

"Shuddup, woman, he were always acting strange."

The woman blinked several times, as if slapped.

Bates ignored the husband. "In what way strange, Mrs. Winters?"

"He was all got up with that Viking stuff he sometimes wears. Nothing like old St. Martin, our previous leader. A gentle soul, he was, and wise. Pushed him aside for Hansen, she did."

"Who did?"

"That Charlotte," Cheryl said, and then she leaned close to Bates: "*Charlotte the Harlot,* I call her. Threw her lover Phillip St. Martin over soon as she met Hansen, she did..."

"Phillip were ailing anyway," Brad said. "Time for a change." The fact that Charlotte had once seduced Brad and that, as a result, she had a hold on him when it came time to vote to elevate Archie, was something he did not choose to share.

"So what happens in this ceremony?" Bates pressed.

Cheryl answered this time: "Well, we thank the departing winter and welcome the fertile spring. But this time, Archie had one of our grove, young Joey, who'd just had a child a few weeks back, appear naked, or nearly so, as the May Queen. A right shock, that was, I can tell you!"

"Naked?"

"But for a girdle of rhododendron branches at her waist, yes," Cheryl replied. "Topless, I guess you'd say, detective."

"She were perfect as the May Queen," Brad interrupted. "The image of fertility, having just had that babe. Not something *we* could have done," he said, cutting a look at his wife. "Us being childless and all…"

Cheryl said nothing.

"I understand Hansen had got into the habit of adding spells—is that the right word?—to your get-togethers."

Cheryl ducked her head. "He believed he could make magic happen. Wanted us to believe that, too. He would focus on one of us, chant and scatter powders…"

"Bloody nonsense, near as I could tell," Brad barked. "Nothing came of it anyway."

"What was he looking to have happen?"

"No idea. Never said. It was all mysterious, like."

Cheryl looked away, smiling.

Bates took this in. "So let's go back to this Beltane ritual. What happens next?"

Cheryl brightened and flushed. "After the ceremony, we all run into the woods and make love, of course. It's the fertility festival!" She clapped a hand over her mouth, but her eyes were dancing.

Novak stopped taking notes.

Twenty-Two

FRIDAY EVENING, FOURTH May, Charlotte arrived at Archie's farmhouse as usual, just after five. But the house was empty. Archie's Land Rover and tractor were both in the shed, but that was normal: work done, he'd have walked down the hill to his local, the thatch-roofed, whitewashed New Inn, as he did almost every Friday evening. They often had supper there. A few minutes later she pulled her car into the car park above the back of the pub and was just descending the rear steps leading to the lounge bar below when she heard loud voices from the door to the men's toilet in a rear annex.

"Up for sale, is what I heard," one voice said, the man's words echoing off the loo's ceramic tiles.

"Higher Pennare? You're jokin!" another voice said.

Charlotte stopped.

"What I heard, okay?"

"Yeah, but. Fine house and all, ancient, and the land Hansen's got there's good, that's certain. But what's he mean to be doin' sellin' up?"

"Haven't a clue. Retirin', I reckon…"

"On what?"

"Dunno, do I? Mebbe he's done a whole lot better than the rest of us. Tight-fisted bastard, Hansen is. Mebbe that's it. Saved up and got no loan to pay off. Plus that old house of his must be worth a pretty penny."

"Goin' off somewheres with that woman, Charlotte, is he?"

"Dunno that either, do I? Heard this from a lady friend of mine at Savills Estate Agents, up in Truro."

"Savills is it? Must be some pretty fine lady with that posh firm!"

"Go on, just a friend, she is…"

"Your missus know about this friend?"

Charlotte turned and climbed back up the steps to the car park and sat in her car, poleaxed. Was this some surprise Archie planned to spring on her? Yes, this had to be a surprise, a reward for the years she'd spent serving and pleasing him. This had to be about the treasure, too, that was it! He had a fortune in his grasp. Not to mention the value of the ancient farm. She thought about reentering the pub to ask him, but felt paralyzed with excitement. She drove home and waited for Archie to beckon her to Higher Pennare.

He did not call.

THE NEXT MORNING was overcast but dry. That was good, Dicky thought. There would be no glare for the photos. Townsend spread a black velvet cloth atop a table he'd pulled toward the hotel room window at the Jamaica Inn so as to catch the natural light. He checked the battery strength on the camera and turned.

"Right then, Archie, what've we got?"

Hansen hesitated, his hand resting on a leather carrying case that itself looked an antique.

"It's okay, Arch, we're just taking pictures." He pointed at the draped table. "If I was aiming to rob you, would I have gone to all this trouble?" He raised his hands. "You want to pat me down?"

Hansen shook his head. "Just bein' careful, is all. Nature of us Cornishmen…"

"And that's always wise, I say…"

Hansen released the latch on the case and, with some effort, pulled out a dirty burlap bag, laid it on the bed, and tipped it open.

It was everything Dicky could do not to gasp. There were two thickly braided gold torcs, almost a matched set. The tarnished bronze brooch he'd seen in Bristol was there, too, along with several others, each intricately incised with a pattern of vines, and in one case, the image of a bird. There were half a dozen bracelets, also bronze, as well as several pieces in silver alloy shaped like miniature shields. Finally, there was a large number of Celtic-era coins, some gold, but most in silver, and these ones fused together by time just like the coin masses Townsend had seen in the British Museum: Archie's "dull stuff," so rare that they alone were worth a king's ransom.

Townsend put on white cotton gloves, and pulled out his loupe, inspecting each piece so intently Archie began to wonder if Townsend thought them fakes.

Finally, Townsend straightened and placed the loupe back in his jacket's breast pocket. Based upon his earlier research, he reckoned Archie's trove was worth between five and ten million pounds Sterling.

"You are, sir," he began, "a very lucky and, I daresay, a potentially very wealthy man. This is a find of historic importance. There have been only a handful of such Iron Age treasure troves discovered in Britain. These two gold neck ornaments, for example, are called *torcs* and are very rare. The brooches are from the same period. These miniature shields I've not seen before, but I suspect they were good luck charms carried or hoarded during times of tribal warfare. I'll need to research them. The coins too, are pre-Roman, Celtic. If they had been Roman, they'd have had the image of an emperor on them. These do not. This discovery is worth a fortune, my friend. How big a fortune, however, depends entirely on what you decide to do next."

"Sell them is what I want. Soon."

"Let me just remind you, then, of something I told you back in Bristol: your best bet to gain the highest price for these items is to report them to the county coroner in Cornwall under the Treasure Act. Might take a couple of years of evaluation, but you'd likely receive full value from the Crown."

"You said you could sell them."

"Oh, indeed I can, Archie. But those transactions are private and essentially illegal and, as a result, you'd get only a fraction of the true value of these pieces.

"How much, then?"

"I honestly can't tell you yet. I'll have to contact certain buyers I know. That's what the photos are all about, so they can see and value them. But, if I may say so, even at the discount you'd have to accept in such sales, you would still be a wealthy man. Very. Maybe a million, possibly more."

Archie sat in a chair against the hotel room wall and passed a hand across his eyes. There was dirt under his fingernails. "Get on with it, then," he said finally.

One by one, Townsend positioned the pieces on the black velvet and took shots from several angles.

"Funny doing this here, at the Jamaica…" he mused.

"Meaning what?"

"Old smuggler's inn, this was."

"So?"

Townsend looked up from the table and smiled: "Think about it…"

JUST AFTER THREE that Saturday, Charlotte stepped out of her bungalow as the car came to a stop in her drive. She looked at the older Ford Fiesta Dicky was driving and said, as he approached her door, "Where's your Mercedes?"

"Too conspicuous. I was followed last time we met. Borrowed this motor from a mate," he lied.

"Followed?"

"Yes. This game has become dangerous, Charlotte. For you, for Archie, and for me as well."

Charlotte pressed a palm against her chest. "Come inside. Please."

Charlotte's house was the antithesis of Archie's. Hers was a stuccoed post-war bungalow nestled on a south-facing slope at the edge of the scrubby heathland of Goonhilly Downs. The house had originally been painted the color of clotted cream, but moss had begun to cling to the rough edges of the stucco and to the slate roof as well.

Where Archie's ancient farmhouse was packed with generations of antiques, Charlotte's was minimalist. She'd decorated her cottage in simple, spare, bright, and cheap furnishings she'd mostly accumulated, as she could afford them, from IKEA in Bristol. She'd designed the space to be bright and airy. Sliding glass doors in her living area opened to the raised bed vegetable garden just outside. She'd built the garden as a landscape feature, the beds artfully arranged to face the sun. Though it was only early May, they were already bursting with early greens, young onions, beet leaves, pea shoots, maturing cabbage, and cauliflower—all cool weather crops she'd soon follow with scarlet runner beans, tomatoes, squash, leeks, mid-season potatoes, and herbs, each as the earth warmed.

Townsend sat on a low, snow white Scandinavian divan scattered with richly colored wool pillows that looked to have been made from pieces of old Persian rugs. The house itself, like so many postwar bungalows, was characterless, but she'd made its interior shine.

Charlotte brought two brimming glasses of white wine and a plate of sliced vegetables with a small bowl of garlic aioli dip and set them on the table next to them.

They touched glasses. Dicky thought, *how intimate this gesture can seem…*

Charlotte placed her hand on his knee. "Tell me: what is the danger, Dicky?"

Townsend paused. "Has Archie any sort of criminal history, Charlotte?"

"No! Oh well, yes, I suppose, if you include selling X-rated videos some years back. But he was never convicted of anything, is what he told me…"

"Ah."

"What is it?"

"My sources tell me he's been in touch with a dodgy character called Reg Connor. Used to be a distributor, I hear, of…um…naughty videos."

"That was before I met Archie, Dicky."

"Oh, I was not suggesting you were involved in the videos."

She smiled, patted his knee, and then leaned back against the arm of the divan, crossing her legs, her skirt slipping higher on her thigh. "I have nothing against naughty, Dicky…"

Townsend cleared his throat. "Yes, well, it turns out Connor's moved on to art and antiques. Your Archie apparently contacted him a few weeks ago, about the same time he met me at the coin show in Bristol. Playing two sides against each other for the best deal, I reckon he is."

Charlotte nodded. "That would be Archie, all right...but he is no longer 'my Archie,' Dicky."

"What are you saying?"

Charlotte rose and went to the doors overlooking the garden. "It all begins to make sense now." For a few moments she said nothing. Then she turned to face him.

"I've been betrayed, Dicky, by the man I've given myself to so completely these past several years. I've been a fool."

"Do you mean he has yet to tell you about the treasure?"

She laughed, but her throat caught: "The treasure's the least of it, Dicky." She took a breath. "He's selling the farm. Hasn't said a word to me about it. I found this out by accident, just yesterday." A tear traced its way down her right cheek.

As if lifted by her grief, Townsend rose, crossed the room, and took her into his arms. She lifted her face and kissed him, first shyly, then almost desperately. She curled her tight little body into his, lifting one leg high behind his and pulling him close.

Early the next morning, the sun having not yet crested the lip of the valley, she awoke beside him in her small upstairs bedroom and smiled. At last, she'd found a man who could find his way to her very core, a man who was as gentle and caring a lover as he was lusty. She had not needed to serve him; he had served her. She felt transformed. It was sudden, but also suddenly and finally, right. So much wasted time. She'd found her match. Maybe Archie had big plans. But now, for the first time in memory, she did, too.

"LET ME GET the photos to some of my buyers, Char," Townsend said as he ducked into his car later that morning.

She loved that he called her Char, the first letter soft: *Shar*. She leaned into the car's window and kissed him.

Townsend grinned. "It may take a couple of days. You do understand, don't you, that you're going to have to obtain the treasure at some point? Others are after it. You should think about how that might happen…"

Charlotte smiled. "Oh, I have, Dicky. I have."

TOWNSEND WAS BANGING north on the A30 and just approaching Exeter when his mobile chirped. He recognized the number.

"Hello?"

"My patience is not unlimited, Dicky-boy."

"Reg! Hi! Hang on a moment, let me pull over."

"Didn't know you were such a safe driver…"

Townsend wasn't. He was buying time to think. He moved left into the slow lane and then onto the hard shoulder.

"Right then, I'm off the motorway." The stopped car lurched from the blasts of air from each auto and lorry that rocketed past.

"Where the hell are you?"

"Devon. Returning from a wild goose chase, I reckon."

"Explain."

"Set up a meeting with Hansen for today at the Jamaica Inn up on Bodmin Moor, right? Got a private room and all and set up to photograph his trove, like you told me. Only he never showed. Squirrely bastard is our Archie, I'm tellin' you, Reg. On again, off again. Trusts no one."

"And you didn't continue on to Cornwall to find him because…?"

"His girlfriend, Reg, if that's the right term for a woman in her forties at least. Met with her briefly a couple of weeks ago, another time Hansen was supposed to be there but wasn't. Told her then that me and Archie were chums from way back. Said I did a quality review of the New Inn at Manaccan for Sharp's Brewery, ran into him there, and he told me to stop by for lunch next time I was in the area. She was supposed to arrange that, but when I got to his farm a week later, no Archie. I think she knows something's up with him, but doesn't know what. I figure she made sure he wasn't around. Tried to pump me for information, she did. Gave me the whole tea and biscuit routine."

"What's all that got to do with today?" Dicky took note of Connor's rising volume. Connor had a volatile temper, his anger soaring like a spiking fever in moments.

"Weekends are when she's at Hansen's place, see?" Dicky said, his voice matter-of-fact. "I figured it was too risky to run down there today. And he's got something else going, I think. I don't know what yet. Said when I rang him that he'd waited all this time for a photo session because he had other plans to make first."

Reg Connor said nothing for several seconds: "All right, Townsend. But you'd better not be playing me. Do that and I promise you the consequences will be extreme."

The phone went dead, and Townsend smiled: *Afraid he's losing it, old Connor is. Threats instead of reason, poor old bastard. Doesn't even imagine I know I've been tailed by one of his people.*

Twenty-Three

"WHAT HAVE YOU got from *Saga?*" Davies barked into her mobile when her call connected. It was early Friday morning, twenty-fifth May, and she was at her makeshift desk at the incident room in the St. Michaels Hotel in Falmouth. "You've had it long enough."

"And a fine good day to you, too. Morgan," Calum West said. "How is Cornwall's loveliest detective inspector this day?"

"Piss off."

"I'll take that as a not too good, then, shall I?"

"Blood. From the boat. What have you got, Calum?"

"You're just no fun, Morgan. You might try it sometime, just for a change. As to the boat, let me remind you: we SOCOs are about preservation of evidence, you CID people are about investigation. We work methodically to make sure you have rock-solid evidence so you can get a conviction, savvy?"

"Blood, Calum?"

"Okay, so the short answer is that the interior of the boat was bleached practically toxic. We found nothing there."

"What's the long answer, then?"

"Ah, you do pay attention, after all, don't you?"

Morgan took a breath, consciously slowing herself. "All right, what else, Calum?"

"My boys found a smudge of blood under the gunwale near the bow."

"The *what*?"

"Gunwale. It's the rim that runs around the upper edge of the hull. In olden days it was the edge of the deck where canons were mounted. Thus, the *gun*."

"I don't need the whole damn video, Calum. What's the blood type?"

"Might have a bit of luck there. It's AB positive. Only three percent of the UK population have it."

"Find someone with it and find the killer?"

"Maybe. Could be unrelated, though."

"You are so cheering…"

"But there's something else. You'll remember that the helm of the *Saga* is on an upright console amidships, yes?"

"Where the wheel is? Yes, I've not entered my dotage yet, Calum."

"Something's missing from the console."

"I'm waiting, but not patiently."

"There's a round mark, just over two inches in diameter. Faint, as if scrubbed clean. And two screw holes. A Ritchie Trek Surface-Mount Compass was mounted there, according to my boys. Inexpensive and commonly used by recreational fishermen hereabouts in case they get fog-bound. Only kind with that dimension."

"Bloody hell! There goes Pythagoras…."

"Pythagoras?"

"Never mind. Long story, involving navigation and a second boat, but which, apparently, was not involved after all."

"Wait. I'm with you, Morgan. Five miles, right? No land?"

"Yes."

"Good reasoning, but easily managed with this compass. But why would someone then remove it?"

Davies considered: "For the simple reason that it would lead us astray. But the next question is why hide the boat up Frenchman's Creek? It was bound to be found eventually."

"Perhaps that was intentional, too," Calum said. "Look, five miles out in the Channel they had no idea the body would be found so quickly. Let's face it: that was pure chance. But they also couldn't bring the boat back to its mooring at Flushing because they might have been seen. But if they ditched it up that creek it looks like someone trying to get away fast, someone who knows little about boats—remember that incompetent knot—but that someone is smart enough to clean the boat and strip it."

"Okay, I like it. Thank you, Calum. One boat, but operated and hidden by whom?"

"That's your department; I'm just the scene guy. But I'm always here for you, luv."

"You coming down for the MCIT meeting in Falmouth this afternoon?" she asked.

"Get to see you, even if only officially? Of course!"

She rang off and stared off across the busy room: PCs were on phones to boatyards and yacht clubs along the

River Fal looking for any boaters who might have been cruising off the Lizard on the morning of seventeenth May. She listened to the hum of their voices, and yet it was Calum's voice she heard, a soft baritone with just that edge of mischief: *Always here for you, luv.*

It was true: ever since the Chynoweth case he'd been there for her, there to pull her back from whatever cliff she was about to jump from in her headlong rush to solve a case, there to support her in the force whenever she was her own best enemy. She wondered whether he'd been a factor in her promotion to detective inspector.

So maybe Calum West really was looking after her, really did care about her, but if he did, what the hell was wrong with him? She rose and walked to the windows overlooking the gardens that led down toward the shore. Weather was coming in from the southwest. Rain soon. She had no experience of anyone caring for her: father and brother dead before she was born, emotionally shattered mother in an asylum, drunken and bitter grandmother who raised her. Her brief marriage? Almost professional: long talks about cases over supper, okay sex. But she'd always known she was the strong one in that relationship. It was one reason it ended…that and his affair with the woman now his wife: younger, pretty in a pale, porcelain sort of way. Sweet, undemanding, unthreatening. No wonder Max had left her. Then she thought about Calum's two impish young daughters and how she'd so enjoyed playing with them at the Bodmin HQ Christmas party. She thought about the death of his wife from cancer, how he'd somehow managed to rebalance himself over time. Maybe it was the girls that had centered him. Or his devoted mother-in-law, Ruth. They needed him and he responded. Had anyone ever needed her? She knew that answer.

She thought, too, about how she and Calum had tussled ever since they'd met and, truthfully, how much she enjoyed their give and take. And it occurred to her that he was the closest friend she had: a friend who told her the truth about herself and who cared about her, if at a distance maintained by their perpetual verbal sparring.

Oh bugger! she said to herself as she returned to her desk and picked up the phone.

LATER THAT AFTERNOON, DCI Arthur Penwarren—"Mister"—sat at the head of the long table in the Starboard Room at the St Michaels Hotel. The rest of the incident team sat along the sides. Rain lashed the windows; an unseasonably vicious storm had crossed the Atlantic and was threatening to uproot trees the length of Southern England.

Penwarren rose and stretched his back. Slender and exceptionally tall for a Cornishman, the DCI privately cursed the world's chairs and tables for being so low. In his office at Bodmin he worked standing up. Though he was still a few years from retirement, his backswept, longish, non-regulation hair already had gone silver at the temples and his lower back was increasingly troublesome. Arthritic degeneration, the NHS doc had said. He seldom did field investigation work anymore, preferring to urge his detectives to lead and lending them his support. Though he believed in that management style, it was also a cover for his gathering infirmity.

"Let me say that I fully understand the difficulty of this case," he began.

Nods around the table.

"And I have made that clear to headquarters in Exeter."

More nods.

Here it comes, Morgan thought: *The But…*

"But it is becoming more and more difficult for me to justify the cost of this investigation with the big boys up there when we have had so little progress."

Silence.

"So let me try to summarize where we are…"

Morgan sighed and crossed her arms beneath her ample chest. *Here we go…the review.* The DCI turned to face the window, as if the jagged lines of rain there were a script from which he read.

"We have a naked and apparently maimed body, found far out in the Channel. We have a woman who claims the deceased is her partner, whatever that means these days, and that he texted her to say he'd gone fishing with a friend. We have a small coastal skiff found up a creek, hidden and bleached so completely that no evidence of foul play remains, although the bleaching itself definitely suggests foul play and the boat is now in evidence."

Finally, he turned to face them: "How am I doing so far?"

No one moved.

"In the meantime, Bates and Novak here"—he nodded to them—"have uncovered evidence that the members of our victim's Druid grove, which I gather is what they call their little congregation, thought their leader an odd sort of fellow, one given to strange augmentations to their official rites, yes? He was not, it seems, universally revered.

"Still with me?"

"If I might comment, Guv?"

"No, you may not, Morgan. I am not finished."

As if as one, the rest of the team took a breath and did not look at her.

"What I suggest is that we forget about boats and harbors and yacht clubs and focus on those who actually knew the victim. We're looking for someone, or some people, who had a reason for wanting Archie Hansen dead, someone with a serious grudge: the Druids, the neighbors, the man's own partner, nearby farmers, the woman at the Royal Cornwall Museum who knew about the treasure but, dare I say it, conveniently failed to interview him? Was she after it?

"Footwork, people: Footwork."

Penwarren folded himself into his seat.

"Guv?"

The DCI rested an elbow on the table, his forehead in the cup of his left hand. "What is it, Morgan?"

"The farm, sir. Who inherits? Terry here says the farmhouse alone is so old it's practically a Heritage Site."

"Terry?"

"Ancient cob farmhouse, Guv, maybe mid-seventeen hundreds, possibly earlier. Very rare."

"And you know this because...?"

"My dad. He's an architect. He specializes in restoring historic houses. Took me along on site visits as a kid, what with my mum dead and all."

Davies nearly stopped breathing. She'd had no idea Bates's mother, like her own family, was dead.

"House and farm like that? Worth a fortune, I reckon," Bates added.

"Hansen's partner, Ms. Johns, says she doesn't know who inherits, despite their having been together for some years," Davies said. "Is there a will? Johns says Hansen was divorced. Where's his family? Do they stand to benefit? May I suggest it is time to have Calum's SOCO boys do a thorough search of that house for any documentary evidence we might discover? Time for us to find his lawyer, perhaps? Bank and phone records?"

Penwarren smiled. He was tired, but pleased, yet again, with this incorrigible but relentless detective. "It's a bit irregular—no surprise, that, given it comes from you, Morgan."

Knowing smiles around the table.

"Calum?" Penwarren asked.

"It's the victim's house and land, not a suspect's, and not a murder site. And therefore it's not within SOCO's remit. We'd need a search made legal."

"Right, then. I'll see what I can do. Meanwhile, Bates and Novak: find out exactly where Hansen's Druid grove members were the day he was found. You spoke to them before. Go back. And take DNA swabs. Each and every one of them is a person of interest. But make sure they understand we're not targeting them because of their religion or whatever it is. That's persecution and it would be all over the media. They're persons of interest solely because of their association with the victim. Meanwhile, somebody remind me who talked to the museum lady..."

"I did, Guv," Morgan said.

"Talk to her again."

"I really don't think..."

"Talk to her, Morgan. Find out where she was the morning Hansen was found. From what I can tell from the HOLMES II file, she's the only one who knew about the possible value of the find besides the dead man. The *only* one. That's a neon light flashing 'opportunity' to me. So let's not ignore the obvious. And while you're at it, talk to this Tregareth fellow. Says Hansen found a chamber beneath his field but also says he doesn't know anything else. Lean on him."

"Can the search include the field and chamber?"

"Like I said, Morgan, I'll see what I can do. You'll be the first to know, after Calum. For now, I think we are done here...."

"Guv?"

Penwarren sighed. "What now, Morgan?"

"This is driving all of us 'round the twist, too."

Penwarren smiled and looked around the table. "You people are the best I've ever had under my command. Carry on."

AT TEN ON Saturday morning, twenty-sixth May, Morgan Davies paced the lobby of the Royal Cornwall Museum, the massive neoclassical granite edifice on River Street in Truro that holds the county's most valuable archaeological, cultural, and historical artifacts. A volunteer at the front desk was trying to locate Patricia Boden, the museum's curator for Bronze and Iron Age artifacts and the British Museum's finds liaison officer for Cornwall.

"She doesn't work Saturdays, usually," the young volunteer said, "but I'm almost certain I saw her a few minutes ago. She's here somewhere."

Davies slapped two palms on the receptionist's desk and barked: "She damn well better be, we have an appointment," showing the young woman her warrant card.

The woman held up a hand as she listened to her phone. "Okay, right, I'll send her right up."

The volunteer stepped back from her desk and blinked several times at the woman looming before her. "She's waiting for you in the Courtney Library."

"Do you have cute little names for all of your rooms?"

"Actually, ma'am, the library is named after…"

"Save it. Where?"

The young woman blinked again. "Upstairs. Shall I find someone to guide you?"

"Do I look blind? Just point me."

Stairs rose from the reception area, and she found the library immediately. It was long room, two stories high. The walls were lined with shelves and file drawers. A circular wrought iron stairway led to the stacks in the oval gallery above. Two women sat at a long table on the main level. The older of the two, at the head of the table, rose: "I'm Hilary Gracefield, the museum's director, and this is Ms. Boden. I believe you two have spoken by phone but not met. How can we help you, detective?" The director was partridge plump and clearly protective of one of her brood.

"I don't think we need a chaperone, director."

Gracefield didn't flinch: "I'll be the judge of that, shall I?"

Davies shrugged: "As you wish."

She turned to the younger woman and, as was her style, skipped preliminaries: "Miss Boden, where were you on the morning of Thursday, seventeenth May of this year? I do realize you may not know that straightaway. If you don't recall, I'll understand. You can get back to me."

"No need. It would have been a workday. I can check right now." Boden flipped open her laptop, punched a few keys, and turned the screen toward Davies. The computer showed she had been at the British Museum in London for a training course. Davies wondered if this whole act had been rehearsed.

"Training about what?"

"Being finds liaison officer, as it happens. There were liaison officers there from most counties. Because of budget cuts, county coroner's offices no longer have a coroner's officer to investigate reported treasure finds with us when we hear of them. The course was about how to use local police authorities to perform that function: how to inform them about the task and so forth. A detective superintendent from the Met presided along with a senior official from the British Museum in charge of administering the Treasure Act."

"So that would suggest that someone can confirm that you were, indeed, there?"

"Just a minute, detective!" Gracefield erupted. "What are you insinuating? That Ms. Boden is lying, or is a suspect of some sort? That's idiotic!"

Davies smiled. Dealing with outrage was an almost daily part of her job. Outrage beaded and rolled off her as if she were greased.

"I insinuated nothing of the sort, director. I asked a simple question. Ms. Boden here is not a suspect, she is merely a person of interest. She is a person of interest because she attempted to investigate a reported treasure find by a man who was subsequently murdered, and in a particularly brutal manner, I might add. Tortured."

"Good Lord," Gracefield said.

Patricia Boden stepped in: "I am sorry. What else do you wish to know?"

"You visited the farm of a Mr...." Davies glanced at her notes. "Tregareth?"

"Yes, that was the name the caller gave when he called Bonhams, the London auctioneers. The call was then reported to the British Museum, and I was contacted by someone at the Met, who passed on what little was known. But I got lucky: there's only one active farmer named Tregareth in Cornwall."

"You visited Mr. Tregareth with PC Novak from the Falmouth station, is that correct?"

"Yes. But I'm sure you know that already."

Davies looked up from her notes. "Indeed. I do. How did he strike you?"

Boden blushed. "Constable Novak?"

"Tregareth!" Davies wanted to slap her silly.

"I didn't believe him when he said he had no idea what I was talking about. I said as much. I'm afraid I'm rather new at all this investigating," she said, glancing at her superior. "It was Constable Novak who managed to diffuse the situation and that was how we came to know that Tregareth's neighbor had apparently discovered an underground chamber on his property. Tregareth was right steamed that his neighbor, Mr. Hansen, had used his name. And he showed us the field where the chamber was found."

"And yet you pursued neither Tregareth nor Hansen…?"

"That's not true! I called Hansen's number several times and left messages but got no reply."

"And despite the fact that you are the county's only finds liaison officer and items covered by the Treasure Act had reportedly been found, it did not occur to you to interview Mr. Hansen in person?"

"I hadn't the time to drive all the way down to the Lizard without knowing Hansen would be there to meet me. I did try to make an appointment!"

Gracefield intervened: "Do you have any idea how difficult it is to run an underfunded, understaffed institution like the Royal Cornwall Museum, detective?"

"No, I do not," Davies said, leveling a look at the director. "Nor do I care. A man who apparently found something old and valuable lies on a slab in the mortuary at the Royal Cornwall Hospital at Treliske, just up the road from this museum. The only person who knew anything about that discovery was the dead man himself and your own Ms. Boden. Thus, as I am sure even you can appreciate, Ms. Boden is a significant person of interest. You deal with past history; I deal with the present, and the present is often unpleasant."

Abruptly, Davies rose and collected her notebook. "This is a criminal investigation," she said to Gracefield, her voice sharp as teeth. "I came to your museum as a courtesy. I could just as well have hauled Ms. Boden up to the incident room in Falmouth for a formal interrogation, which I may yet do. Like I said at the outset, we did not need you as a chaperone. Nor, in that role, did you do anything but obstruct, which I will remember." She passed a business card to Patricia Boden. "By Monday morning I will expect a full and signed statement covering your meeting with Tregareth and your movements and activities up to and including seventeenth May. Are we clear?"

Boden blinked. Gracefield was glacial. Davies nodded once and left.

Twenty-Four

"OKAY, SO SOME of them thought Hansen odd, that's clear," Terry Bates said. "But does that make any of them murderers?"

Bates and PC Novak had just concluded another round of interviews and DNA swabs with the members of Hansen's Druid grove. It was late Sunday afternoon, twenty-seventh May. Novak was driving their police car. They were just approaching the junction with the A394 at the eastern edge of Helston.

"You're a man, what did you think of the women in Hansen's grove?"

Instead of answering, Novak said, "Would you mind very much if we stopped for a few minutes at the Sainsbury's at this roundabout? I need to collect a few things for dinner."

Bates looked at her driver, then at her watch. "Sure. Fine. We've plenty of time."

Inside the automatic entry doors to the superstore, Novak grabbed a wire basket. Bates followed. The produce section was just ahead, and he prowled it like a prey animal, plucking a small shiny green courgette from one bin, a slender purple aubergine from another, a yellow onion, a head of garlic, four ripe tomatoes, a green pepper, a small pot of fresh basil, and a plump lemon. As if he were in another world which did not include her, he strode to the back of the store to the seafood counter, where he ordered a dozen fresh prawns, their shells a bright greenish orange. "Let me smell," he said to the young lady behind the counter. She held them out. "Fine," he said.

In the wine aisle, where he chose a dry French rosé from Provence, Adam Novak scrutinized the label on the back. "Good," he mumbled to himself, "twenty-five percent Cinsault."

Bates finally spoke up: "You cook?"

Novak startled and turned. "Oh, dear. I'm sorry. I did not mean to ignore you; I was trying to be quick. Yes, I cook. Tonight I will make ratatouille with garlic prawns and lemon."

"Hot date?"

Novak's olive skin was too dark to show a blush. He looked at the basket for a moment instead. "No. I cook for me. It's how I separate myself from the police work, how I end my day. It calms me. We can check out now; did I take too long?"

Bates looked at her watch again and smiled. "Less than fifteen minutes. You're a speed shopper. Impressive." As he stood in line to pay, she began to form a very different picture of PC Novak: not a ladies man, after all, but a man's man, comfortable in his own skin, whether as constable or cook. Interesting…

Back on the A394, Novak said, "I have been thinking about your earlier question. I think the women in Hansen's grove were somewhere between attracted to and intimidated by him. I have to wonder if there was more going on between them and him than Druidry. I'd guess affairs. But the one I find most troubling is Mrs. Winters's husband, Brad. As when we interviewed him before, he was dismissive of Hansen, but very high on Charlotte Johns and seemed eager to silence his wife. Did he do something once for Johns and now he's in her debt? Or did they have an affair?"

Bates listened carefully. Novak was confirming her own somewhat vague impressions, but more succinctly. She admired his mind.

Novak had just switched off the ignition in the police lot at the Falmouth nick when he turned and asked, "You like prawns, then?"

She patted his forearm. "Thank you, Adam. That's very sweet of you. But I've a long drive back up to Bodmin."

"Hot date?" Adam echoed.

She opened the passenger door and stepped out, ducking her head in again: "You're joking, right? I'm a policewoman…"

Novak watched Bates cross the lot toward her own car, her reddish hair dancing as she walked. The woman was slender and, at maybe five-foot-four, almost tiny. But there was strength in her. She radiated it. That bit was as attractive as the rest of her, which was saying something. He locked the car and went inside to file his report on the Druid interviews.

Bates sped up the A39 on her way home and thought: *You bloody idiot, Terry....*

EARLY SUNDAY AFTERNOON, as the western sun faded the sky to a pale, watery blue, Morgan strode into the Blisland Inn, just north of Bodmin. The big man behind the bar looked up, smiled, and waved. The place was, as usual, packed tight as a sardine tin with locals, the old friends calling out jibes to their chums. But they were quiet when Morgan entered. She was still a bit new and there was a rumor she was a detective.

The landlord ignored the crowd at the bar and called, "Pint of Keltik, Morgan?"

She nodded, slipped a hand through the scrim of bodies at the bar, paid, withdrew her foaming pint, and found a seat at a small table by the hearth.

Back in March, uncertain as to how her promotion to detective inspector at the Bodmin police hub would sit, and sad to leave Newlyn, the fishing port where she'd lived for some years when she was head of CID in Penzance, Morgan had decided to register her renovated former sail loft with a holiday letting agency, just in case she might want one day to return. The furnished stone building would earn her more in a summer than its mortgage would cost in a year.

Initially, after her promotion, she'd lived in a guest house and, in her off hours, would drive through the surrounding countryside looking for a village that might have some of the comradery she'd felt among the rough and tumble fishermen at Newlyn. One day, a few miles northwest of Bodmin, she'd wandered into the Blisland Inn at lunchtime. There was a welcoming wood fire in the granite hearth near the bar.

"Double vodka tonic, please," she said to the man behind the bar.

He recoiled and pressed a hand against his chest as if wounded. "Madam, please! Spare a moment to regard this award-winning array of local cask conditioned ales we have on offer, the largest in the region, not to mention our collection of hard ciders from Somerset and Devon."

Morgan looked down along the bar, and had to admit she'd never seen so many pump handles—nearly a dozen—for pulling ale or cider up from the cellar. Clearly the inn was a Free House, unaffiliated with any particular brewery, but it was more than just that: it was an aficionado's haven.

"Impressive," she acknowledged. "You the barman?"

"Landlord actually, madam: Garry Ronan, at your service. But may I just ask, given this splendid range of good and honest British brews, how you can even consider something as foreign as vodka? Vodka? That's from Russia, yeah? Our former enemy and dodgy new friend? Come on, then…where's your patriotism?"

The man was big, bearded, and full of playful trouble. Morgan took to him instantly.

She fished in her purse, slapped a five pound note on the bar, and said, "Give me one good reason to change."

Ronan stroked his beard and looked at the beamed ceiling of the pub as if seeking wisdom there. Dozens of antique ceramic "Toby" beer jugs hung from the blackened beams.

"Vodka drinker. Hmm…. Well then, you'll want something clean and smooth, not too hoppy, so not an

India pale ale. Too sharp, that would be, like gin. I'm thinking something in a nice amber, with just the slightest bite, like it had a touch of tonic and lemon."

"Your choice, but I'm only tasting," Morgan said, her head cocked to one side, her hand on the five pound note, the picture of skepticism. "Not buying, mind you."

Ronan placed two beefy hands on the bar and leaned across. "I can see you are a hard one. But I've had harder…"

She chuckled but did not correct him. He had her pegged.

He moved down the bar, considered for a moment, pulled a half pint of "Keltik Magic," and set it before her. There was the slightest lip of creamy foam. "This is from a local boutique brewery run by a chap who knows his stuff. It's a medium amber, a bit fruity, but also smooth, with very light hops. On the house, madam, so as to lure your delightful custom in future."

Ronan admired the woman before him: a fine strapping lady, big but not overweight. Strong bones and sculptured facial features, spiked, bleached hair, just the hint of lipstick, but no other makeup. A woman who did not need to impress with embellishment, is what he thought: impressive in her own right.

"Passing through or new here?"

Morgan sipped and then smiled. She'd never been much of a beer drinker, but the landlord was right: this was delicious and refreshing. Clean, but also smooth.

"New," she said, finally answering his question. "House hunting."

"Buying or letting?"

"You an estate agent then, too?"

Ronan shook his head. "I've been landlord of this pub for quite some years now. There's not much I don't know hereabouts, and what I don't my customers will tell me. What are you looking for then?"

Morgan drained her glass.

"Letting, for now. New job. Looking for someplace with history, but freshly renovated. Not too big. Two bedrooms maybe. Maybe just one. Not far from here. I work in Bodmin now."

"What at, then?"

Morgan hesitated, but this fellow was so open and genuine she decided to trust him.

"Detective. Devon and Cornwall Police."

Ronan nodded. "Reckon that's a good recommendation. Might be I know of something that would suit. Just up the moor a bit to the north. Lovely spot. Fine view of old Brown Willy, highest spot in all of Cornwall. Property's an old stone hay barn renovated to high standard to be a holiday letting, except not too many people want to spend their hols up on rainy Bodmin Moor, except in summer. Weather's too unpredictable, rest of the year. Fully furnished it is, as well. Contemporary, but comfy."

"I can't afford what holiday lettings go for. I've just listed my own house in Newlyn with a holiday agency."

"That's exactly my point: Offer the owner a year-round rental that would earn him more than a few weeks of summer hols, and I bet he'll bite. Great spot it is. Big views." He leaned forward and whispered: "Reckon I can have a word with him…"

"You get a commission or something for this?"

Ronan smiled. "What I get is a new neighbor and a customer I already admire."

"Go on, then," Morgan said, pushing the five pound note across the bar. "Pull me an honest pint."

She was just lifting her dimpled glass and collecting her change when she stopped, the mug in mid-air: "Wait. This is your property, isn't it?"

Ronan laughed: a warm, rumbly laugh: "Reckon you're a detective after all. It is. Have you a name?"

Davies smiled. "Morgan. Morgan Davies. Where's this house of yours, then?"

NOW, SIPPING HER smooth, malty pint and thinking about the Hansen case, she was suddenly aware of a presence at her shoulder. It was Ronan. For a big man he moved through crowds like a ghost.

"Dinner, Morgan?"

"What's actually edible tonight, Garry? And since when does this pub have table service?"

"The Blisland Inn has table service whenever you enter, luv, and I'd recommend the Moroccan lamb with couscous tonight."

"What, no one else ordering it?"

Ronan put a big hand on her shoulder, leaned in and said, so no one could hear, "Long day, Morgan?"

She smiled up at him and patted his warm hand. "Long week, actually. Lamb sounds great tonight. Thank you, Garry."

She watched him reenter the fray at the bar. *Chap's a gentleman, he is. I could get used to that. Maybe.*

The renovated stone hay barn she leased from Garry had felt like home right from the start. It shared many of the characteristics of her former home in Newlyn: the barn's kitchen was newly-appointed with stainless steel appliances and polished granite counters. The cupboards were painted the warm white of Devon clotted cream. A long pine dining table separated the kitchen from the sitting room. The concrete floor was heated by electric coils from beneath, a treat to the feet. Facing the coal fired stove set against the barn's stone wall were two deeply cushioned chairs and a small settee, covered in white denim slipcovers. She'd wondered about that, the practicality of white. *Get them dirty or stained,* Garry had explained, *you just toss them in the washer with soap and bleach. Good as new!* She had to admit the thick cotton twill was a lot more comforting than her leather upholstery in Newlyn.

Ancient granite steps, the stone no doubt cut from moorland granite, led to the second level bedroom and bath, the latter of which included both a shower and soaking tub. Set into the north-facing wall of the bedroom, French doors opened to a small balcony looking out across Bodmin Moor.

But it took a couple of weeks before she finally understood why she felt so comforted in her new home, just as she had in Newlyn: it was the view. In Newlyn her vista included the fishing docks below, the arc of the city of Penzance to the northeast, and the whole expanse of Mounts Bay. At Blisland, she also had wide views, but this time of the grey-green moorland of Bodmin and, to the north, the castle-like granite summit of Brown Willy tor, not so different from the manmade castle upon St. Michael's Mount in Penzance. From her balcony she could see for what seemed like miles. That's when what seemed so right dawned on her: she had *prospect*. She had *warning*. No collapsing mountain of water-soaked coal slag could roar through the fog and nearly obliterate her village and the people who lived there. There was no Aberfan disaster possible here. If trouble of any kind approached, whether natural or manmade, she'd see it coming long in advance and be prepared.

She was safe.

Twenty-Five

ON WEDNESDAY, NINTH May, Dicky Townsend stepped off the First Great Western train from Bristol and walked out to the Maidenhead railway station's forecourt. An Elite Cab idling at the curb took him a few minutes north to Cookham, an ancient stone and brick village on the leafy banks of the upper River Thames and the headquarters of D.K. Chalmers Rare Coins and Antiquities. At the edge of the village, the cab turned right into a long crushed gravel drive leading to what looked to Dicky like a riding academy. Fields punctuated with jumps stretched away to the river bank and riders were taking horses through their paces. Chalmers's business was in an almost windowless brick building some distance from the stables.

Dicky paid the cabbie, and then pressed the entry button mounted on the door jamb, smiled into the camera mounted to one side, and announced himself when the intercom light illuminated. He was wearing the same hired suit he had worn when he first visited Charlotte Johns. The lock buzzed, and he entered what looked like a branch of the British Museum. There were ranks of glass-faced cabinets holding ancient objects from, as near as he could tell, all over the world. He padded down a long, thickly carpeted passage and found an office at the end lined with books and presided over by a portly fellow in his apparent sixties. The man, wearing what looked to Dicky like a bespoke suit, did not wear a tie at the open neck of his starched white spread-collared shirt. His head was shaved and glistened as if oiled. Chalmers did not rise from his ornately carved mahogany desk to greet his visitor.

"Ah, Mr. Townsend. Declan Chalmers. Welcome. I do not normally meet anyone on such short notice, but your Sunday email was, shall I say, compelling…if it was accurate, of course." Chalmers held a lifted eyebrow in question.

Townsend did not respond to the challenge.

"You have traveled some distance to see me today; I thought you might like a bite of lunch upon your arrival. Our private chef has provided a light repast." He gestured to a side table set with platters of salad greens, cheese, sliced meats, and an opened bottle of claret.

"Glass of wine to begin, then?" Chalmers suggested.

Townsend found his voice: "That would be splendid, Mr. Chalmers."

"Please avail yourself. And pour a glass for me, as well, if you would be so kind." His smile was as warm as a wolf's.

It was only then that Townsend noticed the wheelchair folded against the far side of the desk. Chalmers followed Townsend's eyes. "Riding accident. Steeplechase. Many years ago. The stables are my wife's business."

"I'm sorry."

"Don't be. It got me into this somewhat sedentary little enterprise and I'm a lot better at this than I was at riding horses, I promise you!"

Townsend was not sure whether this was a boast or a veiled threat. It was his nature to be suspicious. He set a glass in front of Chalmers and took his own seat on one of two tufted black leather chairs facing the desk.

Chalmers stuck a bulbous, bloodshot nose beneath the rim of his glass, sniffed, sipped, and pronounce it: "Adequate."

"Now, you have, I gather, some photographs for me to examine?"

"I do, Mr. Chalmers."

"Please, it's Declan. And you're…?"

"Dicky."

"Hmm. 'Dicky' as in unreliable? Dicky leg? Dicky heart?"

Townsend looked at Chalmers hard: "Richard, if you prefer." He opened his thin black briefcase and slapped a large brown envelope on the desk. Chalmers nodded. Clearly, Townsend was not easily intimidated. He would be a formidable negotiator. Chalmers removed the enlarged photos from the envelope and studied them carefully for several minutes. Then he pressed a button on his speaker phone and said, "Charles, would you be so kind as to bring us a decanted eighty-two Margaux?"

Chalmers swiveled his chair toward Townsend. "You know about the Treasure Act, I assume?"

"Of course."

"Unless I miss my guess, and I seldom do, this is a very significant pre-Roman hoard. Iron Age. Some bits possibly older. One of the finest I've seen or even read about. It is worth…well…millions, as you no doubt know. Why wouldn't the finder report it to the Crown for full value?"

"In a hurry, he says."

Chambers's face darkened. "Stolen is it?"

"Do you think I'd try that, Mr. Chalmers? I've done my research on you."

Another point in Townsend's favor, but Chalmers pressed: "Then, what? He's not some nighthawk, is he?"

"No, a farmer. Found the artifacts while plowing his own land."

"And that would be where?"

Dicky smiled: "Sorry, *Declan*. Later. Perhaps."

A young man in chef's whites knocked and entered bearing a decanter of red wine and two large crystal balloon glasses. He poured a small measure into one glass for Chalmers and waited. Chalmers tasted and nodded. The young man poured both glasses a third full, removed the other glasses and bottle, and withdrew without a word.

"Why not sell it on your own, then?" Chalmers asked, swirling the wine in his glass as if the movement were part of his thinking process.

Dicky swirled and sipped from his glass. The wine was rich, almost smoky, and velvet soft. He waited to reply, as if savoring it like the connoisseur he was not.

"For the simple reason," he answered, "that while I am a dealer—a small dealer—in antiquities, I do not have the contacts through which to sell something of such great value and import. You do, and are too professional to do something untoward or unwise. In short, I come to propose a mutually beneficial business arrangement: my client's treasure, your expertise, your share."

Declan Chalmers nodded and smiled. "Would you be so kind as to fill two plates while I top up your glass?"

"WHAT DO YOU mean you lost him?" Connor barked into his mobile. 'What the hell do I pay you for?"

Max Marchenko, wiry, ferret-faced former Ukrainian security police thug now resident in western England and employed by Connor, among others, for certain delicate tasks, shook his head. The English, he had long since decided, had no subtlety, no patience. They did not understand that in the fullness of time everyone betrays himself. It was Wednesday afternoon.

"Townsend parks at Bristol Temple Meads Station car park this morning," Max said. His English was excellent, but he had trouble still with verb tenses. "He boards London train. I check platform after every returning train in afternoon. No Townsend."

"His car's still there?"

"No. It is now gone. My guess? He knows already he is being tailed. Gets off up the line at Keynsham station and takes cab back to Temple Meads. He never comes off train here."

"So you did lose him."

"Not exactly."

"Well then how, *exactly*, would you describe it? You angling for early retirement, my friend?"

Max sighed. Connor was his most difficult client, and becoming more so as the old man aged. "I have plenty money set aside for retirement, Mr. Connor, so you either trust me or you do not. This makes no difference to me."

Connor said nothing.

"You want opinion? He goes to Cornwall again. Only logical answer. In Ukrainian security we are taught to think with logic, not emotion. You understand? Like your Sherlock Holmes, yes? Whether this Archie is loyal or intends to betray you, he must acquire the goods first. Logical. You want me down there or no?"

In the office of his converted limestone tithe barn in Wiltshire, Connor stared out a window across the undulating, impossibly green spring fields. Here and there, his neighbor's black and white Friesian cows, their blocky heads seemingly attached to the grass beneath them as if by some magnetic force, grazed the meadow beyond his hedgerow.

"All right, find him, Max. Have a chat, yeah? You don't like what you hear, eliminate him. Got that? He's playing me. I smell it. Only thing that matters is that trove this Hansen's found. Find that, by whatever means, and I promise you'll have a very large addition to that retirement fund you mentioned. Huge."

"But Townsend has been with you for years, Mr. Connor…"

"He betrays me, he's gone. Do I make myself clear?"

Max did not respond.

"And Max, do it elegantly, like you always do."

Twenty-Six

THAT SAME WEDNESDAY morning when Townsend was in Cookham, Charlotte parked her car at a distance, walked to Higher Pennare, and peered around the corner of Archie's farmhouse. His Land Rover was gone. She slipped into the house, went directly to his tiny office, and started up his computer. She was determined to find evidence that he was selling the farm. She stared at the screen for nearly a minute, wishing she knew more about computers, and especially Archie's.

She knew that British Telecom was Archie's mobile phone service provider, and guessed that it was his Internet service provider as well. She went to that site, typed in Archie's name as the user name. Then she stared at the request for his password. She didn't think Archie would be very imaginative about his password: at his age it would be too easy to forget. She tried *HansenPennare* and then *PennareHansen*. Neither was accepted. She tried other combinations and wondered if the BT web page would cut her off at some point. She thought a while longer, typed *ThorsFarm,* and suddenly she was in. She smiled: *So obvious, Archie…*

Charlotte did a search and brought up the current Savills' listings for agricultural properties in Cornwall. There were several, but Higher Pennare was not among them. Were the men at the pub talking nonsense? No, they were too specific. She believed what she'd heard, though she did not know why. The news ate into her heart like a parasitic worm. Perhaps the farm had not yet been listed and that was why it did not appear on the Savills site.

She also checked his email correspondence, but it was limited. That did not surprise her. The messages were mostly about commodity prices, offers from equipment dealers, prices from seed and fertilizer suppliers, correspondence with a few other local farmers, although oddly enough, not Bobby Tregareth. Maybe, with Bobby being a neighbor, he didn't need email to chat with his tenant.

Next, she clicked on My Pictures and found nothing. Finally, just before giving up, she clicked on My Videos. Most of these postings were instructional videos of new farming ideas from the local organization, "FarmCornwall." But well down the list was a video file that caught her eye. It was labeled, "Thor's Whore."

She grinned. *You randy devil, have you been filming us?* She clicked open the file.

But the video was not of the two of them. No. The scene showed a crude raftered room she did not recognize. In the center was a table draped in black velvet with a burning candlestick. And beside the draped table, on a low settee, a woman was giving oral sex to a man, though his head was not in the frame.

They seemed in a state of complete abandon. There was a moment's pause as they shifted position and then she saw them: Archie and Bobby Tregareth's partner, Joey. Abruptly, as if to erase the image from her mind, she shut down the computer.

She sat there for a few moments, then stood, looked around the kitchen she knew so well, left the house, walked down the hill to where she'd left her car, and considered her next steps.

LATER THAT WEDNESDAY morning, just after eleven, Archie Hansen turned off the A39 in Truro, drove down Falmouth Road, and then entered Lemon Street, following it into the center of the city. Joey Tregareth was by his side in his aging Land Rover. She scanned the facades of the grey granite three-story attached Georgian townhouses as they descended the hill, looking for the Truro branch of Savills, the estate agents.

"There!" Joey exclaimed. Hansen heard the excitement in her voice and smiled. Savills was on their left, its storefront painted a rich royal blue. Displayed within its high, white-framed windows were glossy photos of local houses and estates.

"Is this really happening, Archie?" Joey said, squeezing his thigh as he reversed into a parking space.

Hansen switched off the ignition, looked at the younger woman beside him, ripe and plump as a fuzzed peach and just as juicy, and pulled her into a kiss. "Are you ready for this?" he asked when they disengaged.

"Oh yes! No more dreary Cornwall, or Bobby, or that demanding baby, yes! I love you my rescuer, my priest, my Thor." Her eyes glittered.

Hansen held up a forefinger: "No, the boy: he comes with us."

"But…."

"The boy comes. We will be a family. And I will be his father."

"Stepfather, you mean. Are you certain?"

"Thor demands it."

Joey stared, silent and bewildered at the man beside her: her mentor, her guide, her lover. She had no idea he'd felt so strongly about the boy she'd named after him. So much of living was a mystery to her, a mystery to which Archie gave form and order through his rituals and potions. Finally, she nodded, not so much in agreement as acquiescence. Much as she'd wanted a baby when she married, she had soon discovered she had little in the way of maternal instinct. And the fussing child wore her ragged.

"If you wish, my Thor, then it shall be. But what about Bobby?"

"He will never find us. Shall we begin?"

Joey almost bounced in her car seat. "Yes!" She made to open her door but he stopped her. "You will wait for me to open the door. Thor attends to his queen." He circled the car and handed her down to the curbside. A light, almost misty rain, barely visible, had closed in on the market town.

Barbara Hunnicutt, the Savills agent with whom Archie had already spoken by phone, met them at reception and led them back to a small conference room.

"Tea? Some water, perhaps?"

Hansen looked at Joey.

"Water would be nice," she said.

Hunnicutt, slender, mid-forties, salon blond, and fashionably dressed, fetched bottled water and two glasses and set them before them. Archie ignored his.

"I've put together a portfolio of properties between Marbella and Malaga," Hunnicutt began. "You said on the phone you were looking for a proper house, not a flat. View of the sea. Two or three bedrooms. Shops nearby. And a pool. Am I right?"

Archie nodded.

"A pool, Archie?" Joey exclaimed.

"Where you can relax and the boy can play."

"You do understand that such properties will be a bit dear? Did you have a target price?"

"Half a million pounds or thereabouts, whatever that is in Euros."

Joey choked on her water. "Jesus, Archie!"

"Be still, luv."

The estate agent wondered about this mismatched couple, but plunged ahead: "And this would be contingent upon the sale of your farm on the Lizard?"

"Maybe. Maybe not. I have other resources. Oh, and a fireplace would be nice in winter."

Hunnicutt tapped a key on the keyboard on the desk before her and a large flat screen mounted on the conference room wall sprang to life with a mosaic of house images.

"I thought you might like to consider these properties," she said. "Shall I scroll through them?"

Hansen nodded. Joey's eyes widened and her hand flew to her mouth.

"These small villas are in a well-established area just east of Marbella called Mijas Costa. It has none of the tacky high-rises you find in the larger cities," Hunnicutt continued. The first photo was an aerial shot that captured dozens of traditional stuccoed Spanish houses that tumbled down a steep hill toward the glittering sea.

"They're so white they look made of sugar cubes!" Joey exclaimed. All were capped with curved rust-red terracotta roofing tiles and had stone terraces giving views out over the Mediterranean beyond. Many had small pools.

Archie looked at how densely packed the houses were and said, "Not much privacy..."

"If you want to be on the coast, rather than up in the mountains of Andalusia," Hunnicutt explained, "you're looking at two choices: beaches crammed with high rise apartments and condos, or these more traditional, clustered coastal villages with their little boutiques and cafes and restaurants catering to a local clientele—which, by the way, includes many UK ex-pats. But wait until you view the properties themselves. I think you'll see they are brilliantly situated to be very private indeed."

And they were. The estate agent had done her homework and had chosen only a half dozen villas for them to view. As she scrolled through the photos it became clear that each had private walled gardens filled with flowering shrubs and thick-trunked palms, multiple private view terraces and, below the terraces, a small level area with a glittering pool. All seemed to have been very recently renovated inside and out.

Joey was wide-eyed and speechless. The scale of this village, while a bit larger, reminded her of Helford, where her parents lived. These Mijas Costa houses clustered in the same companionable way but were lush with tropical greenery.

The villas ranged from three hundred to seven hundred thousand Euros, depending on the size of the lot and number of bedrooms and bathrooms.

Finally Archie said, "Go back to that third one." The ground floor living area was open, airy, and floored in Terrazzo tiles the color of beach pebbles in Cornwall. The kitchen was modern and bright with white cabinets. A curved wooden staircase led to the bedrooms and bathrooms, three of each, above. Each room had at least an outdoor terrace or balcony with either sea or garden views. The light-filled master bedroom had an adjoining bathroom faced in white marble veined in silver and a walk-in shower big enough for two. It was almost exactly a half million Euros.

Archie had already decided, but he turned to Joey. "What do you think of this one, luv?"

Any one of the villas looked like paradise to her so she said only, "Yes."

"Done, then," Archie said to Hunnicutt. "But I want most of the furniture, too."

Hunnicutt smiled. "Let me see what I can do there, Mr. Hansen. But don't you want to fly down there to inspect the property more closely?"

"In my business I make costly decisions every day...and I trust those with whom I have commercial relations. I trust you that what you have presented is accurate. Are we clear?"

Hunnicutt smiled again, though less brightly. "This is Savills, Mr. Hansen, and here trust is everything."

"Then we have an understanding," he said as he rose. "Draw up the paperwork. I should have the resources in a few weeks. You can have the deposit tomorrow if you wish."

"That would certainly help, Mr. Hansen, to demonstrate your earnest offer."

"Send me the figure. I'll attend to it."

He stood and took the arm of the woman beside him.

"Joey," he said. "Come."

DICKY TOWNSEND CALLED Charlotte Johns as soon as he'd picked up his Ford from the car park at Temple Meads Station late Wednesday afternoon. No one was following him.

"Are you free this evening, Charlotte?"

"Of course, and I must talk to..."

"I have information about the value of Archie's find," Townsend said. "I thought it best to share it with you immediately."

"Yes, good. But..."

"I don't understand why Archie has not been in touch, do you? It was he who came to me. I should think he'd be pestering me. What's he up to?"

"Dicky. Please come. Fast as you can."

"Are you all right?"

"No."

"What is it, love?"

"I'll tell you when you get here.

"It's a long drive. It will be nearly dark."

"I'll have supper waiting."

TOWNSEND DESCENDED THE darkening lane to Charlotte's bungalow after eight that Wednesday night. He'd pushed his aging auto to nearly ninety miles per hour down the whole length of Devon and Cornwall. It wasn't just the news he had to share with her about the treasure, it was the woman herself.

"Come in!" she called when he knocked. She was standing at the cooker, stirring a pot. She wore a reconfiguration of some of the clothes she'd worn for Archie: boots, dark stockings in a lacy pattern, a short black woolen crepe skirt, and a loose white blouse, several buttons undone. "It's another chilly evening," she said. "I've made a Tuscan soup with tomato, Cannellini beans, onion, garlic, fresh spring greens from the garden and chunks of chicken. It's hot and ready."

"That's not all that looks hot and ready, Char," he said, embracing her from behind and kissing the nape of her neck.

"Go on then, you," she said, pushing him away. "We need to talk. Go wash up." She'd decided, among other things, that it was time to abandon her vegetarianism if she wanted to have Dicky. A small price for a big prize.

When they settled at the round table in her kitchen, she poured a chilled Australian chardonnay into both their glasses and lifted hers.

"I have something to tell you," she said as she touched his glass to his.

"As I do you," Townsend said.

"Me first."

He nodded. "As you wish, Char."

"I'm done with him. Archie. He's having an affair with our neighbor's wife. He's videoed them together. It's on his computer."

"Videoed? Jesus…"

There were tears in her eyes and he rose, came to where she was seated, and wrapped her in his arms, saying nothing.

"Your soup's getting cold," she said finally, smiling and scrubbing her eyes dry with the back of a hand. "I won't have that."

"Yes, ma'am," Townsend said. And that was when he realized he was in love for the first time in his life.

Charlotte saw it, too. And she shared it.

"You said you had news?" she asked.

"I do," he began. And during the next hour they talked excitedly about the meeting with Chalmers, the deal he'd struck, and what that might mean for them...until, finally, she pulled him up to her bedroom.

Twenty-Seven

DETECTIVE SUPERINTENDENT MALCOLM Crawley, resplendent in his pressed black officer's tunic with the four glittering white bars of rank on each epaulet, sat rocklike behind a desk the polished surface of which was so completely barren of personal effects that it might well have been the site of a nuclear disaster.

It was Monday morning, twenty-eighth May. DCI Arthur Penwarren hated traveling north to the sprawling brick complex that was the Devon and Cornwall Police headquarters on Exeter's Sidmouth Road. It wasn't the distance and time; it was the almost predictable futility of dealing with senior officers whose only care about a case at hand was their own personal advancement. But he had requested the meeting.

"I am sorry to say, sir," Penwarren began, "that after ten days we have precious little to go on in this Hansen case."

"So we have noticed."

Crawley always spoke in the first person plural, as if he were a royal, or perhaps a spokesman for the entire upper echelon of the force. Penwarren found this routine barely tolerable, but held his tongue. He noticed Crawley had put on weight: a roll of florid flesh spilled from the tight collar of his regulation white shirt. Crawley had been a good detective in his day, but that day had long since passed. The only comfort, Penwarren thought, was that the pretentious bastard had to be close to retirement or, with all that extra weight, a heart attack.

"My detectives believe the only way to gather the kind of evidence we need to move this case forward is to launch a full SOCO search of Hansen's property."

"You are free to search any suspect's property, of course…"

"I am aware of that, sir."

"But you do not have a suspect."

"That is correct, sir."

"And now you want our permission to search the victim's premises?"

"Given the unusual aspects of this case, yes."

Crawley leaned back in his chair and stared at the ceiling. "Let us guess: this must be the recommendation of your resident loose cannon, the witch-loving Davies, are we right? We were opposed to her promotion to detective inspector, you know."

"Thankfully, sir, the Commander was not. Let's also recall that Davies solved the Chynoweth case with the aid of the village wise woman to whom you refer. Without that woman's help, we'd have had another dead child on our hands. I doubt you'd have wanted that on your record when you were angling for the promotion to your current position...Sir."

Crawley sat stone faced.

"So yes," Penwarren continued, "DI Morgan Davies is the lead investigator in the Hansen case, and yes, this search is her recommendation. It is also mine. Look, we have a victim who is not only dead, but appears to have been tortured as well. The question isn't what he had that someone else wanted, but what he knew that only torture would reveal. Apart from interviewing associates, which of course we are doing, the logical next step is to search the victim's home and property for possible reasons for, and evidence of, his torture. West agrees, and is ready to put his team to work there at once."

"Isn't the obvious reason the alleged treasure?"

"Well, yes, sir. That would be the obvious reason."

Crawley arched an eyebrow. He could never tell if Penwarren was insulting him, as he did it so smoothly. Penwarren sat erect in his chair, patrician perfect, as if he'd attended a prestigious boys' school, which of course he had: Harrow, just outside London. Another reason Crawley resented him. What was the man doing in the police force anyway?

"Are you proposing searching his fields as well as his house?" Crawley asked.

"For the site of the alleged treasure find? Yes, of course."

"Of course," Crawley sighed. He gazed across the shimmering expanse of his desktop. Finally he said, "The only thing we know about you with any certainty, detective chief inspector Penwarren, is that you're not after our job. If you had been, you'd have had it by now, given your record. So, despite our reservations, we'll make this happen, yes? Just bring us something we can show the bosses upstairs to prove this was a wise move our part, eh?"

"Do what I can, sir."

"Always the braggart, Penwarren..."

"WE SHOULD HAVE searched Hansen's place days ago, Guv," Morgan barked into her mobile. "It's already been sanitized by someone."

"And you know this because...?" Penwarren was speeding down the A30 from Exeter after his meeting with Crawley, and was calling on his hands free mobile.

"Because I had a look around Hansen's place a while back. Then I sent DC Bates and Falmouth's PC Novak to make a new visit just this Wednesday last. I used Common Law authority. I had Novak—bright lad you should keep an eye on, mind—have another look around while Terry distracted Johns out on Hansen's property. "

"I'm sorry, must be having a signal problem. I didn't catch that..." Penwarren was glad his phone wasn't monitored.

Davies chuckled.

"Hello, Morgan?"

"Guv?"

"Remember: there's always something. I'll call West next. No need to get clearance from Johns. It's not her property. Wednesday morning. Meeting at Camborne first, at eight."

"Why not tomorrow? I feel like we're losing evidence every day, Guv. Someone's ahead of us."

"I understand, Morgan, but I need to get the team together. They do have other assignments, you know…and I'll need Crawley's final okay. I think I have it but I'll go around him, if necessary."

"Will it be Calum's SOCOs or the knuckle draggers?"

"If you refer to our Tactical Aid Group, and I am certain you will refer to them thus never again, detective, the answer is both."

"Sir. Sorry. Calum's nickname for them. It just stuck."

"Unstick it, then. The big boys are professionals, too."

The phone signal died.

THE MEMBERS OF the Major Crime Investigative Team sat at an oval conference table at the Camborne nick at eight on Wednesday morning, thirtieth May. SOCO crime scene manager Calum West stood. Penwarren nodded and West began.

"We'll do this in stages," West explained. "In full Tyvek kit, my SOCO people, along with Morgan and Terry, who've been there before, will canvass the home and outbuildings, right? I'll be taking record photos as well."

"I swear he's a voyeur," Morgan mumbled. Laughter all around, except from Penwarren.

West continued "We'll dust and tape everything for prints, hair, threads, the lot. But there's no telling what that will yield. There will no doubt be plenty of evidence of Hansen and Johns, as they lived there; but we'll be looking for anything else, anything that doesn't fit. Next, the Tactical Aid Group will apply their special expertise to every nook and cranny in the house and the surrounding fields. We'll be focusing especially on the field Mr. Tregareth showed our PC Novak." West nodded to the constable, who smiled and was chuffed about being a part of the investigation. "Beth Thompson, my staff archaeologist, will oversee that investigation. She and the TAG boys are already on their way."

"What if Charlotte Johns shows up?" Penwarren asked.

Morgan answered. "Been keeping obbo on her, Guv, and she's stayed close to her own home since the body was found."

"Well done. But what if?"

"Escort her home again."

"And if she makes a fuss?"

"We remove her to the Falmouth nick, as per procedure: Obstruction."

"Fine. Anything else, Calum?" Penwarren asked, rising from his chair.

"We'll begin shortly after nine, Guv," West said.

"Need me there?"

"Only if you wish."

"Unnecessary. You people are the best. I'd only be in the way. I'll read the reports."

Davies had been watching Calum during the meeting and was struck yet again by how so gentle a man could be so completely and easily in charge. She smiled to herself: *A good and solid bloke, is our Calum.*

Penwarren interrupted her thoughts: "Morgan, how about you? Anything else CID needs?"

"Family, Guv. Hansen's. Divorced, two kids. They're somewhere up north in Cumbria, Charlotte Johns says. I mentioned this before. Does she or their children stand to inherit? She's a person of interest, that's certain."

"Okay, agreed, though I am not optimistic in this case, given how many years have passed. But start with the obvious: the Child Support Agency. Find out if Hansen was paying support to his ex. Cross-check with council tax records up there, and voter records as well. Should be fairly easy to find her."

"I can't be in two places at once, Guv."

Penwarren nodded and turned to DC Bates. "Terry? As I recall you're also a trained Family Liaison Officer, which we'd want when contacting next of kin, even though divorced. You want this one? Might be a dead end."

"I'll take it, sir. Let me see what I can find."

"Long drive up to Cumbria. Book accommodation."

"No need; I've an aunt outside Carlisle, my late mother's sister. I could stay with her if I find Hansen's ex."

"Good, Terry. It's all yours."

Bates grinned. Davies ducked her head to hide a smile.

Twenty-Eight

BARRELING THROUGH NARROW country lanes he knew well, Calum West reached the Hansen farm just over half an hour after the Camborne MCIT meeting ended. The rest of his SOCO team and the CID people would take the main roads following the instructions on their GPS units, and would take longer.

But he'd underestimated Morgan Davies. She pulled up beside him just as he'd finished brewing his customary cup of coffee from the kit he'd installed in his car.

She walked to his open window. "I'm old enough that I still use maps, you clever devil," she said. "Think you could get away from me that easily? And are you sharing that coffee?"

"I've only the one cup, but be my guest. Oh, and never think I'm trying to get away from you. And I've never thought I could get *ahead* of you, either. You're too smart for me."

"Oh, bollocks," she said gulping half of Calum's coffee.

"I just like to get to these sites early."

"Yes, yes, I know; you like to have a look around before the rest of the lads show up. Kind of a meditation on the site. You told me last year in the Chynoweth case. Care to have company on your little walkabout?"

He stepped out of the Volvo. "No man could ask for better…"

"Also bollocks."

"I am only speaking truth."

"You want to get to work or just stand about flirting, you idiot?"

"Sadly, work. Get your Tyveks on."

Then the two of them, suited up, walked around the house and through the farm buildings, saying nothing. She watched West soaking up information as if his eyes were made of sponge.

The concrete yard between the back of Hansen's house and his outbuildings was swept clean as a front porch. West was thankful Hansen didn't have cows, but he didn't like the sterile scene. Davies wondered who'd been so fastidious. In the tractor shed the equipment was lined up in rows and the supplies in the loft were stacked in orderly piles. West had been in far more chaotic barns.

"Everything shipshape and Bristol fashion," he said, mostly to himself.

"And wrong," Morgan added.

West nodded: "A bit too neat. I agree."

"No, sanitized."

"Yes, perhaps…"

DURING THE NEXT few hours, West's SOCO team, looking like rumpled polar bears in their white jumpsuits, prowled the house lifting prints, taping doorways for hair or thread samples, searching closets and wardrobes, pawing through drawers, examining every cupboard in the kitchen and every room in the big old house.

Next, the Tactical Aid Group chaps ransacked the attic and jimmied open the door to the locked room there. West joined them as they entered, looked around the cramped, oddly louche space, and called down to Davies who was trying to make sense of the late owner's uncharacteristically spotless kitchen, so unlike the man mess it had been not many days earlier.

"Morgan?"

"What?" she yelled. "I'm busy!"

"You need to see this…"

Davies huffed up the two flights of stairs to the attic and ducked under the low door, but not quite low enough, scraping the top of her scalp on its header.

"Bloody hell!" she cursed. The impact brought tears, which she scrubbed away. She rubbed her scalp. No blood. When she recovered and looked up, she just stared.

"What do you make of this?" West asked her.

Along one low wall, a shelf held books devoted to witchcraft and Satanism. Beneath it, another shelf was stuffed with a messy collection of plastic bags containing various herbs and powders.

"I don't know what to make of this, Calum, but I know who will…"

"Who?"

Davies smiled.

"No, wait Morgan, not Tamsin Bran. Mister warned you. The Chynoweth case was one thing; she was a person of interest in that one. Now you want to make her an expert witness? Penwarren will have your badge!"

She locked her eyes on his. "Only if he knows, Calum, only if he knows. Look, I don't propose that Bran be an expert witness. But she's less than an hour away. And she knows everything there is to know about this sort of stuff," she said waving her hand around the tiny room. "All we want to know is what this tells her about who Hansen was and what he may have been up to. Some in his grove have said they thought he was dabbling in something darker than Druidry. Maybe this is part of it?"

"Okay, but hang on: Bran's talent is looking into someone's eyes and reading what is in their soul. Hansen's dead."

"Yes, but she knows her witchcraft and will tell us the uses of this stuff in the bags."

"And you're willing to risk your career to bring her on?"

"No, I'm willing to risk my career, such as it is, to solve this case which, as you may have noticed, is going nowhere." She pulled out her mobile and punched a preset.

"Wait, you have Bran's number on your mobile?"

Davies smiled. "We keep in touch. I like to know how the girl, Tegan, is doing…"

The call connected. "Tamsin? Morgan here. Look, I know this is short notice, but could you spare me a bit of your time? Today? Like in an hour or so? You can?

Brilliant! I'm on the Lizard. West's here, too. Higher Pennare farm. It's on the Ordnance Survey Landranger map for Truro and Falmouth, near Helston and just south of Manaccan. Yes, it's the Druid murder. Why did I imagine you wouldn't know? There's a little attic room full of books and potions or something. I need someone who can look at it all and tell us what the victim might have been up to before he was killed. No, it's not official. But I need you.

"Yes? Good. I am so grateful, Tamsin, which as you know, I seldom am." She heard Bran laugh, rang off, and smiled. Never in a million years would Davies have imagined being friends with a witch. But she was.

DAVIES WAS PROBING Hansen's equipment shed with the Tactical Aid Group boys when she heard Tamsin Bran's 1966 Morris 1000 estate wagon wheezing up the drive. The car, with its original sage green paint and varnished wooden side panels, was in mint condition. But its tiny 1000 cc engine had never been meant for highway driving. Davies could almost imagine it trying to catch its breath as it eased to a halt in the farmyard.

Bran stepped out from the right side driver's door and, to Davies's surprise, Tegan St. Claire, the young girl whom Bran had adopted after the Chynoweth case, jumped out of the passenger side, trailing a black cat with one white paw on a lead.

The girl, now eleven and, it seemed to Davies after only a year, a half foot taller, rushed up and hugged her.

"Morgan! Morgan! Look at Desmond! He thinks he's my dog!"

The cat, Desmond, had been a twitchy, somewhat neurologically challenged feline when Davies had seen him last at Tamsin's restored mill outside of Penzance, a cat given to occasionally racing about howling as if possessed. But here he was, trotting along beside the girl as if he meant to be nowhere else so happily. As she walked with him, Desmond kept checking in with his keeper, his head angling to one side to watch for signals from the leggy girl.

"Seems to have a way with animals, Tegan does," Bran said, smiling broadly at her protégé. "Talks to the ponies up on the moors, too. When you told me what you'd found, I thought perhaps our girl's special skills might help."

Davies warmed to the phrase "our girl." Tegan St. Claire held a special place in her heart. Not for the first time she thought: *this is the kind of kid I'd want as my daughter....* Not that, at Davies's age, she'd ever have one. That brief span of her life she'd devoted to policing, and so she held the odd girl dear. Tegan was whip-smart and well-mannered, thanks to Bran, but also possessed of certain skills that set her apart. Tegan St. Claire was genuinely clairsentient. She could see things that were happening far away from her in the present, as well as things that happened in the recent past, even though she had not been there.

Davies explained the scene as they approached the house. West met them at the kitchen door, beaming. He could not help it. Much as he thought Penwarren would go ballistic, he was delighted to see Tamsin and Tegan again. With two daughters of his own, he could see young Tegan was thriving.

"What do you seek from us?" Tamsin asked the two of them in her almost whispery voice. Morgan noticed that the gleaming streak of silver on one side of her jet black bob haircut had widened ever so slightly, but that she was otherwise unchanged: the woman was still disgracefully slender, elegant, exotic. Tegan, while taller, was still the same luminous girl they had met the year before. But her strawberry blond hair had been cut to chin length now and curved upward along her chiseled jawline, just like Tamsin's.

"What I seek of you both is wisdom," Davies said. "A man has been killed. He had a history as a local Druid leader. He seems to have had a secret room in his attic which we have opened. I ask only that you examine that room and tell me what it says to you, if anything. I trust your special knowledge and this could be a great help in our investigation. But Penwarren must never know."

"Yes, DCI Penwarren," Tamsin said, smiling. "He is a truly good man but has not yet been able to embrace those parts of experience which are beyond the reach of his lovely rational mind. But I cannot hold that against him. In the end, he became an ally and a friend, for which I am grateful."

Bran leaned close to Davies and whispered, "He, too, has checked on Tegan…"

"Give him time, Tamsin," Morgan said.

CALUM LED, AND they climbed the stairs to Archie's attic room. Tamsin entered first, looked around, and immediately went to the bookshelf.

Tegan stood just inside the door with Desmond. The fur on the cat's back had risen nearly vertical and he began yowling.

"Things happen here," Tegan said. "Scary things. That I can see. So can Desmond. We will leave. This is best."

Bran listened and then sent the girl off. She scanned the short bookshelf and pulled out a single volume, the one that seemed to have been most heavily used.

"Ah yes," she said. "Paul Huson's *Mastering Witchcraft…"*

"Excuse me?" Morgan said.

She showed Morgan the cover. "If you wanted a somewhat contemporary guide to the darkest of occult arts, this book would be it. It was published in the early nineteen seventies, a time when Wicca and other pagan beliefs were in ascendance. But Huson was no Wiccan. Huson's vision and purpose was to use alleged 'black arts' from ancient times to gain mastery over others, especially for sexual conquest. A charlatan, certainly, and yet this book, and Huson's own practices, are still followed by people on the fringe. The Old Craft, which my ancestors and I practice, has nothing to do with gaining power over others. We, and our sisters and brothers in Wicca, have mostly to do with healing and with worshipping our inherent connection with the timeless turn of the seasons, the sun, and the moon. We do not seek to control others, for sexual conquest or any other reason. But it does not surprise me that this was your Hansen's bible, or that he is dead. I believe some people feared him."

Davies noticed that the tips of Bran's fingers were white from gripping the book, as if receiving information from it.

"Your victim was not a genuine Druid," she said, finally. "He was an opportunist bent upon using the spells in this book, along with the herbs and other materials he gathered here, some of them opiates, by the way, to gain control over others, principally women, perhaps the women in his own Druid grove, but of that I cannot say."

"Why did Tegan leave?" Davies asked.

"I think she saw things that happened in this room and it frightened her, things she is not yet old enough to comprehend. At a guess, I suspect it is sexual. Even I can feel that. I shall not ask her and hope you will not, either. But I will talk with her later if she wishes to share. We have an agreement: we trust each other and share when we need to. I do not press upon her gifts, nor she on mine."

"And the cat?"

Tamsin smiled. "That cat is smarter than us all…"

AFTER TAMSIN AND Tegan left, West said to Davies, "If Hansen was up to no good, why did whoever cleaned the rooms elsewhere leave this one as it is?"

Davies smiled and shook her head: "Because it's a ruse, Calum. It's meant to direct our attention to the practices of the Druid grove, and whomever he might have offended or threatened. Otherwise, that room would have been as sanitized as the bedroom and bathroom and kitchen downstairs…"

Now West smiled. Davies made a face: "What?"

"Not quite as sanitized, perhaps, as someone may have thought," Calum said. "My boys have sprayed luminol over both rooms. We got some blood. Only traces. Maybe useless. Someone was very careful, very professional, I'd say. But not quite careful enough, because I have something to show you downstairs."

IN ARCHIE'S CLOSET-LIKE office just off the kitchen, Calum switched on the single overhead bulb and ushered Morgan in. There was barely room for the two of them in front of Hansen's grimy desk.

"Notice anything?"

"Let's not play silly buggers, Calum; what the hell is it?"

"Humor me. Have a look."

She did. "I don't see a damn thing."

Calum switched on his torch and angled it along the wall where Hansen's collection of antique swords hung. In the slanting light of the beam she could see it: like a section of wall where a painting had long hung but now had been removed, there was a faint shadow, a shadow in the shape of another sword, smaller than the ones above. A sword now missing.

Twenty-Nine

COVERED IN A fresh Tyvek jumpsuit, Rafe Barnes, West's lead scene of crimes investigator, climbed down into the chamber on the southeast edge of the field to which Novak had led them. The Tactical Aid Group boys had removed the corrugated steel panel they uncovered when they'd removed the topsoil. West watched. His staff archaeologist, Beth Thompson, was at his side. She fairly vibrated with the desire to descend, too.

After a quick look around, Barnes called up through the hole: "One of those Iron Age fogous, I reckon boss, but more primitive, if that's the word, than the one in the Chynoweth case last year. Massive flat stone on the floor has been moved, and beneath where it sat there's a niche. Some kind of old round clay vessel sits in the hole. Empty."

"Any chance of getting prints?" West called down.

"The container is pretty dusty, Guv. The stone, too. But we'll give it a go. Holes in the floor of the chamber look like someone anchored some kind of winch to move the stone. There's a come-along in Hansen's equipment shed, by the way. Could be that."

"Most farmers have one, Rafe." He turned to Novak: "What's Tregareth have to say?"

"Only that he never went down there. Only Hansen did, he said."

"All the more reason, then, to try to get some prints or fibers or hairs. He was Hansen's tenant. Reckon a treasure would have set him free."

"Rafe? I'm sending Beth down to look at that clay vessel before she dives down the hole on her own accord. Let her examine it before your lads go to work."

When she reemerged, Thompson's face was flushed with excitement. "Iron Age, Calum. Maybe older. Sadly, also cracked. But the vessel itself is probably very valuable, a treasure of the period."

"I wonder why it wasn't removed?"

Thompson laughed, "Because whatever was in it was far more valuable, boss."

ON FRIDAY MORNING, first June, DC Terry Bates steered her unmarked police car through the rocky gap south of Keswick that her map told her was called "the Jaws of Borrowdale." She was in the heart of Cumbria's Lake District. When the narrow B5289 finally exited the Jaws, the vista below presented a pastoral, mountain-rimmed valley, its verdant bottomland crisscrossed with lush hedgerows. The little river Derwent twisted northward across the valley floor, this way and that, following the contours. She'd never seen any place more picture perfect.

So penned in by mountains was the valley that the sun had not yet reached the valley floor and there was the sharp tang of coal smoke in the morning air. It might be June by the calendar, but you couldn't prove that here in the far north of England: smoke curled from the chimneys of stone farmhouses that were scattered like so many grey dice across the valley floor. In the tiny hamlet of Rosthwaite, she pulled into the car park of the whitewashed Scafell Hotel to check her notes.

After the MCIT meeting at Camborne on Wednesday morning, Terry Bates had gone straight back to the Bodmin operational hub. It hadn't taken her long on the computer and phone to trace Hansen's ex-wife. The Child Support Agency had been helpful, and confirmed that Hansen had indeed been sending a modest support payment for his two children to his ex-wife, and had been doing so for some years. The agency also had a postal address.

Taking full advantage of her police car, Terry had raced north on the M6 to the Lake District the next day, thirty-first May. She stayed in the far right passing lane almost the full length of the motorway, and used the car's hidden flashers and strobes to clear away slower drivers. She loved the freedom and power the official car gave her. In just over seven hours, with only one petrol stop and loo break, she'd reached the Lake District and had spent the night visiting with her dead mother's sister, Annie, near Carlisle.

Now, as she looked at the map on the seat beside her the valley narrowed to the south and split into two steep-sided branches rimmed by soaring fells. There were only two more tiny hamlets in the valley: Seathwaite, up the southeastern branch of the valley, and Seatoller, up the southwestern branch, accessible via a road which climbed up through the Honister Pass at perhaps the steepest gradient in all of Britain, a rise of one foot for every four feet of road.

Just after ten, she stepped into the tiny reception area of the Langstrath Inn, the lone guest house at the end of the narrow dead end lane into Seathwaite. There was no one about. She looked around the sitting room, which had somehow retained the homey comforts of decades past: plush old easy chairs, a morning coal fire left to die after breakfast, a side table with an unfinished jigsaw puzzle. In an adjoining room there were several tables where breakfast had recently been served, but not yet fully cleared. A sideboard held cereal boxes and half-empty pitchers of orange and grapefruit juice and containers of yoghurt.

She pressed a button atop the reception desk. Somewhere far off in the house she heard a jangly ring. Some deeply English part of her felt she was violating someone's privacy.

A minute passed, and finally a woman emerged, via the kitchen beyond the breakfast room, wiping her hands on a stained white apron.

"Oh, hello. Sorry, just tidying up after breakfast. Houseful of climbers we had this morning, all heading up the Scafell Massif, out our back door. Breakfast, packed lunches, the lot..."

The woman was, Bates guessed, mid-fifties. Trim, but looking harried as perhaps anyone would be in the bed and breakfast business: face beginning to show its age, hair close-cropped and dyed the color of a ripe garnet yarn. Bates could see greying roots. The woman pulled off her apron and stepped behind the desk.

"How may I help you? I'm sorry to say that, this being June and all, we are fully booked tonight, but perhaps I can find someone else here in the valley who might provide accommodation...?"

Bates pulled out her warrant card. "I won't be needing a room, ma'am. May I assume you are Margie Hansen?"

The woman recoiled as if she'd been slapped. "I don't use that name anymore. It's Roberts now. But I am, yes."

"I'm detective constable Terry Bates, Devon and Cornwall Police. I've come to talk to you about your ex-husband, Archie."

"Sweet Jesus, what's the bastard done now?"

"I'm afraid I am here to tell you that he is dead, Mrs. Roberts."

She waited for a reaction and got nothing more than widened eyes.

"Might we sit in the breakfast room and talk? Would you like your husband to join us?"

Margie Roberts fluttered a hand. "Up in the hills with the sheep, he is, this morning."

"Herdwicks?"

Margie smiled. "Know your sheep, I see! Tough, those Lake District Herdwicks are, but we also have Swaledales. They're hardy, too, but wool's softer. Combine their fleeces and you get a strong wool blend with a nice sheen, much in demand in the rug industry. We've just been through lambing season and they're all well, thank goodness. Though, without the bed and breakfast business, we'd be hard pressed."

She rattled on, like she was trying to gather her wits, as she led the way into the breakfast room.

"Would you care for tea, detective?"

Bates smiled. "Mrs. Roberts, you can stop working. I am not a guest. I just want a chat. And my name is Terry."

Margie sat in a chair by a cluttered table. Her head dropped and she stared at the hands folded in her lap.

"Dead, you say. How?"

"He was found floating five miles off the Lizard a few days ago."

"Fall out of that boat of his, did he? Never did know anything about seamanship. Told him to take some instruction, I did, but would he listen…?"

"No, Mrs. Roberts, he didn't fall out of his boat. He was murdered."

Margie Roberts stared at the detective, then dropped her gaze. "Thought I was shot of him years ago. But here he is again."

"From what I can see here," Bates said gesturing to the room in general, "you are well shot of him and this new life's been good for you."

Margie brightened. "Meeting Victor was everything. Widower he was, wife died. Cancer. He's a bit older, but not by much. A good and gentle man. We met at a St. Andrews Church fete here in Stonethwaite. My kids were going to the primary school. They just took to him."

"The children?"

"Erik and Brynne. My children from Hansen. Erik's fourteen and Brynne's twelve now. Adore Vic, they do, and they work hard on the farm when they're not at school. This life seems to suit them."

"Well, Hansen was a farmer, too…"

"But that Archie, he was always in some dodgy business or other besides his own farm, though I'll grant he's been regular with his support payments. Grateful for that, I've been, I'm sure. But murdered? Why? Somebody catch up with him finally?"

What struck Terry was how matter-of-fact the woman was, as if she'd expected this news to have come one day.

"Reckon that's the end of the support checks, then…"

"Yes, ma'am, I should think so, but I don't know the law. And then there's his estate. Do you, or perhaps your children, inherit? His farm must be worth quite a lot."

"I've no idea. He certainly never said."

"Nothing in the divorce settlement? You've never seen a will?"

The woman laughed. It was more a snort. "Archie leave something to us? Not likely. Hate to speak ill of the dead, but he was one tight bastard. And bitter."

Terry thought the woman had no compunctions about speaking ill of the dead.

"According to county records, you divorced Mr. Hansen. May I ask why?"

The woman looked off, as if to a far continent. "Porn. He had a mail order business selling naughty videos. And nasty business partners. Worked for some creep called Connor. I reckon Archie made a lot of money with that sideline, and old Connor too. But if he did, I never saw it."

"Ever meet this Connor?"

"Never. Archie was closed as a bank vault."

"Who handled the divorce?"

"Borland and Company. Helston. Archie's solicitors for farm matters, but they were fair and good to me."

The woman shook her head: "I've always thought his support payments came from the money from that porn business. Me and the kids, supported by porn riches. How's that for irony?"

"If it is any comfort, Mrs. Roberts, I believe that business collapsed some years ago. Internet made it redundant. So maybe that's not where the money has been coming from."

Roberts ignored this. "Gave him ideas, those videos did," she said just above a whisper and looking away again.

"I'm sorry. Did he ever hurt you?"

"No. He liked to tie me up, you know. But loose, like. He never hurt me, I'll give him that. It was a game or, I don't know, maybe like theater to him. Then one night young Erik came into our bedroom, saw us, and ran out screaming. That was the end of it for me. I filed for divorce. I had plenty of videos to show the judge."

"Videos?"

"He filmed us." It was almost a whisper.

"I'm sorry."

"Long ago, that was, and far away," Margie said, looking up and regaining her strength.

Terry paused. "I'm sorry to ask you, Mrs. Roberts, but can you account for your whereabouts on sixteen and seventeen May?"

The woman laughed. "You think I killed Archie?! Sweet Jesus, girl, he wasn't worth it. Plus he was helping support me and the children!"

"Perhaps you could check your booking calendar?"

Margie rose abruptly and stalked back to reception. Bates followed. Roberts thumbed through her record book and then spun it around for Terry to see. The hill climbing season had begun and the inn had been fully-booked both nights.

"You don't have anyone who steps in for you when you're away, perhaps?"

Roberts snorted. "Look around, detective. Does it look like I can afford staff?"

"Mrs. Roberts, forgive me, but these are just questions we have to ask, principally to put you in the clear. No one is suggesting you were involved in Archie's death."

"Though there were times, back then, when I wished I could have been…"

Thirty

IT WAS MID-AFTERNOON Saturday, twelfth May, when Charlotte Johns turned into the sloping gravel drive up to Archie's house, and there was Bobby Tregareth walking down the lane. He had his infant son in a sort of sack close to his chest.

She pulled abreast of them and rolled down the window of her VW Polo.

"Out for a stroll with the babe, Bobby? Fine day for it."

"Out lookin' for you, actually, Charlotte, ma'am."

"I'm flattered, Bobby!"

Tregareth blinked. "Question I had for you is all, ma'am. About Druidry. Reckon you'd know."

Charlotte took a breath, wondering what Bobby knew, but said, "Well, come back on up and I'll put the tea on."

Bobby and his son came through the kitchen door of Hansen's house just as the electric kettle flipped off. She filled a teapot and set out mugs for them both.

"Well, sit you down, then, Bobby, and let's see this little fellow."

Tregareth sat at the kitchen table and pulled aside the cover over his son's head. The boy was fast asleep.

"He's a sweetie, he is, Bobby," she said as she stroked the smooth forehead. The infant had almost no hair, just a few wispy reddish-blond threads. Charlotte, childless, admired the boy but kept a distance. She had no idea how to relate to a baby.

"He is that, most of the time, Charlotte, but sometimes also a trial."

Charlotte could see the man was weary. She poured tea and sat beside them.

"How are you faring then, with all of this?"

"A bit difficult he can be, to be honest. Fusses and cries a lot, he does. So I just walk him round the lanes. Like a dog, I suppose. Gentles him somehow. Eventually."

Charlotte smiled. "I suspect being close to that big heart of yours, Bobby, also settles him. But where's Joey when you should be out working your fields?

Tregareth ducked his head. "Gone off to her parents down to Helford again. Their place by the river. Does it often, she does. Can't cope with the boy, is what she says. But truth is it seems like she's been slippin' away from me for a while. Only time she's seems excited lately is when she's off to meetings with your Druid people. Off she goes and then it's up to me to take care of the boy."

There had been no recent gatherings of their grove, but Charlotte said nothing.

"Druidry's why I come by," he continued, "to ask your advice. That okay?"

"Of course, Bobby."

The big, young farmer reached behind and pulled a small, leather-bound book from between his belt and back.

"This here says it's a *Grimoire* and it belongs to Joey. Found it by accident sorting her things a while back. Been writing in it since long before ever she met me, she has, and it's mostly to do with various special days you folks celebrate."

Charlotte took a breath. "Yes, Bobby, a Grimoire is a sort of memoir, a record of events and rites and practices celebrated during the course of the pagan year."

"Yeah, I get that, but there's also rites mentioned in here about, I don't know, looking attractive to men, even getting pregnant. What's she need that for, I ask you? So okay, she wanted a baby something desperate but it wasn't happening until it finally did, you know? Is that a Druid thing, too? A rite to get pregnant? Like a miracle or spell or something? That's what I come to ask you about..."

"A Grimoire is meant to be a private, personal document, Bobby."

Bobby placed a big, calloused hand on his boy's sleeping head and looked away. "I get that, I do. But ever since the boy was born she's been a stranger to me, Joey has. It's like I don't exist for her anymore, except as a caretaker for the babe. It's like she's left but is still here...."

Charlotte softened: "Let's look at the book together, Bobby. Maybe I can help."

It was a common enough diary, and not terribly literate, either, as if written by a schoolgirl. Like Bobby, she did not understand the entries that were outside the realm of the common Druid calendar celebrations. The odd entries were spells their grove did not perform, spells to seduce and control. The more she considered it, the more it looked like Archie's influence.

Charlotte placed a hand on her neighbor's knee. "My dear Bobby, there is something I just discovered that I think you need to see."

She led Tregareth to the cramped office off the kitchen, switched on Archie's computer, punched in his password, and showed her young neighbor the video of his wife and Archie. The baby lay in Bobby's arms, sleeping.

After he'd taken it all in, Tregareth seemed paralyzed. Charlotte placed a hand on his shoulder.

"This is something which affects us both, Bobby, a betrayal in which we are both victims, a knife in both of our hearts. Whatever we do next, Bobby, we must trust each other, stay loyal to each other, and reveal nothing. Understood?"

Bobby nodded, said nothing, and then walked out of the kitchen with the baby.

HANSEN'S KITCHEN WAS aromatic when he came down from his evening bath Saturday night, twelfth May, the potatoes boiling and a thick steak hissing in an old cast iron skillet coated with olive oil and scattered with shallots and freshly chopped rosemary from Charlotte's garden. In a few minutes, she would deglaze the pan with a splash of red wine and a knob of butter to make a silky sauce. She had a pint of Doom Bar waiting for Archie beside his favorite chair.

It was a warm night, at last, and Archie wore only a linen robe she'd given him the summer before. His face was still flushed from the bath. He dropped into the chair and downed half the pint in one go.

Tonight, given the weather, Charlotte wore a short, soft, rayon halter dress in a pink floral print, and had wedge-heeled espadrilles on her feet, the better to display her trim legs. She watched Archie's eyes follow her and did a coy little curtsy.

"Warm enough almost for a summer night, Archie…"

"Plenty warm; come over here."

She laughed: "Not a chance, my Thor, lest I ruin this fine fillet of beef for my hungry man!"

Archie finished off his pint and demanded another.

You sly devil, she thought, *making me come over to you with another pint...*

She left the cooker and poured another bottle into Archie's glass. The foam rose to the top of the tall jar.

She leaned toward him; the halter top giving full view of her unbound breasts. "Do you like the foamy cream I make atop your pint?" she teased.

"Like my cream better in your mouth."

"Soon enough for that," she said, slapping his hand away from her bum.

The steak done, she finished the mash and peas and served. She ate only the vegetables. She kept pouring fresh pints, and soon Archie was drowsy. The warm night helped. This was going well.

"You are tired, my Thor. You have had a long day. Let's us go up to our bedroom…"

She guided him up the stairs, helped him undress, and got him into his big antique oak bed.

"Thor wants you," Archie said, his voice furry with alcohol.

"And he shall have me," she said. She lay beside him, still dressed, and stroked him. But Archie did not respond. He had already fallen asleep.

She rose and fished in his dirty blue farm coverall for his keys and then ascended to the attic. She'd never been permitted there before, and now she thought she knew why. At the top of the stairs she tried several keys before finding the one that admitted her to the dim, cramped space beneath the rafters. She patted the dusty wall and found the light switch. There were trunks and boxes stacked everywhere. She wondered how much ancient Hansen history was stored here, and how many secrets. To her right, there was a low passageway leading to another door, this one barely five feet high. Another lock, another key, and she was in. Had she not already seen the room in the video, its bizarreness would have astonished her—the plastic bags of herbs, the books on spell-casting, the candles, and the settee. But of course she had seen it all.

Heading down the stairs, she reached the ground floor and switched on Archie's computer. She logged in with his password and looked for more videos but found none. But there was an email message from Savills, the estate agents. The message had nothing to do with the farm:

Dear Mr. Hansen,

We have received your deposit for the villa in Mijas Costa, for which I thank you. You will be pleased to know that the owners are willing to sell you most of the existing furnishings for an additional three thousand Euros, a very fair price, I believe. You will be able to take ownership in a month's time. Please let me know if this furnishings price is agreeable to you and give my best to your young partner. I trust you both will be happy in your new home.

Yours truly,

Barbara Hunnicutt

Savills

She marked the message as unread, shut the computer down, and sat for a while.

WHEN HIS MOBILE chirped, Dicky Townsend was having drinks with chums on the outdoor terrace of the Avon Gorge Hotel in Clifton, high above the Avon River. The lights of Bristol city glittered far below.

He looked at the screen and excused himself. "Business," he said.

"Char," he answered when he'd stepped out of hearing.

"You need to get down here."

"Are you all right?" He heard the tension in her voice.

"More right than I have been in years, Dicky, thanks to you. He's not only selling the farm, he's bought a villa on the Costa del Sol for himself and that woman. I need you here with me. We have work to do."

"Tomorrow then?"

"No, Tuesday. I got him drunk tonight and I will fetch the treasure on Monday. I know where it is now. Meanwhile, I have plans for him."

"Right, then, Tuesday. Afternoon?"

"Yes. Good."

"I'll be there, love..."

Thirty-One

"GOOD MORNING, MY Lord, and a fine Sunday it is!" Charlotte said the next morning. Sun streamed in through the window above the kitchen sink. Far away beyond the daffodil field nearest the house the English Channel shimmered. Morning clouds had slipped east and the Lizard Peninsula basked in the sun's glow like a lounger in a deck chair on an ocean liner.

Archie leaned heavily against the door jamb at the foot of the stairs to the kitchen dressed in his usual navy blue farmer's coveralls.

"You all right, then Arch?" Charlotte asked, looking up from the cooker.

"Too much to drink last night, I reckon," he said as he crossed the floor and sank into a chair at the kitchen table. "Little rocky."

"Tea, then, I should think, yes?"

Hansen nodded. He looked around the room. He loved this big old kitchen, the gaping hearth, the stripped pine cabinets and cupboards bleached now with decades of lime wash, the deep white porcelain sink stained with age, the oak kitchen table washed and scrubbed so many times the grain was raised. So much history.

"What's on for today, my Lord?"

"Tilling, mostly," Archie answered. "Potato rows. So the weeds don't take over. Half my fields are in Maris potatoes and the price is high right now. Lucky gamble. Harvest in a fortnight, I reckon. But a long day today."

"Well then, this morning I've prepared you well for your day; I've made a proper farmer's fry-up for my hard working Thor: eggs and sausage, bacon, sautéed mushrooms, fried potatoes and tomato, and fried bread. Set you up nice, this will. Right as rain you'll be while tilling today." She set the loaded plate before him and sipped tea as Archie wolfed down his breakfast. "Follow those Maris potatoes with clover or grain, will you, like last year?" she asked.

Archie looked away toward the window over the sink. "Not sure yet. Depends." Archie finished, rose, and grabbed the lunch box Charlotte had packed for him. From the kitchen window, she watched as he crossed the farmyard, started the tractor, attached the raised tiller, and guided the throbbing machine down the farm drive. Their weekend together was over.

TERRY BATES HADN'T even driven up out of the Borrowdale Valley, late Friday morning, first June, when she was on her mobile to Morgan Davies.

"Enjoying your holiday in the Lakes, Terry?" Davies answered.

"I'm coming straight back tonight."

"Careful how you go, luv: you're not too tired?"

"I've got the lights and strobes. Won't take long."

"Like I said…"

"Yeah, whatever. Here's the short report: I'm about one hundred percent sure Hansen's ex-wife knows nothing about his estate. But I did get one bit of information we can follow up on straightaway: his lawyers are at Borland and Company's Helston branch. Handled his farm issues and also their divorce. Says they treated her right. Reckon it's a good chance he might have used them for his estate, too. Worth a try anyway, yeah? Maybe you can get on to them before they close for the weekend is what I was thinking."

Davies looked at her mobile and smiled. Speaking again, she said, "I'm thinking that you thinking is dangerous, Bates. But yes, I'll attend to it. Any other orders for me, detective constable?"

There was silence at the other end.

"That was me teasing you, Terry…"

"Oh. Right. Well then, no. Carry on, Morgan."

Davies rang off and chuckled. Borland had offices in Penzance and Newquay as well as Helston. Its main office was in Truro, a block from the Crown Court.

"WELL YES, OF course we keep the originals of all legal documents, including wills, in safe storage. That's standard practice," Borland's Helston managing partner, Jeremy Rothenberg, said. He sat behind an antique walnut desk, his hands folded across an ample belly, his thin grey hair oiled to his scalp.

"Our clients only get certified copies, you see. But we could never release last testaments without the permission of the named executor. That's standard practice."

"Even in the case of murder?"

She heard a sharp intake of breath. "Perhaps especially so, detective."

"Then it all depends upon the executor, am I right?"

"Exactly."

"Well then, I wonder if you would be so kind as to identify Archie Hansen's executor, or must I obtain a court order for that?"

"Well, no, but that may take some days. We handle hundreds of wills, and we keep most of them in storage, off site."

"You do not have electronic copies?"

"We are a venerable firm, detective."

"Venerable or just ossified, Mr. Rothenberg?"

"Excuse me?"

"Oh come off it, Rothenberg. Your client's dead. Murdered. Got that? If someone stands to benefit we need to know that. I'm assuming even someone as venerable as you can comprehend that, am I right?"

"Well, if you put it that way…"

"Which I do. Now, how soon?"

"A few days. I'll put someone on it."

"I don't have a few days. Perhaps you should be the one who's 'on it,' Rothenberg. Today. Do you take my meaning? This is a criminal investigation. I expect an answer forthwith. Otherwise, I'm coming after you for obstruction. That's my standard practice."

Rothenberg sat speechless.

"FUCKING OFFICIALDOM," DAVIES mumbled as she switched on the ignition of her car. The fact was she thoroughly enjoyed bullying recalcitrant officials. She could not abide equivocators, whether government or private sector. She saw them all as weaklings. There was a hard, angry part of her that wanted to drive every one of them into the ground like a pile-driver. It was all about lies and excuses. It was all about denying responsibility. It was all about Aberfan. Aberfan and the dead there, for whom the National Coal Board had never admitted responsibility. She wondered if that cloud would ever lift, what it would take to put it finally into the distant past. Calum West understood. He'd lost his wife to cancer, so very young. And yet, somehow, he managed his grief. What elixir had he found to help with his terrible loss? Was that elixir generally available? That Calum…the longer she worked with him the more she appreciated him. A gentleman, he was, and protective of her, too. In any other situation she would have bristled at someone trying to protect her. But with Calum she had no sense that he was being superior, or that he thought her incapable. He just always seemed to have her back and, as a cop, that was precious to her.

CHARLOTTE PULLED THE vibrating mobile phone from her hospital smock and looked at the screen.

"Archie! I wasn't expecting to hear from you," she said when she answered. It was Monday, fourteenth

May, and she was just finishing her morning shift. She'd mopped floors, remade beds for incoming patients, and visited patients she knew. Her job as an orderly was only part-time and mornings were when they needed her most, as patients were discharged.

"Thor wants you. Fell asleep Saturday night. Thor missed what he needed. Come, and bring supper."

"I shall be honored," Charlotte replied. "I'll be there soon, my Lord."

She'd worked at the small hospital for nearly four years, and once, while mopping just outside the locked door to the drugs room, she'd memorized the entry code while watching a nurse punch it into the keypad. When a favorite patient seemed restless or anxious or in pain, she'd slip into the drugs room, take a single .5 mg Lorazepam tablet, and dissolved it in the patient's water glass. Soon thereafter, the patient rested quietly.

On this afternoon, while the nurses were busy debriefing during the shift change, she slipped on a latex surgical glove, punched in the entry code, and removed an entire plastic container of Lorazepam tablets. That many would be missed. She didn't care. No one would suspect her. She was only an orderly.

After work she headed into central Helston.

"Charlotte Johns! It's been ages!" Marge Collins exclaimed as she entered Heathercraft, the fabric and trims shop on Coinagehall Street. "How've you been keeping?" The shop owner was about Charlotte's age, but plump as a currant bun and her hair already gone to silver.

"Got my place all decorated a few years back and I guess that was it for me for a while. I'm not much of a seamstress. Don't even have a machine."

"I could teach you, you know, and I've got inexpensive reconditioned sewing machines, as well," Marge said.

"I'd rather rely on professionals, like you."

"Right then, fine, but what can I do for you today?"

"I need new tie-backs for the curtains in my cottage. I was thinking of something braided in black, to match my black and white striped drapes."

"Black and white? Very modern that is; I don't recall selling that fabric to you…"

"IKEA, they are. From Bristol. Sorry."

Marge waved a hand. "Not to worry, I understand. Hard to beat their prices. We often fill in with the accessories, which is fine. Come to the back; I think I've got just the thing for you."

Leaving the shop with twelve yards of shiny black braided cotton cord thick as a forefinger, Charlotte stopped at Sainsbury's. She got Ling cod fillets, fresh off the boats at Newlyn, which she'd batter and fry along with oven-baked chips. Archie loved fish and chips. She also bought a bottle of Italian Prosecco with which to celebrate. It was the fifth anniversary of their hand-fasting. Archie, of course, would not remember. Tonight, though, she would remind him.

Thirty-Two

WHEN ARCHIE STEERED his tractor into the shed at the end of the day, Charlotte watched as he ascended the steep stair to the loft above, checking his treasure trove. She smiled. As clever as he often was, he could also be so obvious, like a whizz kid with no street smarts.

She met him at the kitchen door with a glistening pint of ale. She wore her red robe with the dragon embroidery. She had on matching red stilettoes she'd got from Marks and Spencer's in Hayle that very afternoon. Archie set the beer aside and tried to run a rough hand up beneath the robe. As usual, she slapped him away.

"Go on then, you randy beast, and clean up. I'll still be here waiting…"

"What you got under that silk robe is what I want to know…"

"One or two things you like is all I'm sayin'."

Archie grinned. "Be right down."

A half hour later, Archie tucked into the fish and chips with gusto while Charlotte picked at a salad. She waited until he was nearly done and on his third bottle of Doom Bar.

"Know what today is, Arch?"

"Monday," he answered, pushing the last of the chips into his mouth and wiping his lips on a sleeve.

"That's right. Fourteenth May. That date mean anything to you?"

Archie looked up. "Huh?"

"Day we were hand-fasted. Five years exactly it's been. Our anniversary."

Archie waved a hand as if clearing cobwebs from his mind. "Bloody hell. Completely forgot…"

She forced a smile. "Men do. But I remembered, and I have a special night planned for you…"

Archie brightened.

Charlotte stood and opened her robe, revealing a shiny red latex bustier and matching thong. She dropped the robe to the floor.

Archie rose from his chair but she ordered him to sit.

"First," she announced, "there must be a toast." Then she winked: "Or perhaps several." She strutted across the kitchen, pulled the Prosecco from the fridge, and carefully removed its pressurized cork. Archie had no champagne glasses so she used wine glasses. Her back turned to him while he admired the view from the rear, she slipped 10 mg of Lorazepram she'd already crushed into the bubbly in one of the glasses and then filled her own. Then she opened the fridge again, bent over to improve Archie's view, and retrieved a small ramekin of caramel-crusted crème brûlée she'd bought in Helston. She crossed the room and set the glass and dish before him with a bow. The bubbles had dissolved the drug completely. Then she lifted her own glass.

"To five passionate years with my Thor," she said. She raised and quickly drained her glass. Following her lead, Archie did the same. Then he dove into the custard.

"The fifth is the 'wood' anniversary, you know," Charlotte said as she refilled his glass. "And I have gathered a few blackthorn twigs from the May tree at the edge of the yard with which to tease you tonight. The soft green thorns will make your skin tingle and yearn."

Archie grinned. "I reckon Thor can manage some wood, too." He always fancied being teased. But his head was already starting to fuzz.

Up in the big oaken bed, Charlotte held Archie's head between her legs as she tied his wrists to the posters at the head of their bed with the shiny new black braided cord. She'd taped the ends to keep them from unraveling. Archie was completely naked and grinning though his eyes struggled to focus.

"Thor wants you," he struggled to say, his voice barely audible beneath her.

She ran a warm, wet tongue down his torso and then tied his ankles to the posters at the bottom. Archie squirmed. When he was fully secured she swished the blackthorn branches lightly along his thighs.

"Tickles..." Archie said, twisting against the restraints. He was already hard.

"Oh, I think I must demand you be quiet while I play with you."

She stood above him, slipped off the red latex thong and forced it into his mouth to silence him. He fussed a bit, but was unable to eject the thong without his hands. And his drugged tongue would not cooperate.

When she saw he was struggling to keep his eyelids open despite his excitement, she raised the blackthorn branches and brought them down sharply between his legs.

"Uh!" Archie grunted, eyes now wide.

"I'm sorry, Arch, was that a bit too much for my big, strong Thor? I thought you were invincible…?"

Another blow from the branches and he jumped again, his upper thighs and groin raising angry red welts.

Charlotte timed the attacks to keep the drugged Archie from slipping away. Each time he drowsed, she thrashed him again. In her head, the attic video was a vivid and continuous loop.

At one point Archie passed out, but she was prepared. She'd lifted one of Archie's treasured old swords from the wall in his tiny office. It was not his broadsword, the one he took to Druid meetings. It was instead smaller, lighter, slightly curved, and razor sharp: an antique Turkish scimitar. She took the grip of the sword in her right hand, steadied the blade with her left, drew it lightly across Archie's torso, left to right, and watched the tiny droplets of blood rise from the surface of his skin.

Archie's eyes flew open and he screamed through the thong. But in moments he slipped into unconsciousness again as the drug dragged him under. She watched the blood trickle in little rivulets down his sides to the sheet below, beneath which she'd tucked a plastic tarpaulin to protect the bed. Finally, she pressed a rolled towel against the shallow seam of open flesh and held it there for fifteen minutes. When she lifted the towel, the blood had coagulated.

She smiled, then went to the bedroom across the hall, removed the bustier, and set her alarm for three in the morning, when the drug would begin to wear off. Then, she would begin again.

Thirty-Three

DICKY TOWNSEND YANKED the steering wheel of his aging Ford Fiesta left and right through the twisting lanes of the Lizard Peninsula and finally turned up the farm track to the Hansen place, where Charlotte told him he would find her. It was just past three that next day. Her VW Polo was in the back and he parked next to it.

She met him at the door in a thin sundress and sandals.

Townsend caught her in his arms and swung her in a circle of joy and then let her down again. Charlotte giggled.

"Bloody hell, I've missed you, love," he whispered in her ear.

"No need to whisper, Dicky, we're on our own."

She took his hand. "I thought you'd be hungry; I've made lunch."

In the kitchen she'd laid out a wedge of aged cheddar, sliced beef, salad greens, brown granary bread, and a bottle of French Sancerre in a sweat-streaked stainless steel ice bucket. She made him sit, straddled his lap, and plunged her tongue into his mouth. She kissed him until he was hard, then jumped off and said, "Lunch?"

"Must we?" he groaned.

"Yes. We have much to consider and do. But we both need fuel, and I've had nothing to eat since last night."

"Why?"

"Busy."

As they ate she asked Dicky about his drive south and, from time to time, fed him morsels from her plate, which he licked from her fingers. Between them, and in short order, they'd drained the wine bottle.

Finally, his mind alternating between lust and the treasure, Townsend said, "You were urgent that I come down. What is it, Char? What needs doing?"

Charlotte laughed. "You men always think something needs doing or fixing. Everything's under control. I have secured the treasure, don't you worry. I have also secured Archie. He's trussed up like the garbage he is, to be disposed of before we can be free."

"I'm sorry, what?"

"He's upstairs. Unconscious. I have been seeing to him, the bastard. Years of catering to his every whim and then to be betrayed? No, his escape fantasy with Bobby Tregareth's partner stops here. As for that woman, I've already showed Bobby the video. None of my business what happens to them next."

Townsend just stared.

"Funny thing about Archie, Dicky," she mused. "He believed he ruled our Druid grove, thought our members followed him when, in fact, I orchestrated everything, including helping them understand his slightly twisted Scandinavian saga version of Druidry. I even had sex with one of the doubters, to bring him around as well. God, what a hopeless excuse for a man he was, nothing like you, Dicky," she said, squeezing his hand across the table, "nothing like the man you are. You're strong, solid, and above all, a gentleman. No woman, at least not this one, could resist that. We have a future to plan once we get these other matters settled."

She leaned forward and pulled his head to her lips. "Come upstairs and see our Archie."

Dicky stood just inside the door to the bedroom and struggled to take in what he saw. Hansen was bound, legs and arms, and motionless. Multiple abrasions and shallow cuts laced his torso and legs. Blood stained the sheet beneath him and clotted to an almost brown color along the lines of his cuts, the wounds no longer fresh.

Like a tour guide, Charlotte explained the scene: "This is what happens when you betray the woman who has devoted her life to you. I keep him alive so I can remind him."

"He's not dead?"

Charlotte laughed. "Oh no, that's just drugs from the hospital. They'll discover it eventually, but they'll never suspect me. He feels no pain, now, unless I awaken him. He is quite peaceful. And I don't think I shall be awakening him ever again.

"Now, as I've been busy here all morning," she said, shooing Dicky back downstairs, "I need a favor. Can you pop up to the Sainsbury's at Helston and gather some things for supper? I've made a list. I want to make a special supper just for us."

There was something about the common domesticity of this request that made Dicky's heart leap even as he fought off the horror of the scene he'd just seen. There had never been a woman who'd reached him deeply, but this one did and he found it both frightening and powerfully erotic.

DICKY DROVE DOWN the farm track and turned left into the one-lane road heading toward Helston a couple of miles away. He'd cleared the little bridge across Gillan Creek in the steep valley below Manaccan when he encountered a car slewed sideways so as to partly block his way. It was the navy blue Audi, once again. The driver, a wiry chap with salt and pepper hair cut like a helmet close to his skull, stepped into the lane. He wore a black suit with a grey shirt open at the neck. Dicky looked into his rear view mirror but found no way to reverse out of the situation. The man approached, opened the passenger door of Dicky's Ford, settled into the seat, and placed a 9mm Makarov automatic pistol on his lap.

"I am Max. Max Marchenko," he said. "I work for Connor."

IT WAS NEARLY nine, Friday night, first June, when DC Terry Bates made it back from the Lake District to the Bodmin Operational Hub. She sat down and trolled, once again, through the slim HOLMES II file on the Hansen case looking for anything that might lead to an opening. She'd read through the files twice before something caught her eye. She punched Morgan's number into her mobile.

"It's late," Morgan answered.

"Just a question, ma'am."

"It's Morgan. How many times..."

"Sorry. Sorry."

"What is it, then?"

"It's about the treasure the Boden woman from the Royal Cornwall Museum tried to investigate—that search that went nowhere, the treasure Bobby Tregareth says he knows nothing about..."

"So...?"

"So, let's say they are both being completely honest. Yeah? And let's accept that Hansen would never have called Bonhams if he hadn't found something valuable he then wanted to sell...?"

"I'm waiting, Terry."

"So all we know for certain is that Hansen found something and tried to flog it."

"Why do you think we searched Hansen's farm Wednesday, Terry?"

"Yeah, yeah, that's fine. But there's a problem. If Tregareth and the museum lady are telling the truth, the only one left is Charlotte Johns. Our forensic pathologist says Hansen was drugged. Heavily. Lorazepam. How does someone as petite as Charlotte Johns drag an unconscious Hansen from wherever he was, stuff him into a vehicle, carry him to a boatyard or someplace, load him into a boat, take him out five miles, dump him overboard, and return all on her own?"

"She doesn't."

"That's my point."

"Accomplice."

"Yes, ma'am…Morgan. If she was involved, and that's not been determined, she could not have pulled it off alone."

"So, someone else to do the heavy lifting."

"I should think so, yes."

"I hate you."

"You've said that before."

"And probably will do again, but you, too, have missed something which has just occurred to me: Lorazepam. Where'd it come from? Our girl Charlotte works at the Helston community hospital."

"I'd go with that, Morgan. And search her own house."

"You would? Oh, thank you detective constable…"

"YOU NEED ME, Mr. Dicky," Max Marchenko said, stroking his automatic pistol as if it were a beloved cat, "because Reg Connor has put a mark on you."

"A mark?"

"You're a dead man, Dicky. Connor's sure you're fiddling him with this treasure thing. He wants you taken out…but 'elegantly,' and the treasure delivered to him. So he calls me, because I do it elegantly. Always."

Dicky was barely breathing, though his heart raced. He stared out the windscreen: *This is not where I thought*

I would die…in a narrow lane in Cornwall, in the middle of nowhere.

"Only, I have code, yes?" Marchenko continued. "Maybe you think this odd in Eastern European killer?"

Dicky eyed the gun. "I don't know what to think…Max."

Max waved his free hand in the air. "Look," he said, "you and Connor, you work together for how long? Twenty years maybe? Loyal soldier for boss, yes? I hear the stories. Whatever Reg needs you to become, you are genius at that, yes? I respect this. But are you not also like his slave? Well paid, sure you are, just like me, but still under the old man's thumb. Am I right?"

Dicky nodded in assent. He didn't know what else to do with someone with a pistol on his lap.

"So maybe you come across someone who has something of great value the boss wants. And maybe you are a little…maybe private about it? Yes, private. That is right word, I think."

Dicky sat in his aging Ford trying not to tremble.

"And boss is not happy. No matter how long you work for him, no matter how rich you make him, he wants more. Always. But now he wants you taken out. This is terrible shame. This is no way to treat loyal soldier."

Dicky forced a smile: "I couldn't agree more."

"But Dicky, I cannot kill a good soldier. Old Reg is losing it and he knows it. His time has passed but still he protects his—what do you call it here?—turf. Yes, turf. How strange, to protect grass! He will do anything. He will kill his closest allies. I cannot be a part of that. So you and I must come to agreement…"

"Agreement?"

"Revenue sharing agreement."

"Go on."

"We are four, yes? You, me, the farmer, the woman. Whatever you get we split four ways. This is not insubstantial fortune, am I right? Everybody happy I think."

"But you've had nothing to do with any of this…"

"Except keep you alive, Mr. Dicky. Except keep you alive…"

Thirty-Four

"SO LET'S REVIEW where we are, shall we?" DCI Arthur Penwarren said. It was not a question. More than two weeks had passed since the discovery of Hansen's body in the Channel, and they were no closer to naming a suspect. The Major Crime Investigation Team sat at the long conference table in the improvised incident room at the St. Michaels Hotel in Falmouth Monday morning, fourth June, four days after the search of Hansen's place.

"Look, Guv," Morgan Davies interrupted. "Let's not get all official, okay? I'll tell you where we are. We're behind. We're behind someone or some people who are not your usual idiot crooks or murderers. They're always a step ahead. They act and then cover their tracks. Take Hansen's house: stripped clean by someone as yet unknown, except for what they wanted us to see. Stuff we know was there before, unofficially of course, is now gone. But they're not perfect. Calum's people have found a couple of things.

Penwarren turned to his SOCO chief. "Calum?"

"A couple of blood traces and a shadow on a wall. Blood type same as victim's. The shadow's where a small sword or large knife once hung. Could be what maimed Hansen. That suggests Hansen could have been maimed right in his own bedroom. Can't confirm that, of course."

"Prints?"

"Hansen's and Charlotte Johns's in the bedroom as expected, as they spent weekends together...and such...."

Morgan smiled. Calum seemed almost embarrassed to acknowledge Hansen's and Johns's "arrangement."

"That's it?"

"Well no, Guv. We have Hansen's computer and the tech boys up Exeter headquarters are working on it. Then there's this weird attic room..."

"So I understand..."

"I have it on good authority," Morgan interjected, "that the books and herbs in this little room are all about black magic and gaining control over people, probably members of his Druid grove. The women. For sex."

Penwarren lifted his hand to his forehead. "I am not hearing this. I am not hearing that you called in Tamsin Bran."

"Did I say that?"

Penwarren shook his head, as if to shake off the whole notion of Tamsin Bran. "Morgan, find another authority: an academic in medieval studies or something. Someone with credentials. Someone whose testimony will hold up in court. Okay? Do it. Now, let's move on. Calum, did your people get prints from the fogou?"

"None on the granite slab that had been winched aside; too crusted with dirt, though the dirt is disturbed, as if someone had lain upon it. Prints on the winch in Hansen's barn are his; no surprise there. But we got two partials on the empty clay vessel in the hole. Not definitive, but they look to match Hansen's, though not sufficient for a proof. We took Tregareth's prints. No match."

"Way I see it, Guv," Morgan pressed, "is that we have identified a very few possible persons of interest: Charlotte Johns, Tregareth, and members of the Druid grove. I reckon the next step is to have Calum's people search Johns's house."

Penwarren made a face. "We don't have enough on her to call her a suspect and make a search legal."

"With respect, Guv. Given the blood type in Hansen's bedroom and his relationship, or whatever it was, with Johns, who else could have been in that room but her? And where did everything that was in that bedroom go?"

Penwarren shook his head. "I can think of any number of scenarios involving others. Do we have any useful prints at the house?"

"We do," Calum answered. Two other individuals. Tregareth's in the kitchen and someone else's in the spare room. Checking for priors, Guv."

"Still…" Penwarren said, almost to himself.

"There is something else," Morgan interrupted. "Something we…or rather I…failed to connect before, Guv."

"Yes?"

"Lorazepam. What Hansen was drugged with. Terry here helped me make the connection: Johns works part time at the community hospital at Helston.

Terry checked with the hospital and they admit they're missing a quantity of the drug: very embarrassing for them and all, and a danger to their accreditation. But they reckon it's a nurse or doctor stole it, since the drugs room is locked with a combination only they know. But I'm thinking maybe Johns found a way in."

Penwarren nodded. "Okay, this is enough for me. Morgan, take Johns up to the interview suite at Pool. I'll clear it. She is definitely a person of interest. Calum, search her place. But not just for the drugs. For anything, including this alleged treasure. Inside and out. Upside and down. Use the TAG boys."

He rose and stretched his long torso: "You have my full authority."

"Two other things, Guv…"

Penwarren smiled. "Yes, Morgan?"

"First, the text message."

"Sorry?" Whatever his other strengths as a detective and as a leader, and they were formidable, Penwarren was not a technology expert. It was a generational thing. He left that work to the younger experts who worked for the force. He'd hoped to retire before technology replaced footwork, but it was moving too fast and he knew he was falling behind.

"The only information we have about Hansen's whereabouts prior to his disappearance is his text to Charlotte Johns saying he was fishing with someone named 'Charlie.' Where'd it come from?"

"His phone, I assume."

Davies struggled not to smile. "No, Guv, I'm asking where he was when he sent Johns that message? At sea? On land? Where?"

"Do we have Hansen's mobile in evidence?"

"No, Guv. Not yet, at least," West answered. "But we probably don't need it. We can examine the message he left on Ms. Johns's phone."

"Phones save these messages?"

"Yes, sir, unless they've been deliberately overwritten by newer messages."

Penwarren fished his own mobile from his jacket pocket and looked at it as if it were an alien being.

"The force has a firm under contract which can interrogate her phone," West said.

"All right. Calum, search Johns's place and find her phone. Morgan and Terry, take Ms. Johns up to Pool and have a chat. Don't be gentle."

"Me, gentle?" Morgan said, smiling.

"Are we done?"

"No Guv, one other thing."

Penwarren heaved a sigh. There were times he loved sparring with Davies and times he did not. This was one of the latter.

"Yes?"

"I'll be meeting with Hansen's executor later today. We are trying to ascertain who would have benefitted from his death."

Penwarren relaxed. "Thank you, Morgan. Well done, as usual."

"WE TAKE HIM out in his boat tomorrow, early, and tip him overboard in the Channel, is what I think is the best plan. But far out, where he's not likely ever to be found," Charlotte said.

It was Wednesday morning, sixteenth May, and she and Dicky were having breakfast in Hansen's kitchen. Hansen was still drugged upstairs.

Townsend was trying to come to terms with two opposing emotions. He wanted to be with Charlotte, but her hatred of Hansen stunned him. During the night—another night of long and furious lovemaking—he decided her revenge against Hansen was just one aspect of her passionate personality. She had cried, too, deep heaving sobs at her betrayal. He'd pulled her close. All Townsend knew, and he knew it with certainty, was that he wanted to be with Charlotte. It was almost as if the treasure had become secondary. And that Hansen didn't matter.

"What's the boat like?" he asked.

"An open skiff. Fiberglass. With an outboard."

"Navigation equipment?"

"Just a compass. He was too cheap for anything fancier. Plus, he only ever fished within sight of the coast. The boat's moored at the little cove at Flushing, near Gillan. Beached at low tide. Hauls it high up on the shingle during winter. A dozen or so others do the same."

"Can you run the boat, at least a short distance?"

"I know how to start the engine and steer the boat, yes. But not much else, Dicky. On the rare occasions he took me out, I was just a passenger, unless he caught something and needed me to take over the wheel."

"Good. That solves one problem. But there's another, bigger one. We need to get him out of the house and to some private spot where the boat can be waiting."

"I know a place, up Gillan Creek. Overhung with trees it is and close to a narrow lane. No houses nearby."

MORGAN DAVIES ARRIVED at Borland and Company's offices in Helston just after noon following the MCIT meeting Monday, fourth June. She showed her warrant card and was ushered through the deeply carpeted reception area to Rothenberg's inner sanctum, a small, wood-paneled private conference room behind his official office.

"Detective Inspector Davies."

"You were expecting someone else?"

"No, of course not, but this is somewhat shocking..."

"Murder often is, Mr. Rothenberg."

"Yes, well, but that is not what I meant: we researched Hansen's documents and, as regards his Last Will and Testament, it appears he made a new will, quite recently, through one of my colleagues, and named us, his own solicitors, as sole executors of his estate. It is uncommon but not unheard of. Perhaps he trusted no one but us."

"Which, I gather, means that you, Mr. Rothenberg, have the power to release the particulars of his will to the police."

"Well, ah, not exactly."

"What then, *exactly*?"

"To share that information with you, detective, I must get the approval of the senior partners in Truro."

Davies could feel her blood pressure rising. "Well, Mr. Rothenberg, then we are in luck, for I see you have a phone on the credenza just behind you. I'll wait."

"Written approval, actually."

Davies slapped her hand on the table so hard the lawyer jumped. "What is it about murder that you don't understand, Rothenberg?" She loomed above him. "I will be filing an obstruction charge against you and this firm. You can expect Detective Chief Inspector Arthur Penwarren to speak to your superiors this very afternoon."

Now Rothenberg stood. "This is harassment!"

Davies pulled open the conference room door but paused and turned. "Call it what you will, but one more thing: don't ever make the mistake of having one of your lawyers cross-examine me when I am testifying in Crown Court. I promise you will regret it."

Thirty-Five

DAVIES AND BATES arrived at Charlotte Johns's cottage in two cars. PC Novak drove for Bates in an official but unmarked four-door Vauxhall Astra. Novak stayed in the car.

A loud knock brought Charlotte Johns to the door of her cottage. It had just gone eight on Tuesday morning, fifth June, and Johns appeared in a red silk robe with a cup of tea in her hand.

"Inspector Davies! Good morning! An unexpected visit, certainly, but would you like tea? I have a pot just brewed…and good morning to you, too, detective Bates."

"Ms. Johns," Davies said, "Given your relationship with the late Archibald Hansen, you are a person of interest in our investigation into his death. As a consequence, Devon and Cornwall Police have obtained a warrant to search your premises for any evidence that might help us with our investigation. I'm sure you can understand the importance and relevance of this order, and I am sorry for any imposition this might cause."

To Davies's surprise, Johns opened her door wider and said: "Please, you are welcome to search my house for whatever might help find answers to Archie's disappearance and death."

It sounded like a prepared speech to Morgan. "Oh, we will not be conducting the search, actually. My colleague, detective sergeant Calum West, will be here shortly with his Scene of Crimes people. They will search your house and property thoroughly, but will attempt to cause no damage."

"They are welcome, detective," Johns said, smiling, "though Archie seldom came here, preferring that I come to him."

Morgan's instinctive reaction was, *that means there is nothing to be found…*

"In the meantime," Morgan continued, "detective constable Bates will escort you to our interview suite just a few minutes north at Pool, if you would be so kind as to get dressed. We have some questions for you. I will join you there shortly, after I coordinate with detective sergeant West."

"But I have done nothing but cooperate with you, detective Davies…"

"As you say, but we will explore that at Pool. You are not a suspect, Ms. Johns, just a person of interest. There are others. In the meantime, our inspectors will search your property for anything that might be relevant to Archie Hansen's untimely death. I'm sure you would want to endorse that effort…"

"Of course," Johns said. "I'll just change. Will you come inside in the meantime?"

"No, we will wait here." Morgan did not wish to leave extraneous prints or hairs that might distract Calum's team.

THE INTERVIEW SUITE at Pool, one of two created within an existing cottage in the village just off the A30, had all the comforts of a cheap suite in a chain hotel for long-stay travelers: two easy chairs, one settee, both rather unforgiving to the human form but meant to last, a coffee table, lamps, generic still life prints in frames on the walls. Instead of a bedroom, however, a control room monitoring state of the art voice recorders and hidden video cameras lay just behind a wall featuring an ornately framed mirror set above a low credenza. The mirror was two-way.

Charlotte Johns sat at the edge of the settee, her hands clasped around her knees, and attempted small talk with DC Bates, mostly having to do with her passion for gardening and organic vegetables. When Davies entered finally, Bates left the room and slipped into the dimly lit observation room, which was manned by a surveillance officer who adjusted the audio and video remotely.

After dispensing with the usual legal formalities, Davies said, "I want to begin by thanking you, Ms. Johns, for agreeing to this interview about the death of your partner, Archibald Hansen."

"Yes. Archie…"

"We are sorry for your loss. It must be very hard to take in…"

"We were so close."

"Yet you never married?"

"We are Druids; we do not marry."

"Close, and yet you did not live together?"

"He preferred it that way. Archie was a very private man. He had been hurt before in marriage. He kept a distance."

"Except when he was with you, is that right?"

"Yes, then he was very loving."

Davies shifted gears, an interrogation technique she used often: "Hansen had a police record. Did you know that? Dealing in pornographic videos, some years ago. Was that part of his 'loving'?"

Johns bristled: "I don't know what you mean. That was before I met him, before his divorce."

"Yes, yes, I understand. But were there aspects of your relationship with him that strayed into practices that ever troubled you?"

"Not at all."

Davies wished she'd asked the question differently. The answer was ambiguous. She switched subjects again.

"You reported Mr. Hansen missing on Saturday morning, nineteenth May. If you were accustomed to being with him beginning Friday evening, as you have said, why the delay in reporting?"

"He did not call me that Friday. Sometimes he just didn't." Johns lowered her head. "It was not always the relationship I'd hoped it would be."

"Yet you stayed."

"Yes. Many people do."

"Why, Ms. Johns?"

She looked up and smiled. "There were offsetting benefits, detective."

"Financial?"

"No. Use your imagination."

"I see."

"I doubt you can."

"Well then, let me ask you this: Did Mr. Hansen ever betray you? Was he unfaithful?"

"Of course not."

"What if I told you our Scene of Crimes people confiscated the computer in the room just off his kitchen and our tech experts in Exeter discovered evidence of infidelity?"

"Impossible. He was loyal to me. I made sure he was. I attended to his needs."

"I am going to show you a video on the screen against that opposite wall, and I want you to tell me if you recognize anyone…"

Davies clicked the remote on the coffee table and the video appeared. Johns watched, expressionless.

"And?" Davies asked when it ended.

Johns sat motionless before finally responding.

"Yes," she said finally.

"And these people are?"

Johns stiffened. "They are, as I'm sure you already know, detective, Archie and Joey Tregareth, his tenant's wife."

"Did you have any knowledge of this relationship?"

"No."

"You've never seen these images before?"

Johns looked away. "No."

"Then may I ask why your own fingerprints are on his computer keyboard? Because, you see, our computer experts in Exeter say this video was viewed just a few days before your partner's death."

Johns smiled again, a bitter smile this time: "Maybe he liked watching it. Like those movies you mentioned...."

"So you deny using Hansen's computer?"

"I do not. I do not have a computer; we share—shared—his. He would start it up or whatever you call it and bring up Google for me. I also use the computers at the library, too, though I am not very adept."

"For what, may I ask?"

"Organic gardening tips. I am an avid gardener and vegetarian."

"Gardening. Very satisfying, I'm sure."

"Yes, it is."

"And as we're on the subject of digging in the dirt, what about the treasure...?"

"The what?"

"You know, the treasure Archie found in that underground chamber in one of his fields a few weeks ago. A fogou, those ancient chambers are called. Learned about them in a previous case, I did. Date back to the Iron Age. Can you imagine? That's thousands of years ago, even before the Romans invaded. Amazing. Anyway, we have evidence that Archie tried to get a London auction house to sell what he'd found. But he didn't get anywhere. Turns out it's illegal to sell them privately, because that sort of stuff belongs to the Crown. According to our information, he used Bobby Tregareth's name instead of his own."

"I haven't a clue what you're on about, detective. It is preposterous. He'd have told me straightaway if he'd found something. We were partners and had been for years!"

Davies nodded toward the television screen. "Despite that?"

She ignored this. "And as for that Bobby Tregareth, I should be wary of him if I were you. Slippery character and none too bright. Unreliable with his rent payments, Archie said, and chasing my skirts whenever he came to visit. Farming partners, they were, him and Archie, working fields nearby. Often came for tea on weekend afternoons, checking me out when he knew Archie wasn't here. Flirting."

"Did he indeed?"

"Yes, and these questions are getting tiresome and intrusive. If you've had enough of delving into my private life, perhaps someone can take me home?"

"I have just one more question, for now at least, Ms. Johns. Given Mr. Hansen's text message to you on the day he disappeared, we need to examine your mobile phone and place it in evidence. We can get a warrant, but it would be simpler if you would relinquish it voluntarily. You'll receive a receipt and it will be returned."

"I'm sorry, I can't. I've lost it somewhere, I can't imagine where. But it hardly matters, as Archie was the only one who called me on it. Are we done now?"

"Certainly, Ms. Johns, and I thank you for your cooperation." Davies twisted briefly and nodded to the control room to end the session. Then she rose from her seat and opened the door of the suite. "Someone will be right with you, Ms. Johns. But let me ask you this: Why would a strapping young man like Bobby Tregareth lust after a woman as old and worn as you, a woman nearly twice his age? I find that curious..." Davies smiled and left the room.

In the corridor outside, Bates waited. "I'd hate to be on the wrong side of an interview with you," she said.

"Pressure and surprise, pressure and surprise. It breaks them down," Davies said. "But she's a tough one, either innocent or one hell of an actress. I'm about to identify her as our prime suspect, but there has to be someone else. She could not have arranged this killing herself. Meanwhile, call Calum. Ask him if his team have found a mobile. If not, have him bring us her credit card and phone bills. We'll start there."

Bates nodded. "On it, Morgan."

Davies hesitated, then put a hand on Terry's shoulder. "I know you are, Terry. Apart from Calum, I've never had an investigating officer I trusted more than you. You'll go far. Meanwhile, Johns is trying to implicate Tregareth. It's plausible. Could be he helped her and now she's distancing. Let's talk to him next. Send Johns home and meet me at the Falmouth nick."

CALUM WEST PACED the sitting room of Charlotte's bungalow in his Tyvek jumpsuit. The sun streamed in through her patio doors and the heat gain had him beginning to feel like a poached chicken inside his coveralls. His team was finding nothing of value. There were no blood traces. There were few identifiable hairs or fibers attached to door jambs or furniture. There were few fingerprints in the house and all them were Johns's. The place was otherwise spotless. Either the woman was obsessive about cleaning—and it certainly looked that way—or she was hiding something. But what? There were a few somewhat provocative clothes in her bedroom but Calum had seen worse. Private lives. Where was the evidence of Johns' daily life? His people had taken into evidence all of the woman's bills and other paperwork, which they'd found stuffed into one drawer in a dresser in the kitchen, the shelf of which displayed what looked to West as hand-thrown earthenware platters and serving plates. The paperwork would be copied and returned.

Outside, his people searched around the house, beneath the shrubbery, and well beyond the home's property limits. Like the interior of the house, the grounds were well-kempt and the woman's vegetable garden, even at this early stage in the growing year, was thriving in artfully-built raised beds, a picture of neat and efficient cultivation. There were Oriental salad greens, collards just coming into their own, pea shoots already reaching for the sky on their trellises, wintered-over leeks fattening, a patch of fast-growing radishes just forming their cotyledons, and young lettuces bursting with new leaves.

West looked over the garden and could think only of his dead wife, Catherine, and of her love of gardening. Before she'd succumbed to cancer, she'd had him build a small glassed-in greenhouse so she could start tomatoes early, and his daughters, Meagan and Kaitlin, haunted that greenhouse almost daily waiting for the first fluted leaves to appear, as if their appearance would cancel their mother's gathering infirmity: life in the face of death. He'd ignored the greenhouse since Catherine's death and her garden had gone to weeds. It made him feel guilty to let it go but the thought of working in it paralyzed him. But his daughters were pressing him. So was their Gran, Ruby, who looked after the girls. They all wanted continuity. He'd have to get on to it, and soon.

Thirty-Six

TERRY BATES SWUNG Morgan's unmarked white Ford estate into Bobby Tregareth's farmyard at eight in the morning, Wednesday, sixth June. The small house, whitewashed stone and probably Victorian, had a broad view of the lower reaches of Gillan Creek and out toward the Channel, which, on this morning, was choppy. There were several outbuildings in the farm compound. Morgan was hoping to catch Tregareth before he went out to tend his fields. His tractor was still in his barn, a good sign. She knocked at the kitchen door facing the farmyard and, eventually, Tregareth appeared, barefoot, unshaven, and in pajama bottoms only.

"Who are you and what do you want at this hour?" Upstairs, a baby was wailing. Tregareth looked like it had been a long night.

Davies showed him her warrant card. "Devon and Cornwall Police, Mr. Tregareth, Criminal Investigation Division. I wonder if we might have a word?"

"What's this to do with?"

"The death of your neighbor, Mr. Archie Hansen."

The baby's cries intensified.

Bobby nodded. "I need to attend to the boy. Come in and sit."

When he returned, still barefoot, but with the baby, he had on a khaki work shirt and farmer's blue coveralls. He cradled the fussing infant in the crook of a beefy arm. With his free hand he began heating water to warm a bottle of formula. Bates rose to help him. The baby seemed comforted at last in the big man's arms.

"Where's your wife, then, Mr. Tregareth?" Terry asked as she busied herself at the cooker. "Joellyn, isn't it?"

Tregareth walked to the kitchen window and stared out, as if he might find his wife out there: "Gone off, she has. Hasn't called."

Bates crossed the kitchen and gave him the warmed bottle. "And left you with the baby?"

"Never much cared for the baby once she'd had him," he said as the infant began nursing.

"How old is he, then, this lovely boy? What's his name?"

"Just coming up on nine weeks, he is. Legally, he's Archibald Robert. She calls him Archie, but I call him Robbie."

Both women let this sink in. Finally, Davies spoke.

"Some weeks ago, Mr. Tregareth, a woman from the Royal Cornwall Museum came to see you…"

"Yeah. Thought I'd found a treasure or summat. Like I'd ever…"

"And you reported that your neighbor, Mr. Hansen, had come upon an underground chamber while plowing and had you help him get into it, am I right?"

"Yeah," Bobby said, adjusting the bottle as he fed the baby. "Yeah, but I never went down into tha' hole.

He wouldn't let me, see. Said I was to keep mum so English Heritage wouldn't shut down his field and all. Good field it is, you see. Plenty fertile."

"And so you deny," Davies continued, "ever calling Bonhams to try to get this treasure, as you call it, sold?"

"Who's Bonhams when they're at home?"

"London auction house, Mr. Tregareth. Famous."

"You're talkin' riddles, you are. I know nothing about a treasure but what that museum woman said. Like Archie'd ever have told me anyway, if he'd found something?

Tregareth bounced the boy to make him burp. Bates got a tea towel to put on the man's shoulder.

Davies switched subjects abruptly: "Well, of course Hansen's dead now and there's this video of him and your wife…"

Tregareth thrust the baby back to Bates.

"How'd you know 'bout that?"

"We collected the late Mr. Hansen's computer during a search of his house. Our tech people got into it. I am sorry to have to bring this up."

Tregareth took the child back into his arms and paced the kitchen, head down. Finally he straightened, looking away, and said, "When I was a boy, before we came to the Lizard, my dad farmed up near Falmouth. The rail line ran right along the east edge of our fields. I would go down there by the tracks and wait for the trains. As they whizzed by, the sound they made was like, *wheee-oooh.*"

"It's called the 'Doppler Effect'," Davies said.

"It's been like that with her: that fading away sound..."

Davies let a moment pass and then asked, "How did you know about the video, Mr. Tregareth?"

"That Charlotte. She showed it to me."

"Charlotte Johns? Why?"

"Reckon she was angry and wanted me to be angry, too. But then things fell into place: why the wife's been cold to me and all, and why she left here when she heard Hansen was dead. Never twigged they had something going. Never. She said her absences were about that Druid stuff."

"Of which you were not a part?" Davies asked.

"No. Her world, not mine. Very involved, she was. Joey had a secret book I come across by accident a while back—a *grimoire* it's called. Summat like a diary about all that Druidry. Full of her secrets, it is. Rites and spells to do this or that. Like being attractive to men or getting pregnant and so forth. Seemed just plain odd to me. But now, well, it makes a bit more sense. Maybe you should see the book? That Charlotte looked at it, she did, but she told me little about its meaning."

"You have it? That could be most helpful," Davies said.

The big man rose, gave the quiet infant back to Bates, and went upstairs, returning shortly with the book.

Davies scanned the Grimoire and found most of it unremarkable, the majority of entries associated with seasonal pagan ritual days, as would be expected. The entries about how to become pregnant were strange, but then the whole memoir seemed bizarre. She could see a simple woman, superstitious and credulous, open to any suggestion, accepting whatever was told her. It offended her. She passed the book to Bates.

"May we take this into evidence?"

"Well, what good is it to me?"

Davies rose and stood directly before the farmer. "Did you kill him, Mr. Tregareth? Did you kill Archie Hansen, perhaps in a fit of rage over that video?"

Color rose in Tregareth's face. "Listen here, lady," he said, his voice barely controlled. "I'm a farmer. I grow things. I don't kill them. You got that?"

"Not even a man who was having it on with your wife?" Davies pressed.

Bates watched as Davies provoked Tregareth.

"What do you want from me, lady, a bloody confession? Well, you're not getting one, you hear? You know anything about tenancy? Of course you don't; big shot detective and all. This here's the lowest rung of farming. It's where you start. That Hansen owned the land I farm, understand? I farm it at his sufferance and pay him rent. The farming is what keeps us and I put a bit aside so's that one day I'll have my own land. But meantime, you reckon I'm gonna thrash the bastard when our lives depend on him? Huh? I got more than just an unfaithful woman to consider; I have a son!"

Though she was uncertain whether to do so, Bates intervened, giving the baby back to the farmer to calm him: "When did she finally leave, Bobby?"

Davies glared at her but said nothing.

Tregareth sat down at the kitchen table across from Davies and took a deep breath, calming himself and holding the now sleepy child to his chest.

"Hard question to answer, that is. Reckon the leaving started just after that Druid festival, Beltane, first May: May Day. She just seemed to pull away after that. Avid partner she'd been before that, if you take my meaning. After that, it was like that train I mentioned: the sense of her speeding away. She'd been a Druid long before I met her, she had. Seemed harmless enough practice to me and never seemed to affect us."

"And you didn't join her in these activities?" Bates asked.

"Like I said earlier, no. Plus, dance around in silly white robes? Not for me, that. Mind you, I respect their beliefs—all about cycles of the seasons and our place in the natural world. Farmers, well, we already understand that, we do. But no need to make it a religion or something."

"Archie Hansen led her group, her 'grove,' I understand they call it?" Davies asked.

"Yeah. Last couple of years. Way I heard it he and that Charlotte pushed out the old fellow who'd long been their leader—Phillip St. Martin, his name was. Was Charlotte's lover before Hansen came along, if you can credit it. Nice enough chap, I understand, but getting on in years."

"How did that go over with the other members of the grove?"

"Don't know, do I? I'm not one of them."

"What about your wife? What did she think?" Davies asked.

"Oh, she were all for it." He looked away for a moment. "Reckon she would be, given what's happened..."

"Where is she now, Bobby?" Bates asked gently. "Where is your wife now?"

The baby had fallen asleep. Tregareth closed his eyes for a moment. "Don't rightly know, do I? But I reckon she's at her family's place, just down in Helford, by the river. Thatched cottage hard by the Shipwright's Arms."

"Address?" Davies asked.

"Number four, Orchard Lane. But why are you asking?"

"Archie Hansen, the man with whom she was having an affair, is dead," Davies answered. "I'm afraid that makes her a person of interest in our investigation, just as it does you."

"But Joey could never..."

Davies held up a hand: "I did not say she was a suspect, Mr. Tregareth. Just a person with whom we need to have a chat. Like we just did just now with you, and we are grateful for the time you have given us. We truly are."

Even as she said this, Davies marveled at the farmer's loyalty to a wife who had both cuckolded and left him. A small part of her softened. But, given his passionate responses, she had no doubt that he could have killed Hansen. The question was how and when. With Charlotte Johns's help, almost certainly, but how to connect those dots...?

Thirty-Seven

DAVIES AND BATES were just descending from Manaccan to Helford that Wednesday afternoon when Davies's mobile vibrated.

It was Calum West.

"I'm busy," she barked into her phone.

"Do you think the rest of us are just sitting about on our hands, Morgan?"

"What have you got?"

"I am thinking a bit of time at a finishing school might not have been a bad investment in your youth."

"I had no youth. And no one to invest in me. And I'll never be 'finished.' What have you got, dammit?"

Aberfan, again, Calum thought. It was actually one reason why he kept teasing her: to lift her from that childhood horror. He'd so far been only occasionally successful. But he wasn't about to give up. She meant too much to him...not that he'd ever let on. He reckoned he might even love the prickly, brilliant detective, but the slow death of his own wife from cancer was still fresh, and still hurt.

"I've been thinking about that rare blood type on the *Saga's* gunwale smear..."

"I'm listening, but do get on with it."

"I can't imagine a scenario in which someone close to Hansen is not involved."

"What about the farm girl who found the boat?'

"Took a blood sample. The kid was quite brave. She loves the whole mystery element and was thrilled to help."

"And?"

"Not a match. So I'm thinking there are very few people associated with Hansen and that one of them is a match to this rare blood type. Doesn't make him or her a murderer, mind you, but certainly a person of interest. So I'm suggesting we keep the focus narrow."

"And this is because you've been promoted to detective inspector, is it, sergeant?"

"Stop it, Morgan. It's because I am trying as hard as you are to make sense of this maddening crime scene. I'm suggesting I have my people check the blood types of each of the members of that Druid group. That should all be in their NHS records."

"Druid *grove*."

"Yeah. Whatever. I've looked over the HOLMES II interview files and I can't help but think something's not right there."

"You mean besides being Druids?"

"Now, now, detective: Druidry is an ancient and revered Celtic tradition. No, it's something else…"

"What's that?"

"Hansen's sudden ascension to priest. He comes out of nowhere, yeah? And then he's their leader. Why? How?"

"Tregareth says it was Charlotte Johns's doing."

"Which makes me wonder: how do the others feel about that?"

"They voted him in."

"Don't you wonder who or what swayed them?"

TERRY BATES PULLED their car into the little car park at the top of Helford village just as Davies rang off. She was smart enough not to enquire about the call but guessed the content. As they crossed the lot, Davies ignored the parking fee ticket dispenser. They descended the steep hill and fetched up beside an old stone cottage so festooned with hanging flower baskets and curbside flower pots it looked like a florist's shop.

"Bloody horrible fate, this tarting up is, for an honest old fisherman's cottage," Davies grumbled. "Had a heritage, this house did. Prettied up now, like the past didn't exist."

AN ATTRACTIVE WOMAN of perhaps thirty, slender with chin length hair dyed rust red, answered their ring.

"Joellyn Tregareth?" Davies asked.

"No, Beatrice…*Bea*…actually. Her sister. What can I do for you?'

Davies flashed her warrant card. The woman's eyes widened.

"We should like to talk to your sister. Is she here?"

"Bea, what is it?" a loud voice called from another room. In short order, Joellyn Tregareth bustled into the foyer.

"Who are you and what do you want?" Her voice screeched like chalk on slate. She was older than the sister and just this side of frumpy.

Clearly, Beatrice got all the good genes, is what Morgan thought.

"They're police, Joey," Bea said.

"We'd just like a chat with you about a few things."

"Nothing to do with me," she spat.

"What's nothing to do with you, Mrs. Tregareth?" Davies replied, her voice level despite rising anger: "Your abandonment of your child and husband, or Archie Hansen's death? Which is it?"

"Good Lord," her sister gasped.

"Shut up, Bea, and disappear."

The younger sister fled down the hall in the direction of the kitchen.

"Bobby is not my husband and I am not 'Mrs. Tregareth.'"

"You've arranged a divorce so soon?" Bates asked, astonished.

Joellyn turned on the constable: "Never married the man, got that? Not legally. Just 'hand-fasted' him within our Druid grove. Doesn't count, legally."

"Seems to count to him, though," Davies said. "We've just come from him. Probably matters to your son as well, or will one day...."

"I don't have to answer your questions."

"Actually, legally, you do regardless of your informal...what did you call it... 'hand-fasting?' We can chat here or we can haul you up to the police station in Falmouth and put you in an interrogation room. Not very comfy, really, those rooms. Actually, they're just repurposed jail cells. But it's your choice. By the way, what is your actual surname? Just in case you already have a criminal record..." Davies nodded to Bates for her to begin taking notes.

"*Masters,* and I have no record..." she snapped, just as her sister emerged from the kitchen with a tea tray and cups, as well as a plate of biscuits.

"Christ, Bea, this isn't a bloody tea party!"

"I just thought, as we were making it anyway..." the younger woman began.

"I'd love tea," Terry Bates said, smiling and accompanying Bea into a sitting room overlooking the creek that emptied into the Helford River. The tide was full and the water glittered.

"She's not been herself," Bea whispered to Bates.

Davies entered next and Joellyn Masters followed, as if drawn by the power of her own anger.

Three of them settled into chairs. Joellyn remained standing.

"You left your...your what, 'partner?' Is that what you call him? And that was when, Ms. Masters?" Davies asked, helping herself to the tea. Bea jumped to fill the other cups.

"What does it matter?"

Terry Bates took a teacup from Bea and wondered at Joellyn's belligerence.

"Just answer the question," Davies said.

"The day after I learned Archie was dead."

"And how did you learn about his death?"

"Bobby told me. He'd heard from Charlotte."

"It must have come as a great shock, given your relationship with him, Joellyn..."

"What relationship?" the woman demanded.

"Oh, dear," Davies said. "Did he not tell you he was videotaping the two of you? You know, upstairs in his attic? Having sex? You didn't know?"

Bea stood abruptly and tipped over her teacup. "Joey?"

"You're hopeless, Beatrice. Always have been, Sit down and do try to keep silent." The sister immediately did so.

"Bobby Tregareth, I'll have you know," she began, her voice suddenly almost pitiful, "is a beast. Alcoholic. Abusive. A wife beater. A sexual attacker; a rapist of his own partner, me. If I did not comply, he beat me and he is so much stronger than I am." A tear wandered down the woman's left cheek. "He's horrible."

Behind her, Bea rolled her eyes and shook her head.

Terry Bates came to her side. "Did it never occur to you to report this abuse, Joellyn? You could have been in grave danger, you and the baby both."

"No one believes a battered woman," she answered, her voice clipped and dismissive. "But Archie looked after me."

"Well, that video suggests he certainly did," Davies said. "And I reckon from the video you looked after each other equally well..."

"You know nothing about this."

"You're probably right, Ms. Masters. But here's what I do know: in my experience of twenty five years on the force, a jury in a domestic violence case would find it very hard to believe an adulteress and liar like yourself who made a claim against a guiltless farmer who loves you still, poor bugger, and who dotes on your son. And so, Ms. Masters, I think we are done here. But we will want to see you again, more officially, in an interrogation suite. Tomorrow would be good. We'll arrange to collect you and take you to Pool."

"Wait! You don't understand!" Joellyn shouted: "We were starting all over, Archie and me! He's put his farm up for sale with Savills and bought us a house in the Costa del Sol!"

"Wrong verb tense, Ms. Masters: Archie's dead," Davies said as she turned to the door. "That dream's done and dusted. Time for you to start a new fantasy, but perhaps one which does not involve slandering the very good man who loves and cares for your son. Just a suggestion, yeah? We'll be back for a proper interrogation."

Davies marched out of the cottage, Bates following. There might as well have been steam coming out of Davies's ears. "Makes you hate being a woman, a slag like that." A local parking citation was tucked under the wiper on their windscreen. Davies pulled it off and threw it to the ground before settling into the passenger seat.

"Here's what I don't get," Terry Bates said as she guided their car through the narrow lanes out of the Helford River valley. "Why'd she marry—or whatever she did—to Tregareth in the first place?"

"Immature romantic with limited prospects, is my guess."

"Sorry?" Bates asked as she turned onto the B3293 toward Helston.

"Well, look at her. Hardly a pin-up beauty, yeah? Reached a point where she'd have latched on to anybody who'd have her. Turned out to be Bobby Tregareth."

"Jesus, Morgan, am I hearing this from you? That's so completely sexist!"

Morgan smiled. "There's sexism and then there is realism, Terry. I reckon this was Joey seizing the day while she had the chance. When she saw another chance, a better one, with Hansen, she seized that one, too. And poor Tregareth's the casualty. Him and the baby."

"Tregareth said she wanted a baby something awful, at least until she had it. Why do you reckon she abandoned her own son?"

"Ever had a baby, Terry?"

"Of course not."

"Nor I, but I reckon the caretaking engulfs you. You're either made for it or you're not. I reckon Joellyn isn't. She's far too self-absorbed to care for a child. Bobby Tregareth stepped in and she despised him for his patience and strength. His caring shows up the fact that she doesn't have what a mother needs. So she creates a legend that he's a beast...not that she wants custody of the boy, mind. Leave the baby with the beast. Not too clever is that Joey. If Bobby Tregareth's an abuser, I'll put my ticket in."

On the way back to Falmouth, Morgan thought again about Calum West: a widower, two young daughters to raise, a job with long and unpredictable hours like hers. Yet he still made time for his girls. She'd never given it much thought until Bobby Tregareth came along. She stared out the passenger window at the hedgerows flashing by. *Pretty heroic, when you think about it. Quite a good man. And how about you, Morgan? Would you have had what it takes in the same situation?*

But she already knew the answer.

Thirty-Eight

THURSDAY, SEVENTEENTH MAY, dawned soft as the best of spring days. The air was still, the barely lightening sky wide and clear with just a touch of haze. An aging Land Rover Defender, its diesel engine barely idling, chugged along the single lane road that followed the creek's northern bank. It pulled up beneath a stand of sessile oaks whose gnarled branches overhung the water. The tide was coming in and had nearly filled the basin.

A shallow draft outboard skiff waited below. The woman in it clutched a low branch to hold the boat to the bank. The man driving the vehicle got out, opened the Land Rover's big rear door, and hauled a large parcel wrapped in black plastic down to the road. As he dragged it over to the bank, the plastic tore and the back of the body within scraped on the macadam. As the man slid the bag down the steep slope to the boat below, the air was filled with the sharp tang of crushed wild garlic blossoms. With the woman's help, the man wrestled the bag into the belly of the skiff and they covered it quickly with an old brown tarp. Another black plastic bin bag lay in the stern, filled with bloody sheets, among other items.

The woman stepped out of the boat and climbed the bank to the lane above.

"I'll leave the car in the tourist car park at St. Anthony-in-Meneage, near the church. It's only a few hundred yards ahead," Charlotte said. "No one will take notice of it there. Coast Path walkers use the car park all the time. I'll be back shortly. Stay low and quiet."

Charlotte was hurrying back up the lane to the hidden boat when she came upon old Dorothy Trugwell walking along the lane toward her cottage, the former parsonage at St. Anthony. She knew the old woman from the hospital, where she'd been an occasional patient. Trugwell was overweight and in her late seventies. Her doctor had recommended exercise to ward off late-onset diabetes. She used a canc to keep herself steady for her walks. She considered the wheeled walker the hospital had given her an abomination.

"Fine morning for a walk!" Trugwell said she chugged past Johns without looking up. It was as if the old woman was on autopilot.

"That's why I'm doing the same," Charlotte answered, wanting to throttle the old girl for even existing.

A few minutes later, the skiff slipped out the mouth of Gillan Creek and into the English Channel.

COMMS NOTIFIED DAVIES and Penwarren as soon as they got the report from Helford's Godophin Road police station a few hours after Davies and Bates had interviewed Joellyn Masters in Helford that Wednesday, sixth June.

Car pitched over the edge of a ravine above the creek south of Manaccan, rolled several times before landing upside down in shallow water. An older model Ford Cortina. Driver, a woman: Joellyn Masters, according to her license. Being transported by South West Ambulance to Royal Cornwall Hospital, Truro.

Davies called Calum West as soon as she got the message from Comms.

"Where are you, dammit?" she barked.

"I'm on the way down from Bodmin. I get the same Comms feed as you do."

"I only interviewed her a few hours ago, Calum!"

"Things happen, Morgan."

"Come off it: things just 'happen' to someone associated with a murder, whom I've just interviewed?"

"Calm yourself, my dear. My SOCO team are on the way already. I'll be there in under an hour. Will you?"

"Bloody hell, where else would I be? I'm at the Falmouth nick and leaving now."

"It's not a race, Morgan. Careful how you go…and when you get there, let my people do their job, okay?"

THE CRASH SITE was just south of Treworgle Mill at a sharp left turn beneath a steep decline in the narrow road on the way to Newtown-in-St-Martin. Traffic had been diverted and now Davies was on her knees examining the skid marks the woman's tyres had left on the lane. She didn't hear Calum West approach.

"Communing with the macadam are we, Morgan?"

"Don't sneak up on me like that!"

"It's just I've never seen you on your knees before…Interesting perspective."

She rose. "Have you no sense of the *gravitas* of this situation, you idiot?"

"I find it useful to focus on data. Helps solve crimes, you see. And is she dead?"

"That's so crass and I don't know." She stood and brushed off the knees of her trousers.

"Just asking. The tyre marks are interesting. The question is what caused the driver to brake hard and yank to the right. This driver didn't just stray off the road in a moment of inattention or recklessness."

"Okay, you're not an idiot after all. Some obstacle, Calum. Something in the way, that caused an avoidance reflex. Please note, if you will, the farm gate directly opposite the point where the car went over the edge."

"You're sounding positively Sherlockian, but do go on..."

"The steel gate set into the stone wall is open, yes?"

"Yes."

"No responsible farmer would leave it so."

"No. I'm with you."

"Now look at the ground at the gate. What do you see?"

"Tyre tracks, no surprise there."

"Correct. But what kind of tyres, and whose? Look Calum, someone jerks her car to the right directly opposite a farm gate. Why? Because something lurched through the gate and surprised her. You got another theory?"

"Dog? Cat? Sheep? Cow?

"You can be so contrary."

"Just considering alternatives."

"Are you saying I'm not right?!"

"Not at all. Plus, I see no hoof or paw prints at the gate, so I think you are on to something. I just want your conclusion to stick. Let's just remember: I'm about protecting evidence."

"And I'm about collecting it."

"And my team's job is to make sure your evidence holds up, so you and the Crown Prosecution Service can win. You with me on this?"

Morgan stared at him, hands on hips. "What are you, my keeper?"

"You could do worse, you know...."

"Go to hell."

West laughed. "Working with you is like already being there, luv."

"Whatever. So, genius, what's your own conclusion?"

"I agree with you. Something or someone triggered this event. And if it was another vehicle, why flee? Why not call 999 and report the incident immediately?"

"Fear? Expired license? No motor insurance cover? Young driver on a Learner's Permit?"

"All good reasons to leave the scene. But a 999 call could be anonymous."

"Which leads us to one more option."

"I know."

"A deliberate act."

"But why?"

"How about adultery, for starters?"

"Pardon?"

"The victim was having it on with Archie Hansen, Calum."

"And this was going to be entered into my evidence record, when?"

"Relax. It's probably waiting for you on your computer up in Bodmin. I just learned about it myself, earlier today."

"So we're looking at three possibilities, then, yes?"

"Well done, Calum. Someone unknown who fled, and two others: a cuckolded husband, or whatever he is in their religion, if that's what it is, and an angry, jilted woman."

West walked across the lane and climbed down to the men in the ravine, taking reference photos as he went. "How we doing, Rafe?" he asked his most senior investigator.

"Nothing down here but a wrecked Cortina and a lot of blood, Guv. Car's too damaged to say if it might have been hit. But the tyres are fine. No blowout."

"All right, wrap it up. I need your team to take tyre print castings up on the road."

"Got that kit in the van, Guv. Be right there."

Using broken branches for handholds, West ascended the ravine. He paused twice. Though only in his late forties, West's heart had taken to fibrillating with exertion. He'd told no one. He stood for a moment at the top before crossing the lane. Davies noticed.

"You okay, Calum?"

West waved a hand. "Too much desk time. Getting out of shape, I reckon. I'm fine." He crossed the road. Davies was looking uphill.

"What are you thinking?" he asked.

"I'm thinking we need to know who owns this field. I've already sent PC Novak a text. He's at the Falmouth nick and is good at research. Bates was there, too, and I've told her to come. She'll be here within the hour. I need to let Beatrice Masters know what's happened to her sister and Terry is a trained Family Liaison Officer."

"Why the sister? What about the husband?"

Davies looked at West and simply raised an eyebrow.

"Oh, right. Of course. He's a possible suspect."

"And I need to know more about him first, like whether he farms this field. Plus, there's something else I need to know."

"Yes?"

"Who might have known Joellyn Masters would be driving along this lane this afternoon."

DAVIES'S MOBILE RANG as she watched the SOCO boys make tyre print castings. It had just gone four in the afternoon. "Yes?" she barked.

"Massive internal injuries, Morgan," Jennifer Duncan said from the mortuary at Truro. I haven't begun the post-mortem yet but from what I've seen so far, death would have been immediate, or nearly so."

"That's a blessing."

"Not for her, Morgan."

"No, of course not. I'm sorry. I'm just trying to get my mind around this. I was with her only this morning."

"Morgan, you didn't drive her into that ravine...."

"Yes, but what or who did…?"

"She just took a turn too fast? The medics at South Western Ambulance told me about the site."

"Neither Calum nor I believe that she simply drifted off the road. Something or someone startled her. Her reflexes kicked in. There is possible evidence. We're working on it."

"Okay, but take care of yourself, Morgan."

"What's that supposed to mean?"

"Your heart, Morgan, your well protected heart…take care of it. You interviewed her only hours ago and now she's gone. I'm sending you hugs, though I suspect they'll be rejected."

"Maybe not today, Jennifer. Maybe not. I owe you a pint, girl. Thank you for caring."

"I prefer whisky. Talisiker, from the Isle of Skye. I'm expensive."

"Gorgeous blond like you? I should have guessed!"

WEST HAD BEEN listening and put his arms around her. She relented only a moment, then pushed him away. "Everything in my bones says this was no accident."

"I think your bones are not just lovely but smart. Let me photo these castings when they're dry. Then I'll have the boys take them to Falmouth and scan the prints into our database. We should have the brand for you fairly soon. Maybe tomorrow."

They both heard the screaming police siren approaching at speed and then Terry Bates roared up the hill. Davies looked at her watch.

"Jesus, Terry," she said as Bates climbed out of the car, "that was just over half an hour!"

Bates grinned. "Isn't that what the lights and sirens are for?"

Thirty-Nine

ONCE AGAIN, THAT same Wednesday, Davies and Bates stood at the door of the whitewashed cottage in Helford and waited for an answer to their ring. It was well past six in the afternoon but the June light was still bright.

As before, Beatrice answered.

"Detective…um…."

"Davies. Morgan Davies. And detective constable Terry Bates. May we have a word? It's important."

"Yes, of course, come in. Tea?"

Morgan could have murdered for a pot of tea at this point this day, but she declined.

Beatrice led them into the front sitting room overlooking the tidal channel beyond the lane bordering the house. The channel was empty now and wading birds poked their elongated beaks into the mud flats for morsels.

The three women remained standing, as if uncertain what to do next. Finally, Beatrice sat on a divan covered with an old-fashioned cabbage rose printed slipcover.

"I'm sorry," Beatrice said, "but my sister is not here, if you were hoping to speak with her. She goes to that shop at Newtown-in-St.-Martin every afternoon to pick up a few things for our supper. But she's late returning. I can't imagine why. Although," and at this she leaned toward Morgan, "I think she has a bit of a thing for that chap Gordon who runs the shop. Just a flirtation, mind you, what with, you know, her other situation. With Bobby."

"Yes, Bobby. And her son."

Beatrice stared at the folded hands in her lap for a moment. "I don't understand that, honestly. Bobby has always seemed a good and gentle soul to me. But she says not. Could he be two different people and we didn't know?"

"I'm sure I could not say, Beatrice. Are your parents at home?"

"Oh goodness, no; they're in Tuscany. They have a little villa in the hills there, near Montefollonico. Go there every year this time. New wine vintages about to be released you see. My father was a very successful London wine distributor. Still writes a column in the Sunday *Telegraph*."

Davies took a breath. "Ms. Masters, I'm afraid we have unhappy news for you and for your parents both: your sister was involved in an auto accident on the road to Newtown-in-St.-Martin this afternoon. Her car went off the road and into the ravine near Treworgle Mill. Her injuries were severe. She did not survive."

Beatrice vaulted from the divan and clasped her arms across her chest, as if to keep from exploding.

"No! No, this cannot be! I won't hear of it!" The woman was trembling violently and Bates rose and took her into her arms and held her there. The sister shuddered uncontrollably.

Finally, she pulled away and dropped to the divan as if she could no longer support her own weight. "No, no, this can't be," she whispered. "Mum and Dad…they'll never accept it. They'll blame me." She stared at the floor as if already chastised.

"You live here with your parents, Beatrice. I am wondering why…?"

"What does it matter?" She seemed glad for the change of subject.

"It's just a question."

"All right, if you must know, though I don't know why: I was engaged to a soldier. Special Forces. Pathfinder Platoon. They do reconnaissance behind the lines. Gather intelligence. He disappeared in Afghanistan last year. Assumed dead, they said. The worst part is the never knowing…"

Beatrice was no longer trembling. She sank into to the cushions, her body limp with resignation.

"My parents never approved of him from the start."

"I'm sorry, Beatrice. Truly." Davies said, kneeling beside her. "But why would your parents have left you to deal with Joellyn alone?"

Beatrice lifted her head and smiled, a smile as dim as dusk. "Because they reckoned I was used to it."

"To what?"

"Look, Joey was beastly to me all my life, running me down so as to lift herself up. Blamed me for getting the looks and the brains. But she was still my older sister, okay? Someone I tried to look up to, which was what my parents expected. But when she found Bobby, we were all so relieved, Mum and Dad and me. Then she came back and it was tantrums and vitriol once again. She blamed everything wrong in her life on Bobby, but she focused her bitterness on me, like I was the only target she could reach. The atmosphere here has been toxic ever since she came back. Reckon that's one reason Mum and Dad set off for Tuscany early: just to escape her. Joey said Bobby had driven her off. Fact is, they never thought Bobby Tregareth was suitable anyway, though he's proven a fine man and a loving father. A very fine man," she said, looking off toward the window. Davies watched the woman's face soften.

Beatrice turned suddenly: "Does Bobby know yet? He'll be crushed!"

"No. I'm off to see him next. And please do not inform him. That's my job. But may I ask, Beatrice, whether you have a car?"

"No, no. We just use the old Cortina, Joellyn and me, for errands and such. My parents have a Volkswagen estate. But they drove it to Tuscany so they could load it up with cases of wine."

"Thank you, Beatrice. Let me say that we are deeply sorry for your loss, and we mean that. No matter your relationship with your sister, it must come as a terrible shock. Detective Bates will stay with you here, to help you through this tragedy, and for as long as you wish. I think you will find her a good companion. She is a kind soul. Just like you. When you think it's safe, Terry, call for transport and we'll get you home."

There was silence for a moment.

"How about that tea now, Bea?" Bates said at last, taking the woman's hand. "I reckon we could both use a cuppa or three, don't you? Got anything stronger?"

DAVIES HAD JUST reached the car park above Helford when her mobile trilled. She leaned against her car and flipped the phone open.

"What?"

"PC Novak, ma'am."

"Don't 'ma'am' me, dammit, constable."

"Just being polite, ma'am. How I was brought up."

"Outgrow it. Am I polite?"

"Not especially, ma'am."

Davies couldn't help but laugh. "Then the name's Morgan. Got it?"

"Right: Morgan, then. Now we have that sorted, did you wish to know the substance of my call?"

This one's no wilting lily, Davies thought, smiling to herself. "What have you got, Novak?"

"Name's Adam, Morgan."

"Don't get cheeky with me, Novak. You're not there yet. What have you got?"

"That field above the accident site: it's owned by the late Archie Hansen."

"I'll be damned."

"That may be, Morgan; I couldn't say. But I have another surprise for you: it's leased by Bobby Tregareth. Legal tenancy. Tregareth leases most of his land from Hansen, according to county records. Hansen's a major landowner on the Lizard. Or was."

"Novak?"

"Morgan?"

"Thank you."

"Was that you being polite?"

Davies laughed again. "You won't be a PC long, Novak, trust me. And then you'll be under my thumb as a detective. This is just a warning. Prepare yourself. But well done and thanks again."

She'd just climbed into her car when her mobile rang again. The trill was getting on her nerves. Time for a new ring tone.

"Davies!"

"Good afternoon, Morgan."

"Do you have the tyre data, Calum?"

"No. But soon. I have something else. That blood smudge on *Saga's* gunwale?"

"I'd practically forgotten…"

"Yes, well, sometimes it takes a while to get results from the NHS data base. But your AB positive may be Brad Winters."

"That weasel? I don't see him in the picture…"

"I said 'may' be."

"What about Tregareth and Johns?"

"Neither one's a match. Nor Tregareth's wife or whatever she was."

"Yes, well, her."

"Morgan, listen: I know her death hit you close to the bone, given you'd just seen her, but we'll find the bugger who triggered it, okay? We will. My lads will have those tyre prints identified very soon. Meanwhile, given this latest death, the DCI wants another MCIT meeting at Falmouth tomorrow morning."

"What's Penwarren think, we're bloody magicians?! We'll have it all solved?"

"Mister has people he has to report to as well, Morgan. We should be thankful he's left us in charge of this case. He could have muscled in. Probably under orders to do exactly that, but it's just not his style. He trusts us."

"Yes. Yes, he does. And we are lucky. I appreciate that. So many officers who reach his rank are total prats..."

"It's his senior officers who are the prats, Morgan. I know them. SOCO deals with them all the time. Penwarren's our buffer, our bulkhead against waves of officialdom crap. He's always on our side, and especially on yours. He protects us."

Davies said nothing for a moment. "I know. And you protect me, too, Calum. I am grateful to you both."

West laughed. "Don't be an idiot, Morgan; we look after you because you win! It's completely self-serving. You make us look good. We don't give a damn about you, personally. It's all about the case!"

"Fuck off, West," she said. But the smile was clear in her voice.

"Fucking off now, Morgan. Back to you soon about the tyres. And Brad Winters?"

"Tomorrow, Calum. More important things today. I have to inform Tregareth."

"I don't envy you that job, Morgan."

"It won't be the first time, Calum."

"Yes. But still…"

MORGAN HAD BEEN waiting in her car for nearly half an hour when she heard the chugging diesel engine of Bobby Tregareth's tractor as it pulled into his farmyard.

She met him as he climbed down from his cab.

"Hello, Bobby, where's the boy?"

"Come look," Tregareth said, beaming.

He opened the side door of the tractor cab and there was the baby, fast asleep in a wicker basket on the floor. It was lined with a soft blanket.

"Loves the tractor, he does. Puts him right to sleep, like rocking, and keeps him warm as well." Tregareth's grin was wide with pride.

"I need to have a word, Mr. Tregareth."

"Yes, of course. Here," he said, lifting the basket. "Hold him while I put the rig away."

He engaged the tractor's clutch and lurched it into the shed beside his other farm vehicle, an old Land Rover.

"Come inside, then," he said when he took the basket back from Davies. "I'll put on the kettle and this one will need a bottle when he wakes up as well. Overdue, he is."

"He looks very peaceful."

"Reckon he likes this life. Maybe make another farmer out of him, eh?"

"Could be."

Morgan let Bobby get to work in the kitchen. The boy still dozed in his basket, twitching from time to time in response to noises, but never quite awakening.

Bobby poured tea into two stained mugs, brought a container of milk and a box of sugar cubes and settled into a chair at the kitchen table.

"This about Hansen again? I'll tell you, I don't even know what my status is on my leased land, now he's gone. No one's called. I want to keep my rent current and all, don't want to be delinquent you see, but where to send the payment? Went into town, I did, and set up an account at Lloyds in Helston to show I'm keeping up...."

Davies looked at the child in the basket, and then looked at Tregareth.

"No, Mr. Tregareth, this is not about Mr. Hansen. It's about Joellyn. She's been in a car accident. I'm afraid she did not survive."

Bobby Tregareth stood up abruptly and was motionless for a moment. Then he went to the basket and picked up the boy, as if to protect him from the news.

"How?" he said, finally.

"Veered off the lane not far from here, on the way to Newtown-in-St-Martin. Plunged into a ravine. We don't yet know how or why. But we will find out, Mr. Tregareth, I promise you."

The boy began to fuss. Tregareth placed a bottle into a warming saucepan.

"First her coldness, and then her and Hansen together, then Hansen's death, and then she abandoned us, the boy and me. And now this…" Tregareth was rigid as a statue with shock.

"Would you like us to arrange to have someone stay with you tonight, Mr. Tregareth? Someone to talk to? A friend or neighbor, perhaps?"

"Friends, like at the New Inn, they've steered clear since she left. I hear she's been saying I'm violent and abusive. Reckon they don't know what to think, so they keep a distance, you know? But I've got my boy," he said, cradling the child in his thick arms. "We'll be fine. Just like we have been these past weeks. Him and me; we're a team."

Davies watched the farmer as he slowly paced the kitchen, waiting for the bottle to warm.

"I am sorry to have been the messenger with this news, Mr. Tregareth. We may want to talk with you again tomorrow. Will you be here?"

"That's Thursday, yes?" he said as if trying to get his bearings. "Reckon I'll be in my fields, as usual. Seeding clover behind the potatoes. Just ring my mobile. Robbie, he'll be with me."

"You'll be okay tonight?"

Tregareth looked at her.

"I have my boy."

Forty

MORGAN SPENT WEDNESDAY night at the St. Michaels Hotel. It was too much to drive all the way up to Bodmin only to come back for a meeting in the same hotel in the morning. She awoke early and spent a half hour alone in the spa's sauna, emerging energized. Just as the MCIT meeting began Thursday morning, Terry Bates passed her a faxed message. It was from Rothenberg at Borland and Company.

She glanced at it. "Bloody hell," she said under her breath.

DCI Penwarren didn't hear her. "I suggest we start with the accident yesterday and work backward. Jennifer," he said to the forensic pathologist, "your conclusion?"

"Cause of death: massive skull trauma," Duncan said. "Also multiple internal injuries. All signs that she was crushed. Death almost certainly instantaneous. I'll leave it to Calum's people to fit that to the scene."

Davies was still trying to digest the information in the fax as West spoke: "Jennifer's findings are consistent with the scene, Guv. The ravine is steep and there are trees which were damaged by the woman's tumbling car. Her body was found outside the vehicle.

We have determined that impact with the first tree shattered her windscreen and the sudden jolt flung her out through that gap. But the vehicle kept rolling. It looks like it rolled right over her and kept going until it reached the streambed below.

"Good Lord," the DCI said shaking his head. Penwarren had never been able to harden himself about deaths. He stood and went to the window overlooking the Channel.

"If I may continue?" West said, after a moment.

"Yes. Of course."

"DI Davies and I studied the surface of the lane and the rest of the scene at the top. And I think Morgan will agree that we believe Ms. Masters did not drift or skid off the road. We believe the victim was startled by something or someone and she made to avoid a collision and that this reflex pitched her over the edge. In addition we noted fresh tyre tracks at the edge of a farm gate directly opposite the point at which the victim veered. As of this morning, I have the brand: General Tyre 'Grabber ATZ,' commonly used on farm vehicles."

"Tractors?" Penwarren asked, still staring out the window as if for enlightenment.

"No, sir, working, multi-purpose farm vehicles, off-road and on: Land Rovers, Toyota Land Cruisers and such. According to our on-site searches of their properties, both Hansen and Tregareth have old Land Rover Defenders."

"As do most farmers in the county," Penwarren said. "Rugged and indispensable is what I understand. Workhorses. So what?"

"The question, Guv, is what tyres are on their wheels?"

"Okay, stop," Penwarren said. "Before you check these vehicles, find out who sells those tyres locally. Let's not give anything away just yet."

"Of course," West agreed.

Penwarren returned to his seat and looked at Davies, who'd been staring blankly throughout West's report.

"Morgan? Are you with us?"

Davies blinked. "Of course, Guv."

"You confirm West's findings?"

"I'm sorry. I'm afraid I was preoccupied."

"Morgan?"

She pushed the faxed letter across to Penwarren: "This is from Hansen's lawyers. His beneficiary is not his partner, Charlotte Johns. It's Archibald Robert Tregareth, Bobby and Joellyn's son. In the event of Hansen's demise, everything goes to the boy, in trust first to Joellyn Masters and then, should she die, to Mr. Tregareth himself."

No one spoke.

"Which is to say," Davies continued, "Tregareth has at least two motives for killing Hansen and Joellyn as well: his wife's adultery and the boy's inheritance."

"Hang on, Morgan," Terry Bates said. "When I read that fax, I thought, how would Tregareth even know he benefitted? You had to practically get a court order to obtain the will from Hansen's lawyer."

"I know. I was getting to that. And you're right, Terry, he almost certainly couldn't, though we don't know for sure. But the real question is, why the boy in the first place?"

"That, I think I may know," Terry said.

Davies lifted an eyebrow. The rest of the team looked at Bates.

"You know that book Tregareth gave us to take into evidence, Joellyn's so-called 'Grimoire?' And those odd codes in the back? I've been thinking about them. I think they're maybe, among other things, dates when she was fertile and the 'A' stands for Archie. They're times they had intercourse, I think, and one of them is almost exactly nine months before the child was born. I hadn't twigged it before I passed the book on to Calum's people for the evidence file, but driving here this morning the codes just clicked in my head."

Penwarren stood again, as if he could not contain his energy in a chair. "So you're proposing that this boy, 'Archibald,' is Archie Hansen's son, not Tregareth's?"

"The dates could be coincidence, Guv, is all I'll say at this point. But the boy's given name certainly gives me pause. Only a paternity test would answer this question. I'm a Family Liaison Officer and I know a bit about this sort of thing. And what I'd like to suggest is that Dr. Duncan here," she said nodding to the forensic pathologist, "should test Joellyn's DNA."

"I've got the samples," Jennifer said.

West stepped in. "And then we'll need a swab from Tregareth, as well, to complete the match."

"No we won't," Davies countered. "Jennifer, are there still samples of Hansen's DNA?"

"Of course, we always keep specimens."

"If you've got Ms. Masters and Hansen, you don't need Tregareth. Their DNA should be definitive. If the tests match the boy's, then Hansen's the father. The question is how do we get the boy's DNA without forewarning Tregareth?"

"Isn't that obvious?" Penwarren asked.

Penwarren's strength as a detective had always been his ability to leap forward in an investigation, ahead of the evidence-gathering. What Penwarren saw that others often did not were stories. Where others patched together bits and pieces of data, like jigsaw puzzle pieces, Penwarren saw whole pictures. They were almost like movies in his head, movies about how something might have happened and who might have been involved. Others tried to do the same thing, but Penwarren's scenarios often turned out backed by the evidence in the end. There was nothing clairvoyant about the DCI. In his mind he had characters, he had settings, and he had potential scenes driven by possible motives. It was just a matter of pulling together the final narrative and for that, for that glue, he depended upon his detectives.

"Put Tregareth in the interview suite at Pool, Morgan," Penwarren said. "We'll have a Family Liaison Officer adept with infants look after the boy there during your interview. She'll get a cheek swab. Lean on adultery as his possible motive. We have no evidence he knew about the inheritance anyway and I cannot imagine Hansen, given his plans with Tregareth's partner, ever having told him. Don't bring it up. The boy's mother abandoned Tregareth and their son the moment Hansen was found dead. Fill in the blanks."

"But can we take a swab from the child and use that, Guv?"

"Of course not. Not without permission. But you'll also get a sample from Tregareth as part of the Pool interview, Morgan. That's triangulation. And anyway, the child's DNA will be on his nursing bottle, which we'll take into evidence. The swab will be known only to us and, unless I miss my guess, we'll never need it."

"Not exactly normal procedure, Guv," Davies said.

"I've been taking lessons from you."

Davies smiled. Most of the time, Penwarren was their nearly avuncular leader, letting them forge ahead and giving them his official sanction, and sometimes his protection, as they pursued an investigation—like the Chynoweth case in Penzance the previous year, which had little to do with official procedure. But every once in a while a case kicked him into overdrive and he became the laser-focused detective once again, as if there were lightning flashing around his greying skull. "Pull him in now, while he is vulnerable. And Calum: study the tyre castings. See if there are any unusual markings. Start with Tregareth's vehicle, then follow up with Hansen's."

"Done."

"Mr. Novak. Find out where those tyres are sold locally and see if they have customer records."

The young police constable smiled. "Sir."

"Good. Now, where the hell are we on the alleged treasure?"

"Nowhere, Guv," Davies answered. "Figuratively and literally, we haven't a clue. Maybe Tregareth has had it all along, stashed somewhere. Maybe Hansen had it and hid it and we'll never know. Maybe Johns knows. I'm sorry. We've all been busy with these deaths. Treasure seems such an abstract matter when people are dying left and right."

"No. It's not. This treasure is at the root of these events. Hansen's death, Ms. Masters's, were specifically designed to steer us away from the obvious motive: the treasure. Thoughts, anyone?"

To everyone's surprise it was DC Novak who spoke first. "For what it is worth, sir, I believe that museum woman, Patricia Boden, was following up on a genuine lead. And when Tregareth showed us the field where the chamber was—which the SOCO team subsequently confirmed—he was telling the truth about Hansen's discovering it. What I don't know is whether he, and not Hansen, removed the contents and subsequently flogged them to London using his real name, out of naiveté or possibly by intent, or whether it was Hansen all along. But I am convinced the treasure exists. Somewhere."

"Thank you, constable." Penwarren said.

Davies sat up. "No, wait: the timing's all wrong. Hansen found the chamber weeks ago and enlisted Tregareth's help for him to enter it. But if Tregareth was the one who looted it, it would be he, not Hansen, who'd be dead now, I should think. At the time, he was the only one who knew about the chamber besides Hansen. Hansen would have seen the stone had been moved and gone straight after Tregareth."

"What about Charlotte Johns? Maybe he told her," Penwarren suggested.

"She hasn't the strength to have moved that massive granite slab; she's tiny, practically a bird. Plus, if Hansen told anyone, and I doubt it, given his character, I reckon it would have been Joellyn Masters, what with their apparent long-term plans."

"Plans?" Penwarren asked.

"Sorry, Guv, I haven't had time to enter this information in the HOLMES II system yet: According to Joellyn, interviewed just before her death, he'd bought a house on the Costa del Sol for the two of them."

"A new life in the sun," Penwarren mumbled.

"And then he was dead."

"Wouldn't that make Johns a suspect?"

"Of course, but so far we have nothing on her. Not a bloody thing. If she's involved then she is one extremely clever woman. Nothing attaches."

"I wonder if I might raise something else?" Terry Bates asked.

Penwarren nodded to her.

"Besides Joellyn Masters's claim, is there really any evidence that Hansen had actually bought a place for them in Spain? Was this some fantasy of hers? I'm thinking that if we interview the estate agents—Savills, Joellyn claimed—we might find an answer."

"Good. Go after that, Terry," Penwarren said. "Report to Morgan."

"Right."

"But I keep coming back to the treasure, people," he continued. "Morgan, you say Johns wouldn't have had the strength to uncover the alleged hoard within the chamber. But what if she pulled Tregareth in? What if they're in this together? Hansen's death would have benefitted them both, or at least that's what they might have thought, not knowing about the will. She'd shown Tregareth the adulterous video, yes? Why else but to recruit him? And then she offers to split the fortune with him. Yes, it's time to lean on Tregareth."

"DON'T KNOW WHAT you'd want me for, but this isn't what I expected for a police interrogation," Bobby Tregareth said, settling into the settee at the Pool interrogation suite, late Thursday morning. "Right comfortable, this is."

"Maybe you've seen too many detective shows, Mr. Tregareth," Davies said. "We try to care for the people we question these days, especially those who've suffered a loss, and this isn't an interrogation, just a chat." She'd already read him his rights, but the farmer seemed unintimidated, almost bemused. She wondered whether he was still in shock. He looked at her. "What are we supposed to talk about, then?"

"To begin, your partner's death yesterday. Are you up to that, Mr. Tregareth?"

The big man took a long, deep breath but looked straight at Davies. "Reckon I am."

"Let me just say, for the record, Mr. Tregareth, that we had Ms. Masters's sister, Beatrice, identify Joellyn's body at the hospital in Truro earlier today. She was your partner's legal next of kin, as your 'handfasting' is not recognized legally as a marriage, and Joellyn's parents were in Italy. I am sorry. Then again, I suspect that by doing so Beatrice shielded you from even more pain."

Tregareth nodded. "Good person is Beatrice. Kind. Caring."

"Yes, that is my impression as well."

"Joey was never very nice to her. Couldn't understand that."

"Sometimes that happens between sisters."

"Yeah, I reckon."

Abruptly switching subjects, Davies asked: "Where were you late yesterday afternoon, Mr. Tregareth?"

"Me? Out by Nare Point. Field I lease there, one of Archie's. Seeding red clover. It'll be fallow awhile, then I'll plow the clover under and plant potatoes next. Perfect conditions." Tregareth did not connect with the reason for Davies's question.

"Anyone see you there?"

"Nah, Nare Head's not near anything except the Channel; field's right up against the cliffs and the Southwest Coast Path. Love working that field for the views over the water."

"How far is that from Treworgle Mill?"

Tregareth looked at the ceiling for a moment, as if a map was printed there. "As the crow flies? Only a few miles, but no direct lanes, see. You have to go up and around through Manaccan. I've a field up that hill I rent from Archie…rented, I guess I should say."

"We know. It's just opposite the spot where your Joellyn went off the road. There's a farm gate to that field, am I right?"

"Sure." Tregareth was suddenly wary.

"It was open yesterday afternoon. We wondered about that."

"Often is. Arable it is, not a field with livestock, you see. Easier to get the tractor in and out without holding up traffic if the gate's already open. But what's this leading to? I wasn't working that field yesterday."

"It's leading to tyre tracks, Mr. Tregareth. Tracks at that gate that match the brand on your Land Rover Defender. When were you there last?"

Tregareth shot from his seat. "What the hell?"

"Sit down, sir. Please. And just answer the question."

"More than a week ago, nearly two. Sowing maize for fall, I was. But what are you saying?"

"I'm saying only that your partner died on that road. We are trying to discover how."

"Look, all I know is that I got the boy to care for now, all alone. Why would I want Joey dead?"

"How about adultery, Mr. Tregareth? How about her having sex with the late Archie Hansen? How about that video? That didn't affect you?"

Tregareth waved a hand before his face, as if shooing flies. "That was all that Druidry stuff. Had her in some sort of spell, I reckon Hansen did. I'd have never held it against her had she come back to us."

"But she didn't, did she? She left you, and the boy, without so much as a 'by your leave.' How'd you feel about that?"

Tregareth stiffened. "The boy and me are fine. Companions, we are. Happy."

"If you reckon this is all Hansen's doing, did you kill him? Did you kill Archie Hansen and dump his body in the Channel?"

"That's bloody nonsense. How'd I do that anyway? Got no boat, have I? Besides. I told you people before: we depended upon him to lease us our land. Kill him? Why?"

"Because you loved Joellyn?"

"No. Yes, but no."

"How about getting your hands on that treasure Hansen found, maybe you and Charlotte Johns working as partners? Why else would she have shown you that video if not to obtain your help? Just think, you'd never have had to worry about those lease payments again."

Tregareth blinked and shook his head. "That's bloody daft, that is," was all he could manage to say.

"On the other hand, she says you fancied her, says you visited her every chance you could when Archie was off working, especially after your partner turned cold on you. Sniffing around, she says you were."

Tregareth snorted. "That skinny old slag? Other way around is more like. Slinking around me like a cat if I came for a neighborly tea midday while working a nearby field to Hansen's. It was, 'More tea, Bobby?' And anything else I can do for you? Lots of, what do you call it...cleavage. Reckon Hansen wasn't enough for her and she wanted more. But I had my Joey."

"But you didn't, Bobby. She'd left. No shame in wanting the comfort of another."

Tregareth 's head shot up. "Another? Never. Thought Joey'd come back, I did. If only for the boy. But she didn't. And now she's gone. We're on our own now, I guess, him and me."

He lifted his head. "House feels hollow without her, but I reckon we'll get by."

Davies relented. Without definitive marks from the tyre castings she had no other lines of interrogation. "I hope so for both your sakes, Mr. Tregareth."

"Where's my boy? Where's Robbie?"

"Just outside in the next room and well cared for, I promise you. The family liaison officer will take both of you back home straightaway. I just need to take a swab from inside your cheek. It's standard procedure and nothing to do with you being a suspect. Just part of the process. We test everyone."

"What for?"

"DNA."

Forty-One

JUST AFTER NOON, Thursday, Dicky Townsend parked by the stone-girt harbor at Porthleven, roughly six miles through twisting lanes west of Helston, and walked up to the end of Mount Pleasant Street where the whitewashed Ship Inn was built into the cliff face like a watchtower high above the port's mouth. Within the harbor's sea wall, brightly painted coastal fishing boats rested at anchor in their protected pool, as if mustering strength to fight for fish out in the Channel again the next day. The inn's ground floor was devoted to storage and the keg cellar. Townsend climbed up a steep flight of granite steps set into the cliffside to the pub's door on the second level. There was a hearth, cold on this summer day, set into one stone wall. The windows were open to the soft air. The low ceiling was plastered with faded old bar mats from long-forgotten beer brands. Charlotte Johns was seated on the red cushion of a high-backed pine settle by a window overlooking the water. She wore a scooped neck blouse that invited inspection. It was lunchtime and the pub was bustling.

He ordered his usual, a double whisky, paid, and then went to the niche where she sat nursing a glass of white wine. "Crowded today; may I share this table with you, ma'am?" She nodded. "I can recommend the fish pie here." And by this, Townsend knew it was safe to talk.

"Darling, this silence has been hard," he whispered.

"It is necessary."

"Because?"

"Because much else has happened and I am at risk. We are at risk. You cannot phone or text me; I've buried my mobile. That's why I called you from a public phone box. Our friend was found soon after he went swimming. Very soon, apparently. The police have questioned me. They also know about the video of Archie and Tregareth's partner. I believe I am being watched. That's why I chose Porthleven; they won't follow me here. Just out shopping, I am. Bought some lovely fresh bream from Quayside Fish."

"Will we share it tonight? Shall I find a paired white wine?"

Johns wanted to squeeze his hand but refrained. "No, not yet. There are other developments: Tregareth's partner, Joellyn, was in an auto accident. She died."

"Jesus."

"Given that video, I'll be a suspect, which means more interviews."

"But…?"

"No, of course not. Nothing to do with me. Shall we order lunch?"

"What about the artifacts? Have you protected them for us?"

"Yes. I promise you."

They never ordered lunch, and when she finished her wine Charlotte said, "I can only phone your mobile from a public phone box just now. I will try to keep you appraised and, when it is time, I'll send you instructions about our items. Be patient. All this soon will pass. Then we will be free."

She walked back to her car alone. After a short interval, Dicky followed. He found Max Marchenko leaning against Townsend's aging Ford Fiesta in the lot by the harbor.

"You should have a better motor than this old wreck, my friend," Max said. "My recommendation? German car. Audi or Volkswagen are best bet. Reliable. Fast. In case you need to escape…"

"From what, Max? From you?" Townsend was unafraid. He was unafraid because he still knew nothing about the treasure. He had nothing to hide.

"If you want, Max, go tell your boss that although I am in this case up to my neck, I know nothing yet about the artifacts. Okay? That's the truth. He doesn't like that? You don't like it? Shoot me. I'm doing the best I can, going softly, softly, so as to leave no trace. There have been two deaths so far, murders apparently. The police are all over this. Doesn't Connor follow the news?"

Marchenko patted the gun in his pocket and smiled. "I know when someone is lying, Dicky. We had training. You are not lying. Mr. Connor, he is making my life very difficult: full of demands and threats. I am thinking I do not need him anymore. We don't need him anymore. I am thinking his health will take a turn for the worse. His heart, of course. It is weak. I will arrange this because we are partners, Dicky, you and me. Yes?"

"Yes. We are partners. It's just that this may take a bit more time."

"Life is long."

"I certainly hope so...."

"WHAT WAS IT made you vote to retire Philip St. Martin as the leader of your Druid grove?" Terry Bates asked Brad Winters. Davies was with her. They'd arranged to interview Winters at his Helston florist shop Thursday afternoon. His wife was out making deliveries.

"The old boy was losing it. Mind getting soft. Kept missing meetings."

"And so you voted in favor of Hansen, a relative newcomer? Terry Bates asked. "That's what the other members of your grove say, according to their statements."

Winters twisted in his high chair behind the flower arranging table: "I wasn't alone in voting, was I? And anyway, who else would they choose?"

"What about Charlotte herself? Or you, as one of the long-standing members?"

"They thought I wasn't up to it." Winters mumbled. "I didn't know enough of the history yet."

"Who told you that, Brad?"

"Charlotte. She did."

"Were you lovers, you and Charlotte, Mr. Winters?"

Winters's head snapped toward her.

"Where'd you hear that?"

Davies, sitting in a chair by the refrigerated flower case, smiled: *bingo*. Bates had run on intuition and scored.

"And did that relationship, sir, influence your decision against Mr. St. Martin and in favor of Mr. Hansen? I'm just wondering, because we're all only human, any of us, yes?"

Davies wondered whether this sweet-talk form of questioning was something Bates had learned when she was in training or something that came to her naturally. Whichever, it certainly worked on Winters. Davies herself by now would have been bullying the man into a confession. Bates was waiting.

Winters said nothing for a moment, then seemed to collapse into himself: "She can be very persuasive, Charlotte can. And seductive. I weakened. Just the once. A few years ago it was. After a Beltane celebration. It was supposed to be so innocent and natural, but she held it over me, said she'd tell my wife about our goings on unless I helped her. After pressing me to vote for Archie, that was the end of it. She wasn't the least bit interested in me, really."

"And she's made no demands of you since? Never asked for a favor again? Did you feel rejected? Did you want her back?"

"No, and I felt well shot of her."

"If the experience was so painful for you, why did you remain in the grove?"

Winters smiled and shook his head: "The wife. She loves all that stuff, especially that fertility celebration, first of May." He stared off toward the shop window. "Not that it ever made a difference for us and now we're too old for a child..."

Bates said nothing, letting Winters sit with that thought. Then she said, "May I just ask you where you were Thursday, seventeenth May? Sometime after noon?"

"Dunno. A while back, that is. In the shop here, I reckon. Thursday's a big delivery day for new flowers, what with weddings and funerals coming at the weekend and all. Lots of arrangements to make."

"Can you prove you were here, Mr. Winters?"

Winters blinked. "Sure! I can check the books. We keep a record of our hours, you see, for accounting purposes. What's this about then?"

"It's about murder, actually. It's about your rather rare blood type being found on the boat that was used to kill Archie Hansen."

"What? Wait, I never...!"

"Calm down, Mr. Winters. We want to believe you, we do, but it's our job to collect evidence. So let's have a squint at those records, shall we?"

Winters bolted from his chair: "We've got both computer records and paper receipts that one or the other of us has signed," he said over his shoulder. "I do most of the designing and arranging; Cheryl's the bookkeeper, mostly. Very orderly, she is. I'll get it all..."

"SO, THAT'S THAT, done and dusted. Well done, by the way, Terry."

"Yes, he's in the clear, assuming the records are accurate, and the handwriting on the receipts looks genuine. But where does that leave us?"

Davies smiled. "It leaves us with a new, as yet unidentified suspect or accomplice. Time to press West for prints or any other evidence that doesn't fit with who we already have in our sights. Someone else is out there, hiding, Terry. Maybe in plain sight."

Davies leaned back in her seat while Bates drove back to Falmouth. "So much of this business is about intangibles: perception and intuition. We like to think it's all about the accumulation of evidence, but that's really only for public consumption—and the Crown Court's. The rest of it is something just below the level of thinking. Something almost primitive. Something about sensing danger and untruth. Something we're meant to sort out."

She looked at her driver. "Did you think for a minute Winters was involved?"

Bates's eyes stayed on the windscreen; it had started to rain. The clouds rested atop the hills to the west as if burdened. "No," she said. "Never once. Waste of time, that was."

"No, no, not at all. Terry. That's one down. But how many more to go?"

Bates's mobile rang, a tinny version of a Dave Brubeck Quartet tune, Paul Desmond on the sax: *Take Five.* Davies loved American jazz. Was Bates another fan? Bates passed the phone. Davies didn't recognize the number.

"Detective Inspector Morgan Davies here."

"Oh dear, I thought I was returning a call from a Constable Teresa Bates…"

"You are. She's engaged. How may I help?"

"This is Barbara Hunnicutt with Savills in Truro. Constable Bates had enquired about a sale we arranged in Spain for a Mr. Hansen."

"Yes. I know. What is its status?"

"Well, I'm sure I don't know, honestly. He sent a cheque the day after our meeting as security against his purchase."

"Were you also handling the sale of his farm?"

"Not me personally; one of our agricultural specialists was. But neither of us has been able to reach him to follow up."

"That's because he's dead, Ms. Hunnicutt."

"Oh no! Oh, I am so sorry; it must have been very sudden!"

"It was. Murder. So, I'm afraid that sale is null and void."

"Good Lord, his young partner must be devastated!"

"Hard to say; she's dead too. Separate incidents."

"Oh! Oh no! This has never happened before…"

"I'm afraid it happens all too frequently, madam."

DICKY TOWNSEND CHECKED his phone messages. There was only one, an unidentified source. He heard Charlotte's voice: "Harvest the radishes, send them to market, and deposit the proceeds in our joint account."

Forty-Two

WEST WAS WAITING for them when Davies and Bates returned to the incident room at the St. Michaels Hotel late Thursday afternoon. He was grinning.

"Oh, what the hell is it now, Calum?" Davies snapped. "It's been a long day."

"The long and winding road..." he sang, badly.

"You can be so tiresome," she said.

"Ah, but that's the whole point, isn't it?"

"What is, before I find something sharp and jagged?"

"Tyre-some!"

Davies sank into her chair. She knew he wanted to play but she wasn't in the mood. She just stared at him. Bates stood to one side, watching.

"All right, have it your way, Killjoy," West said. "There's a match between the casting and a tyre. A superficial nick, from a sharp field shard, perhaps, on the inside wall of the tread. Little more than a blemish, really. Lucky we found it at all, actually."

"So it was Tregareth, after all!"

"Actually, no. The scar matches Hansen's Land Rover. Right rear tyre."

"But..."

"...Hansen is long dead, yes."

Davies stood. "Someone else was driving. Steering wheel?"

"Wiped clean."

"Gearshift?"

"The same."

"Door handle?"

"Also."

"*Anything?*"

"No."

"Bugger!"

"Find out who had access to the Land Rover's keys and you'd probably have..."

"Opportunity, motive, and means. I know. I don't need a tutorial, Calum. And I can think of only one possibility...."

The conference room door opened and DCI Arthur Penwarren entered. "Late notice MCIT meeting, people. Sorry for the surprise but happy to catch you all here. Where's Novak?

"Falmouth nick, I'd guess, Guv," Bates said.

"Get him over here. He's part of our team now."

Her smile could have lit a stadium. Davies noticed and shook her head.

"We got a tyre match, Guv," Calum said. "It's Hansen's Land Rover, not Tregareth's."

"Could it be an old print?"

"Too much rain."

"Could Tregareth have had access to Hansen's vehicle?"

"Possibly. With Johns' help."

Penwarren said nothing for a moment. "It becomes increasingly clear that Johns, if she is our suspect, and the facts do keep revolving around her, could not have pulled off Hansen's death alone. But who helped her? Who else but Tregareth? He had plenty of motive…"

"I've tried to put him in the picture, Guv," Davies said, "but he never fits. Hansen cuckolded him, yes, but Tregareth was too fearful of losing his livelihood to have gone after his landlord. I can understand that. His wife was an adulteress, sure, but it is perfectly clear he wanted her back, wanted to have an intact family for the boy. I don't see him running her off the road, and he claims he was far away, on the coast, anyway."

"Any corroboration?"

"No. But when I questioned him he had no idea I was trying to place him at the scene of Joellyn's accident; the details flew right by him. He was just full of enthusiasm about how he was managing that field on the coast. And I don't think it was an act. The man's a passionate farmer. That, and his boy, come first. He actually keeps the baby with him in the tractor, wrapped and nestled in a basket on the floor."

"I'll have to believe you, Morgan, given we have so little else. But on the subject of Johns, I've got the report from the telephony experts. They acquired her mobile transmission records from British Telecom. Most helpful BT were, especially when leaned upon." Penwarren tossed a sheaf of papers on the desk. "Johns was honest when she said her mobile was new and she barely used it. Not many calls."

Davies pinned the printout on the cork board near her desk and the four of them stared at it. "Do we know whose numbers these are?" Davies asked.

"That one's Johns' and this one's Hansen's. They're calling or texting back and forth, though not that often. Short, businesslike," Penwarren said. "There are a few outliers, but I doubt they are important. We're dealing with older people with Hansen and Johns; I don't think they had yet fully embraced this technology."

Davies smiled. She knew Penwarren counted himself in that group.

As they studied the numbers, Novak, who'd just been a few blocks away, arrived and joined them.

After a few moments of study he pointed to one entry: "That last call from Hansen's mobile to Johns. Is that the one Ms. Johns reported? Hansen texting her to say he was off fishing with Charlie?"

"Must be; it's dated seventeenth May," Davies answered.

Novak chuckled and shook his head.

Davies looked at him. "What's so funny?"

"Someone's careless..."

Calum peered at the printout more closely, then nodded to Novak: "Nicely done, constable. Sharp eyes."

Davies studied the printout then wheeled and punched Novak in the shoulder. "You bastard, you've twigged it!"

"Someone want to put me in the picture?" Penwarren said, clearly annoyed.

"Go ahead, constable...it's all yours," Davies said.

"Look at the time of Hansen's last text message. It was sent from Hansen's phone to Ms. Johns' phone. But look at the time date: it was sent *after* Hansen's body had already been found and reported to the Coastguard. Explanation? Someone else sent it, not Hansen."

"Someone very clever," Davies said, her normally stentorian voice almost a whisper.

"But perhaps too clever by half," Penwarren added. "Johns herself?"

"Or someone helping her."

"Guv," Calum said, "our telephony people in Exeter can determine the exact source of a mobile phone transmission by targeting the mast from which that message was sent. If they know enough about this text message, they can locate the source geographically. Transmission masts transmit and receive data from three thirds of a three hundred and sixty degree circumference around each tower. The masts divide that circle like a pie. But if other transmitting masts are nearby, they, too, can be analyzed to pinpoint a specific source for a given call or text message. They can triangulate, is what I'm saying. They can put the call on the ground."

Davies went to her own desk, pounded the keyboard of her laptop, and finally looked up. "There are masts at St. Keverne, on the Lizard, as well as in Helston proper and at the southern edge of Falmouth. There's your triangle, Calum."

Penwarren picked up a phone and gave Exeter the mast locations.

"They'll be on site here tomorrow," he said after ringing off. "All it takes, apparently, is a couple of murders to get their attention...."

Almost immediately, his mobile rang. "Yes? Who? She does? Is she reliable? Right then, have her interviewed and we'll take it into evidence."

"Guv?" Davies asked.

"That was Comms. There's a possible witness, a Dorothy Trugwell from St. Anthony-in-Meneage. Older lady, apparently. Says she knows Charlotte Johns from her own stays at the hospital at Helston, and saw Johns while walking along the Gillan Creek lane near her village the same morning Hansen went missing. Never thought of it until she read our request for information in *The Cornishman* this past week."

"That lane's part of the Southwest Coast Path," Bates said. "Is Johns a walker? We'll need to know." Davies went to the Admiralty coastal chart on the big cork board by her desk. "Guv, that creek's just around a low headland from the little harbor at Flushing where Hansen's boat was anchored."

"So if she was not out for a walk early on the very morning Hansen went missing, what was she doing there?" Penwarren said. "Bring her in again; Morgan, she's yours. Meanwhile, if they have a room, I'm staying here tonight."

"Me too, Guv. No sense in going upcounty...."

"Well, I hope you two will be nice and cozy; I've got kids to attend to," Calum said.

"Calum," Penwarren said, "you look after them brilliantly. Don't think we haven't noticed."

Morgan grinned. She wasn't sure why.

Forty-Three

"THIS IS BEGINNING to feel like harassment," Charlotte Johns complained. She was perched at the edge of the settee in the interview room at Pool once again. It was just coming up on eleven, Friday morning. "The love of my life has drowned. Why must you persecute me?"

"Relax, Ms. Johns. No one is harassing or persecuting you. This is simply another interview. And, for your information, Archie Hansen did not drown. No water in his lungs, you see. He suffocated face down in the water."

"Oh my God, how horrible…"

"Yes. I should think so. But we doubt he was even aware. The pathologist's report says he was heavily drugged at the time: Lorazepam: a powerful sedative. Drugged unconscious, in fact. Curiously, a quantity of that same drug went missing from the hospital where you work just before Mr. Hansen disappeared. Were you aware of that?"

Johns laughed. "Look, I'm an orderly. That's a fancy word for a charwoman, okay? I clean rooms, clean toilets, make beds, swab floors. I need the money. At the hospital I have access to nothing but cleaning materials and linens. There are very strict rules, as there should be, of course."

"So you know nothing about this particular drug?"

"Sorry. Nothing."

"Never heard of it before?"

"I am not a pharmacist, detective."

Davies consulted a sheaf of papers before her, one of her favorite ways of distracting suspects, and then looked up: "Have you ever driven Mr. Hansen's Land Rover, Ms. Johns?"

The question gave Johns only momentary pause. "Of course not. He never lets me near his farm equipment."

"But Mr. Hansen is dead. Have you never had need for his four wheel drive vehicle, perhaps since his death?"

"I have my own motor, detective. I do not drive farm vehicles. What's more, I wouldn't have the first idea where to even find the keys to his vehicles."

"Really? Because our scene of crimes people noted in their report that the keys for the Land Rover, as well as Mr. Hansen's two tractors, hang in his barn on a marked rack just above his neatly labeled spare parts. Very orderly chap, Archie was."

"As I've said before, I was not permitted in there."

"In all your years together, never?"

"Correct. He was very particular about that."

"Why do you suppose that was?"

"I couldn't say."

"Couldn't or won't? You and Hansen were together for some five years, yet you lived separately. Why?"

"You asked that before. As I said then, he preferred it that way. The arrangement suited us both."

"Did it really? Or was it, Ms. Johns, that he didn't love you, that you were simply one of his playthings?"

"That's nonsense! He was my priest. I was his priestess. Our intimate life was rich and full of love!"

"Full of love, Ms. Johns, or just sex? There is that video of Hansen and his neighbor's partner, Joellyn, you see, having it on in Hansen's attic. Looks like he had a more varied sexual life than you knew, so I can't help but wonder, as any woman might, about the sincerity of his love for you?"

Charlotte shook her head. "That would be that slut Joellyn's doing, that would. What they did in that video? That wasn't even a technique he enjoyed. Trust me, I know. And that Bobby Tregareth? I don't think he satisfied his Joey. So she came looking for more from Archie, is what I think."

"Perhaps you're right. Or perhaps she was more…ah…accomplished than you in that particular technique, as you put it. But never mind; let's say you're right, that Joellyn didn't satisfy Mr. Tregareth. Do you reckon that was why Bobby lingered with you of an afternoon, over tea, as you've previously stated?"

Charlotte shook off the jibe and smiled: "Sure. Needy, he was, that's why he hung about gawking, always looking down my blouse."

"And yet he says that's not true. Never happened."

"Well, he would do, wouldn't he? Makes him look weak, poor devil."

"I'm sure I can't say, Ms. Johns. I've no previous experience with lechery, you see."

Johns looked at her: "Doesn't surprise me."

Davies marveled at the woman's poise: she was formidably unflappable. So, as was her practice, she decided to go straight for the woman's throat: "I wonder if you are aware, Ms. Johns, that your partner, Archie Hansen, signed a contract to purchase a small villa on the coast of Spain for himself and Joellyn?"

Johns' head snapped up: "What? That's impossible!"

"Yes, well, that's true enough, now, as they are both dead, an interesting coincidence when you think about it. But we actually have the sale documents, you see. Archie had put Higher Pennare up for sale for quite a tidy sum. Hadn't he said? Both transactions were being handled by Savills in Truro: sell the farm, buy the villa. Savills was kind enough to email us a link to the property in Spain. Quite charming it is: tropical plants and a pool as well. The estate agent confided that Archie and Joellyn planned to take Joellyn's boy with them."

"Tregareth's child? Don't be daft. Archie was through with children after he lost his own in the divorce several years ago."

"And, of course, you were too old, am I right, to have a child with him? But maybe he wanted a second chance with someone younger?"

"Bobby would never have let that boy go…never."

"What makes you so certain? Because according to our DNA analysis, the boy isn't Tregareth's son. He's Archie's."

Johns looked like she'd suddenly been flash-frozen. Davies's mobile vibrated silently in her suit jacket pocket. She'd kept it on purposely.

"Would you excuse me for a moment, Ms. Johns? I'm sorry for this brief interruption."

Davies stepped into the hallway.

"Morgan?" It was Calum.

"You were expecting someone else?"

"Oh, be still. I have news about that text message from Hansen to Johns."

"And that would be...?"

"The telephony analysts from Exeter are here on the Lizard. And they've zeroed in on that signal allegedly sent from Hansen's phone. They've triangulated from the three masts in the area. The primary transmission came off the mast at St. Keverne. It stands on high ground about three miles south of Hansen's farm...but closer to Johns's place at the edge of Goonhilly Downs."

"I'm listening."

"We're here at Johns' place now. The crew here says the transmission to the St. Keverne mast could only have come from her bungalow, there being no other houses anywhere nearby out in this barren heathland. Bleak it is out here, I'm telling you, just acres of gorse and bracken, not a tree to be seen."

"Spare me the nature lesson, Calum..."

"Okay, what the Exeter boys say is the message could only have been sent from the upper story of Charlotte Johns' house. There's no reliable signal on the ground floor."

"Which is to say?"

"Either she sent it or someone else did, but from her own house...and, of course, after Hansen's body had already been found. Will you take Johns into custody?"

Davies hesitated…"No. Not yet. There's still a big piece missing."

"I know. She couldn't have pulled off the dumping at sea on her own. What about Tregareth?"

"No. He doesn't fit. Not at all."

"Why? He had plenty of motive."

"I can't explain. It just doesn't add up. I trust him. There's someone else. I can smell it."

"Okay, Morgan. And I trust you. But you'll need an explanation for the Guv."

"I'm still working on Johns; an arrest would only silence her."

"You're the boss. I'm with you, Morgan."

"Thank you, Calum, thank you very much; I'm learning I can count on you."

"You're not in this alone."

"Always have been."

"Maybe time for a change…?"

Morgan rang off and returned to the interview suite. She wondered what it would be like not to be alone.

"ARE YOU A walker, Ms. Johns?" Morgan asked when she'd taken her seat again. "I am. When I lived in Newlyn, I often hiked along the Southwest Coast Path to get some air and clear my head. Gorgeous coastline hereabouts in Cornwall."

"No. Walking alone frightens me."

"Even in broad daylight? Like, for example, early in the morning of seventeenth May, at St. Anthony-in-Meneage? Lovely spot for a walk, that is, hard by Gillan Creek and on the way to the viewpoint at Dennis Head, just around the headland from Flushing where Archie moored his skiff. Know the spot, do you?"

Johns shook her head. "Can't recall being anywhere near there."

"And yet someone else can. Someone who recognized you, apparently."

"She must certainly be mistaken."

"She?"

Morgan thought she'd caught Johns, but the woman's comeback was slick: "The only person I know in St. Anthony-in-Meneage is Dorothy Trugwell. She is very old and a frequent patient at the hospital in Helston. Comes to us when her visions get the best of her. Completely unreliable, she is. Has to be on her medications, but often forgets to take them."

Forty-Four

IT WAS WHILE the telephony experts were gathering up their gear that West saw it. He'd been gazing out the sliding glass door of Charlotte's sitting room toward the raised bed vegetable garden beyond when it came to him. It was all about his late wife and her passion for gardening and their work together each spring to grow fresh vegetables for their kitchen At this stage, late spring, he saw that the vegetables in John's gardens were thriving: lettuce, spinach, cabbage, cauliflower, carrot tops, and young peas climbing on trellises. But it was the earliest of the garden vegetables, the radishes, which seemed to be struggling, almost stunted. They should have been way ahead of the rest of the garden by now, their green leaves flourishing, their red orbs fattening, ready for harvest. Instead, they looked like they were only just beginning to set true leaves, the first round cotyledons withering, like they'd been poisoned. It was all wrong.

West found a garden fork in the shed behind the house and began digging in the radish bed. He dug furiously until the fork hit metal. His chest heaving and his heart thumping from the effort, he pried out a heavy biscuit tin. It was wide and deep, the images on the big tin commemorating the 1981 marriage of Prince Charles and Lady Diana. He reached down to pull it out of the soil, opened the lid, called Morgan's mobile, and got her voicemail. "I've found the treasure. In Johns' garden."

Then he collapsed.

DICKY TOWNSEND AND Max Marchenko had cased Charlotte's bungalow for police activity and now stood before her garden.

"What is radish?" Max said.

Townsend ran his hand through his thinning hair. "An early vegetable."

"Many vegetables here."

"Yes. All but one. Look at that bed: the radishes were there. Now they're gone."

"And the treasure, too?"

"Yes. The police, I reckon. We have lost this one, Max."

"Mr. Connor will not be pleased. He has been in touch, repeatedly, ever since the news of Hansen's death."

"I thought you were through with him, Max."

Marchenko smiled. "I keep my options open, Mr. Dicky. I will not betray you, but I think a plane ticket to, say, Canada is in your future. Yes? That or my gun to your head."

"I COULD KILL you, you idiot!"

"Morgan," Calum West said. He had been sedated and was just coming back to the present at the hospital in Helston. The fibrillation was under control and his condition had stabilized.

"I'm sorry..."

"You're sorry all right! Give me no clue your heart was dickey? I should have twigged it when you were climbing out of that ravine after Joellyn's car went over. I don't know whether to hug you or slap you! And what about your girls and their gran, Ruby? What would they think if you'd suddenly checked out? That's just irresponsible, that is!"

Calum managed a grin. "That's where you're wrong."

Davies ran her hands through her cropped hair and shook her head. "All right, how am I wrong because, you know, I almost never am..."

"You've been in the force almost twenty-five years, right? Me, almost as long. Plenty of young vultures sniffing around our aging carcasses, waiting to pounce."

"Aging? Excuse me?"

"Shut up for once, will you? I let on I've got a dicky heart and guess what, I'm retired. The force couldn't care less. Disposable, I am. Piece of meat to them. How's that good for my girls or for their gran, eh? So we keep this quiet. Private."

He looked at Davies hard. "Got that, do you?"

Davies rested her head in her hands. "You are so impossible."

"Why does this matter so much to you?"

Davies looked around the hospital room as if for an answer.

"I suppose, you imbecile, because I may care for you. A lot."

"God help me..."

Morgan smiled and placed her hand against Calum's cheek. "You may need the combined help not just of God but of the Druids and all the other pagans hereabouts to survive me."

Calum took her hand and kissed her palm. Morgan had never known a kiss so tender or more heartfelt.

Epilogue

"A BLOODY TRAVESTY, this is!" Morgan Davies shouted, pounding her fist on the table at Bodmin around which the Major Crimes Investigative Team had gathered after the verdict in the months-long trial of Charlotte Johns. Fall was nearly upon them, and the leaves on the trees on the Channel side of Cornwall were already yellowing. Calum West watched his partner's fury. The woman was incendiary. In more ways than one, he'd learned recently.

"Conspiracy to murder? That's the best the Crown Prosecution Service could come up with, the best the damned judge could do? *Conspiracy?* Twenty years? The woman's a pathological liar, a torturer, and a murderer!"

DCI Penwarren let Morgan burn out. He was used to her fury against injustice.

"The judge, Morgan, had little choice. Because we knew Johns could not have acted alone, he had no alternative but to instruct the jury to back down to conspiracy. But recall the judge's words," Penwarren said, picking up the transcript:

I have had extensive opportunity to see you give evidence and have heard you testify over a period of many weeks. I believe you are a consummate actress and your performance demonstrates your ability to lie with apparent conviction and yet, clearly, you experience no remorse for what you did. I have no doubt at all that the arrangements for Hansen's torture, abduction, and disposal were of your making. What you orchestrated was a horrific and slow death.

"That's pretty damning, Morgan."

"But it doesn't put her away for good! And where's the prosecution of Joellyn Masters' death? The Crown dropped that one entirely."

"And for good reason: we had nothing but an ambiguous tyre print. Nothing. They were wise to pursue the stronger case."

Penwarren sighed. "Look, Morgan, you and I know only too well how little true justice there is in this world, much less in our legal system. And I know you also know that I understand the true source of your anger. But the jury did convict her and they wouldn't—they couldn't—have done so unless the judge had reduced the charge. So no, it's not the verdict we sought but let's remember, the woman will be nearly seventy when she gets out."

"Come off it, Guv, she'll be out sooner."

"I wouldn't count on it, Morgan. Others have weighed in on this case…."

LATE IN THE afternoon a few days later, Morgan Davies and Terry Bates drove into the yard of Bobby Tregareth's farm. Patricia Boden from Truro's Royal Cornwall Museum sat in the back seat with the lawyer,

Jeremy Rothenberg. They climbed out of the car and Davies knocked on the kitchen door at the back. Davies was surprised to find that Beatrice Masters answered it, the boy Archibald in her arms. Something savory was simmering on the cooker.

"Oh, hello! You'll be wanting Bobby. He's just texted to say he's on his way home. Will you have tea while we wait?"

Beatrice put the child into a springy suspension contraption in which the boy could work his plump little legs and bounce. The child seemed supremely happy.

Just as Beatrice served, Bobby Tregareth came through the back door, kicked off his Wellies in the mudroom, and padded into the kitchen in his socks.

"What's this then?" he said when he saw the visitors. "Bea?"

"They've come to see you, Bobby."

"About what?"

"Come on then, love, and take a seat," Beatrice said as she set a mug on the kitchen table. Tregareth remained standing.

Morgan closed her eyes for a moment. Bobby Tregareth seemed to have found the woman who fit him best. It had never been Joellyn. It was meant to be Beatrice all along. She wondered when each of them noticed. Who was first? Or did it just emerge in the midst of their dual tragedies. She opened her eyes and watched the new couple: *I'm getting mushy and romantic,* she thought. *This is all Calum's fault.*

"We…all of us," Morgan said finally, gesturing to the others who'd accompanied her, "we think we have some news for you Bobby…and Beatrice."

"What's that then?" Bobby had learned to be wary.

"Perhaps you'd like to sit down?"

"Fine I am, right here. What's this about?"

"Bobby," Beatrice said, her hand light upon his shoulder. "Sit. These are not our enemies."

Morgan nodded thanks to her and took a breath as Bobby finally sat. He'd not touched his tea.

"We are here to tell you, Mr. Tregareth," she began, "that your son, Archibald Robert Tregareth, is the sole beneficiary of the late Archie Hansen's estate. You are the boy's fiduciary manager. This means that all of Hansen's property, as well as his cash assets, whatever they may be, belong to your son and to you as your son's legal representative."

Tregareth blinked several times. "I'm sorry," he said finally, "but can you spell this out in plain English?" He looked at Beatrice. "For both of us?"

The lawyer, Rothenberg answered: "It means that the land you have leased is now yours and your son's, as is all of Hansen's own land. His house as well. They are all yours and at your disposal, for the benefit of your son. My legal firm represented Mr. Hansen and we will be happy to help you sort this all out."

Tregareth was dumbstruck. Beatrice wrapped her arms around his neck but said nothing.

"I…I'm sorry," Tregareth stuttered, as if trying to gain control of his tongue, "…I."

"But there is something else," Patricia Boden added.

"I remember you," Tregareth said. "You're that museum lady...."

"I am, yes sir. Do you remember that chamber Hansen found?"

"Course I do. Beginning of all this sadness, that was..."

"I understand, and you have my sympathy, truly. But I think the outcome may alleviate some of that sadness. As it happens, Mr. Hansen found items in that underground chamber of great value. Relics from the Iron Age: jewelry, coins. The police recovered them from where they were hidden and returned them to the Crown."

"Good, and good riddance, I say. Nothing but trouble we had after he found that hole."

"You may wish to change your mind about that, Mr. Tregareth," Boden continued. "It will take a couple of years for the British Museum's full evaluation but, Hansen being dead and your son his beneficiary, the full value of that Iron Age hoard will come directly to him. It is of course, now your son's land and therefore whatever was found there belongs to him."

"I'm sorry. What does that mean?"

"At least a million, Mr. Tregareth, and likely much more."

"TRY THE KELTIK," Davies said. "Smooth, almost comforting, as ales go."

"I'm not much of a beer drinker," Terry Bates said as they stood at the bar of the Blisland Inn.

"I wasn't either, until I moved here. Trust me."

Publican Garry Ronan was suddenly beside them. "I don't know whether I can permit two such lovely women in my pub at once. Could cause fisticuffs among the regulars!"

Bates lifted an eyebrow. Davies laughed.

"That's just Garry being Garry, luv. Take no notice."

"Oh, I am cut to the quick!" Ronan complained.

"I know it's hard, but do try to control yourself, Garry. This is my rather splendid assistant, detective constable Terry Bates. I won't have her getting any bad impressions of you or my village local, you hear? Now, what's on for supper, and make it good."

Ronan threw a bar towel over his left forearm, in the manner of a waiter and bowed. "I should think the Shepherd's Pie would do you. Fresh local lamb, new Maris potatoes, veg, all savoury and luscious."

"You make it sound X-rated, you knave," Davies joked.

"You shall not be disappointed."

Davies and Bates found a small table by the hearth; fall was upon them and there was a wood fire smoldering in the grate. Davies grabbed an iron prod and shook the fire to life.

Bates stared at the creamy foam in her pint jar for a bit, then looked up.

"Something about this afternoon at Tregareth's I wanted to ask you about."

Davies sipped her pint and smiled. "I was wondering when you'd get around to it. It's why I asked you here."

"The DNA evidence."

"What of it?"

"It was never entered in the trial and you said nothing about it to Tregareth this afternoon."

Davies stared at the fire for a few moments.

"Did you see those three today? Bobby, Beatrice, the bouncing boy?"

"Yes, but…"

"Do you honestly think Tregareth's never noticed that youngster's bright red hair? He knows Hansen's the father. It simply doesn't matter to him. He loves that boy and, unless I miss my guess, he loves Beatrice as well."

Morgan looked at Terry and smiled: "What would you have said?"

Keep reading for an excerpt from the next book in the Davies & West Mystery Series.

Trevega House

A Davies & West Mystery

An excerpt from Book 3 in the Davies & West Mystery Series

Prologue

IT WAS, ALMOST everyone in Boscastle later agreed, a great mercy that death was so quick.

That late spring morning, the sky sapphire blue and the grazing meadows emerald with new growth, Roger and Anne Trelissick, on their way to the shops up in Camelford, had just reached the top of the long gravel drive from their home, Bottreaux Farm, when an empty dump truck going far too fast failed to negotiate the B3266's steep ninety-degree left turn toward the village. The truck lifted and tipped over to the right, became almost airborne, gave in to gravity, crushed the Trelissick's Land Rover where it waited to enter the main road, and rolled once more before resting finally upside down in one of their fields, scattering the cattle that had been grazing there.

Incredibly, the driver survived. Roger and Anne Trelissick did not. Roger died instantly, Anne before the emergency aides could cut her free from their mangled farm vehicle.

The Cornish village of Boscastle was nearly a year into a reconstruction project following an epic and massively destructive flash flood, one of the worst in British recorded history. In a single afternoon, thanks to a bizarre meteorological convergence, nearly half a billion gallons of rain fell in a few hours and funneled from the hilltops into the Valency River Valley uprooting trees, rolling boulders like so many marbles, carrying dozens of cars out into the Atlantic, and ultimately destroying many buildings that had stood firm beside the harbor mouth for as long as five centuries. The task of rebuilding, of clearing the rubble, re-channeling the river, dredging the tiny harbor, and reconstructing underground utilities, had involved removing tons of mud, rock, crushed cars, and other debris. The heavy lorry and dump truck traffic roaring up and down the steep valley had thundered daily for months, right through the winter and spring. To residents trying to rebuild their lives and businesses, it was the thunder of hope. As spring advanced, apple and ornamental plum trees were blooming and the emerging new leaves were the freshest bright green. Life returned.

To everyone's amazement, the flood had killed no one.

Until the Trelissicks.

While the police picked their way around the accident scene, one of the emergency service officers, Jimmy Poundstock, a Boscastle native, pulled out his mobile and called Janet Stevenson, the young vicar at Boscastle's Forrabury Church where he worshipped. Stevenson listened, said a silent prayer, and went out to her car to fetch the Trelissick's only child, Lilly, a strong-minded girl who demanded to be called "Lee," from the primary school she attended on Fore Street, just below the church. But she stopped beside her car first and placed a call to Nicola Rhys-Jones and Andrew Stratton. She knew that the couple, she a painter and he an architect, both ex-patriot Americans and dear friends of the Trelissicks, would come immediately to care for the girl. Lee had spent part of her Christmas holiday with them at their new home near St. Ives taking painting lessons from Nicola. They were practically family to Lee and they, too, were flood survivors.

WHEN IT BECAME clear, a week later, that the little parish church would never be able to accommodate what turned out to be almost the entire village for the memorial service, the event was moved to the newly restored Wellington Hotel. This did not trouble the vicar; she knew her parishioners and she knew Roger and Anne. They'd have wanted a joyful remembrance with lively, heart-soaring music and plenty of refreshments, both in ample supply at the Welly. She offered a simple celebratory prayer to the assembled crowd and reminded those gathered that another Trelissick, young Lee, remained and needed their love.

It was Jack Vaughan, the bearded singer and musician locally called the "Boscastle Busker," who finally cried *Amen* and ordered the gathered musicians to play. He sat Lee beside him in the family room of the hotel's bar and the celebrants first sang *Amazing Grace* in full throat. Then they launched into their weekly singing of the seafaring songs, a tradition so old no one could recall its beginnings.

Jack, who raised money from his music for a cancer treatment center, wanted life and normalcy to prevail over tragedy and he knew and loved Lee and her parents: what better vehicle than their regular Wednesday night sing? As if to a lifeline, Lee clung to the tradition as well. She slapped her palm against Jack's knee to the tunes, brightening with each familiar song, and at the bar the drinks flowed. Jack had organized a similar community gathering a few days after the flood the previous year. That time they'd held it in the middle of the street by the hotel because the bar had been destroyed by a tributary stream called the River Jordan, which tore through the lower floor of the hotel. They'd built a bonfire from the wood remnants of the bar and a local brewery donated kegs of ale to the stricken village.

But now, toward the end of the sing, as was their custom, the villagers began, slowly and then with more heart, for it seemed more appropriate than ever before, their traditional closing number: "The Shipwreck of the Mary Carter." The guitars thrummed, a flute and a fiddle sang, and the voices rose until they reached the final stanza:

Rise again, rise again,
Though your heart, it be broken,
And your life about to end;
No matter what you've lost,
A home, a love, a friend,
Like the Mary Ellen Carter,
Rise again…

Jack scooped Lee into his lanky arms and held her as she finally cried. Everyone else applauded, their eyes brimming, too. The whole village was Lee's family this night. Jack handed the girl to Nicola and Andrew and, once again, everyone cheered. With them, they knew, she'd be safe.

One

IT HAD TAKEN almost an hour of climbing for him to reach the moor top. The pale granite tors along the summit ridge were so weathered that their edges were rounded and their strata so eroded that they looked like stacks of petrified flapjacks. They rose from the heather, gorse, and bracken-cloaked slopes like the bones of some ancient beast stripped bare by eons of relentless storms. The ancients had revered these tors, given them magical names, built settlements nearby and fortresses atop, and buried their chieftains beneath cairns and quoits on the high ground facing west to the Atlantic.

He leaned against a rock face and took in the view far below: the lush meadows of the farm, the stone mansion house, and the assortment of outbuildings that dotted the Trevega Estate north and south along the coast. As he watched, he beat his right fist against the stone like a pulse until the knuckles were nearly worn raw. He barely noticed. Anger rose like a fever:

They don't belong.

"YOU ALL RIGHT, Lee?" Nicola asked. The now eleven-year-old at the table was staring out the kitchen window as if into another plane of existence.

It had been many months since Lee's parents had been killed, but the girl had surprised everyone by being as resilient as a willow whipping in a high wind. She missed them, of course, but she also accepted her loss with a strange equanimity unlike any other child her age might have done. Something of an old soul, Lee reckoned that her loss was a bit like the turn of the seasons: there was death in winter and rebirth in spring. The loss of her parents, she reasoned—because she was a thoughtful girl—was like the natural cycle of things: the world turns; things change. Sometimes change hurt. That was also to be expected. But she had Andrew and Nicola now and that was everything. Their love was warm as a thick down duvet on a stormy Cornish night. And she had this new home by the Atlantic cliffs.

It was a chilly Friday evening despite being early summer, and Nicola was spooning out beef stew from a heavy Dutch oven. The updated but cavernous old kitchen on the ground floor of nineteenth century Trevega House was redolent tonight with the comforting aromas of their own farm beef, onion, garlic, rosemary and thyme, carrots, parsnips, potatoes, and new peas. Atop the stew were eight fluffy dumplings.

"No, I'm fine, really," Lee said, finally.

Nicola had got used to this sort of delayed response; it was as if the girl chewed for a while on the gristle of every question, giving it thought before composing an answer. At her new school, she stood back from the chatter of her classmates. Her teacher was concerned that she did not blend in. The truth was that Lee could sense what her classmates really felt or cared about and for the most part it bored her silly. What she cared about were the lessons and there she excelled.

"It's just something I saw out on the coast path this afternoon," she continued.

The Southwest Coast Path, one of Britain's many National Trails, edged the cliffs and hollows along the whole length of Cornwall and Devon's Atlantic and English Channel coasts for some six hundred thirty miles. The Trevega Estate bordered the cliffside path above the Atlantic and ranged for nearly half a mile north and south along a gently sloping grassy plateau a few miles south of St. Ives. The plateau itself was the remnant of a shelf of beach from eons before, when a prehistoric ocean lapped at its shore. Now it stood high above the Atlantic and was crisscrossed by stone field walls, some of which dated to the Iron Age and possibly before. The verdant meadows, sequined by drifts of tiny white English daisies no higher than the grass blades, supported Trevega's large herd of Black Angus cattle, a hardy breed and a major source of income for the estate.

Having finished serving, Nicola sat and sipped from her own wine glass. A shapely woman a bit taller and more broad-shouldered than most, she had thick brown hair so dark it seemed almost black. It fell in gentle waves to between her shoulder blades. Raised in a poor Italian enclave in North Boston, her maiden name had been DeLucca. During an arts fellowship in Florence, Italy, she had met and later married Jeremy Rhys-Jones, the son of Sir Michael Rhys-Jones, an investment banker. The marriage had not gone well. She lived now at Trevega, the family's "country house."

"So what did you see?" she asked.

"Someone walking north. I'd just come 'round Mussel Point on the way to Zennor when Randi noticed this walker far away to the south above that gully at Tregarthen Cliff. I was watching the pink thrift dancing in the wind at the cliff edge—they're beautiful right now. The wind came at us from the south and maybe Randi caught a scent. He barked once, then twice, his warning bark, you know, and when I looked up,the figure had turned and was hurrying back the way it had come."

"It's a public footpath," Andrew said, looking up from his plate.

"Plus, our big Siberian husky can be pretty intimidating," Nicola added.

"But from a tenth of a mile off?" It was like the girl thought them both idiots. She shook her head and continued eating.

"What did you see of this walker? Male or female? Tall or short?" Andrew asked.

"No idea, Drew. Dark trousers, olive green anorak I think, hood up because it was sprinkling."

"Probably just a tourist at the end of a walk, avoiding the rain and heading back to the Tinners Arms for a pint," Andrew said.

"Yeah. Probably. Yeah, that makes complete sense." Lately, Lee liked things to make complete sense. So much of her life recently hadn't.

"Did you continue on to Zennor?" Nicola asked.

"Me?" she said, laughing and shaking her head. Lee had let her previously close-cropped sandy hair grow to a bob after her parents' death and now it danced along the line of her fine-cut jaw. As she matured, her features were becoming chiseled and angular, as if cut from the granite cliffs all around her.

"No, me and Randi, we turned inland around Treveal Farm and came straight up our valley to home. When Randi speaks, I listen. He's very wise, Randi is."

"Randi and I," Andrew corrected.

Lee made a face. "Like I didn't know?" Lee had gained a good three inches in the past year and a half and had loose, gangly limbs that suggested she hadn't quite got used to her new body. She'd also begun to develop a certain resistance to what she thought was expected by the adults in her life, no matter how much she loved and needed them.

But Nicola heard Lee say "home" and it warmed her heart. She'd never had a child, nor had Andrew. In their mid-forties now, they never would. But they had Lee, and they could not imagine a finer daughter. Not that they had a clue how to raise one, especially a rare one like Lee.

Nicola and Andrew had lived together ever since the flood. Nicola's former father-in-law, who was among other things a financial advisor to Charles, Prince of Wales and Duke of Cornwall, had arrived in Boscastle with the Prince's entourage a few days after the catastrophic flood to survey the damage. While the Prince moved through the shattered village talking with residents, Sir Michael stepped away to check on his beloved ex-daughter-in-law, Nicola, who had lived alone in a cottage near the harbor's mouth ever since he had arranged for her divorce from his abusive son, Jeremy. But the flood had torn her house apart and there was no sign of her.

When he found Nicola at last, battered, in shock, but alive, and met the man who'd rescued her, the visiting American architect Andrew Stratton, he begged the two of them to move to his family's country estate, Trevega House, just south of the historic artists' colony of St. Ives. The estate had been neglected, and he directed Andrew to begin its restoration. Andrew recruited his stone wall-building mentor, Jamie Boden, to join him, along with his partner, Flora Penwellan. They all now lived on the estate.

This particular evening, Drew, as Lee always called Andrew, clutched a glass of red wine in his right fist but did not lift it. Nicola noticed his hands were raw and gave his arm a squeeze. She could tell he was exhausted. He hadn't had time to bathe and his thick mass of curly salt and pepper hair was tinged with grit. He and Jamie had been heaving stone all day to rebuild a collapsing wall in the estate's old gardener's cottage so it could be converted to a rental unit. Lee, too, school now being out, had helped them most of the day. The girl had loved stone work ever since she'd watched Drew and Jamie working on that new wall behind the tourist car park in Boscastle, the unfinished wall that was washed away as if it were made of nothing of substance in the flood that had nearly destroyed her home village and so much else of what Lee once believed was rock-solid and permanent in her short life.

NICOLA PUT HER fork down and turned her attention to her partner: "How'd you and Jamie get on with that wall at the gardener's cottage?"

Andrew shook his head; grit fell from his hair. "That Jamie is a genius. I was sure we'd have to tear down the whole west-facing wall and remove the roof, it was all so weathered, but old Jamie just said, 'trust the stone.' He rammed a vertical supporting timber beneath the roof's end-rafter and we've rebuilt the upper half of the exterior stone wall beneath it, as if the roof were floating above us. It's taken a few days but when we're done he'll ease out that support and the old timber and slate roof will settle down onto the new wall right as rain, completely stuck and sturdy. That's what he says, anyway."

"And you, Mr. Architect," Nicola teased, "Did you serve as his structural engineer?"

"No way; I'll never stop learning from that wily old man. And this young lady," he said, nodding at Lee, "she was with us all the way. Her spatial sense is amazing."

"What's that mean?"

"This girl of ours can see in three dimensions. She can turn space around in her head and tell you where a particular stone will fit as if it were meant to be sewn there. It's a rare talent, Jamie says."

"Wow!"

"Whatever," Lee said to her plate.

"She could be an architect," Andrew added.

The girl smiled but did not look up.

"Where's Jamie's Flora tonight?" Nicola asked.

"Off to one of those pagan meetings she goes to once a month," he said. "'Moots' they're called. I don't know if Jamie's a believer or not; he doesn't say. But tonight he's off to the Tinners for supper and a pint or three with the neighbors while she's out. Bit of a reprieve from the witchcraft for him, I suppose."

Nicola locked her ebony eyes on him: "Listen, you: I believe in her and in her faith and skills. She lifted a great burden from my soul after the flood…and made it possible for me to trust and love you. If that's witchcraft, I'll take it."

"It wasn't my inherent charm?"

She relaxed: "Yes, well, maybe a bit of that too…."

Andrew marveled at the woman beside him: her feisty Italian edge was never far beneath her smooth, slightly olive skin. Andrew's ex-wife had been tall, slender, and cold, but his Nicola was a comforting warm armful when they curled up together at night. He especially loved waking up early in the morning to see her long dark brown hair, burnished with tints of copper in the sun, splayed out across her pillow. That's when he wanted her most, but he let her sleep and slipped off to brew tea for them. It was little ritual of theirs, having tea in bed to begin each day, a still point of catching up, looking forward, and being together before their worlds started turning again.

Lee watched the two of them banter and considered how lucky she was that these quirky grownups had adopted her. The formal process was not yet complete, she knew, but what seemed like half the population of Boscastle had turned up for the hearing at the Family Proceedings Court at Bodmin to support Nicola and Andrew's petition. Lee's own grandparents said they were too old to look after the precocious girl and endorsed Andrew and Nicola wholeheartedly. It was only a matter of time now before the order would be final. It hardly mattered to Lee, though; Andrew and Nicky were her anchors now.

What she did not know, and what they had not told her yet, was that the settlement from the accident that killed her parents, when it finally wound its way through the courts, would likely protect her financially for the rest of her life. Others of the company's drivers were on record reporting that the truck that had lost control had continually leaked brake fluid. In response to their warnings, the owners had simply topped up the reservoir as needed and ignored them. A corporate manslaughter charge would be heard in Truro Crown Court. Psychiatrists for the injured and emotionally shattered driver had already been deposed and they doubted the young man would ever be the same.

As for Bottreaux Farm, Lee's home, the rich land above Boscastle had been rented quickly by a neighboring farmer, and the farmhouse itself had been purchased and turned into a posh bed and breakfast venue…where no one spoke of the tragedy. The proceeds of the sale, and the rental income, went to a trust fund for Lee established by Sir Michael.

AS SHE ATE, Lee could not stop thinking about Flora's pagan moots. She just knew somehow, like an itch beneath her skin, that she was meant to attend those meetings, too. There were things she knew, things she sensed, but she did not yet have the words or the courage to talk about them. Only Flora understood.

Flora Penwellan had worked behind the bar at the Cobweb Inn at Boscastle dispensing drinks, food, and sage advice in roughly equal measure for as long as anyone could remember...until the flood nearly destroyed the pub and swept her finally into Jamie Boden's arms. The two had flirted with each other for years but had both been too shy, and thought themselves too old, to act on their attraction. In the end, all it took to bring them together was a disaster that could have killed them both.

Jamie Boden was as wiry and tough as a goat, lean but strong from years of stone work. His weather-beaten, freckled face possessed an almost perpetual look of mischief and his unruly thinning red hair, touched now with threads of white, was like a storm swirling around his head. Just encountering Jamie Boden made you smile.

Full-figured Flora—"strapping," some might describe her—was what locals called, privately, a "village wise woman," one of several in this part of Cornwall... someone you could count on to lift an ache from your soul or a curse from a neighbor, among other maladies: in short, a witch. And, although she was almost sixty, she had also been Lee's closest adult friend both before and after the flood. It was simple: they loved and respected each other. Plus, Flora had already sensed that Lee was unusual. She kept an eye on the child as if the girl were her own, and now that they all lived on the Trevega Estate that was easier to do. She loved that Andrew and Nicola had wrapped their arms around the orphaned girl and given her their hearts, but she did not believe they understood, at least not yet, how different the girl really was. And it was Flora's job, she believed, to protect and nurture that difference. It was, she felt, the last big task of her life.

That, and maybe Jamie.

HE CLIMBED BACK over the ancient stone hedge and stood at the edge of the coast path, admiring his handiwork. It had been harder than he'd expected and he was winded, even a bit frightened by what he'd done. But he smiled nonetheless:

It's a first step. There will be more.

And then he strode south, careful not to be seen.

Two

NIGEL LAWRENCE, THE thick-set young farm manager for the Trevega estate, knocked at the kitchen door of the big house early on Monday morning. He and his wife Annabelle and their toddler Jesse lived above the valley in the estate's farmhouse. Low-slung under its lichen-encrusted slate roof and looking like it had grown out of the rocky landscape rather than having been built upon it, the stone house was more than a century older than Trevega House, almost a museum piece. Nigel managed the estate's cattle for Sir Michael.

"Nigel!" Nicola said, opening the door. "Come in! Tea?"

"That would be fine, Nicola, thank you. Andrew about?"

"Of course. Just changing into his work clothes. Be down any minute."

She poured him a mug. "Something more than tea, Nigel? Toast?"

"Nah. My Annabelle fixed me a breakfast to last all day."

"A fine and lovely woman she is, Nigel."

She paused and added, "Plus Annabelle saved me from Jeremy. I'm forever in her debt. And yours."

"I'm so sorry we didn't know sooner that he was beating you…I'd have throttled the bastard. So unlike his dad, Sir Michael, who's such a good and noble soul."

"All in the past now and long gone, Nigel. Anyway, I should have said something back then, but I was too afraid. Annabelle helped me to find my voice. Then again, look at all the good that's happened since…Yes?"

"Mighty glad we are about you and Andrew. And Lee, too, despite her terrible loss. Landed safely with you two, me and Annabelle think. Reckon we'd like her as babysitter for our little Jesse sometimes, if she's interested. Loves her, that little boy does. How's she faring, then, our Lee?"

"Hides a lot inside, I think, Nigel. But she soldiers on. She's a strong girl."

"And smart, too, I reckon. Comes up to the farm and wants to learn all about the herd. Lovely company she is as well, and the animals they take to her. You should see it: they gather around her, their big ginger heads bobbing, and they lick her boots. She has a way with them."

Andrew came down the back stairs to the kitchen. "Nigel! How are you, my friend?" He thrust out his hand.

Nigel had not yet quite got used to this overt American custom. Diffident nods were more a Cornishman's habit of greeting. Given its smuggling history, wariness was culturally ingrained. At some point in the distant past maybe you had to worry if someone who extended one hand might have a knife in the other.

"Reckon I'd like a word, Andrew," he said, taking the proffered hand. "On a farm matter." He looked at Nicola. "Outside, maybe?"

"Of course!" Andrew said.

"So much for tea," Nicola groused. "Go on, you two…"

A crushed gravel terrace separated the back of Trevega House from the overgrown formal garden a few steps below. Renovating the garden was Nicola's next task. The rear terrace was where they parked their vehicles, near to the kitchen door. Nigel stopped in the middle of the yard, as if there were a mark there where he should stand and speak.

Andrew joined him. "What's up, Nigel? What is it?"

The farm manager looked across the yard and then turned to Andrew.

"Reckon it's murder, Andrew."

"What?"

"One of our bullocks dead this morning in a field down by the coast. Throat slit. Couldn't even have bawled out for help, the poor devil," Nigel said, his voice catching, as if his own child had been slain. "It was Lee who told me. She'd been out walking early with Randi. Came right up to the farm, she did, told me, then left. I moved the rest of the cattle from that field. They were gathered around the dead one nudging it, wanting it to live."

Andrew put his arm around the man's shoulders and led them farther away from the house. "Good

Lord, Nigel, why? What's the point? Do we have enemies?"

"None what I know of, truly, Andrew. Folks hereabouts are proud of how you're restoring Trevega. The old place is full of life again. That's good for everyone in the district. They're always talking at the Tinners about all that you and Jamie are doing. Admiring, everyone is."

"But this?"

The farm manager raised his hands. "No idea, honestly. Such a beautiful, harmless beast."

Nigel was a stocky Cornishman in his mid-thirties, ruddy-faced from the weather and so heavily muscled it was as if he didn't just raise cattle but wrestled them as well. He ran a hand through his thick black hair and looked off across the overgrown garden.

"This could be just someone's filthy prank," he said without conviction.

"Maybe, but I think we'd best report it to Sir Michael anyway," Andrew said.

"We've plenty more cattle, Andrew."

"Still, he'll want the police in. Don't move the beast, okay? And let's get your veterinarian to have a look as well. We'll need something official."

"Already called the vet."

"Why am I not surprised…?"

"Has Lee been back yet?"

"I didn't know she'd been out, honestly."

"You'll go look for that girl, won't you? She were powerful upset finding that bullock. Troubles me more than that beast, to be honest. Find her."

Acknowledgments

The Davies & West mystery series is set in contemporary Cornwall. I love this far southwestern tip of England, a place of mystery itself—wind-whipped on its Atlantic side, pastoral on the Channel side—a place where Stone, Bronze, and Iron Age sites litter the landscape. I know this world well, but that does not mean I'm an expert. For expertise, I depend on a splendid team of local advisors who make sure everything I write, from police procedure to ancient archaeology to contemporary paganism, is spot-on accurate.

First among these equals is and must be Devon and Cornwall Police Crime Scene Manager detective sergeant Martin South, a gentleman of deep experience, even deeper patience with an American novelist, and by now a dear friend. Other members of existing and former members of the Devon and Cornwall Police to whom I am indebted for this particular book include Neil Best, former Criminal Investigation Division (CID) detective inspector; David O'Neill, former CID detective sergeant, and Falmouth-based CID detective sergeant Helen Shears. On matters of forensic science and autopsy procedure, I thank Dr. Amanda Jeffers, forensic pathologist, and Kevin Hammett, mortuary manager at the Royal Cornwall Hospital in Truro.

Archaeology plays a key role in this story, and on that subject I was capably guided by James Gossip, senior archaeologist at the Historic Environments Service of the Cornwall Council; his team of volunteers from the Meneage Archaeology Group who generously invited me to carry very heavy buckets of rubble at the excavation of an underground chamber, a "fogou," on the Lizard Peninsula in Cornwall; and Chris Hoskin, the owner of the farm where that chamber was found and a generous host. In addition, I am grateful for the friendships made with members of the Cornish Ancient Sites Protection Network (CASPN), who invited me to join their annual walk connecting three sacred wells on the Lizard Peninsula and taught me so much along the way.

As guides to the deep and continuing culture of paganism in Cornwall, I thank Ronald Hutton, professor of history specializing in paganism and magic at Bristol University, and Andy Norfolk, Cornish expert in Druidry.

At the center of this mystery is the discovery of an Iron Age hoard, a treasure trove worth millions. For guidance on both the law and the valuation of such ancient relics, I thank Roger Bland, Keeper, Departments of Prehistory & Europe and Portable Antiquities and Treasure, and Dr. Michael Lewis, Deputy Head, Department of Portable Antiquities and Treasure, both with the British Museum in London; Mark Harrison at English Heritage; Anna Tyacke,

Finds Liaison Officer, Royal Cornwall Museum; and Christopher Martin, Chairman, UK Antiquities Dealers Association.

And for a springtime local flora tutorial and walk through the valley of the Helford River, I thank botanist Amanda Scott, a delightful guide.

That's a lot of help, but it doesn't mean I've got everything right. Moreover, I may have adjusted some facts to suit the story, though these instances are rare. As always, therefore, I must say that if there are errors, they are mine alone. I trust that my friends, for these advisors have become my friends, will forgive me.

And finally, a deep bow of gratitude to the entire creative team at Northstar Editions: my project manager and steadfast advisor, Stephanie Konat; gifted cover designer Laura Hidalgo, editor extraordinaire Patricia Eddy, proofreader Karen Alcaide, and book formatting genius Adam Bodendieck.

Will North
June 2017

* ALSO BY WILL NORTH *

The Long Walk Home
(Romance)
Forty-five year old Fiona Edwards answers her Welsh farmhouse door to a tall, middle-aged man shouldering a hulking backpack—unshaven, sweat-soaked and arrestingly handsome. What neither of them knows is that their lives are about to change forever.

Water, Stone, Heart
(Romantic Suspense)
Nicola and Andrew have each come to the Cornish village of Boscastle to escape their troubled pasts. When they meet, they're bristly and sarcastic—yet are attracted to each other. What neither of them know is that a ferocious storm is brewing, one that could destroy them, and the entire village. And that storm is about to hit.

Seasons' End
(Contemporary Romance)
Every summer, three families spend "the season" on an island in Puget Sound. But when local vet Colin Ryan finds Martha "Pete" Petersen's body in the road on the last day of the season, he uncovers a series of betrayals that will alter their histories forever.

Harm None
(British Murder Mystery/Davies & West Series: Book 1)
When an American archaeological team discovers the skeletal remains of a missing child, British Detectives Davies and West unearth a growing list of suspects. Just as they close in on their prime suspect, another child goes missing.

Trevega House
(British Murder Mystery/Davies & West Series: Book 3)
Three years after surviving a catastrophic flood (***Water, Stone, Heart***), twelve year old Lee Trelissick has settled into a safer life with her adoptive parents. But before long, preternaturally wise Lee announces "Someone wants to do us harm. Someone evil." She's right. Can Detectives Davies and West protect the girl and stop the killer before it's too late?

Made in the USA
Las Vegas, NV
25 September 2023